CONTEMPORARY AMERICAN FICTION

CLOSE QUARTERS

Larry Heinemann was born and raised in Chicago. He served a tour of duty with the 25th Division in Vietnam as a combat infantryman. *Close Quarters* has been called *the* seminal work to come out of the war. C. D. B. Bryan called it "the best book by anyone who fought there." A worldwide Dutch-language edition was published in 1986.

His shorter fiction has appeared in *Harper's* magazine, *Penthouse* magazine (as part of their Peabody Award-winning Vietnam series), and the *TriQuarterly*, as well as in *The Best American Short Stories of 1980*, *The Best of the TriQuarterly*, the recently published *Soldiers and Civilians*, and elsewhere. His non-fiction has appeared in *Harper's* magazine, the *Chicago Daily News* and the *Chicago Sun-Times*. Mr. Heinemann has received literature fellowships from the National Endowment for the Arts and the Illinois Arts Council. His second novel, *Paco's Story*, is also available from Penguin.

Mr. Heinemann lives in Chicago with his wife Edie and their two children. He is currently working on a non-fiction book about post-traumatic delayed stress and the "tripwire" veterans of the Olympic Peninsula and the Pacific Northwest.

CLOSE

QUARTERS

LARRY

HEINEMANN

PENGUIN BOOKS

3/8/90

Bechu

I wish you

luny good ... in

my heart.

Larry H

PENGUIN BOOKS
Published by the Penguin Group
Viking Penguin Inc., 40 West 23rd Street,
New York, New York 10010, U.S.A.
Penguin Books Ltd, 27 Wrights Lane,
London W8 5TZ England
Penguin Books Australia Ltd, Ringwood, Victoria, Australia
Penguin Books Canada Limited, 2801 John Street,
Markham, Ontario, Canada L3R 1B4
Penguin Books (N.Z.) Ltd, 182–190 Wairau Road,
Auckland 10, New Zealand

Penguin Books Ltd. Registered Offices:
Harmondsworth, Middlesex, England

First published in the United States of America by Farrar, Straus and Giroux
1977
Published in Penguin Books 1986
Reprinted 1987

Sections of this book appeared, in slightly different form, in
Penthouse magazine and *The Story Workshop Reader*.
The characters and events herein are
fictitious and any similarity to persons
living or dead is purely coincidental.

LIBRARY OF CONGRESS CATALOGING IN PUBLICATION DATA
Heinemann, Larry.
Close quarters.
Reprint. Originally published: New York: Farrar
Straus, Giroux. 1st ed. 1977.
1. Vietnamese Conflict, 1961-1975—Fiction.   I. Title.
[PS3558.E4573C5   1986]   813′.54   86-9466
ISBN 0 14 00.8578 5

Printed in the United States of America by
R. R. Donnelley & Sons Company, Harrisonburg, Virginia
Set in Bodoni Book

TO MY FATHER, JOHN,

AND TO EMERSON

No story is told, no book is written, in a vacuum. There are many people to whom I owe acknowledgment, and hearty thanks and abundant affection, for sustained encouragement and advice and every sort of help, and first among these is Edie, my wife, and John Schultz, my good friend.

I also wish to express my thanks and affection to (then) First Sergeant Alva (said to have been a full-blood Navaho Indian), who called me into his Orderly Room office the day I left for overseas and told me to "remember, this is not a white man's war," among other things. First Sergeant, this is to let you know that your advice has served me well.

May God's luck be with you.

Larry Heinemann
Chicago

UGLY DEADLY MUSIC | 3

MOON OF ATEVO | 70

TORQUE | 78

THE PERFECT ROOM | 172

BY THE RULE | 209

COMING HOME HIGH | 271

CLIMBING DOWN | 314

BUZZ, BUZZ!

—Hamlet (II, ii)

CLOSE QUARTERS ·

U G L Y

D E A D L Y

M U S I C

I stood stiffly with my feet well apart, parade-rest fashion, at the break in the barbed-wire fence between the officers' country tents and the battalion motor pool. My feet and legs itched with sweat. My shirt clung to my back. My shaving cuts burned. I watched, astonished, as the battalion Reconnaissance Platoon, thirty-some men and ten boxy squat-looking armored personnel carriers—tracks, we called them—cranked in from two months in the field, trailing a rank stink and stirring a cloud of dust that left a tingle in the air. One man slowly dismounted from each track and led it up the sloped path from the perimeter road, ground-guiding it, walking with a stumbling hangdog gait. Each man wore a sleeveless flak jacket hung with grenades, and baggy jungle trousers, the ones with large thigh pockets and drawstrings at the cuffs. The tracks followed behind like stupid, obedient draft horses, creaking and clacking along, and scraping over rocks hidden in the dust. There were sharp squeaks and irritating scratching noises, slow slack grindings, and the throttled rap of straight-pipe mufflers, all at once. And the talk, what there was, came shouted and snappy—easy obscenities and shit laughs. It was an ugly deadly music, the jerky bitter echoes of machines out of sync. A shudder went through me, as if someone were scratching his nails on a blackboard.

The men walking and the men mounted passed not fifteen feet in front of me. A moult, a smudge of dirt, and a sweat and grit and grease stink covered everything and everyone—the smell of a junkyard in a driving rainstorm. Each man looked over, looked down at me with the blandest, blankest sort of glance—almost painful to watch—neither welcome nor distance. This one or that one did signify with a slow nod of the head or an arch of the brows or a close-mouthed sigh, and I nodded or smiled back, but most glanced over dreamily and blinked a puff-eyed blink and glanced forward again.

The tracks, flat-decked affairs with sharply slanted fronts and armor-shielded machine guns (one fifty-caliber and two smaller M-60s), were painted o.d.—olive drab, a dark tallow shade of green—with large dun-colored numerals, faint and scratched but plain. The smooth straight sides and some of the curved gun shields bore thin bright gouges from Chicom claymore hits and deflected small arms. The confusion of scratches and scrapes was wonderful and brutal as fingernails dragged across the nap of velvet. Some of the tracks had nicknames: "Lucky Louie" and "Stone Pony" and "White Hunter" and "One Bad Cat" and "The Kiss-off" and "Scratch ⫲⫲ ⫲⫲ I." Body count.

That summer the number would become fifteen and

later twenty-six, and later still we would lose count and give up the counting, saying among ourselves, "Who fucken cares?"

The last track, the seven-seven, pulled into the motor pool, towing the very last, the seven-six. The seven-seven left the seven-six near the mechanics' quonset and pulled up and parked with the rest. A pathetic, odd moment of stillness settled over us as it finally shut down. Thick waves of engine heat rose through all the chicken-wire grillwork. The ground guides stood in front of the tracks, motionless and stoop-shouldered in ankle-deep ocher silt. The men still mounted, the drivers and gunners and TCs—track commanders—gazed at their hands or wiped dusted faces with dusted arms or stared down the broad slope at the rubber-tree woodline across from the perimeter wire, squinting darkened, puffy eyes.

With the tracks facing me on line I saw that all the machine guns—ten fifty-calibers and twenty M-60s—were still loaded and pointing down. It was the frankest kind of gesture. Down where the terror would be, pointing always at the closest trees, the likeliest part of a hedgerow, the nearest rice-paddy dikes, which everyone called berms. The driver of the downed track, wearing a football-helmet-looking thing, a CVC, roused himself. He pulled himself out of his hatch and stood on the seat, sloughing off his dark glasses and bulky flak jacket and CVC, leaving them where they fell. He wore a pistol holster clipped to his trouser belt and two leather cartridge belts buckled round his waist, studded with rounds. A thick dust, almost crusted, covered his short curly hair, the razor rash on his face and neck, and the sparse hair of his arms. A glistening sweat smeared the sides of his chest and back where his flak jacket had clung to his body in folds, and his eyes shone a glassy pink against his gritty black face. The sweat soaked through in patches and dripped in runnels from his chin and fingertips and belly. He worked his jaw and cheeks, harking up phlegm, then spit a gob of white foamy spit to leeward at the woodline down the way. It disappeared into the dust. He heaved his chest, catching his breath, all the while working his hands open and closed until he reached his fists to his eyes, leaning his head back.

"Geeee-ahhh damn!" he bellowed. Everyone in the motor pool jerked their heads, then looked away or turned their backs completely, but still listened. The man swooped down, landing in a dry puff of dust, but caught himself from falling over with his fists. He turned quickly and drew a long-handled spade out of its strap among the other pioneer tools—shovels and tanker bars and other long-handled junk. He brought the spade back over his head and began beating on the front of the track with the blade end, like it was an ax.

"You goddamned half-stepping fuck-up track!" He said it low and slow and mean. "I'm gonna tear you apart with my bare fucken hands. I'm gonna pour mo-gas on your asshole and burn you down to fucken nickels, you short-time pissant mo-gas-guzzling motherfucker!" The blade end of the handle cracked and flew off on the upswing but he kept beating on the headlight mounts and the engine-hood catch and so forth, shouting and cursing, the sweat flying from his forehead in an arc and his back rippling under the dirt. Then suddenly he stood mute, his arms hanging limp, his gaze fixed upon his boots and the dirt and the cracked and splintered tip of the spade handle. He let it slide from his fingers, then climbed the tread next to his hatch. He reached in for his shirt and steel pot and walked stiff-legged toward the mess hall and did not look back. I did not see him until later that night when he was drunk and incoherent, lying on his cot smoking dope and blowing large billowing smoke rings. The next morning he packed his duffel, sold his pistol and cartridge belts, said his goodbyes around, and went home.

The rest of the platoon, singly and by twos and threes, slowly went to work dismounting the guns for cleaning, and after a moment only one man was visible. He leaned against the sloped front of his track, stripped to the waist with a stub of cigar between his teeth. His trousers, soaked through around the belt, were covered with dirt and grease, stiff and puckered at the knees. He wore a faded web belt low on his hips; a knife on the right, a green plastic canteen on his left, and a forty-five-caliber automatic pistol in a black holster hung in front of his crotch. He told me later he wore the pistol for protection the way some people kept something thick in their breast pocket, "like a Bible or a fuck book, ya know?" He walked toward me with a slow ambling gait, smiled to himself as he passed, and went over to a fifty-five-gallon drum sunk in the ground, the Enlisted Men's Club piss tube. His hair shone with sweat, was matted and wild-looking. He had brown teeth and dark wrinkles around his mouth, gray watery eyes, and tiny inflamed scars across his stomach, like the deep and sweeping scratches of cats. His whole face seemed pulled together around the eyes, as though someone had squeezed it. He stood with his feet well apart, looking straight down at the stream of piss. There was a rich humus smell about him, not plain dirt or soft crumbling chunks, but powdery and damp, a thing that clings to everything it touches.

"Excuse me," I said. "Could you tell me where I can find the platoon leader?"

"Say? The El-tee?" His words came easy and weary and dry. "See that track on the end there?" He pumped his thumb over his shoulder without looking up. "He's aroun' back some fucken place. Ya can't miss him. He's the dude

with the silver spoon in his mouth. You new, huh? M'
name's Cross."

"I'm Philip Dosier. Well, I'll see you later."

"I don't doubt."

I walked around the side of the six-niner, making sure
all my buttons were buttoned, pulling the slack out of my
rifle sling, and adjusting my steel pot down over my eyes,
garrison style, then walked around to the back. All the
activity was there, all the way down the line. The ramp of
each track was open, some swung all the way to the ground,
some held level to the floors inside with water cans or
wooden boxes. Everyone was stripped to the waist and bare-
headed, going about his work with slow languid motions
because of the heat; shaking out blankets and poncho liners
in a cloud of dust and chaff and lint, or cleaning the
stripped-down machine guns in cans of gasoline, or policing
up brass cartridges by the armfuls and tossing the cartridges, cans, and all into fifty-five-gallon drums set out for
junk. The gas truck, a deuce-and-a-half with two fuel tanks
on the back marked "Mo-gas," had begun moving up the
line, refueling. I thought gas-powered tracks were obsolete.
I had never seen any before, except the two on display at
the Patton Museum at Fort Knox.

Lieutenant Greer sat in the shade inside the back of his
track on one of the low metal benches, folding a map. He
was a husky, meaty-looking dude with short, shaggy, filthy
hair and freckles and red wrinkle marks from his CVC
across the forehead and under the ears. He wore back-in-the-
world fatigues covered with dust; a brass armor insignia on
one collar, his silver lieutenant's bar on the other, and a
pair of amber-tinted driving goggles around his neck.

The first time I came down with heat exhaustion a
couple months later, May or June it might have been, Lieutenant Greer called the dust-off chopper himself. He laid

me out on the litter and held me up, leaning me against his thigh, and poured canteen after canteen of tepid water over my head. He held his canteen cup while I washed down half a handful of salt tablets, spilling mouthfuls of water down my chin and chest. I vomited twice, finally dry-heaving on my hands and knees while he soaked compresses on the back of my neck with more water. When the chopper came, the Colonel's command chopper because the dust-offs were busy with Bravo and Charlie companies, the Lieutenant walked me over to it and gave me a hand up, saying thanks to the Colonel. I sat among the racks of the Colonel's radios until he landed me at the battalion aid station, and late that afternoon the Lieutenant came over to fetch me back to the platoon. Toward the end of summer when Greer went home we threw a party for him at the platoon tents, everybody getting ripped and red-eyed drinking quarts, drinking his health. He shook everybody's hand and wished us good luck and left, staggering out into the moonlight, and I never saw him again.

The inside of his track was very neat, much neater than any of the rest. There was a collapsed litter strapped close under the armor deck, three radios, ammunition cans neatly stacked on the floor under the TC hatch, waterproof duffel bags full of clothes along one wall, and boxes of fragmentation grenades and claymores, command-detonated antipersonnel mines about the size of the top of a shoe box and curved outward. The Lieutenant's M-1 carbine and a sandbag filled with magazines hung on a hook behind his head.

I saluted and nervously introduced myself. After a moment of silly questions and silly answers and that same stupid lecture about bringing him my personal problems, the Lieutenant called on the radio for Seven-zero, Staff Sergeant Surtees, the Platoon Sergeant.

Surtees was a heavyset Negro who wore the only shoulder-holster forty-five in the platoon and the only man, other than the Lieutenant, wearing a shirt, the sleeves rolled in precise folds with all his insignia and rank patches: E-6 chevrons and 25th Division patch and name patch.

He smoked big cheap cigars which he rolled in his fingers as he talked to the platoon in formation, and would pause to spit tobacco for emphasis, but he could never get the hang of it and so always had spittle dribbled on his shirts. He loved to say, "E'ery swingin' dick," and here he would take pause to spit on his shirt, "in this platoon is chicken shit," and then would bug his eyes, trying to flash fire. When he had an announcement for the whole platoon, that the mail was in or chow was ready or the water trailer had arrived he would call us on the radio and say, "Rom-e-o, Romeo. This is Seven—ze-ro!" and then say whatever it was he wanted to say.

In the fall when his 1049 came, his transfer to Division, it took him fifteen minutes to gather his gear and sign out of the company. Word came down to the tents that Surtees was shipping out and a bunch of old-timers went down to see him go. When he slid into the jeep for the ride up to the airport, Quinn, a dude who transferred into the platoon that summer, walked up beside him, dropped a small package in his lap, and said, "It's a special belt, see? Ya take yer dick an' strap it to yer leg, get it stretched out good an' long, say 'bout fifteen or twenty feet. Then some night when yer good and fucked up on that NCO Club booze, just real down home fucked up and horny, why just whip it out, rub it up, an' shove it up yer fat nigger ass." Then everybody laughed, even the driver, who hardly knew him.

Sergeant Surtees stood in front of the Lieutenant at mock attention and gave me the "Teamwork, fight like hell, and sleep on your own time" speech that he would give every new replacement. "Falling asleep on guard duty is a court-martial offense; incorrect radio procedure will not be tolerated, the FCC monitors all frequencies; and you will at all times address me as Platoon Sergeant Surtees. Is that clear, Pfc?"

"Yes, Platoon Sergeant Surtees," I replied. I didn't know any different. I was still garrison. I had just come from Fort Knox, the armored cavalry, where I called *everybody* sir or sergeant.

Then he said, "Well, Lieutenant, wheredaya wanna put 'im?"

Greer stood above us on the ramp brushing dust from his shirt, looked down the line of tracks, and said, "Put him on the seven-three. They're first in line, I guess. Got a note here from the Sergeant Major that three more'll be here this afternoon, so you make sure you're at Battalion to pick them up. Otherwise, they're liable to get lost in one of the line companies. That's all, Sergeant. Glad to have you with us, Pfc."

Surtees walked me down to the seven-three, talking the whole way. "Putting the poop" to me, as he said. There were two men inside. One sat spraddle-legged over an ammunition can filled with gasoline on the driver's-side bench with his trousers rolled to his knees, scrubbing caked carbon from an M-60 bolt with a toothbrush. The other swept the metal floor with a short-handled Viet broom and stacked ammunition cans under the TC hatch, bent over at the waist because of the headroom.

The inside of the track was painted a light foam green. Everything was covered with road crud, mud-splattered and filthy. It was crowded and awkward and smelled sharply of gasoline, but there seemed to be room enough.

"Trobridge," Surtees said, "this man is on your track. Replaces Murphy." Then he turned and walked away.

The man bent over backed out and stood up, wiped his hand on his trousers, put it out to me, and said, "I'm Sergeant Trobridge, the TC. This here is Pfc. Atevo, my number-one gun." Atevo dropped the bolt into the can and shook hands firmly, nodding. The backs of his hands were red and raw from the gasoline. "And the dude that drives this thing is around here someplace. Cross? Hey, Cross!"

"Yeah," came a voice.

"Come around back and meet the new man. What did you say your name was?"

"Dosier. Philip Dosier."

"Yeah, Dozer. Name's Dozer, Cross!"

"Already met 'im. He'll do."

With that Atevo reached into the gas can for the bolt and motioned with the toothbrush for me to sit down. Trobridge slumped down next to me to take a break.

Atevo was about my size. He had a light, bushy mustache with tips that twisted around the sides of his mouth nearly to his chin, large and dark boyish eyes, and a dusty olive tan. Beside him a twelve-gauge pump-action shotgun leaned against the gas-tank armor. The gun was covered with dirt and a powdery rust that a person could rub off with his fingers. He wore a bowie knife on his belt in a black leather scabbard—riveted, not stitched.

The knife itself, easily the biggest blade I had ever seen, was gunmetal black with a dark wood handle. A gift from his uncle, he told me once, hand-forged and blade-heavy. "So it will always hit," he said. But he never threw it by the blade, always the handle. "All you will have time for is the draw and throw," he told me. He had a clear, keen eye and a good arm, and again and again I saw him throw it into a dirt-filled sandbag to the curved hilt. "But you must throw a knife only if you know it will strike its mark," he would say as he yanked it loose with a flick of his wrist.

"For to throw it is to disarm yourself, and to disarm yourself is to be naked." He carried a whetstone in a small cedar box. He would spit on the stone, move the knife forward and draw it back and move it forward, keeping time with his breath. Sharpening both edges. Sometimes he would strop it on the leather toe of his boot for hours, especially after we had smoked some smokes, then test the cutting edge against the calluses on the heel of his hand.

Trobridge was on the chunky side with a flabby face and thick wetted lips. He always sweated more than anybody and wore thick black-rimmed GI glasses that slipped to the end of his nose, so he was always pushing at them, and for some reason he never tanned. He had a smallish waist, and wide fleshy hips, and since he wore his trousers high on his waist, the fatigues did not bag the way they did on the rest of us.

He was one of those fat, sloppy, cushy dudes who would walk into his Basic Training company mess hall for the first time, and there would stand one of those barrel-chested, bad-ass-looking NCOs. He'd have his bad-looking Yogi Bear hat set at an angle down over his eyes and his arms folded across his chest, real badlike, and a pair of light-blue-tinted PX aviators. He'd spy Trobridge up one side and down the other, and say in a deep, gruff baritone, the humor and irony just dripping out of his mouth, coming in gushes, "Hey, *Fat*boy? How much you weigh, *Fat*-ass?" And Trobridge would stand there in his brand-new rumpled and shiny olive-drab fatigues, not knowing whether to shit or piss or go blind, and he'd answer, "T-t-two hundred and seventy pounds, sir," in a high-pitched voice. "Don't call me sir, *Fat*boy!" "Yes, Sergeant." "We gonna run about a hunnurd poun's offa yer ass, *Fat*boy. You gonna sweat an' grunt a hunnurd poun's off 'r die in the a-tempt." Then Bad-ass would turn on his heel and lay his eye on the cook

13 |

behind the serving line. "Dursey, no potatoes fer Fatboy," he'd say, then he'd whirl around, coming down nose to nose with Trobridge. "An' Ah catch you with potatoes on yer breath, Fatboy, an' yer gonna wish you was never borned. You got that, Fatboy?" "Yes, Sergeant!" "Okay, *Fat*boy," he'd yell, and snap his arm straight, pointing to the serving line. "Eat it!" And every morning when the company would fall out for the mile run Bad-ass would scream in Trobridge's face, "You drop out, Fatboy, and you git this size-ten boot straight up your ass. You drop out and you'll be in the front leaning rest poundin' out eight-count push-ups until every hair on yer ass is white as ash. Now double-time! An' let me hear you grunt, Fatboy! Grunt!" Trobridge was just the perfect sort of no-talent loser the Army sops up the way a desert soaks up a two-day rain. Not a week later it looks as though nothing happened at all. He gets room and board and a new pair of boots now and again, and the Army baby-sits him for twenty or thirty years, telling him when to go to bed and when to eat, what to think and how to say it, and his desolate and destitute imagination never knows the difference.

Cross came around the back with a double armful of chilled beer, so the four of us sat in the shade inside a while, drinking and talking. Where are you from? How come you wound up here? What's happening back-in-the-world? Were you drafted?

Besides the machine-gun ammunition stacked under the TC hatch where the fifty was, there were wooden boxes of frags and claymores and M-16 magazines, a captured AK-47 wrapped in clear plastic hanging from the radio, neatly folded ponchos atop a pile of neatly folded blankets and poncho liners, and two cloth hammocks tied front to rear just under the armor deck. A pair of Ho Chi Minh sandals and a red bandanna held at the neck with a twenty-four-carat gold ring hung from the rubber eyepiece of the infrared scope. There were duffels and waterproofs, spare barrels for the machine guns, wooden boxes, cardboard boxes, cooking gear, canteen cups, everything. I sat facing the gas tank, decorated with tits and thighs cut from magazines and covered with acetate and green cloth tape. The four-color paper was beginning to fade into yellows and washed-out pale greens. And behind me was the envy of the whole platoon, a genuine Igloo water cooler strapped to the top of the battery box. Cross had swiped it from the PA & E dudes, Pacific Architects and Engineers, across the road from the motor pool. They were the civilians who operated the camp's water purification gismo, among other things, and had it made. We could see them from the motor pool, taking a nap in their pickups or breaking for lunch or knocking off for the day or sitting on the veranda of their office, listening to the machinery hum and catching flies.

On the ground behind the ramp two bags, a beat-up waterproof and a duffel sealed with a padlock, leaned against each other with an M-16 and a steel pot on top.

Atevo kept scrubbing gun parts and we kept talking. He laughed down at the gas can when Cross spit tatters of cigar into the dust, saying something about "that fucked-up nigger, Surtees." Atevo let the parts dry in the sun, wiped them down with an oil-soaked shaving brush, and slapped the two M-60 machine guns back together. Then he turned his attention to his shotgun next to him. He broke it down quickly, cleaned it, passing a rag through the barrel, oiled it, and reassembled it, reloading all the shells. When he finished he stood up, put on his shirt not bothering with the buttons, grabbed his steel pot, and jumped off the back.

"Hey, Dosier, Cross, you want to go eat?" he asked.

I nodded and got up. Cross slouched lower on the bench and shook his head no.

"Atevo, why don't you take Murphy's gear up to the Orderly Room on your way?" Cross sat with his legs outstretched, pointing to the bags.

"Okay." I took the duffel and the steel pot, which was covered with a cloth camouflage cover, faded and stretched tight to the helmet like everyone else's. Atevo walked ahead with the waterproof and rifle. We stood in the shade of the Supply Room tent along with the rest while the First Sergeant and the Supply Sergeant filled out forms. There were a dozen or more sets being turned in. It took longer than I expected because there were questions and answers and stories.

"It was raining and I couldn't see, but . . ." said one.

"That was two months ago, seems like, back in January somewhere. The afternoon we got those six gooks in the open, for Christ's sake," said another.

"These are the two that got it at the same time. They were sucking a smoke and the round hit right between 'em."

One guy had had his leg taken off by an RPG, whatever that was, and another guy had written from the States to say he and some other guy were doing fine and bragging about the Fort Ord Hospital pussy. When it came our turn Atevo said, "Sergeant Sean Murphy. KIA, eighteen February. Issue gear is in the duffel. Personal gear is in the waterproof," while the First Sergeant wrote it down. I tossed the duffel with the issue gear on the pile behind the counter. Atevo set the waterproof in the back of the Supply Room deuce-and-a-half, then we went to eat.

As we walked along the ditch that split the company street I asked Atevo, "What's KIA?"

"Killed in action. Dead." He said it with a quick turn of his head.

I wanted to ask about Murphy—his story—but I looked at the side of Atevo's dusty, fuzzy face, the droop of his mustache, the way he hefted the shotgun easy over his shoulder, and thought it better to keep my peace.

*

That night after dark Cross wangled a case of beer out the back door of the EM Club, which was a tent with a dirt floor and some benches and picnic tables, and the three of us, Cross and Atevo and I, went down to the seven-three. It was cooler than the club or the tents. They had both showered and changed clothes and looked rested, except for their puffy faces and darkened eyes. Cross opened three cans right away, tapping them with the pointed tip of the opener to settle the foam, then making one small cut on one side for air, two full cuts on the other for the drinking; then he brought out the squat stove and fired it up for a snack, a can of beef and potatoes from the leftover box. We drank the tepid chalky beer for a while, watching the beef broth simmer, then Cross said, "Well, how 'bout some smoke?" and reached under the bench to pull out an ammo can. There were several packs of cigarettes, Kools and Marlboros and Salems, and baggies filled with dope.

"Uh, Cross? What's smoke?" I asked.

"Say?" But then he let out a low chuckle and mumbled something about fucken new guys. "Why, smoke is M.J. Mike Juliet. Ya know—grass. Same same smoke. Light up, it won't kill ya. 'Bout the only thing round here that won't. Guaran-fucken-tee!" He snapped his Zippo and I sucked the smoke down into my lungs.

"This here is one of the exotic de-lights of the East. Make a short man see over fences, a tall man see into the clouds, fat dudes crawl under screen doors. It'll slick up a wet dream, screw up a bad dream, fuck up a dufus. Cures heartburn, jungle rot, the Gee-fucken-Eyes, all them things. An' there ain't no muss, no fuss, no puke to clean up after. Smoke is m' little buddy." I felt a cough, a pain. I blurted out the smoke, coughing from way down, hacking. Cross laughed and slapped his knee so hard he dropped his ash.

"Hey, m' man, ain't ya sipped smoke before?" he asked.

"No-o-o," I managed to say between coughs.

"Here, here ya work it too hard. It's a thing ya ain't got to sweat for. You be good to smoke an' smoke'll be good to you. Ease up, we got boo-coo and we got all fucken night."

After that we sat quiet, smoking and drinking. There was just the hissing of the squat stove and the outgoing H. and I., harassment and interdiction, from the battery of 105 howitzers down the road. I was getting stoned for the first time in my life. Then it occurred to me that the beer was warm.

"Hey, Cross," I said. "You ever get ice?"

"Say? Ice? Yeah." He nodded his head slowly. "Every now an' again. We scrounge it from the icehouse they got at the Tay Ninh Base Camp, sometimes. There's a gook icehouse on the convoy road, the other side of Charlie Papa Alpha. It's a fucken rip-off, but every once in a while a trooper gets a taste in his mouth, or some fucken place, for a cool brew. Yeah, we get ice. That's what the Igloo's for, but you'll get used to warm. You get so you don't mind anything."

He spooned out the beef and potatoes onto a cheap tin dish. I watched the dead ash of his smoke; the beer cans we threw into the dust and moonlight; the cans from the afternoon were still lined up on the deck above my head. Then came the question, from way down, way back. The stupid question, the only question.

"What's it like?" I said. "Outside the wire. In the field. What's it like?"

Atevo sat across from me, wearing his dark canvas slouch hat with the frayed, floppy brim down over his face.

He leaned his head back and looked at me with reddened stoic eyes, and said nothing. Cross put aside the tin plate, wiped the mess-kit fork on his trouser leg, and put it aside.

"Heh-heh-heh," he said, "Dosier, m' man, I wondered when you was gonna ask that. An' the answer is: it ain't different a-tall. It don't smell any more fucked up, it don't rain any harder, the gooks ain't any uglier, not by no long shot. 'Bout the only difference is, there ain't no wire. Outside it's just us chickens. And this whole fucken place, from the Red River Delta to the Me-kong, every snatch of sand, every hill and ARVN fort, all the banana groves and rice paddies and hamlets and fucked-up mud hooches, right down to the last squint-eye on this whole fucken farm, you could roll it into one tight-ass ball and none of it is worth the powder to blow it away with. There ain't one, not one square inch of muck within five or six thousand miles of here that I would fight anybody for, except what I'm standing on. And that includes this rubber plantation and fucken Saigon and the goddamn American Embassy. I been here goin' on ten months, m' man. I be goin' home May twenty-first. It ain't soon enough to suit me, but who cares, dig? An' in all that time I never met a squint-eye that I would call anything but gook. 'Come 'ere, papa-san. Lah-dee, motherfucker.' 'Me no VC. No VC.' 'You boo-coo VC, you lyin' slant-eyed, skinny-legged dink. I said come 'ere.' Gooks don't know how ta do shit. Can't get the hang a black-jack, don't even know how to plant somethin' simple-ass, like corn. Fucken-A, m' man, back home all ya got ta do is toss it outa fucken winda and the shit sprouts like weed. I swear, when I leave here you got the run a this fucken ranch. I'm gonna stay in Frisco and stay fucked up. I'm gonna sit me down and just sit, and when I get tired I'll move to a different chair. An' the first dude who fucks with me, I'm gonna crack his hat in two.

"You take Murphy. He'd been here 'bout as long as

me an' a better gun you won't find in this fucken platoon, except maybe Atevo here. One night, 'bout a month ago come ta think about it, after weeks and weeks a contac' ever' fucken day, he got some wild hair up his ass and got ta chasing this gook on foot; jumped outa the hatch there and tore off toward the fucken woods, screaming at the top a his lungs. One of the goddamnedest things I seen *anybody* do. An' that chicken-shit gook turned on his fucken heel and shot Murph square in the neck. That's the fucken AK right there. Murph died waitin' on the dust-off. That's why I got the ass at Surtees, 'cause that spook just took his sweet fucken time callin' them in, and Murphy bled ta death. I tell you true, Dosier, I get about half a chance I'm gonna do a number square on his nappy fucken head."

He sat slouched on the bench with his feet out in front of him, flicking ash with his ring finger, leaning his head back against a waterproof and staring up through the crew hatch. His voice trailed off as though it were the end of an early-morning party, with wine bottles and beer bottles lined up along the windowsills and across the floor and everybody out of cigarettes. His words came mumbled and graveled and slow. The pain seemed to draw away from his eyes and settle in his voice and hands. He lit another smoke with a flick of his Zippo, popping seeds, and sucked on his beer. His story wandered through the nights when it rained and the nights when it was clear as water, "where you can't just tell what a thing is, but know just exactly where it's at, ya know?" and the platoon's first pathetic firefights, and down to the firefights they had just come in from.

"Shit, boy. We was at a fire base north a Suoi Tre when a call comes in from the artillery base a couple clicks—that's kilometers, boy—up the way. The dude on the radio said the perimeter was overrun. I know, I was listening. By the way he was talkin' it musta been the gook hordes that's been in the papers all these years. Well, Romeo and a couple tanks from the 34th Armor took off lickity-split through the fucken woods, with Bravo and Charlie Company right behind. And that kid bustin' jungle in the lead tank was busting some bad jungle too. Knocking it back boom-boom-boom. Hell of a lot better than these fucken crackerjack boxes do. We busted through that woodline and Jesus H. fucken Christ, but shit, boy, it looked like every dink in Cochin China was inside that perimeter. The artillery dudes and straight-leg grunts and the gooks was doin' it hand to hand. There was skirmish lines every which way all over the fucken place. That's when Seven-six, Sergeant Bendix, caught a fucken RPG that blew him right outa his hatch. Blew everybody away but Ivy, the driver." And Cross took me down to the seven-six to show me, talking the whole way.

He showed me a ragged hole about the size of my fist in the upraised TC hatch cover, and concentric spirals from the bits of shrapnel coming out from it, like the chamber and grooved rifling you will see if you look down the barrel of a gun.

"It was just about every man for himself," he said as we walked back to the seven-three. "Gooks tried to climb the seven-seven there, and Tweezer and the rest were beatin' them back with a tanker bar and shovels. We got on line with the grunts and dudes from artillery, I pulled into low gear, and drove standin' up one-handed, dingin' gooks with my forty-five and pullin' pins on grenades, counting one thousan', two thousan' three, and dropping them over the side. The tanks was firin' point-blank canister rounds, and seven-one backed one gook upside a tree and ran his ass down, tree and all. An' when some ya-hoo called a cease-fire and the fog cleared there was gook body count and KIA all over everything. Shit, but shit, m' man, the Colonel come down and jus' about creamed his fucken jeans, said there was something like six hundred fuckin' body count. An' it coulda been, I swear. Ain't that right, Atevo? You betcha. We was down about a third of our dudes. An' just about every night after that we had business, mortars and RPGs and probes and sniper fire, and had to drag the seven-six with us every place. Then one night . . . well, who knows, maybe Murphy just got tired. Wore out, ya know? Anyway, one night he goes straight over the top. He jumped outa his hatch like somebody had kicked him and took off with the shotgun after this gook, screaming, '*You cocksucker*.' " Cross pulled out his wallet and the picture of Murphy's wife he had kept, water-ragged and frayed and finger-smudged, a young woman with short combed-back hair in a two-piece bathing suit. He told me about the letter he promised Murphy he would write, but didn't. "It was easy to lie to Murph. Easier than I thought."

"And where does Trobridge come in?" I asked.

"Ol' Four Eyes'd been a gunner on the seven-zero, suckin' on Surtees' hin' tit for his third stripe, so the next morning Surtees put him in the hatch here. An' that fucken Trobridge is a *prime* cunt-head, too. He got a three-inch gash from his me-dulla ob-long-gotto clear around to the bridge of his fucken nose, dead square between his four fucken eyes." Then Cross's speech got crisp and mean. He told about the body count Romeo left in piles and the fucked-up ambushes, and then he told all over again of all the hate he had for Surtees. " 'Bout the nex' firefight we get into, I'm gonna settle his fucken hash, I swear," he said. Then his voice trailed off again into whispers and mumbles.

". . . Ever get so your body just shivers?" he said, loud again. "Like you was pullin' on a bottle of that God-awful junk gook booze. . . . Shivers so bad it's like malaria shakes. Fever and cold sweats and you can't even hold your hand straight, and you feel like you got to puke. That's all that happens anymore. Jesus, but goddamn I hate warm beer," and he tossed his half-finished can under-handed out into the dust with the rest. It clattered and jangled among the others and I could hear it fizz, the beer spilling out on the ground. He reached above his head then, and yanked his hammock loose and started unbuttoning his cuffs.

"Well, why don' we call it a night, huh?" he said.

"Yes," Atevo said, gathering up his shotgun and flak jacket and slouch hat. "It is getting late."

I got my M-16 and steel pot and the two of us squeezed between the seven-three and seven-one, sidestepping, Atevo saying to Cross, "See you in the morning."

"Roger, roger, roger," Cross said back, his croaking voice trailing off into whispers and mumbles again.

We walked through the motor pool under a vaulted black sky, the stars clear and abundant, with Atevo leading by a step or two. He never used a flashlight, like some did, because the motor pool and the battalion command bunker and the Headquarters Company Orderly Room and the Recon tents, and the paths among them, were in plain view of the woodline, and I got that habit from him. We passed the silhouettes of tracks and deuce-and-a-halfs and the medic and recoilless-rifle jeeps. He stopped at the gateway in the wire where I had been standing earlier—his shotgun over one shoulder and flak jacket over the other, like a short thick cape.

"Let me tell you the first thing you must know," he said. "Do not walk so close. Keep five meters back, and when you go in front I will be five meters behind you."

"Okay," I said, and felt stupid.

We walked along the hard dirt path, Atevo going quick and quiet, passing among some of the officers' tents and the aid station and battalion headquarters. We passed along the darkish rain gulley that meandered down the company street where the housecats—the vehicle mechanics and radio mechanics and cooks and clerks—held reveille. The Recon tents were tethered together in a row among the other clusters of tents, the canvas stretched and filthy, nicked with unmended shrapnel hits, the ropes frayed and slack.

A blackjack game still chugged along in the next tent. I found my cot by feeling along the edges of the other cots for the one with no feet, sixth on the right, and laid myself out on my sleeping bag. I had scrounged it, a mangy, lumpy, sweat- and grease-smelling, quilted affair, from the Supply Room tent. I could pull ticking out of the rips by the handful. I settled myself among the lumps, with my shirt for a pillow and my poncho liner to my chin because of the mosquitoes. Then I looked up and whispered to Atevo across the aisle, "Hey, Atevo? Cross sure is a funny dude."

"Been here a long time," came his soft-voiced answer. "Might as well know the rest of that story. The dink that shot Murphy? Cross was right behind. Shot him seven times. That's where he got the bandanna, and the ring, too." I could not help but let out a breath that was everything but a whistle.

"Well, good night, Atevo."

"Night, Flip."

Ivy, the driver of the seven-six, thrashed quietly in his cot next to Atevo's. He sat against his duffel with his knees well up, mumbling drunkenly and tossing the butts of his smokes and beer empties at the back doorway.

"Yeahhaaa," he said, almost in a sigh. "He fucked that cocksucker *alllll* up."

In the next tent behind my head the blackjack players whispered their bantering curses and kibitzed.

"Hit me, but not too hard," one of them said. A card snapped and a hand slapped it down. "Whoa."

"Gentlemen," came another voice, "the fucken dealer will now take one bad, bad hit." Snap. Slap. "And guess what, suckers? The dealer will pay the fucken point and the point *own-lay!*" Then came the shuffle of raked-in cards and raked-in paper money.

I lay awake, getting comfortable among the lumps, staring up at the darkened peak of the tent and thinking to myself: my God, what have I let myself in for? Gas-powered museum pieces. But at least it isn't the straight-leg infantry. At least I won't have to grunt and pound ground.

*

Early morning.

Empty beer cans and cigar butts crowded around the back doorway. The mumbling and snoring of drunken sleeping men covered with dusty blankets and poncho liners, like lumps of rubble under tarpaulins. Here and there a tan arm dotted with swollen mosquito welts, reaching to the floor. Between cots, dusty, muddy duffel bags and waterproofs and cheap footlockers covered with damp trousers, and rifles and pistols and grease guns and bandoliers of M-16 magazines and grenades, piled like apples. Loose ammo and freshly opened letters and busted claymores and canteen cups and beer cans, crushed one-handed, and mess-kit forks and C-ration snacks along the low sandbag walls. The soft scratching of rats under the packing-crate and shipping-pallet floorboards. Shirts with rolled sleeves used as pillows or hanging on nails pounded into the tent poles. The smell of spilled beer and urine ammonia and a smashed bottle of Aqua Velva. Heavy green socks stuffed into the green canvas uppers of boots to keep the bugs out. Playmates and fuck books and *A Child's Christmas in Wales*. A bottle of back-in-the-world ready-mix martini and the ass end of a salami dying in a puddle of its own grease. Unopened beer cans and plastic pouches of dope. A furry black mongrel pup curled in a shirt under a cot, stretching its legs and yawning. The almost rain of cool soggy night air still clinging to the bushes and weeds and low places.

It was just sunrise. I sat around and got up. After a moment of yawning and rubbing my eyes and looking for a cigarette, I went out back to piss. I stood spraddle-legged at the edge of the ditch with the fuzzy shadow of the woodline at my feet. The tops of rubber trees down the slope steamed with mist, but the sun, just now at eye level, would burn that off soon enough, and the day would be hot and humid and muggy, and smell of rain.

Atevo came out with his blanket tight around his shoulders, and soon a crowd of men stood shoulder to shoulder, pissing in the ditch. The sleep wrinkles deep on their faces, and fingers fumbling with fly buttons and ciga-rettes and Zippos. Atevo and I got our guns and went to the mess hall, one of the few buildings in the battalion that was not a tent. Everybody else went back to their cots.

"It is bad to sleep too much," he said.

When we walked in the serving-line door, Haskins the breakfast cook, a tall and fat black dude with short fingers, stood behind the griddle stirring eggs with a large spatula that he whipped around in the air like a baton, flicking the sticking egg back in the pool.

"Haskins, damn your eyes, what's for breakfast?" Atevo said.

"Screw, 'Tevo. Ain't nuthin' ready. Coffee's in the tub, like aluz. Move out, Pancho."

Atevo slammed the barrel of his shotgun across the serving line, chest high.

"Haskins, you'd look awful funny splashed up against that back wall."

"Wall now, young trooper, rumor has it that Ah'm a pretty quick dude with a fucken egg, so if ya don' move back, yo're just liable ta find out how fas' Ah am." He moved the shotgun aside with the spatula. "By the bye, ma compliments to Romeo for the smoke. You dudes shore know how ta do a thing right." Then he looked over at me. "Who's the fucken new guy?"

"Dosier. My name is Dosier," I said.

"Yeah, Ah seen ya 'round. Welcome ta the shithouse. How'd ya like a nice housecat job? Ya cook? Ah'll trade with ya. Ah fucken hate it. Cookin' jus' plain sucks."

"I don't know. I'll think about it."

"Wall, if ya de-cide lemme know. Y' know, Ah gets hos-tile fire pay, same's this bird? Fifty-five a month ta get up with the fucken chickens an' wrassle these little mothas. If ya wanna eat, set down fo' a while, it'll be right inna coupla minutes. Take it light." We got our coffee and sat down, but after a moment I got up and took my coffee down to the motor pool.

The only way I could tell the seven-three from the other tracks was the coiled black jump cable strapped to the front. That morning and almost every morning Cross would jump-start the seven-four and the seven-seven, that track being the hard-luck track with batteries, going through four sets in two months. I squeezed between tracks and sat down on the bench. Cross was asleep in the hammock. He slept straight on his back, his hands jammed under his thighs, his head and eyes close to the underside of the armor.

"That you, Dosier?"

"Yeah. Coffee?" A hand came out from under the blanket and grabbed hold of one of the hand straps. He flipped himself out of the hammock and sat down. I handed over the canteen cup and he held it in both hands, sipping. He spit out the first mouthful, then gave it back.

"Jesus H. fucken Christ! Ain't Haskins ever gonna get

the hang of makin' coffee?" He reached around into the Igloo cooler, took out a beer, and opened it, squirting a chalky foam. Then he took a sip.

"That's more like. Dosier, m' man!" and he reached over and slapped my knee. "Today I'm gonna teach you how to drive. You wanna learn how to drive this fucken crate?"

"Well, I guess."

"Heh-heh, 'well, I guess.' Okay, you're elected. After breakfast Rayburn's taking the seven-zero out for a road test down to Check Point Hotel. We'll go when he goes. 'Sides, we can get laid a little, get some gook beer," and he looked at me out of the corner of his eye. "Maybe some ice, too."

When we got to the serving-line door at the mess hall the line went around the side of the building. Cross moved right to the door. Several men standing there began to grumble. Cross stopped at the door and turned to them.

"Hey, housecat, ain't ya never heard of NCOs bucking the line? This trooper's with me." And we went inside, took trays, and stood in front of Haskins.

"Wall, kiss ma ass!" said Haskins. "Cross ya mutha, what's yo pleasure? We got scrambled. We got fried. We got Rice Crispies. Got powdered milk. Got apples. Got C-ration jelly. Got *real* coffee. We got fucken oatmeal. Any y' birds want some a this here oatmeal? Just have ta throw it out! Dosier, y' better take yoself some a them salt pills. All right, y' housecats, step up an' state yer purpose. Ya don' look too good, Cross. Here, have a egg. 'Tevo told me 'bout Murph. It's too bad, he was a good ol' boy. Ya gonna write his ol' lady? Ya tell 'er that Haskins, the number-two cook, is sorry. Tell 'er God bless. Do that, will ya, Cross?"

"Sure Tim. Take it light. . . ."

"Roger that." Then Haskins turned his attention back

to food. "All right, ya bunch a losers, show me a straight line. Keep the grab-ass down back there. Don't be slammin' the fucken do'. We got scrambled. We got fried. Move along there, truck driver. Now listen up, radio, y' slam that do' one mo' time an' ya goes hungry. We got Rice fucken Crispies. We got OAT-MEAL. Which one a ya clowns wants ta tes' fly some a this goddamn oatmeal? Ah don' make it 'cause Ah like it. Who wants what? Put ya tray up 'ere, clerk-typis'. Don't jiggle so, goddamn. Scrambled! Fried! Attention, Kool-Aid lovers! Kool-Aid is out!" and he threw his arms out to his sides, the spatula dripping grease and scrambled egg, looking like Jocko Conlan calling some housecat safe at home plate. "Cut that grab-ass back there . . . !"

Cross ate slower than I did, but finished before me and sat tipping ash into his instant potatoes, waiting. When I finished we went back to the motor pool. He threw his forty-five onto the deck and turned around, putting one hand on the driver's-side lift hook.

"Dosier, m' man, this here is a M-one-one-three, o.d., one each type, never fail, never float, armored personnel carrier. It is powered by a single two-eighty-three-cubic-inch Chevy V-8, with vacuum governor, and something like a ninety-gallon gas tank. The configuration of three automatic weapons makes it an armored assault vee-hicle, and it carries a basic load of eight thousand rounds. We carry firepower, not troops. Let the fucken line companies do that. To climb up, put yer right foot on the tread, grab this lift hook, swing yer other foot to this bolt head, and swing yerself up." He stood on the deck. "Now come on."

After several timid tries I made it. He motioned me into the driver's seat. He sat next to me on the chicken-wire grill over the engine with his feet dangling over the front. There were two flak jackets on the seat, sandbags jammed tight on the floor, and the two brake handles. I started it up. The straight-pipe muffler throttled and roared. Cross had cut the vacuum governor, advanced the time, tuned the carburetor, and it idled wonderfully.

"Now, when you want to go right pull on the right brake, the left brake for a left turn. It's just like falling outa bed. Okay, take it around the motor pool a couple times to get the feel." I pulled it down into gear and let out the brakes. We rolled forward.

"Now, when ya turn, kick it in the ass so's ya got the torque to make it. When ya get through the turn, ease up on the brake an' the gas an' it'll do the rest. Don't let it fuck ya over, lean on it." When the rear cleared the other tracks I pulled right and fed gas.

"Pull harder," he yelled over the engine noise. "More gas. Lean, goddamn, or ya ain't gonna have room. Okay, let'm slide out. Not bad, m' man. Yer on yer own. Don't let anybody fuck with ya, not even me. Yer gonna do fine."

After several laps around the motor pool the turns got smoother and the straightaways more flat-out. Rayburn, one of the best mechanics in the battalion, came down to road-test the seven-zero, Surtees' track. He waltzed through the break in the barbed wire with a jaunty, springing step, holding his M-16 by the carrying handle. He hopped up on the seven-zero, slid into the driver's hatch, cranked up, and moved out without so much as a minute's warm-up. Cross told me to wait for Rayburn's dust to settle some and handed me his CVC, that football-helmet-looking thing.

It was a communications helmet with built-in ear-phones and a microphone that swung down in front of my mouth, and the push-to-talk/release-to-listen button just under the left ear. A CVC never deflected small arms or shrapnel that I ever saw, but it kept me from beating myself senseless on the armor.

Cross climbed into the TC hatch behind the fifty, slipped Trobridge's CVC over his ears, and motioned me forward with a sweep of his arm and a "Move out" over the radio. I followed Rayburn past the dug-in, sandbagged ammunition dump and the mo-gas dump, hung a wide, sloppy left at the perimeter road, passing behind the Romeo tents. Several men stood at the wash table and waved, hooting and pointing, and Cross grinned and waved and hooted back. I drove slowly, holding the black plastic grips on the brake handles tightly. The vibrations jolted my hands and arms and chest. The CVC muffled the grinding and shrieking and thumping of the treads, the throttled roar of the engine, but after that day I always had a buzzing, crackling, rushing hum in my head.

"Move out a little faster," Cross said over the radio.

I leaned my shoulders forward against the cushioned lip of the hatch and grasped the handles even tighter. We rolled off behind Rayburn and the seven-zero, roaring and cranking, throwing dust into the air in funnels that swept over the perimeter bunkers and piles of concertina wire, and settled into the village. We passed the battery of 105 howitzers and part of the village cemetery caught inside the wire.

"Hey, Dosier, stay in the tread marks. Never drive out of the tread marks of the track in front of you. It's the only place on the road you can be sure ain't mined. Always drive in the tread marks. Never forget."

At the east gate near the helipad an MP sat back in his jeep, fanning himself with his MP helmet liner. Cross made me stop back a way to load my rifle and put on a bulky flak jacket. It was cumbersome and cold, sweat- and salt-stained under the armholes and down the zipper, and it stank of grease and gasoline. We pulled up to the MP.

"You gotta note?" he said.

Cross leaned over the armor shield. "The guy behind us has it." The MP got up and opened the gate.

I cranked through and hung a right into the village, Dau Tieng, the company town for the Michelin Rubber Plantation. On both sides of the road were row houses with thick garden walls and tile roofs and women standing in doorways with babies slung over their hips. Work crews sat on their heels or stood in groups around the flat-bed trucks and pickups, waiting for the honchos and drivers. To the left was the truck scale, the motor pool, and gas pumps, and on the right was the office building with air conditioners in every window. There were ditchers and old beat-up Ford tractors and harrows and crates of whatnot and a slick of grease and oil and water along the ground. Small children stood in groups, waving, or trotted alongside as I slowly rolled along.

"Hey, Cross," I said over the radio, "how come you told him that? Isn't he gonna be pissed?"

"Well, m' man, if I told him we was goin' ta get laid, wha' daya think he'd say? Sure, he'll be pissed, but wha's he gonna do? Lock us out? MPs give me the ass, anyway. He gets his pussy, why shouldn't we get ours? Fuck an MP," he said. And that closed the subject.

We passed among several large windowless buildings set close together, three or four stories high and covered with corrugated tin. To the side of one building a Viet in a pith helmet and shorts stoked a furnace fire with rubber-tree logs, but I never found out why. My eyes smarted, I nearly sneezed in the sharp and thick, foul and ice-cool smell of the raw latex and processed latex and furnace-fire smoke. The same sort of saturated, gamy stink that my brothers and I rolled up our car windows for and held our breaths for when we passed through southside of Chicago and Gary on our way to visit aunts and uncles and cousins in Michigan.

Then I rumbled, slow and careful, across the Saigon River bridge, a French-built, rusted and spindly-looking, one-lane affair, surrounded by four bunkers—two French and two GI—covered with greenish slime and dust. As I cranked along the timber-covered roadway the bridge creaked and moaned, and I could not help gritting my teeth. The French concrete bunkers on the near bank had gun slits and embrasures and iron doors; the GI bunkers had piles of tangled concertina wire and claymores set out in gangs.

Over the bridge, I headed for the rubber-tree wood-line, Check Point Hotel, where Rayburn had already parked. Along the gravel road the track shook and bucked and banged through potholes and ruts, and I felt everything in my hands and feet and forearms. The wind blew in my face and I could feel the tingle of dust that still hung in the air. I squinted and narrowed my eyes. The dust still stung my eyes and they began to tear. I hit a suddenly abrupt hole. The track snapped up on the back edge and snapped my head back. I banged a bicep on the lip of the hatch and it began to ache. Then the vibration of the road began to irritate. My arms and chest and stomach and thighs shook and quivered. I could not focus my eyes. Then Cross told me to slow down. Rayburn had parked the seven-zero on the right against the woodline. I pulled up slowly on the left and shut down.

Rayburn stood in the shade of the woodline, sipping from a quart bottle of beer and talking to a young boy who squatted in the dirt with a plastic mesh shopping bag full of melting ice and beer. The boy was counting MPC, Military Payment Certificates, GI funny money, which he stuffed into the pocket of his shorts.

Rayburn was one of those tall, lanky dudes with thin arms and long hands and bony fingers, spotted with blood blisters and small cuts that never healed. When he smiled anyone could see that he didn't have a good tooth in his head, made worse by a thin stringy mustache. But he always carried an amazing variety of tools and small parts in his pockets—a small crescent wrench and vise grips and rare, odd sizes of sockets for the wrench—spare cotter pins and spark plugs and 13/16th nuts for the tread pins and grease fittings for tread tension cylinders—and he never went anywhere without Trojan rubbers with the reservoir tip. "If ya need one an' ain't got it, you are taking a big chance with your generations," he would say.

Next to Rayburn a Saigon Cowboy-looking kid sat astride a Honda with the kickstand down, and a girl sat on the back, wearing a light-colored, tight-fitting blouse, her arms around the kid's belly. Rayburn stood talking to him, looking at the girl and gesturing into the woodline with the mouth of the bottle. Cross jumped down and walked over. I climbed out of the hatch and sat next to the fifty barrel with my feet dangling over the front, rubbing my stinging arm. Among the rubber trees, planted in precise rows like corn, was that same cool tang that lay close to the ground around Dau Tieng, but it was the faintest whiff mixed with other woods' smells, not heavy and foul. And if you struck a rubber tree, it oozed a whitish sticky sap, something like milkweed.

I rubbed the sore on my arm and watched the woods, listening to Rayburn tell Cross, "Surtees got a wild hair up his ass about some 'funny fucken noise' in the transmission. So I told him I'd be downright proud to road-test it for him. But shit, hey, you know and I know and *everybody* knows that every fucken track in the whole fucken battalion makes 'funny fucken noises.' Then again, what the fuck? The pay's the same whether I'm out here getting laid or taking my morning nap on the welder's bench or busting my ass stripping down the seven-six."

"Could dig it," Cross said.

"Hey, Dosier? How come you sittin' up there?" said Rayburn.

"What?" I said.

"Come on down, man, it's daylight. There's nothin' out there but the hired help. They may be VC, but shit, man, they got to make a wage just like the rest. Come on over, you make me nervous up there," he said.

I walked over with my steel pot and rifle.

"Dosier," said Cross, "I want ya ta meet Claymore Face, the greatest piece of ass this side of the Saigon River. She ain't much ta look at but she puts out like crazy. Just put a paper bag over her head. Claymore Face, flash a little tit for the man. Dosier here is a Chicago boy, boo-coo hard-core and a number-one fuck."

She sat on the back of the honda, holding the brim of her cone hat down over her face, giggling and feigning snatches at Cross's crotch. When Cross pushed the hat back over her head I saw that she had pox scars from her forehead to the neckline of her blouse, like someone had beat on her with the business end of a wire brush, like she'd had acne vulgaris since the day after she was born. She giggled some more and tried to hide her eyes.

"You Sha-caw-go?" she asked between giggles. "Know gangster?"

"*Know* gangsters?" retorted Rayburn. "Why, *Clay-* more Face, he *is* one. Why you think they slammed his ass into Romeo. Fucken-A, back on the block he's known as Deadeye Dosier, ain't that right, Deadeye? Why shore and kilt him a bear when he was just fourteen, ain't that right?"

"Rayburn, you're crazy," I said.

And Claymore Face, who looked like she'd been around the block a couple times herself, said, "Him boo-coo dinky dau, huh, Deadeye?" and smiled. There wasn't a tooth in her mouth. "You like short-time?"

"No, no, thank you, not this morning." I bought a beer

and stood with my back to the woodline looking back at camp and the plantation water tower and the river and a cloud of dust coming up the road. Cross and Rayburn settled on a price with the kid on the Honda, and Rayburn and the girl walked into the rubber, Rayburn carrying a blanket draped over his shoulder, the girl walking behind, swinging her hips and waving a bandanna over her shoulder. I stood next to Cross and we turned our backs to the road when the Dau Tieng–Tay Ninh convoy went by, escorted by two platoons of tracks from Alpha Company, six or eight men crowded on top of each track.

When Rayburn came back, Cross handed the kid three dollars, MPC.

"Hey, Rayburn, you got rubbers?" Cross said. Rayburn reached into his trousers and handed Cross a small foil packet. Cross walked into the woodline unhitching his web belt.

"Where you at, Claymore Face? Huh, sweetheart? Oh, where ya hidin'?" She started to giggle and waved the bandanna over the clump of bushes.

I looked down at my hand. I had a blister on the inside of the knuckle of my ring finger, my first blister.

When Cross went home, a couple months later, I became the seven-three Delta. I sat on the same two flak jackets as Cross and got the same scratched gouges that never healed and blood blisters and yellow calluses, and an ache in my wrists and the small of my back that I never got rid of.

*

When we pulled into the motor pool Trobridge was standing on the ramp of the seven-two next to our space, his glasses slid to the end of this nose, his hands splayed on his wide hips.

"Where the fuck have you been?" he said when I had backed in and shut down.

"Say?" said Cross. "Why, gettin' laid, a course! Why you ask? We leave ya behind or some shit?"

"You were not authorized to leave this motor pool," Trobridge replied, pushing his glasses up. "Military vehicles are never to be used for personal business."

"Say?" said Cross again, climbing out the back. "Aw, go piss up a rope, Highpockets." He reached for his shirt and forty-five and left for the tents.

Trobridge watched him go, then turned and looked over the top of his glasses at me, standing among stacks of C-ration cases and ammunition cans on the armor deck above him. He told me that I had the afternoon off; that I had ambush that night. Atevo took me down to the open-air Viet shop where this wrinkled-up, beady-eyed papa-san and his old lady sold junk trinkets and souvenir ashtrays and genuine cheap tin dishes and footlockers. I bought an Australian-type bush hat, grayish with brown and off-green and russet splotches and a stiff plastic sweatband. I spent the better part of the afternoon working the brim until I had the front and back curled up, Gabby Hayes fashion.

Around four the ambush gathered in the mess hall for early chow. We slid into two tables near the big two-tub stainless-steel coffee urn the battalion had brought with them from Fort Hood. The cooks boiled the coffee in a vat on the stove, campfire style, and fixed the Kool-Aid in the urn, since there were more Kool-Aid drinkers than coffee drinkers. There were Atevo and myself; McNertney, a Canadian, the TC on seven-two, who would walk point; Weatherjohn, the platoon RTO, radioman, who was grenade nuts and whom everybody called Whiskey j. ("I put up with the Whiskey part, but not the Juliet," he told me); and last of all was Jerry Stepik, the platoon medic, one of the payday blackjack players and a real card sharp. Trobridge, the dude in charge of the ambush, ate by himself at the NCO tables on the other side of the serving line, which was just as well.

We slouched in the cheap kitchen chairs, eating little, drinking coffee and popping No Doz, laughing and talking and throwing our cigar and cigarette butts on the floor. I sat quietly near one end of the table, leaning forward over my tray and breathing deep and rhythmically, trying to get my stomach to settle. I darted my eyes, glancing from face to face as the conversation skipped back and forth.

Whiskey j., who had clusters of warts on the backs of his hands and long, straight black hair, used his canteen cup and the salt and pepper shakers to explain how to booby-trap claymores with trip flares or frags with the shorter fuses from smoke grenades. Then he slipped a pineapple grenade from his flak jacket, hefting it in his hand, and said, "What's fucked up about this frag, Deadeye?" He rolled it across the table at me.

I didn't know.

"The pin's in. Here," he said, snatching it up again. "See, you got to straighten the cotter pin, and when we go out tonight and sit, why, you yank the ring and pull the pin all but half a cunt hair. See?" He held the grenade in one hand, holding down the spoon handle, and yanked the pin free and tossed the pin and ring on the table. Then he snatched it up again, pinched the halves together, and worked the pin back in, twisting it until the pin just hung there, holding back the spoon just barely. "See? Now the mother's ready. You just set it down in your lap, and every-thing is right there and ready, except the bang. Why, you can even John Wayne it and pull the son of a bitch with your fucken eyetooth."

Around five the cooks finally threw us out, pissing and

moaning about the butts on the floor and the mess. We left in a gang and went back to the tents. I laid out my flak jacket, which would be worn zipped and snapped, hung six grenades on the slits about the breast pockets, and attached my field bandage pouch to the left epaulet so it would keep the machine-gun sling from rubbing my neck. I oiled my M-60 from the seven-three and wiped down the two fifty-round belts of ammo with an oiled rag. Atevo would hump the other two belts.

The others went out back to lean against the bunker in the shade and took turns standing at the ditch to piss. I stayed in the tent, trying to nap, but I was too nervous to be comfortable and the tent was hot. I just lay among the lumps of my sleeping bag, wetting my lips and squirming in the sweaty heat, and tried to imagine what going on ambush would be like. I could hear the voices outside and the ha-ha-ha shit laughs and Atevo, sitting Indian fashion, stropping his bowie on his boot leather. Just at dusk when I finally began to get drowsy, Trobridge arrived to get us and everybody came in to get ready. Trobridge carried his M-16, so slopped with gun oil his palms shone. Mac humped his automatic M-14, something like a BAR, which everyone called an E-deuce. All Whiskey j. carried was a knapsack and claymore bag filled with grenades, both the old pineapples and the newer smooth-sided sort, and Ivy's black leather cartridge belts crisscross, Pancho Villa style, and that thirty-eight. Steichen, a short stocky dude who did not eat dinner, carried a short-barreled M-79 grenade launcher and a gas-mask bag full of canister rounds—double-aught buckshot shells in 40-mm casings—which made the seventy-nine a sawed-off shotgun, a scatter gun. Stepik, the medic, had a forty-five and his aid bag. Atevo took his shotgun and two M-16 bandoliers with slits cut for the shells. And everyone wore flak jackets hung with grenades, knives or bayonets, and slouch hats or berets or bush hats. We trooped over to the Orderly Room, where the El-tee held an inspection, going from man to man, tugging straps and asking questions, and finally giving his assent for us to go.

Steichen broke out two camouflage sticks, dark brown and foam green, the only camouflage sticks in the company. He rubbed in wide vertical lines on his face from ear to ear, then passed them along. Atevo drew the crude outline of a hand in green and smeared the rest of his face brown. I let them do me up. Atevo and Steichen argued kiddingly about stripes versus splotches, but Whiskey j. settled it with a flip of his buffalo-head nickel. Atevo did the honors with wide diagonals from my hairline to my collar. He rubbed the sticks hard, burning my shaving cuts.

"A bare face will shine in the dark and be seen," Atevo said, capping the sticks and passing them along. "The same as the glow of a cigarette." The camouflage pulled at my face like drying mud. It felt sticky and strin-gent and the odor was mildly suffocating. The smell of camouflage was just one more thing I would have to get used to, like the bitter taste of ten-year-old C-ration instant coffee and the itch of damp wool socks and sleeping on the narrow metal bench underneath Cross's hammock when we were in the field. We loaded into the back of a deuce-and-a-half for the ride to the MP shack and bunkers and concer-tina wire at the north gate.

The dusk was red and cloudless. We moved in behind the sandbag-and-timber MP shack and along the grassy ditch and settled in, waiting for darkness. I sat with my back to the wire, my feet in the ditch, under the tight heavi-ness of the flak jacket and belted ammo, worn criss-cross fashion, looking down at the M-60—the "pig," they called it.

Guns and grenades and shineless grotesque faces.

Whiskey j., hefting the radio and holding the phone mike up to his ear, stood next to Mac, who had his E-deuce at order arms and stood, hip cocked, leaning on the muzzle and flash suppressor. Steichen sat cross-legged near me with his seventy-nine in his lap and rubbed a canister round like a new baseball. Atevo and Stepik sat back to back in the grass, leaning against each other, and Trobridge spent the whole wait in the MP's shack sitting in a chair, watching the woodline and rapping in whispers with the MP sergeant. They all daubed the sweat from their faces with their forearms, talked in low voices, and kept checking their pockets. I was warm and sweating under my flak jacket already. All I could think of was that in a moment I would crack open the feed tray, lay those first fifteen rounds in, cock it with that click-clack-click sound, loud as horses, and walk through the wire. I had asked Atevo and Steichen, what do I do? And they had said: turn and fire. Don't squeeze and don't hesitate. Yes, but what do I do? Hit the prone and put out rounds, they told me. Get grazing fire, keep the muzzle low, down where the ankles are. If we get hit, don't sweat and don't run. But we got nothing to worry about. Gooks in this neck of the woods is too dufus, this time of year they're still half-stepping it around Suoi Tre and French Fort and Fire Base Grant, up that way. What Cross called puppy-shit country, " 'cause it's runny and yellow and smells fucked up."

Finally it was dark and word came down for the Romeo Apple Pie to move out. One by one we got on line. The MP unlocked the gate, rattling the chain. The softest echo reverberated against the far woodline and everybody shuddered, whispering curses at the guy. "Sorry. Sorry," he whispered back, but Stepik and a couple others mumbled in stage whispers, "Lot a fucken good 'sorry' is." He pushed the gate open a crack and one at a time we filed through—first Mac, then Trobridge. When Whiskey j. came up to the MP he said, "My man, we get hit within five hundred meters of this gate, an' I'm gonna come back here and do you in. If I got to crawl and push myself along with stumps." Then he put the phone mike to his mouth and whispered, "Romeo Apple Pie leaving the wire. See you all in Montreal."

Just before Steichen stepped off behind Whiskey j., he snapped the safety off and turned to me and said, "Do what I do. Step light. See you in the morning." I put the sling of the pig over my shoulder and brought the butt of the gun up into my right armpit. I waited for a decent interval, counting the soft footfalls, then took a breath to settle down and stepped off. I waited to hear Atevo. I listened and listened and listened, all the while moving away from the wire. And still I did not hear him, until I glanced around and there he was, coming along behind, quiet as you please.

It felt as though I had walked through a wall. The air was different there, the ground sounded funny under my feet. I felt the air thicken; moisten; chill. I wanted so bad to turn around and walk backward for a moment, to look and see that sliver of space between the gate halves fall back, like the lip of a well I have fallen in. The stone circle falling up and up until the sky is a small hot speck. I tightened my hand around the slippery plastic. We moved quickly from the road through the ditch and clumps of bushes and tall grass into a hedgerow of bamboo. Then Mac started to take his time, so we moved slowly. I kept trying to adjust the pig, hunching my shoulders and holding them stiff or dropping them down, holding the trigger and pistol grip with my right and using the off hand to hold back the branches. The bamboo stalks were thick, and moving among them was difficult because they did not give, but hung stiff nearly to the ground. I lost Steichen as soon as he went inside the hedgerow. I felt the sweat on the back of my neck, along the sides of my face. There was little sound besides my own breathing and the bamboo clacking together in the wind.

The gun, the ammo, the grenades and flak jacket, everything hangs painfully on my shoulders. I begin to sweat in earnest. It tickles. It burns. It screams at me. It rolls down my face, dripping bitterly into my eyes. My legs and feet itch, my back and arms, even my scalp. Abruptly we move into a stand of rubber trees. I look behind me. Atevo moves among the shadows, a man-shaped silhouette. There is a light breeze and the trees shake noisily. The leaves flash green and silver and green. We move through several rows in a northerly direction. I see the patrol in front of me, stretching out for fifty or seventy-five meters. Way ahead, framed by the last two trees, there is a clearing. The patrol stops, but Steichen motions me closer. There in the moonlight is an acre of cleared ground with rice berms and a small truck garden. We move out, walking in turned earth. The patrol staggers itself on either side of the berm. Steichen is on the right. I am on the left. Atevo is on the right. Halfway across Mac turns east along another berm. I am still on the left, closest to the opposite woodline. We are nearly into the rubber again, then there is a faint soft clicking, a rustling. I turn my head in the direction of the noise. Someone shouts, *"Gooks!"* and immediately there is a long, shuddering burst of automatic-rifle fire, clean and crisp. There are gun flashes in the woodline and I freeze. I am frozen as though the air has been sucked out of my lungs. Then more shots and grenades and more shots. I seem to be lifted from the ground. The noise gets fainter and fainter, like the sound of trains. Rounds are going by my ears, near enough to touch, buzzing, whining like quick hard thorns. I can see myself lying on the ground screaming bloody murder. Suddenly my gun is firing. The recoil shakes me stiffly. Those first fifteen rounds are gone—into the dirt in front of me. Rounds keep coming out of the woodline, right for my chest, my head, kicking up dirt around my feet. I am still standing. I drop to the ground and roll to the side and with fumbling fingers try to unhook the belts of ammo. Everyone else is behind the berm. I don't have to look back to know it. Here I am, cursing and fumbling, trying my level goddamn best to shoot back, but my hands, my eyes, my voice—everything is haywire. I am going to be killed. Soon they will get the range for real and blow me away. I feel so stupid. I am so panicked I cannot speak, not even to scream. I breathe in gasps, sucking the acrid gun smoke and sweet humus smell and sweaty salt odor of my own body deep into my lungs.

Then it changed.

I would load and lock that gun if it was the last natural act of my life. They are going to kill me, but what is it going to look like, the new man so fucked up he couldn't get off more than a couple rounds? I open the feed tray, lay the first rounds of ammo in, and close it with a snap. I turn the gun to the side and cock it, then set out the bipod legs and settle the butt plate snug against my shoulder. I start at ankle height at the edge of the woodline, dropping my shoulder to elevate the muzzle. The sputtering gun flashes light the whole area in front of me. I hear the rounds slamming into the woodline, slapping through the leaves and low branches. The woodline returns fire. I hear the rounds going by my head, making that dull *thup* sound as they hit the berm behind. Then it happens. Hangfire. I take a breath and cock the gun and try again. Only a couple more. Rework. Reload. Another breath. Work, you mother. A couple more rounds. Another breath. Load and lock again. Rework and reload and rework. Piss on it, I'm dead. I inch back until my feet touch the berm and I pull the gun in front of me for cover. I begin to laugh. I'm pathetic. They're going to kill me right here. Not just a little dead, not a quarter cupful, but gallons and gallons of dead and gone. Doesn't your life flash in front of you? Isn't this where you scream and pray to God?

Shit, if I do scream they *will* kill me.

I hold so tight to the stock that my arms shake. My eyes are slammed shut.

Boogie man, boogie man, where you at?

I squeeze down close to the ground. "Hey, cease fire! We're GIs, goddamn it! GIs. Cease fire!" someone shouts. Then come more shouts and echoes and louder shouts. The shooting on both sides stops. Someone touches my leg.

"Flip? Hey, Flip? You okay?" comes a whisper. Without bothering to answer I gather up the gun, throw it over the berm, and lunge headfirst after it. I stretch out on my back where I fall, breathing open-mouthed, forcing down long, deep drafts. My arms shake, my fingers open and close just to feel the muscles work against the earth. I am soaked to the skin and fiery hot. There is something jammed in my throat. I feel as though I will have to puke or choke on it. My whole body shudders against loose dirt. My stomach rattles my breathing into short terrified gasps. Atevo lays his hand on my chest and whispers, "You okay?" His hands are all over me, lightly touching my legs and sides and head, feeling quickly for a tear or the sticky warm wetness of blood. He slides his hands under the small of my back and lifts me, saying, "Breathe out all the way. Hold it. Now slowly breathe in."

I turn and look at his face smeared with dirt, the narrow whites of his eyes, and the stars behind that shine and sparkle in that slick sort of way. My eyes sting with salty sweat and the sprinkle of reflections, white hot and shining so close. It is all I can see; the handful of glowing crystals and the black outline of Atevo's face and the wild hair hanging down from under his slouch hat in brownish greasy curls.

"Come on, Flip, get your shit together," he says at last.

I roll over to the berm. Steichen has set my gun across the top with thirty rounds still hanging from the feed tray. The three of us watch the woodline. In front of us I can see the litter of brass, four of my six grenades, and the other belt of ammo. The woodline is just as before, but I can make out soft scufflings and murmurs. In the moonlight I look straight down at the place I had fretted and nearly cried. The dirt is molded around the soft image of a struggle and pinched where the rifle fire ricocheted. There are soft clumps of turned earth, a random scatter of brass to the right, and scrapes in the dirt where my feet and hands clawed, pulling me back. I see the pitiful thrashing, the pleading, the stupid kicking and screaming, the quick death. I am looking down at the ghost of my own corpse.

Steichen whispers, "Hey, man, what happened?"

"The motherfucker misfired," I say. "I worked it and worked it, but it just wouldn't go. Is anybody hit?"

Steichen sidles over. "No, hey, but how's this for stupid. They're ARVNs." He points to the woodline with his chin. ARVNs. South Viets. Our allies.

Trobridge crawls down to us, scuttling on his belly, to explain that the three of us will cover the others when he gives the word. We are pulling back to the woodline and going back to camp.

He bellies back to Whiskey j. and Stepik and Mac and a moment later there is a shout and the four men get up, turn their backs to the ARVNs, and run. There is a moment of foot stomping, hustling, and grunting, then silence. Trobridge shouts again, but I do not hear what he says. I get up with Steichen and Atevo, and swing the pig to port arms, and run flat out. I want to run and run and run. I want to crash through the woodline, hit the trail, and keep going. I want to shout and scream, yell and run. I have never known the simple release of turning my back on a terror and taking to the woods. Atevo and Steichen and I fly past the others and jump behind another berm. We roll into the prone with our guns at the ready. Trobridge and the others take off again. They run past us in a random sort of way back to the woodline. We watch them, and the moment they break through the bushes and into the woods, we get up and run after them. I yank the pig close to my chest and run flat out, bent slightly at the waist, and I begin to feel better the closer I get to the rubber trees. I hear a pop behind me and then there is a sudden burst of light above us.

Flare!

I let go the gun and fall to the ground and freeze, my hands over my eyes to save my night vision. I can hear the flare crackling overhead, the phosphorus boiling white hot and dripping foamy gobs to the ground a hundred, ninety, eighty feet below. I open my eyes and see the black and silver shadow of my arm as it quickly passes and passes again in front of me. The flare hits the ground and bounces. The small white nylon chute catches fire, burns brilliantly for a moment, then goes out. It is immediately black dark. The three of us get up one last time and run. I snatch up the strap of the pig on the fly and we run, trampling onions and cabbage and bean plants and poles, until the low-hanging branches of the trees brush against my face. I stomp on someone's flak jacket. Atevo and Steichen and I stand in a daze, catching our breath while the rest of the patrol gathers behind us. We trot back through the rubber, Atevo leading the way, all the way back to the jungle. We stop and sit down. I feel as though I will throw up. I wish I would. We stay there while Trobridge calls Battalion. He tells them we are coming in by the quickest way, then we move off and do not stop until we reach the edge of the bamboo hedgerow.

Trobridge has us wait while he gets close enough to the MP to whisper. When he is inside he signals twice with his flashlight, and one at a time we go through the bushes, along the ditch, and step inside the wire, home free. When it comes my turn, I watch Steichen running in a crouch along the ditch, then sidestep through the gate. The two flashes come and I am off.

I don't remember whether I ran or walked or what, but the next thing I knew Trobridge threw the light in my face.

I see nothing but the ringed whiteness of the light, the rim of the flashlight, and the ring on his finger.

"Name?" I can't tell if it is Trobridge or the MP.

"Ugh, yes, sir," I say.

"Name. What's your name?"

"Dosier. Get that fucking light out of my face." I push the flashlight away with a parry of the gun.

"Watch your language, trooper."

"Take that flashlight and shove it up your ass." I push past them nudging someone aside. I can see nothing, just shadows of arms and on the periphery—lights flickering like worms. I walk away from the gate. I don't know where anybody is. I don't care. I want to get away from this madness, get this crap out of my eyes. I walk up the road until I bump into someone. I am muttering to myself, spitting on the ground, trying to get the bile out of my mouth.

"Hey, trooper, are you well?" someone says. It is the Colonel. I can make out the brass chicken on his collar and the shine on his chin and nose.

"Yes, sir, pardon me, sir," I say. Fuck him, I'm thinking.

I step to the side and then there stands Cross, his cigar glowing, clenched in his teeth, and his thumbs hooked on his pockets.

"Cross?" I say.

"Dosier, here let me carry that," he says, and reaches for the gun. I gladly give it to him. He takes me by the arm and leads me to the deuce-and-a-half that has come down to pick us up. Steichen gives me a hand up. I sit on the bench and unzip my flak jacket and open my shirt, holding them open to let in a cool rush of air. Cross throws the gun onto the back and climbs after. I sit with my head between my legs to see if I will finally throw up. I want to get the puke, that bitter tang of creamy yellow bile, out of my throat. It is giving me a headache, making my ears ring, my jaws ache. Cross passes me a canteen; the water is tepid and brackish. I drink some and pour the rest on my head, and rub the back of my neck. Then he gives me a cigarette. I take it and lean back, shoving my feet out in front of me. My shirt and socks and hair are sopping wet, as though I have been caught in a quick spring storm.

We hear Atevo cursing Trobridge for the flashlight, and someone unloading a fifty in one of the bunkers, slamming the feed tray shut, clanking the belted ammo against the tripod. Atevo mounts up. Trobridge comes and we ride back to the company.

Atevo and Steichen and I were sitting on our cots wiping down when Trobridge traipsed in and said that the patrol was to form up in the mess hall. The Colonel wanted to talk at us. When we got there the Colonel, the Major, and the El-tee stood near the head of the Colonel's table, talking in whispers and drinking Kool-Aid from mess cups. One of the cooks offered us sandwiches from a platter, limp lettuce and thick-sliced ham on that no-taste GI white bread. We took a sandwich apiece and ladled out coffee and slid in at the back of the rest of the patrol near the provision-room wall.

Colonel Sadler was as plain-looking as a piece of unfinished wood with a white sidewall haircut, and he always looked rested whenever I saw him. He lived in a gray forty-foot trailer just behind the operations bunker, had his own shower, and the only air conditioner in the battalion. It was *his* chopper that landed the first time I got dusted off for heat exhaustion. And the Major—I never did catch his name—was a rough-and-tumble-looking guy with a fraternity haircut who always followed the Colonel around with clipboards and pockets full of messages and rosters. He folded the Colonel's shirt sleeves and held his doors and cut his meat at dinner, no doubt.

Finally, the Colonel and Major and the El-tee put down their cups, walked to the middle of the room, and stood at parade rest, one behind the other. The El-tee stood stiff, harassed and embarrassed, while the Major barked, "Listen up!" to get our attention, then the Colonel cleared his throat and spoke.

"Sergeant Trobridge," said the Colonel, looking down his nose at him, past the chicken feathers on his collar and his Airborne wings and Ranger shoulder patch, and the crisp inverted creases on his folded shirt sleeves.

"Yes, sir!" Trobridge sang out, and got up, standing at a brisk, chin-wrinkling attention.

"Sit *down*, Sergeant," said the Colonel, coming up on his toes. "How long have you been a noncommissioned officer?" he asked, enunciating each consonant and vowel in full voice.

"Sir!" said Trobridge. "I have been an E-5 for a month and a half, sir. Date of rank, thirty January, sir."

"Hmmm," the Colonel said. He rocked back on his heels and slapped his hands together behind his back and dropped his chin, looking lost in thought, the way they do. "Young sergeant, this ambush was your responsibility. As far as I have been able to judge, your patrol was something like five hundred meters off its course. The one fact I am certain of is that you were ambushed by an ARVN compound that has been located at those coordinates since before this battalion arrived in-country. Now, just to teach your young ass a lesson I should send you and your troopers right back out, but I am not going to do that"—and a visible sigh of relief went through Steichen and Atevo and Whiskey j. and the rest of us—"because those goddamn ARVNs, apparently, were not advised by Brigade of your route or destination in the first place.

"However, be that as it may," he said, "I have received a communication from the brigade evac hospital that your ambush killed three outright and wounded fifteen. Sergeant Trobridge, as far as I'm concerned, you have fucked up, and this is the last time I want to see you under these circumstances, but on the other hand I feel I should offer congratulations to all of you for conducting yourselves in a soldierly manner. You men are a credit to this battalion," he said, the way they do. "That's all."

"Ten-shun!" barked the Major, and we all stood up. The Colonel and the Major gathered up their steel pots, which they wore command-bunker style, slightly down over both ears, and made for the door. The El-tee stopped to say something to Trobridge, who did not look well at all, and left quickly.

Atevo and Steichen and I leaned back on our chairs finishing the sandwiches, eating the meat, leaving the bread; grateful we wouldn't have to saddle up again and go back out. Off to one side Trobridge and Mac leaned over their table, talking loudly. I could hear the gladness in Mac's voice, too, along with the brag.

"There, you see!" said Mac. "I fucken told ya I got them three little mothers with the first burst. They was crouched down by that bush there, an' me an' ma E-deuce swung around right then and there an' blew their shit a-way.

I keep telling ya, Highpockets, I *never* miss," and he let out a long, loud horse laugh.

I ladled out another canteen cup of Haskins' strong campfire coffee and took it back to the tent, one of the last to leave the mess hall. I sat in the dark on the edge of my cot with a green PX towel draped around my neck, unlacing my boots one eyehole at a time, sipping coffee and smoking the last cigarettes in the pack. I felt very small and lonely.

Every year my brothers and I couldn't wait for the first big snow. When it came we would roll snowballs for snowmen. The three of us would top them with a beat-up felt derby hat Pop had won at a carnival ring toss. Pop said he had me on his shoulders and I kissed each ring for luck. We always put the snowmen in the middle of the front yard and when we were older they were as high as the house. But when we were still very young we would sprawl in the snow and on signal flap our arms and legs and wag our heads to make figures, just in front of the sidewalk. Snow angels, with wide shirts and drooping sleeves and big-eared heads and halos. We would get up carefully and jump to the sidewalk with all our might so the angels would seem suspended. Then we'd stand and look at them until one of us grabbed some snow for a snowball and broke the spell. We'd race down the street, making snowballs as we ran, winging them at each other and passing buses and cabs. And it was snow angels I was reminded of when I peeked over that berm, my breath hot and hissing with fright, and stared at that terrified, splay-legged image of a struggle in front of that woodline, only our snow angels were white and as deep as the snow.

I kept sipping coffee and puffing on wet-lipped Camels and glancing over at Atevo and his gear spread out on his beat-up footlocker. His face was plaqued and folded with wrinkles, fine hairline creases that followed the close grain of his skin, and smeared with camouflage. His hands were wrinkled, too, sprayed along the palms—the wrinkles fanning out where the movement of his thumb stretched and opened them. He slept with his eyes open, the poncho liner to his chin and his trouser cuffs loose around his ankles. He always slept that way, breathing slowly and heaving his chest with his head straight. And his gear—the shotgun propped against the footlocker with the slouch hat hung on the muzzle and the homemade bandolier cartridge belts and black bowie knife and his filthy flak jacket and steel pot— right next to his hand within easy reach.

And I glanced up and down the two rumpled rows of cots, the two lumpy rows of sleepers. What in the world am I doing here? My parents raised me on "Thou-shalt-nots" and willow switches and John Wayne (even before he became a verb), the Iwo Jima bronze and First and Second Samuel, and always, always the word was "You do what I tell you to do." The concept around our house was everybody takes his own lickings. But what in the name of God had I done to get this one? This wasn't going to be a simple whipping. This was going to be a thrashing with the buckle end of the belt. Why, oh why wasn't I born the Crown Prince or some senator's brat, having myself a whipping boy? But I'm dumb. I'm a fool. Always wanting nothing more than to get along, just hoping to get by—a true son of the empire, trusting enough to buy that sorry myth of having to pay my dues—and so hauled off by the ears to sit on this cot and struggle around these woods, taking the cure. It was going to be a long year, too, or a short one. And the former dues payers? The spectators and cheerleaders who have already cashed in and haven't missed a meal since? They will gather around my marker once a year and plant flags and mumble prayers, blessing my hoary soul, and salute my corpse, bawling and honking into their handkerchiefs, while I lie in state at Arlington National Cemetery. Stuck in the fucking Army until the goddamn Judgment.

You've got to be nuts to do an ambush, to want to do it, to get your sorry ass talked into it. It sounds so simple—walk out, walk in, like falling out of bed. Every night, for months, a different route, a different spot, every night a brand-new can of worms. Listen, not even your own house back on the block looks the same at night. Everything was shades of gray and silver and black, even with an illumination round from a 105 floating down from two thousand feet. But after a while you catch on to the game. The deeper shadows among the bushes or the silhouettes glowing on the woodline or the lighter, almost white of the line of the horizon. And you learn to step light. The closer you get, the more quiet you've got to be. Toe-heel-toe. Stop. Listen. Watch. Does it smell funny? Move again. Listen. Stretch your neck and put your ear to it. What's the sound behind that sound? Gooks or rats or a swarm of mosquitoes? Keep moving, keep looking, keep listening. Hear that? Music from a radio in that ville over there. You get to the ambush site and set up slowly, one man at a time. Then you sit. Hour after hour, the woodline and the lonely bushes and the sorry clumps of kunai grass and the clouds that come and go. Everything becomes so familiar. Everybody sits within an arm's reach, behind camouflage, in a defilade if you can, all the claymores out, the grenades in your lap, and the pistol grip of the pig in your hand. It is the oldest skill. You think about everything: God and the devil and pussy and *what*-the-*fuck*-am-I-*doing*-here. You sing a song to yourself or crack a joke. You squirm because you've got to take a leak, but you hold it until your stomach aches, and wait for morning. And sometimes, if you're an FNG, a fucken new guy, you nod out, thinking the same things you were thinking before—God and the devil and pussy, damn I wish I had some pussy. Then something starts you awake. There is a flash of light, like somebody has cracked you across the face with the narrow side of a two-by-four. You startle. And there it is just the way you left it. The woodline and the bushes and the kunai grass. You sit there red in the face, not because you've nodded off, but because you have jerked awake and made the mistake of being heard. But it is a trick of the mind. It is only your eyes that have moved. You sit there dumb, like stones and logs, as still as lake water in the moonlight. The movement is underneath—the cool water rising, the warm slowly sinking. All you heard was your heart beating, slamming against your chest, screaming again and again.

Every time we went out we sat watching the cart trails or a footpath or a rice paddy, until first light or the first rush of blood in our ears when all of a sudden there he was, skylarking down the trail right at us. And then we blew him away with a claymore, and watched him fly and bounce and roll. Some quiver, some wiggle, some are stiff right away. Every night for weeks, months. Years maybe. Mac and his E-deuce, Atevo's shotgun, Steichen's seventy-nine. Rain or shine. From camp or some fire base or other, into the jungle or the rubber or the paddies north of Trang Bang. We would gather at the seven-four to sip some smoke, slap on some camouflage, and go. And after the first dozen or so I got used to the pig and preferred it. That and the two hundred rounds. I would come back in the morning, the second man back from point, my flak jacket smeared with mosquitoes, hating the rain. My eyes going bad and my mustache coming along. Out and back, just like falling out of bed, until I couldn't have told you the day or the date. My eyes went deeper and deeper into my head and my hair got a shade lighter, my hands got water-wrinkled and leathery, and I had a strength in my wrists I was sure could crush a wooden post. I would sit out there nights in the pouring-down rain or the insane moonlight and wonder why, why am I doing this? But after a while that faded, too, like clouds fade sometimes, slow and billowing, but billowing like a fire sucking the smoke into itself. I would sit there snug enough in my flak jacket, my belly and back sleek with sweat. My thighs and arms shivering, my stiff and wrinkled fingers around the pistol grip, and the grenades snuggled down comfortable, like breaking in a big ugly chair. Then early in the morning we would pass around the No Doz and the canteen. And when we could see each other plain and the dinks could see us plain, we got up in a gang, stood around working our legs and gathered in the claymores, and walked in. We got on line and moved off by the most direct route, calling the El-tee to say we were coming in. And as we moved off, the papa-sans came behind with their oxcarts, and the herd boys came behind them with the cattle and buffalo that dragged their nose-ring thongs between their legs. We walked with a long interval, stretched out fifty meters and more. We did the last hundred meters with our backs to the perimeter watching the woodline, stepping around and through and over the several concentric semicircles of armed claymores. When we passed between the tracks, Atevo and I made for the seven-three, Steichen for the seven-four, Mac the seven-two, and Stepik and Whiskey j. the six-niner. Like the fingers of a hand first pointing, then reaching flat to grasp. We would throw off the guns and hats and flak jackets and shirts and steel pots, and walk with a shuffle over to the artillery's mess tent for breakfast. The Romeo ambush was always the last to eat. We would straggle through the chow line voiceless, beyond complaining and wishing and sleep, into bizarre swirling dreams, coming down from that tight, circling ambush high.

Our eyes wide and tight, staring down at cold, shriveled eggs, the dregs of instant potatoes, and no milk. Atevo and Steichen and I would sit on the cook's bunker outside the doorway, no shirts and all, stinking that morning mildew stink. The camouflage still on our faces, the streaks of grit thick and kind of artful, like the small subtle folds of sand that an inlet surf leaves when a slow tide gives way. We would sit there side by side just like we had done all night, wordless, eating soundlessly, but feeling the close heat of the other bodies. The dreams would come faster and faster, the forks moving slower and slower. And every once in a while there would be some lifer, some dufus straight from the plane with starch still in his teeth, some first looey with a command-bunker housecat job and something folded and stuffed sideways, who'd peek out from under the awning of the officers' mess, as though the tent were part of his cap, all shaved and smelling so good with his buffed-up boots shoved out in front of him. And he'd whip his act on us. "Hey, you troopers! Where's your steel pots? Who is your platoon leader?" And the three of us would look around as though he was talking to somebody else.

"You three right there! The uniform of the day is shirts, rifles, and steel pots." We would stare at him, stare at each other, gather up our coffee and paper plates and mess-kit forks, and move back to the tracks down on the line where we could eat in peace. And dufus would sit there jacking his jaw till we were out of earshot.

After chow the three of us would smoke a smoke to mellow down. Steichen would go back to the seven-four, Atevo and I would crawl under the seven-three with our blankets where the grass would be cool until noon or so, and nap. Not sleep. It was never sleep. We would lie on our backs with our arms over our eyes, and dream the same dreams as before, the weary dreams and wet dreams and bad dreams. Karen with her ballerina thighs who had died of pneumonia the Thanksgiving before, and Jenny's freckles and the scar across the bridge of her nose, the lilacs and jonquils that grew wild in the apple orchard and abandoned nursery out back of the house, and the Grand Trunk night trains whistling past the Techny Junction tower. And then one night, one morning, there was suddenly nothing left, no thought, no wonder, not even the dreams. Just the image over and over again of one foot in front of the other and clusters of sweat pimples and the mildewed taste of salt, moist crawling things and hard-beating rain and mushy turf.

*

Two days later when the ambush stumbled in the gate, the Romeo tracks were waiting for us. The battalion was going back to the field. The ambush climbed aboard, grumbling and pissed. I mounted the pig on the right-side gun shield and sat next to Atevo with our feet dangling in the crew hatch. By the time we arrived at the west gate I had reached inside and fetched a blanket to sit on, because of the jostling and nagging and bouncing ride. When I finally dismounted that night my kidneys ached and my ass was sore, and I walked with a bowlegged limp like a rookie horseman for three or four days.

The Romeo platoon spread out among the other battalion headquarters tracks—the Colonel's operations track, the maintenance and medics' tracks, and the Mortar Platoon's tracks. Alpha Company led. Bravo and Charlie companies fell in behind. When the column finally made a move we hung a right through Dau Tieng, made the river, hit Check Point Hotel, and drove into the rubber. The column cranked along between rows at a walking pace until we came to a large clearing of plowed ground and rubber-tree saplings. Romeo was ordered to keep moving, to go to such-

and-so coordinates and report on the bomb damage of an air strike that had been called in the night before. Cross dismounted and went with the El-tee to see the Colonel's map for himself, then drove point as he always did.

We traveled along a cart trail at a good clip with working rubber on one side and jungle on the other, until the El-tee called and told Cross to hang a left into the jungle. Cross slid down through the ditch and up to the first tree he came to. The front of the seven-three climbed up the side of it, scraping the bark for four or five feet, the tread cleats digging all the while. Then came a quick crunching sound and the tree fell back, uprooted, and we drove over it. The other tracks followed. Cross sat low in the hatch and drove from tree to tree, knocking them back, and soon things were falling out of the canopy; shaken down, pulled down—long sinuous vines, sometimes whole sheets of them, and large chunks of trees long since dead. The deck around Atevo and I became littered with small bewildered insects and branches and twigs and jungle junk. We continuously brushed away low branches and hordes of cobwebs and red pissants. I never gave a thought to the fact that VC might be there. I concentrated on the jungle that was constantly appearing in front of us. Cross drove with his head down so the trees, the trunks and branches, would glance off his football CVC. We made headway by jerks and lunges, rising up the sides of trees, crashing down on top of them with a sudden sharp bounce. Cross drove in low gear, constantly in the high RPMs for leverage. I never plainly saw the ground, only a black background for the shades and hues, the walls and fountains, and balcony upon colonnade upon catwalk of green. Then suddenly in the middle of the afternoon we broke into a clearing. Off to the left, nearly out of sight around a corner, was the air strike. The platoon split into two columns fifty or seventy-five meters apart and moved off. Atevo brought up the box of grenades. Cross drove standing up holding the forty-five in front of his face at arm's length. When we got within easy grenade range the tracks came on line.

The bombs had fallen half in, half out of the woodline, baring what was left of a VC base camp—two beat-up bunkers. The jungle had been gouged out, like a squash. The craters clustered together, overlapping, and a clear, pale green water, like you see in old quarries, seeped in. A litter of grayish dust and chunks of trees and clay and tattered canopy covered the grounds and the splintered tree stumps.

Seven-one and seven-five pulled off a couple long, sweeping bursts with their fifties, reconning by fire, just on the off chance we would draw fire. The gunners, with Atevo and me among them, dismounted and made for the bunkers. We picked our way among the craters and tatters of cloth and a scattering of crumpled tinware, pieces of heavier metal—which I took to be gun parts—odd-shaped chunks of filthy, bug-crawling rice cakes, and various other unrecognizable junk. The place smelled of turned earth and damp, musty clay, and a sniff of cordite soaked into the dirt, like a heavy mist. The tracks pulled into a loose perimeter—a laager—around what was left of the two bunkers, and the TCs joined the search. Almost immediately someone shouted, "Tunnel!" Surtees trundled over to take charge and called for Lavery, Seven-seven Delta, a well-built, shrimpy black kid. The platoon tunnel rat. Lavery leaned down next to the tunnel entrance, cupped his hands around his mouth, and shouted, "Chieu Hoi!"

It means, literally, "open arms" and was the government program by which turncoat VC were rehabilitated. In the field it meant, "Give up." Something the same as happens in Westerns when the posse has the mine shack zeroed in and the hero says, "Okay, Sundance, we got yer ass surrounded. Come out with your hands up!"

No one answered. So Lavery slid back along the ground, and waving everybody back, prepped it with two frags. Then he rolled down his sleeves, chambered a round in his forty-five, and crawled into the tunnel entrance head-first with his flashlight. The fire teams went back to the searching. Atevo came across some blood trails, copious dark puddles teeming with flies, leading to a footpath. We hailed the El-tee, standing on top of the six-niner. He called back for us to follow, but not to go out of earshot. We were just pushing through the woodline, Atevo with his shotgun and Steichen with a canister round in his seventy-nine and me with my sixteen on full auto, when somebody shouted, "Gook!" The three of us hit the prone and waited, then looked behind us to see two troopers from the new seven-six half pushing, half carrying a VC. We went back to the laager. The blood trails could wait. Besides, I wanted to see my first Charlie.

His muddy, bloody shirt and shorts hung from him in shreds. He was small, almost boyish, with oddly cut hair—long on top and shaved at the sides—his face a mass of blackish, yellowish bruises. Blood oozed from his scalp and forehead and cheeks and down his throat. He bled in slow thick trickles from his ears and eyes and mouth. When they sat him against the El-tee's track his wrists bent back and his head lolled to the side. The look on his face in no way showed fear—not even recognition, now that I come to think about it. He clenched his teeth, but his lips hung open, drooling and bleeding around the gums. Stepik pulled out a litter and blankets and laid the man out, giving him sips of water, then began to bandage him as best he could. While Stepik cleaned the blood and applied the compresses, he tried to talk to the man, in a light tone of voice like you would soothe a frightened dog or a lathered, skittish horse, but the man did not seem to hear. The El-tee tried. The man did not even blink his eyes.

At dusk the tracks backed into a tighter laager around the bunkers and we broke for dinner. Cross and Atevo waited for dark, then put out a dozen or so claymores in three concentric semicircles, a handful of trip flares, and dummy claymores booby-trapped with Whiskey j.'s short-fused frags. Before they finished it began to rain. The overcast was low to the ground and I could just make out the light on the El-tee's radio not thirty meters behind. Then came the noise, so soft at first it was almost like humming. Atevo and Cross and I sat on the back between the pig gun shields, watching the darkness and the rain and the faint outline of the craters in front of us, when the man began to moan. I jerked my head around and stared into the darkness with the others. It was that effortless open-mouthed sort of crying—half breathing, half cursing. All he had to do was open his mouth and exhale. He lay there thinking about the pain, the only thing he had left in the world, oozing from his scalp and under his fingernails, the sweat that dripped from the wrinkles on his neck, and the stupid rain. The moans washed back and forth, coming out of the darkness like fingers and hands, flying past us to the other side of the clearing and back. Was he just doing it to hear himself? Did he listen and compare? A whisper came from the other side of the laager: "Shut him the fuck up." Stepik crawled over quickly and pulled the blankets closer around his chin. The man shook his head. Stepik gave him some water, pouring it slowly over the lips, dripping it around the bandages on his eyes. He took the water, all that was offered, and shook his head still.

"Shit, buddy," said Stepik in a whisper. "Come on." The whole laager sat there looking over their shoulders, gazing into the darkness where the sound was the thickest, when one of the three-man listening posts in the jungle came over the air in slow and careful whispers. "Lima Papa. Two. I got movement."

I jerked my head and looked at the lighted dial of our radio, then out to the front over the three rows of claymores and the bomb craters. There was a long silence. Cross picked up the mike. "Hey, Step, get him quiet."

"Whadaya want me to do?" Stepik asked.

"Either shut him up, or shoot him up."

Stepik crawled away from the radio and back to the man. The man heard him come and a second man behind him, and began to thrash slowly and squirm. Stepik had the second man hold his head down and one arm while Stepik held the other arm tight between his knees, like he was shoeing a horse. Then he reached quickly into the aid bag and took out four quarter grains of morphine. Stepik jabbed his arm four times and squeezed the syringes. Both of them held the little man down. Slowly, the noise subsided, got quieter and quieter, until it was nothing but a rustle of the blanket pulled smooth.

I could feel my stomach go numb, feel the smooth and slack and warm plastic of the pig's pistol grip in my sticky fingers, feel the trickles of rain soaking through the flak jacket to my shirt.

"Cross," I whispered. "You've killed him."

"So?"

"But he was wounded. He was a prisoner." I looked at Atevo, but he just looked back at me, blinking his eyes.

"Look, Dosier," said Cross. "He was giving away our position—why you think the LP was whispering? He was dying anyway. I seen it enough to know it when it comes stumbling out of the woodline. And besides, it was a gook. You give gooks a break like that and you ain't gonna last. Listen, I took a chance for Murphy, I'll take a chance for Atevo, and I'll take a chance for you, but don't ask me to take a chance for gooks. Dosier, look: the only thing more fucked up than being here, is getting killed here. Savvy?"

The rest of the night we listened to the LP calling in

movement. The next morning we ate early and gathered in the claymores and trip flares and booby traps. Stepik and Whiskey j. took the litter and the body and the blankets over to the craters. I stood next to the seven-three driver's hatch, winding in a trip-flare wire around a stick, and watched them slide the body feet first into the water. They folded the blankets and collapsed the litter, and I wondered how Stepik could do it. We mounted up and moved off, and while we busted jungle I kept looking back at Stepik, sitting next to the El-tee with his forty-five in his lap and his aid bag over his shoulder.

*

We busted jungle until we came to a road and headed for the village of Suoi Dau, near the Nui Ba Dinh, the Black Virgin Mountain. We rode out of the rubber into open rice fields, through the suburbs of Tay Ninh city, back into the rice fields, and then Suoi Dau. South of the village was an ARVN fort, a battery of eight-inch guns and 175s, and an airfield. At the other end of the runway was a creek, apparently the namesake of the place, and a wood bridge and road going past an abandoned brickyard. The road continued to French Fort and Fire Base Grant and more rubber, and farther north more jungle and the Cambodian border.

We roared through the village and alongside the runway almost to the creek. Cross pulled up with a jerk ten meters past the end of the runway and before any of the other tracks were in place around the airfield we had shut down and sat inside in the shade. Trobridge took off his flak jacket and helmet, but stayed in the hatch, watching the bushes across the creek. A while later Steichen and Stepik came up the road with their steel pots and weapons. Stepik brought along two decks of Red Cross cards, and the five of us set out some ammo cans covered with a mangy piece of plywood and blanket and cut cards to see who was going to deal blackjack. We huddled around the board with our knees up, bare-chested and sweating even in the breeze, when the Coke and beer and dope and pussy merchants arrived. They came in small groups, like a parade, stretching out along the outside of the perimeter and hawking to the crews as they came. Claymore Face, the platoon punchboard, was there, too. She snagged a couple takers and took them down to the creek embankment one at a time while the others stood along the top in a gang, hooting and laughing and lobbing rocks.

"Hey! Whip it to her, Lavery!" somebody said.

"Goddamn Claymore Face, you sure got the *ugliest* cunt for a hundred clicks around," yelled someone else.

"Yessireee," said Lavery, coming up the slope and grinning. "Terrible! Just pitiful! Like fucken a washrag soaked with vinegar. Who's next?" He made a show of hiking up his pants one more time for the crowd, picked up his shirt, and walked away, blowing kisses down toward the creek. And we could hear Claymore Face's squeaking, high-pitched squeal, "Yoo-hoo!"

Two small girls not even into puberty yet walked up to the back of the ramp, each dragging a plastic mesh basket dripping with ice, one filled with Cokes, the other with beer in quarts.

"Hey, Sebbo-twee! Gaa-damma, you wann Coke? You wann bee-a! Got dope, too." Cross looked up from his cards. We all looked up. She was barefoot with filthy splayed toes, black pajamas, and long black hair under her cone hat.

"Well, shit. If it ain't No-tits. Whatcha got, No-tits?" he said, putting down the deck.

"Boo-coo cold, Sebbo-twee," she said and opened the top of her basket.

"How much?"

"Twenny-fie Coke. Numba-one boo-coo cold. Bee-a fordy cen'. Ace bee-a, gaa-damma," she said, staring at us.

"Too much," said Cross with a wave of his hand.

Steichen said, "Yeah, too fucken much. We ain't no rookies. Beat it, No-tits."

"Okay. Okay. Twenny for Coke. Thurdy for bee-a."

I bought the first round, paying No-tits in MPC. She hooked the church key over the top of each bottle and with a sharp rap of her hand that made a sharp, sucking *pok*, opened the bottles and handed them up. Then she squatted on her heels next to her friend to wait for the empties. They sat thigh to thigh with the baskets between their knees under the shade of their cone hats. We went back to the game, throwing the empties back and calling for more; Cross shuffling and dealing and slapping down the hit cards.

"Hey, Sebbo-twee! You hurry up, heh? No-tits got buznus, eh?"

"Yeah, sure sure, No-tits. Don't get yer balls inna uproar," Cross said, not looking up from his hand.

We drank all the beer they had and played blackjack and bought a five-pound sack of Cambodie dope. No-tits and her friend left with the collapsed mesh baskets under their arms. Alpha and Bravo companies arrived from Tay Ninh and a little later Charlie Company showed up with battalion headquarters. They spread themselves out between the airfield and the ARVN compound. About the middle of the afternoon a flight of choppers came in from the southeast. The El-tee called over the radio that General Somebody-or-other from Division was on one of the choppers and everybody should get their shirts and flak jackets and steel pots on and straighten up for a minute. Then he threw a green smoke grenade for the wind direction. The three choppers came in low overhead, skimming along the runway and taxiing down to where the Colonel stood with the Major and the rest of his suite. There was a moment of saluting and handshaking and welcomes and small talk, bowing and scraping for the General, the way lifers do. Then they walked over to the Colonel's track, where the lawn chairs and beer cooler and map table were. I watched them in Trobridge's field glasses, lounging in the lawn chairs and yakking and swilling the Colonel's beer, poring and puzzling mightily over the French-made maps that didn't even show the road from Dau Tieng to the Tay Ninh high road. They stayed and stayed while their chopper crews sat twiddling their thumbs, and we sat in our shirts and flak jackets and steel pots, working up a sweat in the shade. Then as quickly as he came, everybody saluting and bowing and scraping for the General again, he left. Two minutes later the three line companies and battalion head-quarters left, with Romeo right behind.

Cross and Stepik and Mac and a couple others decided to stop in Suoi Dau for ice and beer. At the first hooch, across the road from the guy who sold beer, a woman sat on her haunches, swinging a baby in a low-slung hammock tied between the doorposts. Off to the right in a copse of trees was a huge pile of damp rice chaff, covering a couple hundred pounds of ice. Cross pulled up along the ditch in front of the hooch and everybody pulled in close behind him. Then, without shutting down, he jumped down and walked into the yard straight to the woman.

"Mama-san!" he yelled. "Gimme some ice." He slowed up and shot his arm out, pointing to the pile of chaff. The woman jumped up, jabbered something into the hooch, and an instant later some kid came streaking around the back and began shoveling through the pile with his hands. Every track in the platoon sent somebody down with a sandbag and MPC. Atevo and Steichen and others went across the road to get the beer—warm or cold, it didn't matter. The kid stood holding up the ice, hefting it from hand to hand for Cross to see; his legs and arms wet and clinging with chaff, his elbows dripping water. Cross looked at it and judged it too big, so the kid took a hand scythe and chopped off a little. The woman stood next to Cross waiting for the money. When the kid had a piece that looked like it would fit into the Igloo, Cross counted out a couple bucks and walked back through the crowd with his ice held up in one hand. Everybody started talking at once, flagging their MPC in the air, razzing the kid, who jumped back into the ice and chaff. Then the crowd was joined by the El-tee with Surtees right behind, his hand hanging limp from his shoulder-holster forty-five like he was leaning on a fireplace mantel.

"Cross!" said the El-tee with exasperation. "Just what in the goddamn fucking hell are you trying to pull?"

"Say?" Cross said. "Sir?" He looked over and raised his eyebrows.

"Don't give me any of your 'say what?' short-timer 'sir' crap! You heard what I said," he said, rolling his *r*'s. And behind him Surtees nodded his head, flashing that harmless flame. "I do not give a good squat if you go home tonight!" the El-tee said, pointing his finger into the air. "You mount up! And lead out! And don't you stop until I, Cross—me—Romeo Six—tells you to fucking whoa! Do you roger that, Specialist?" he bellowed.

"Now, El-tee," said Cross, handing up the ice to me. "It's gonna take two minutes for this platoon to get ice. *That* battalion ain't gonna be going so far I can't catch up. You oughta know that, El-tee," he said.

By the time they finished talking back and forth enough ice and MPC had changed hands for every cooler in the platoon and Atevo was back with double armfuls of beer quarts. Cross turned away from the El-tee to mount up. He winked at me and climbed aboard, and when word came from the last track, shifted into gear and drove away. I slid the ice into the Igloo and chopped it up with my bayonet and laid the beer in and when we got to the fire base it was good and cold.

We caught up with the rest of battalion before they got to the Suoi Dau cutoff and followed them south to Fire Base Judith, halfway to Trang Bang. Judith was off the road a couple hundred meters the other side of a Chieu Hoi village. During the day the Chieu Hois took classes and worked their fields, while their women fanned themselves and weeded truck gardens. And at night everybody was VC, just like always. Romeo pulled into the laager on the north, in front of a battery of 105 howitzers. To the front were dry rice paddies, which would be flooded and planted with seedlings before we left, and five or six hundred meters in the distance, a cart trail and a jungle and rubber-tree woodline. There were more hamlets and villages around, but we did not sweep more than a handful. Romeo sat security for the howitzers and pulled search-and-destroy missions—S & Ds—day sweeps, we called them. Ambushes were the same, except that Trobridge stayed back at the El-tee's suggestion. Mac took charge and Atevo walked point.

The night we pulled into the laager it rained. The next day was clear, but every day after that it rained and rained, until everything was soaked and mildewed; until I didn't care whether I was wet or dry.

It seemed as though we stayed at Fire Base Judith until the end of May, but we had Chieu Hoi pussy almost every afternoon and beer by the case from the artillery.

M O O N

O F

A T E V O

It is well after dark. There is a light drizzle, the least it has rained all day. Atevo and I join the ambush at the El-tee's track with guns, grenades, claymores, and camouflaged faces. Cross lounges in back of the seven-three, good and stoned, waving to us. He has not said a word to anyone since the night before—just keeps smoking his smokes and staring at the tits and thighs. Atevo's shotgun is heavily oiled because it is raining and the gun is not blued. When everyone gathers we line up behind him and step off. We shiver in the wet blowing rain, soaked to the skin already, but it does not matter. We will be warm enough after we have walked a hundred meters. We move through the laager, among the 105 howitzer pieces and the aiming stakes and crew bunkers, to the space between the seven-seven and the seven-eight. One at a time we move past them and the semicircles of claymores, following the road east, walking in the ditch. Atevo's boots make no sound. His clothes make no sound. He moves quickly, toe-heel-toe, with the shotgun in front of his face. We come to a cart trail. Atevo crosses and waits a moment, then waves us on one at a time. We keep to the ditch, bent at the waist to keep our silhouettes low on the horizon. The patrol spreads out considerably. We are making for a small stand of jungle, teak and wild rubber on high ground with bushes crowded round thick as hair. For a thousand meters there will be nothing but flooded rice paddies and open pasture, footpaths along the berms and cart trails along the embankments.

Atevo stops the patrol a hundred meters or so short with a slow wave of his arm. Then he moves out, crouching close to the ground with his slouch hat back on his head and the shotgun closer in front of his face. Every few meters he stops and listens, cocking his head to one side and cupping his hand around his ear. He squats motionless for the longest time, staring hard at the woodline, waiting for the slightest telltale. He moves away until his silhouette blurs in the drizzle, then disappears. After a long moment the sound comes—the signal—a clicking of teeth clear as anything. The site is clean, come on. Each man sets out his own claymores, sets up slowly, then settles in behind a loose pile of grenades, with the pins pulled halfway, and claymore detonators and his weapon across his lap, safety off. When the last man settles down the silent sitting begins.

The rain comes down through the trees. The moon, hazy and zinc-colored in the clouds, shines rippled silver. The sounds change. They seem to splash with a quicker ring. Next to me Atevo sits Indian fashion. His back straight. His eyes wide and moving. He barely breathes. I reach over and touch his knee firmly. He turns his head. I tap my wrist. He reaches up and curls a hand around a

mosquito buzzing in his ear. He squeezes his hand into a
fist, then wipes it on his trouser leg and returns it to the
muzzle of the shotgun, shielding it from the rain. He looks
closely at his watch, then shows me one finger, wipes the air
with the flat of his hand, and shows me two fingers more.
Midnight.

We sit dreamy and dreary, watching the rain. The
crowded splashing ebbs and washes in the breeze. It rains
harder for a time, then slacks. The moonlight dims and the
rain picks up again. Then the not-quite-rain sound. Not the
rustling of crickets and hares, not a night sound, but the
stride of farmers, ploddish some, quick and silent some.
Bare feet squeak in the grass. A silver and black shadow
stands upright in the rain. All at once there is a sudden
exciting hustle and rush of breath. He fires. The rounds
snap—*thuck-thack*—hitting somewhere. Just that quick
someone sucks a quick, loud breath through their teeth,
someone shouts, "Geé-za-shit!" and everybody splashes and
curses, grabbing for guns and fumbling for claymore detonators and short-fused frags. I pull off a long burst, sitting
bolt upright, making for the ink-flak shadows of the gun-
flashes. I sweep left, then farther left to cover the flank.
There's no telling where they are. No telling.

When I have gone through a hundred-round belt and
half my grenades the firing ceases. Then I am low-crawling
hand over hand across the mushy grass, holding my bayonet. A little man drags himself away with his rifle under one
arm, held level, pushing at the grass with his good leg,
pulling with his free arm. I catch sight of the tip of the
muzzle and the front sight blade in the downpour, like a
hole in the earth. He catches sight of me. There are two
quick roaring flashes in my face. My eyes burn. I must be
blinded. My ears ring. It is like coming out of a cave at a
dead flat out run into the brightest, brilliant desert sunlight—hot sweat and tearing eyes and everything all at

once. It is like being locked in a room of scalding-hot air. I get up on my knees and fall forward, knife first, past the muzzle, brushing it aside with a jerk of my elbow. The little man tries to scuttle away. I grab his shirt and feel for the collar, shoving him into the soggy mud. He reaches for my arm, my eyes. I raise myself straight-armed above him, bringing the bayonet roundhouse high. I gather the shirt tightly in my fist; tightly around his neck. All I have to do is bring the knife down, drop it straight into his chest, and snap the breastbone. It would be like slicing twine. I work my fingers on the handle, feeling for a good grip. I can see nothing but his eyes, blinking from the rain. He has one hand tightly around my wrist, the other raised to parry the bayonet. I could puncture a lung, coming straight down through the shoulder, or get his heart from the side, or simply stab him in the throat at the carotid.

I let the bayonet slip from my hand and come down with all my weight on his chest, my hands around his neck. I squeeze his Adam's apple with both thumbs. I lift his head and push it back into the turf with a muted splash. My fingernails work into the back of his neck. The little man grabs both my wrists. He gurgles and works his jaw. His mouth stretches open and he wags his tongue. Lift. Push. Squeeze. Like working a tool smooth. His head splashes harder. His nails gouge my wrists. Lift. Push. Squeeze. Something cracks and my thumbs work easier, deeper. His mouth, his tongue, make thick wet murmurs. Lift. Push. Squeeze. His body shakes as though someone is trying to yank it out from under me. His face and lips and jaw go slack. His head and hands go limp.

*

There is only the moon now and again, and the rain and the cool, grassy mud. The trees, skirted with bushes, stand behind me above a sea of rice fields and pasture grass. I feel the soggy cool night air at the back of my neck, the water soaking into my boots, and I shiver. My eyes, my eyes ache. The rain-soaked body lies on its back. He will not drop his arms. He will not close his eyes. I sit cross-legged between him and his AK. The rain drips in a runnel from my bush hat, soaking my trousers. He is splashed with a thin wash of mud. His knees are raised and the muscles are still tensed. His hands in the gesture of a grasp, as at a rope. I reach down into the grass between my legs, feeling for a single root, and each blade makes a muted snapping noise when I pull it up.

The rest of the ambush sits behind me among the trees, rifles ready, a few grenades left. Atevo's shot, they whisper. Atevo's dead, they tell me. They stare at me, at the body and the AK, and try to cover Atevo as best they can.

The little man will not let go his arms. I thought a body just gave up and stretched out. He will not let go his knees, his hands. Clouds pull in front of the moon. The rain slows, stops finally, then drips from the trees. The little man and Atevo and I, and the rest of the ambush, sit and wait for the platoon to come out to get us. I sit close to the little man, close enough to touch, but I cannot now that he is dead. His skin was hot and clammy, slick and sticky. I wonder how cold he is now? With his head thrown back the tongue swells in his throat among the odd ugly bulges and broad rounded creases. I stare at his face in the moonlight for hours. His hair is thrown back and soaked to the scalp.

I look away and back. I cannot get comfortable. My wrists ache. My back is sore and cramped. My knees are kinked from all the sitting. My eyes burn. He could have crawled away. I could have let him crawl away. Why didn't I do him with the bayonet? Strangling him was like wringing out a wet rag, folding and squeezing, refolding it thicker, squeezing it more. It was like crushing a melon in half and that junk, seeds and all, oozing out between my fingers. The bony knees and calluses on the black heels and the stiff animated tendons at the back of the hands—that ugly, wobbling, cool-water-ripples image of a man laid out with his tongue shoved back in his throat—that wide-eyed, black bowie knife, wrinkled leather, flat-faced grin of Atevo's—that grinding, grinding migraine ache and those darting slivers of silver light back of my eyes—that make-way-for-a-new-deck gesture.

I want to see this out. I want me and Atevo and this little dude here to ride in the same car. Just slap your hand round something soft, my man, and twist and yank and grit your teeth, come on.

After first light Cross and the seven-three and the rest of the platoon drive out to get us. I hear them, see them a mile off, coming like crazy, throwing sprays of muck behind them instead of dust. I am pale and chilled. My legs tingle. There are rolls of skin and sweaty dirt under my fingernails. My hands are water-wrinkled. The nail gouges on my wrists have gone to soft scabs, itching and stinging like paper cuts. When the platoon pulls up the ambush rouses and moves off for their tracks. Cross gives me a hand up. Whiskey j. and Steichen and Stepik and the El-tee lay out Atevo on his poncho and snap it up. I stand there working the circulation back into my legs. Stepik hands me half a handful of Darvons and a canteen of night-cooled water. Cross gestures for me to sit inside the seven-three. The rest of the platoon stand around the little man with their PX Kodaks and Nikons and Minoltas and Canons, snapping shots and pushing at the arms. They say, "Jesus, is *this* gook ever dead," among themselves and snatch glances at me. I sit on the bench across from the tits and thighs. I listen to Steichen dig a narrow, shallow grave—the sucking sounds of the shovel as he strikes through the turf and rich black muck—laying each shovelful aside. I smoke a smoke and drink the water in sips, feeling for the Darvons. Whiskey j. comes with Atevo's shotgun and floppy slouch hat, and the AK. He says that Atevo never knew what hit him; tells me Atevo was dead before he splashed; tells me the AK is mine. He says the greasy plastic pouch of dope and the two hundred piasters are mine too. Mine by rights. I tell him no. No, thank you. You want them, they're yours, I tell him. He nods and puts the shotgun, cartridge bandoliers, and slouch hat aside, and leaves with the rest. The El-tee comes over, ignoring the smoke I have cupped in my hand. He wants to talk about the body count. Yes, sir, hand to hand. He says something about a Bronze Star. No, sir; no, thank you. Fuck a Bronze Star, sir. And he leaves. My legs still tingle. The Darvons finally come and my breathing eases. They bring Atevo to the seven-three and lay him out with the palm-shaped green and brown camouflage still on his face, and the neatest small puncture over one eye. Then everybody mounts up and we ride back to the fire base, flying as the crows fly. I sit inside with Atevo and his shot-gun and bloody slouch hat. My shirt and trousers cling to my skin. My boots make squishy sucking noises. Atevo's boots jog and dance, keeping time with the track as it sways and jerks and slides along. I smoke another smoke, holding on to one of the hand straps, and stare up through the square-looking crew hatch. A constant spatter of mud flies up from the treads, sailing in a backward arc. Atevo's poncho is bunched up for toting; the sky a clean blue color, like it always is after a rain.

*

Back at the perimeter Stepik gives me more Darvons and I nod out in the damp grass under the track. That night we sit playing blackjack by the light of the squat stove.

"Cross?" I say.

"Wha'?" he answers, not looking up.

"I wanna drive," I say.

Stepik sits by the Igloo cooler with the deck in the flat of his hand. Whiskey j. leans back against the tits and thighs, listening to the radio on the headset.

"Hit me," Cross says to Stepik. "Sure, Dosier, t'morra."

"I don't want any more ambushes," I say. "I wanna be a Delta."

"I could dig it," he says. "Stepik, hit me again." Stepik snaps the top card and skims it across the lumpy blanket. "I'm good," says Cross. "Inna mornin', Flip."

TORQUE

The next day Cross let me drive just as he said he would. A couple platoon tracks escorted some deuce-and-a-halfs south to the town of Trang Bang. The trucks would fall in with the Cu Chi–Tay Ninh convoy, make their way to Dau Tieng for resupply, and be back in Trang Bang the next afternoon. When we moved out I leaned my shoulders against the cushioned lip of the hatch for leverage, squinting fiercely in the dry dusty wake of the seven-two and gripping the slippery brake handles tightly.

Cross squatted behind me on the upturned driver's hatch cover, eye to eye with Trobridge, who stood low behind the fifty. Cross shouted encouragement and coaching at me, smoking his smokes and waving to the Viets in the roadside hamlets and razzing Trobridge with snide remarks and gestured epithets. Trobridge kept making like he was in charge, shouting instructions at me over the crew phone: "Close up, damn it. Close up!" And Cross bent low next to my face, screaming, "Ease off! Keep a good fifty meters! Watch those tread marks! Fuck Four Eyes!" We hit real asphalt just outside of town and everybody started honking their pathetic tweep-tweep horns, like we were a wedding party, pounding down on oxcarts and pushcarts and mamasans with long, pitiful honks and buzzing past them like there was no tomorrow. The traffic clambered for the roadside as we cranked past, like a fox clearing a henhouse. We crunched and clanked along on bare, raw tread cleats, sliding through the curves and corners like Mario Andretti or A. J. Foyt or "Burn 'Em Up" Barnes. Then we zoomed across Highway 1 and hauled ass into the fountain-square traffic circle just this side of the marketplace and skidded to a halt ass-up against the stone curb, like a bunch of Saturday-night cowboys. We stood on the decks, head and shoulders and bootlaces above everybody else, brushing the settling dust from our faces and flak jackets.

Cross said, "Not bad, m' man. Not bad in the least for your first time outa the chute. You catchin' on!"

I stood on the driver's seat, out of breath but exhilarated, and stared back down the road at the Viets, picking themselves and their oxcarts and truck vegetables and whatnot out of the gutters.

While we waited for the convoy Cross and Steichen and I took a stroll through the market with our flak jackets and side arms and frags. I bought a pair of cheap plastic sunglasses, first thing, to keep the dust out of my eyes. There were pony carts and pedicabs, oxcarts and Hondas, rows of one-man stalls covered with homemade awnings, and the buzz and hum of gobbledygook chatter. There were baskets of grayish, brownish rice and boxes of truck—carrots and beans and squash and such; stacks of GI blankets and jungle fatigues, mess kits and C rations, and canteen cups and green plastic canteens. Inside the high-ceilinged open-air warehouse, where it was cool, were hundred-pound sacks of rice and bolts of cloth and brand-spanking-new Hondas and Japanese transistor radios and more black-market gear. We walked single file through the crowded foot traffic and I kept a firm grip on the shotgun. We watched fascinated, at least I was fascinated, as women in tight-fitting blouses squatted on their heels and fanned themselves with their cone hats, hawking in high-pitched atonal singsong voices to the crowd pushing by. And the buyers stood hat to hat handling and squeezing and sniffing and haggling, I guess that's what it was, and the stink of bodies and pony shit, rotting garbage and gas fumes was not to be believed. Cross and Steichen only went with me because I wanted to see, but we had not gone the length of one aisle before I got uneasy and nervous because of the close crush of the crowd, the nauseating smell, and the stories I had heard of VC brats slipping a live grenade into a GI's pocket. So I turned around and the three of us pushed our way out.

In an open-air arcade about the size of a hotel elevator foyer a group of ARVNs stood playing pocket pool on an old beat-up pool table. They were PFs, Popular Forces, whom everybody called Ruff Puffs. The five of them, with longish, straight black hair and shirttails hanging out of their hand-me-down, back-in-the-world GI fatigues, drank beer and lounged street-corner style against the arcade wall or leaned on their cues, waiting their turn to shoot. They looked young—fourteen or fifteen—but Viets always looked several years younger than they were, until they got to be twenty-five or so, then they always looked older. Especially the women. As we walked by they came to life and called to us, "GI! GI, numba fucka one, eh? You know to pool? Play some pool, GI?"

Cross stopped and leaned back against a rack of carrots. "No, not pool, but do you dig poker? Same same, roger?"

"Oh, too much same same roger!" they called back, quizzing among themselves but trying to sound as though they understood.

We settled into a table at a sidewalk bar near the tracks and the main road where the Cu Chi convoy would pass. The Viet came out from behind the bar where he sold black-market C-ration instant coffee and cocoa, and Viet beer, called Thirty-three, in quarts.

"Hey, Chingachgook!" Cross yelled. "Got any cold?" The guy nodded. "Well, okay. Three bottles and don't bother with the opener, we'll do that." He went behind the bar and rattled around and came out with the bottles, wiping off the dirt and rice chaff and ice slivers with a filthy rag. We sprawled out on the iron chairs near the curb with our guns on the table among the bottles. The ARVNs came out of the pool hall and sat down at the next table. After a moment of gibberish between them and the bartender—they flashing their money in grand style; the bartender grinning and nodding and yessing back—they slid their chairs to our table and moved in. No helmets, no gear, no guns. Underfed, doe-eyed, skittish and fretful, with pegged pants and black high-topped gym shoes or shower thongs. Christ, no wonder we're over here busting our ass. They wagged their money in our faces and called for another round.

Cross pulled his chair closer to the curb and gestured for them to go ahead if they had their hearts set on it. We all sat and drank their beer and they pawed the guns and buddy-buddied us, with their hands and arms around our shoulders, and wanted to know, in their broken GI pidgin English minced with French and gestures, why we called the bartender Chingachgook, for that was not his name.

"Well, ya see, Ruff Puff," said Steichen, "he reminds Cross here of his great white father, the last of the fucken Mohicans and a champion bartender from Washington. He lives in this boo-coo numba-one hooch, painted white with a twenty-four-hour generator. Dig? Chingachgook here same same three brain cells, white apron, goofy-looking feet, shit-eating grin. Everything same same." And all of us looked over at the bartender as he flitted from table to table, bowing and scraping, pouring drinks and shooing flies. I watched the road and the oxcarts and pony carts and the mama-sans humping produce and rice over their shoulders and drank my beer in sips. The Saigon–Tay Ninh bus whizzed by, crammed and piled with people and chicken crates and rag-wrapped luggage and duffel bags. Right behind it, driving in the dust was a small black car, a two-door with a running board. The bus went straight on, but the car hung a left around the fountain and pulled up to the curb in front of us with a crunch of tires. Inside were five unarmed rounded-eyed white men, wearing dark trousers, sunglasses, and short-sleeved shirts.

The driver stuck his head out the window. "Eh, monsieur," he said, looking at us. "Monsieur, could you assistance me, *s'il vous plaît?* How is it that I may get to Go Dau Ha?"

"Say?" said Cross. "Well, what the fuck you wanna go to 'Go Da Ha' for?"

"Ah, monsieur," the guy said, widening his eyes. "It is my brother's Peugeot. His auto, you see, is there and we must pick it up this afternoon," he said, nodding his head at every word.

"Who's he trying to kid?" said Cross under his breath. Then raising his voice, "Negative, Pierre, you don't wanna go there, not for no Poo-joe anyway. There's nothing but gooks in 'Go Da Ha.' Dig? A Maserati might be worth an afternoon in there, but not no Poo-joe."

The driver turned his head to the three dudes sitting in back and whispered, *"Que ça c'est,* 'dig'?" The guy in the middle with his knees up jerked his head and shot Cross a look. Then he mumbled something to the driver. The driver laughed weakly and turned back to Cross and explained in more detail. His brother, a man with thinning hair who wore oxfords and boutonnieres, was an officer in some Saigon corporation. There had been some obscure but urgent business. There had been an accident, anybody could tell that by the way he slapped his hands together. The car had been abandoned. On and on he talked, thick-tongued, rolling his *r*'s. The five of them kept looking at our bare arms and bellies and flak jackets, the guns and bottles and grenades, and I couldn't look away from their round eyes and short sleeves and white faces and windblown hair. Cross sat forward, leaning on his knees, holding the beer between his legs, and nodding where he thought it was agreeable. When the Frenchman finished, Cross said "Bullshit" out of the side of his mouth and repeated the same advice. The Frenchman nodded sternly, pulled his head back inside, and jammed the car into gear, tearing around the fountain traffic circle to where a Viet cop, white mice we called them, sat on a chair, watching the traffic. The dink stood up and touched his cap and they talked among themselves. There was more head nodding and pointing and gestures, then the car tore off around the traffic circle one more time and hung a left toward Tay Ninh. We sat with our heads down, blinking, as the dust settled behind them. The Ruff Puffs sitting among us didn't seem to have taken the slightest notice and kept up their gibberish conversation, pawing our shoulders and knees and drinking manfully from their quarts. And when the dust settled we looked around at each other until Steichen said it.

"Did we see what I think we saw? Five Frenchies in a black two-door? And not a gun among them?"

Yeah. White shirts and round eyes and white faces. Besides the PA & E dudes, reporters and journalists, the Dau Tieng Captain Kangaroo Red Cross man, and that kind —who always seemed to be underfoot and nothing but in the way—those five Frenchies were the only round-eyed white men we saw. And it had happened so quick. Poof— here in a cloud of smoke and dust, and five minutes of incomprehensible conversation. Poof—gone in a cloud of smoke and dust. But that was always the way things happened. Quickly, quickly, ambush quick in a whirl of dust.

We would be busting jungle all morning and break through the treeline onto sudden odd terrain; a weed-grown, unused rice field a couple miles across; a two-acre clearing filled with VC graves—a year old, a week old, and every month in between; or a French-colonial-style hooch with tiled walls and no roof and vines and saplings growing around the veranda. There was the time that Steichen literally tripped over an ammo cache and the platoon wound up the afternoon locating a company-sized base camp, complete with bunkers and tunnels and smoking cook fire and damp laundry hung out to dry. At Fire Base Carolyne one morning, an old, ragged papa-san stumbled out of the woodline and when we checked for his papers he didn't have any. He swore up and down he had just escaped from a VC prison camp and he pointed, limp-armed, north into the deep rubber. He showed us his scars, but no one believed him until the battalion interpreter choppered in and palavered with him and took him away. Then there was the time we were pulling a sweep through some rubber with Bravo Company and all of a sudden, there, to my front and not thirty meters down range, was a woman walking backward in the high brush, snapping pictures with a 35 mm. She must have come out with Bravo Company. I tried to shout and wave her off, but she just kept backing up and taking shots. If we got contact she'd be right in the middle, but when I saw she wasn't going to budge I thought to myself: well, if this picture-taking snatch wants to be an asshole and work the bushes for us, like a setter flushing pheasant, she can be my fucking guest.

*

A couple days later Cross's orders came. Cross and Steichen and Stepik and I stayed up all night, drinking and smoking and playing blackjack by the light of the squat stove.

The game was always blackjack. We played it because it was simple and quick, and there were no IOUs, nobody could play light. Two cards; one down, one up. A six-seven-eight combination paid double the bet. Ace and a face card blackjack paid double and won the deal. Five and under twenty-one paid double. Six and under paid double that. Three sevens paid triple. We would smoke our smokes and tap our fingers on the blanket, holding our money crap shooter's style, doing the odds in our heads and counting the cards like bridge players; then scoop in the MPC slicker than a black-tie croupier with a mahogany money shovel. We would watch the hands and eyes and listen to the voices dropping lower and going slower as we smoked. After a couple months I could tell a new guy just by the way he played—shifting his pale eyes from his up card and down card and hit cards to the bet money to the dealer, who slid the hit cards from the deck and flipped them over with a twanging snap, and skimmed them across the fuzzy wool blanket.

In the field we laid a blanket over a mangy-looking piece of plywood and a couple ammo cans and played by the yellowish hissing light of the squat stove. In camp we sat around a blanket-draped footlocker in the tent and the hands went fast. Every three or four hands the dealer reshuffled, offered the cut, buried the first card face up, and called out, "Put your money down." Everybody watched the cards and the bets and the dealer's hands, calling for hits, going double on pairs of aces or face cards or tens, and standing pat. And the games went on for hours and hours—into the small hours, the ones that don't come to the knees—with towels draped over our shoulders for the heat sweat, the sweat sweat.

The dudes in the next tent would shoot craps. We could hear the talk among the shooters and bettors and side bettors, quick and witty, as they called bets and odds; the shooter rubbing and rattling the dice between his palms, calling, "Come on, lady! Come on, black lady! Be sweet," he'd say, pounding down on the *t*. Then would come the dance and the closed-fisted shake and the long, low under-handed roll and follow-through. The shooter would shout, "Hey!" The dice would skitter over the planks, strike the side of a footlocker, and snap back to the sound of "Whoa," and "Yeah," with a snap of the fingers when they came to rest. Then the winners would call in the money, saying, "Pay up, suckers."

But the blackjack players played it cool, played in dry-throated whispers. And the payday games were the jack-pots; the other games just practice. Payday games could have better than a thousand dollars, MPC, stacked on the blanket. And the deal was worth boo-coo dust. We'd cut high card for the deal and crinkle our money so the bills wouldn't stick together. After hours and hours of nasty-tasting smokes and beers in quarts and listening to the PA & E's night generator, it was just the players, just the sharks, the dudes who did it for the money. We'd play and play, munching C-ration crackers and tins of cheese, and watch the cards and watch our luck—the lady whispering the odds in our ears—never letting the eyes wander. And once or twice I saw some dude jerk his hand away from his cards, like he'd been burned, and gather up his money and walk away and get awful quiet, like he believed what he saw. You could just about see it come on his face, that fear of lost luck working its way into his bowels, squeezing down on his asshole—pucker factor, we called it—tensing his back, squeezing his buttocks tight as he sat.

We played until breakfast. Cross shaved and dressed in his cleanest fatigues with the red bandanna around his neck, held at his throat with that twenty-four-carat gold ring, the AK across his back, and the forty-five web belt over his shoulder. When he and I walked to the LZ, the landing zone, Steichen and Whiskey j., even the El-tee, came over to say goodbye. The chopper came, sweeping a rush of dust ahead of it as it landed. We walked over and Cross threw his waterproof aboard.

"Hey, Flip, here," he said, and handed me the web-belt forty-five. "The sight is a little to the left." Then he grabbed me by the shirt. "Flip, m' man, you take good care—hear me? You grit your teeth and do your time and get on this chopper and go home—just like me—whatever happens after. Hear?"

"Yes, Cross," I said. He took my M-16 and climbed aboard, sitting on the door gunner's bench. The chopper rose and turned and swept across the laager, out over the seven-six. The door gunners pulled their sixties up and Cross went home. He told me he would write, but never did.

*

The next day the platoon drove out to pick up two downed tracks for Bravo Company. The ground was dry and grass-covered. We drove at a jogging pace through the turf, into jungle and out again, past the spot where Atevo died and along cart trails. The two Bravo Company tracks were parked back to back in knee-deep grass. We pulled into a tight laager and stayed the night. The morning broke clear. After breakfast I took the long-handled spade and the seven-three's roll of toilet paper into a grove of trees. The paper was damp. Trobridge had left it out all night.

As I finished up Trobridge began calling my name.

"Goddamn it, Dozer, mount up."

"I'm taking a shit. That okay with you?" I yelled back.

"We got to hook up with one of the Bravo tracks."

"Okay! All right! Be right there," I said, hiking up my trousers.

Several of the tracks were already moving around. I poked my head out of the trees. Trobridge stood on the deck with his CVC and glasses, his hands on his hips, looking dufus and dimwitted and exasperated. Suddenly there was an explosion, the concussion sharp and hot. An orange flash and a rush of black smoke. People were running, leaping over grass toward the seven-six, John Granger the chess player's track. Then came the hiss of dirt spraying across the grass. Stepik and a couple others were already scrambling up the side. I could see the top of Granger's CVC. Nickles, the TC, stood in the grass a little way off, stumbling and weaving like a drunk. Stepik and another man reached into the driver's hatch and grabbed Granger under the arms and pulled him out.

I ran over, not thinking that I could do Granger or Nickles or the others any good, but Granger was a Delta, I was a Delta. I didn't even know him that well, he was newer than I was.

Trobridge yelled to me, "Get the hell back here."

The grass around the seven-six was laid back, like trampled, windblown winter wheat. There was a broad crater deep enough to stand in. The tread and sprocket and five road wheels on the driver's side were blown away. The armor just under the driver's seat was torn open along the weld with sharp streaks of muck sprayed up the side. Pieces of the tread and road wheels were scattered around. The mine had gone off right under Granger's foot. The concussion had come up through his hatch.

Stepik screamed at me to help with Johnny as they handed him over the side. I turned to him and reached, but when I saw him my hands jerked into fists and my thighs began to quiver. He screamed with pain and flailed his arms and tried to kick away, rolling his head. The whole left side of his body—his scalp and face and down his neck, the flak

jacket, his arm and hand, his hip and thigh and boots—
hung from his body in bloody tatters.

I turned away and looked at the seven-three, but then
turned back, took a breath, and grabbed hold of him around
his bloody knees. We laid him out on the litter, then Stepik
got down on his knees and went to work, cutting Granger's
clothes and boots off and tearing open bandages. Johnny
didn't even know who we were. He squirmed around on the
taut canvas, wincing and mumbling, "Billy, Billy, don't
run so fast. Bill?"

I leaned against the seven-six, the armor damp from
the mud and dew. I had my back to Stepik and Granger's
squeaking murmurs, looking down at a crumpled scrap of
road wheel still bolted to an axle. The explosion had
vaulted Nickles completely out of his hatch and he had
landed on his head. Don Tipton and a new guy named Patrick had broken legs and bad concussions. The other Deltas
in the platoon were there too, milling around, trying to help
with the wounded, gathering around the bomb crater and
climbing up the side to have a glimpse inside the driver's
hatch, when Surtees trooped over. Above the hushed conversation and Patrick's high-pitched hysterical crying ("I
can' feel my leg. It's gone. Tell me it ain' gone, eh?") and
Nickles sitting in the grass with his eyes rolled back into his
head, mumbling his mouth, I could hear the El-tee twenty
meters away, talking in quick breaths as he called the dust-
off.

Even as Stepik cut Granger's clothes Surtees started
in. "Do this and you do that," and "Get ready with that IV.
Hold it up, goddamn," and "Better break out some more
fucken field bandages," and "Bring Nickles over here,"
and "Can't you work any faster, you chicken shit?" until
Stepik looked up quickly out of the corner of his eyes and
said, "Get out of my light, asshole. Go call the dust-off. Tell

'em we got four litters, and make sure you call them this time, hunh? Aw, fuck it. El-tee?" he yelled across the laager. "El-tee, tell the dust-off we got four bad litter cases, eh?"

"Roger," said the El-tee. He stood on top of his track and repeated the message into the radio.

Johnny stopped thrashing and got quiet when Stepik put the bandage over his eyes, like a horse in a barn fire, but Stepik kept up the talk, speaking softly, quietly, holding him by the arm to still the wiggling. Then he moved over to Tip and the new guy, and Nickles, who was only dazed. While he worked Surtees moved around behind him and stood puffing his cigar, watching. I wondered if the same thing happened the night Murphy had been shot.

The darkness and the tall grass and brush and the two bodies and Cross on his knees next to Murphy, whose wife had small breasts and plumped hips, pinching Murphy's neck at the artery to keep the bleeding back and shouting for the medic, "Where's the fucken medic?" And Stepik coming on the run through the weeds, hustling and grunting, his aid bag flapping against his thigh, with Surtees right behind. Surtees stands behind them with his hand dangling over his shoulder holster, hip cocked, his buffed boots shining smooth in the moonlight, puffing on his ragged cigar and spitting on his shirt, repeating again and again, "Yes, sir, what we needs just this minute is one of them medevac choppers, a dust-off, don't ya know." Cross talks to Murphy, who's choking down breaths and coughing spatters of blood, and Cross shows him the AK and the red bandanna and twenty-four-carat gold ring and the filthy sandals, and keeps saying, "Be easy, be easy," while Surtees looks over Stepik's shoulder, like some half-wit idiot brat just tall enough to get his nose to the top of the candy counter, but still can't decide. Stepik keeps shouting without looking up, "Get a dust-off. Get a dust-off. Get a dust-off, goddamn you." But then come the back-and-forth glances in the moonlight, the gritted teeth and bitter sighs, when both Cross and Stepik know and agree with a look of the eyes that even if the dust-off comes now, this instant, Murphy will die. Cross puts his ears to Murphy's face and listens closely to those bloody, thick-tongued whispers and nods his head and whispers back, blinking his whitish eyes the while, saying, "Yes, I'll do that. Yeah, no sweat. Take good care. Goodbye."

I knelt down next to Granger and talked and tried to soothe him and watched the blood soak through the bandages. Granger squirmed uneasily on the taut litter canvas, like he had an itch and couldn't get comfortable, tensing his thighs against the bandages and rolling his bloody, mudshining head slowly from side to side. He mumbled something about playground swings and a locked gym door and then the dust-off came, sweeping in close behind us. The medics jumped out with more litters and an armful of stiff mesh-wire splints, and laid out the gunners to work on them. Then the litters were loaded in the chopper and they left, skimming the grass with the blades pounding away. When it was finally out of earshot, circling away to the south, Surtees grabbed Stepik by the sleeve and turned him around.

"Don't you *ever* talk to me like that again," Surtees said. "I am an NCO, the Platoon Sergeant, and you can't talk to me like that."

Stepik stood his ground, repacking the aid bag. "I'm the medic, Surtees. Kiss my ass. But while we're on the subject you might as well know, when your turn comes around you're gonna get the same number you gave Murphy. Roger? Now the El-tee can't hear us and these dudes don't, so this is just between us chickens. You get the same same as Murphy. I will shoot you up myself." And he turned and walked away. When things calmed down we mounted up and towed the three downed tracks all the way back to Dau Tieng. That night the Deltas gathered around the seven-six with beer and smokes and tool bags, stripped it clean, and we turned in the rest for scrap. The seven-six didn't have five hundred miles on it.

*

Romeo started driving the Dau Tieng–Tay Ninh convoy and we drove it, out and back for weeks, months maybe. Years. Out with the engineers' sweep team at first light to clear the road. Back in the motor pool in the late, hot afternoon, sipping smokes all the while. Tiger Tango, the major at Brigade in charge of base-camp resupply, said that Romeo pulled the fastest convoys, and there was never a nickel's worth of difference among the bunch of them.

Out the west gate and gingerly over the Saigon River bridge. Through Check Point Hotel and into the rubber where the road was always shaded and muddy, even in the dry seasons. Past the bullpen where the rusted-out Michelin water tower was and out into the rice fields and bamboo hedgerows. Over the culverts at Check Point Golf and past that dippy-looking roadside shrine at Check Point Foxtrot, which got more shot up and more shot up as the year went on, until sometime after the first of the year it fell over altogether. We'd hang a hard right at Charlie Papa Echo where there had been a Chieu Hoi village once upon a time, and then head due north along the Trang Bang–Tay Ninh high road and more rubber. It was uphill from there to Charlie Papa Delta and that burned-out, burned-to-the-ground Alpha Company track slumped in the high grass near the creek, and the abandoned plantation house, with its high ceilings and louvered doors and stone parquet verandas. Next came the Suoi Dau cutoff near Charlie Papa Charlie with its quick downhill and Monza-looking S curve we took at better than full tilt. On the other side of Charlie

Papa Bravo stood the Cao Dai temple, complete with a stone fence and dormitory, across the road from a marketplace that always smelled fucked up, and a barb-wired schoolyard. There were these huge, craterlike potholes in the road out front of the lumberyard with stacks of cut lumber, teak and mahogany logs along the ditches, and sawdust muck. We cranked by Charlie Papa Alpha, a beat-up-looking, falling-down Esso gas station with an open-air grease rack where we bought or bartered white gas for the squat stove, and the dink icehouse that was set back from the road in a palm grove. Then came the black-topped intersection near downtown Tay Ninh, where we were never allowed except once, for a nighttime call-out. The convoy hung a left there and whizzed by the ARVN fort with its tangle of concertina wire, all run-down and French-looking like the Saigon River bridge. We passed another Chieu Hoi ville where the VC brats trotted alongside, hustling beer and Coke in cans, the first I'd seen. And finally the convoy would crank and crash past the strip of car-wash and hand-laundry whorehouses outside the Tay Ninh Base Camp gate, where the housecats got laid. Then the seven-three and six-niner, the ice truck and mo-gas and diesel tankers and the rest, would fly through the gate, going flat out and low to the ground. Some dufus MP would be standing behind the crash post in front of the gate-bunker doorway, and he'd be flapping his arms, waving his clipboard for us to slow down, but waving it like a damn checkered flag and I'd flash him a grin as I flew by. And big deal, the tracks could only do thirty miles an hour, top end. We drove flat out, I tell you; flat out, I say, and the driving was pure kick.

Romeo would pull up along the ditch in front of the 34th Armor, across the road from the icehouse. Then we'd dismount and crowd into the mess hall for a late lunch, road-ragged and sweated up, brushing the dust off each other and stinking that gritty road stink.

The first time I took the Tay Ninh gate the MP, bless his little heart, hopped in his MP jeep and followed me. Just as I swung my no-radius U turn in front of the 34th, so to be facing the gate just in case, he drove up with a screech of brakes. He pulled me over like a highway trooper, Yogi Bear hat and .357 Magnum and all, and climbed the driver's-side tread, bringing his bad-ass housecat clipboard with him.

"Just what in the gawddamn fucking hell do you think you're trying to pull, trooper?" he asked.

"Say?" I said from under the CVC. My ears still rang with engine noise and radio noise and road noise and the rattle of the straight-pipe muffler. The dust of the other tracks settled thick around us. The front of the seven-three leaned forward on broken shocks.

"Listen," he said again, trying to bad-ass me. "When I tell you to slow down, that's just exactly what I mean. The speed limit inside the wire is twenty. I see you do this again and I'll issue you a Delinquency Report." A ticket. Get three of them and you get an Article 15. Company punishment: KP, guard duty, confined to quarters. MP puppy shit.

"Say, m' man, you ever drive point for a convoy?" I said.

"That's not the issue here," he said back.

"Well, Mike, *I* ain't gonna slow up on no convoy. Not for you or the El-tee or Westhisface, not even the fucken Commander in Chief himself, 'cause 'bout the minute I do there's gonna be a hundred-truck convoy get shoved up my ass. Look, Sport, when I hit your gate I ain't leadin' anybody, I'm being chased. Roger?"

*

Quinn comes to the platoon. He comes from the 5th Mech. in the 1st Brigade, a legend among line outfits in the

25th Division. He knew maps, compass, recon, S & D, ambush, and maintenance inside and out. He taught me to look in the oil-filler caps instead of the dipsticks. He was shorter than I was and stockier. He used to wrestle middleweight in high school. He had an easy evil grin of white teeth. At Fire Base Georgianne I saw him take a full bottle of Darvon, pull the capsules apart, take out the little tabs of pure Darvon, and down the whole handful. He didn't say a word for two days. Another time we were running a convoy back from Tay Ninh. Seven-three was point and Quinn was back in the convoy, driving the seven-four. I came flying out of the Monza S curve pacing a herd of buffalo when one of the buffs made a turn right in front of me. I couldn't stop. I wouldn't stop. I didn't even slow up. Chunk, chunk. The seven-three ran right up her back with the right-side tread. That's how the seven-three got its nickname, the "Cow Catcher." I screamed *"Olé!"* and called the El-tee. He called Quinn and told him to put the buff out of its misery and take the farmer's name so the Army could pay him back. But Quinn didn't find the buff I ran over till later, because he ran over one of his own. He stopped in the ditch and jumped down to empty his forty-five into it, then reloaded and wasted another magazine. We sat in the EM Club that night while he told us, smiling and laughing his little laugh, licking the corners of his mustache with the flat of his tongue, and doing all the gestures. Then there was the time he went to Saigon on a three-day pass, shacked with some broad, and parlayed it into three weeks. We had to laugh about that. He got some captain to sign a letter he sent to the El-tee explaining how he was "unavoidably detained," and couldn't get a flight back, and the El-tee believed him. We laughed about that, too.

There were the times we skinny-dipped in the river at the laterite pits outside Tay Ninh. There was Steichen, who could barely swim, and Whiskey j., who always brought his air mattress, and Quinn and me. Quinn and Whiskey j. would do high dives off a tree branch that hung over the water. A dink chick would come down and sit under a bush and watch Quinn and he laid his rap to her. At first we thought: well, she's just Quinn's free pussy. He even talked her into coming in with us, but she would only strip to her waist. One afternoon we were taking a break on the river-bank, shaking the water out of our ears—Quinn and the chick taking a break in the bushes—when an old papa-san came putt-putting by in a dugout canoe. We grabbed our guns and bush hats and stood on the slippery bank, not another stitch on. "Hey, papa-san!" we yelled, and waved him over. "Papa-san, lah-dee. Lah-dee!"

"No VC," he called back slowly, waving his skinny arms. "No VC," he said.

"I said come 'ere," I shouted again, and held up the shotgun, making a broad gesture of chambering a round so he could see it plain. He took one look and swung that dugout around and came ashore, then whipped out his wallet to show his ID. "Stow it, pop," I said. Quinn and the girl came out of the bushes, the girl behind Quinn and covering her breasts with cupped hands. Whiskey j. said, "Take us for a boat ride, pop," and Steichen and Whiskey j. and I jumped in. "GI wan' *boat* ride?" the old man said with much relief. "Give numba-*one* boat ride." "Hey, Quinn," I said, "come on." Quinn looked at the girl, trying to hide her face in her hair, hiding from the old man, and then back to me and said, "No, Die-wee, I don't need no boat ride and why don't you dudes put some clothes on." As we settled into the dugout and pulled away from the bank, Quinn and the girl disappeared into the bushes again where they had a blanket. It lasted on and off for three months, whenever we were up that way.

I remember one night at Fire Base Carolyne we had

our hands full with sniper fire and two- and three-man probes, looking for claymores to steal. Every time somebody had a target and opened up with a fifty or a pig, Quinn started up with the fifty on the seven-four. This went on for the better part of two hours, Quinn always putting out rounds in the same general direction. Then after a long pause, everybody listening and watching, guns at the ready, grenades up, Quinn stood up noisily in the hatch, cocked the fifty one more time, and said out loud, "Fuck this standing around," and squeezed off a long, long burst. There was a crackling, a grinding and screeching, an ugly tearing sound that started in a low register and rose into a high-pitched crunching, and then a rubber tree fell out of the woodline and crashed to the ground, the uppermost branches and leaves falling on Quinn and the fifty and the TC hatch of the seven-four. He started laughing and slapping the side of the armor shield. He laughed and I began to laugh and soon the whole perimeter was laughing, even the El-tee. That ended the firefight and the Lord only knows what the dinks thought it was.

Another time we were running convoy and the road was crowded with dink kids, begging C rations just like always. Quinn was a gunner on the Cow Catcher by then. He took a full boxed meal and dangled it over the side just out of reach of this one kid, all the while tossing fifty-caliber cartridges at the kid's head—first with a light snap of the wrist, then flicking them, harder and harder, sidearm hard. After the kid had humped a good half a mile, fighting off other kids and ducking fifty brass, Quinn flipped it out to him. Big deal. Ham and lima beans, GI white bread, crackers, and apple jelly.

The first night Quinn came into the tent everybody but the hard-core blackjack players sat along the aisle on the ends of their cots, talking and smoking smokes and sipping

Kool-Aid. He stood in the doorway dressed in fatigues and a dusty black T-shirt with his aviators up on his head, taking everything in. Then all of a sudden he raised his waterproof over his head, two-handed, and called out, "Who called this fucken Quakers' meeting?" and tossed the waterproof over several ducked heads to an empty cot.

Later, after he had sat for a while and smoked and slugged Kool-Aid to wet his whistle, he said he was a poet.

"Yeah, I'm a fucken poet. Ain't that some shit? Now I sent this one to the Rollin' Stones, but those assholes never said nothin':

"Napalm, napalm,
That's the game.
Kick his ass,
And take his name.

"The name's Quinn, m' man, an' I need s'more smoke. Yeah, then there's the one that goes to the tune of that fucked-up subway song. I call it the 'Ballad of the Dumb Lieutenant' and it goes like:

"Well, let me tell you the story of the dumb lieu-
tenant,
How the troopers had to pay and pay.
He was so fucken stupid that it wasn't even funny,
But we managed to laugh, anyway.

"Now comes the chorus:

"But did he ever return?
No, he never returned,
And his fate is still unlearned.
He's prob'ly on a ambush

By himself in soldier heaven.
He's the man who never returned.

"The second verse is even trickier than the first:

"We was sittin' 'round talkin' 'bout a one-man am-
    bush,
The fool piped in and said he'd go.
So we scrounged him some frags and a thirty-eight
    special,
And bowed, and showed him to the door.

"But did he ever return?
No, he never returned,
And his fate is still unlearned.
He's prob'ly walkin' point
All by himself in soldier heaven.
He's the man who never returned.

"I'm gonna send *this* one to the Rollin' Stones, too, and if I don't hear nothin', then fuck that bunch of house-cats," he said, and grinned his white-toothed grin and rocked back on his cot, spilling Kool-Aid on the floor. We must have sung that song a hundred times, serenading the whole battalion with a regular shivaree—clapping our hands and stomping our boots, clacking steel pots together and slapping rifle butts against the tent poles and rattling M-60 ammo belts.

*

I am dying inside. It is a lump of phlegm, a slab of lard, a gob of yellow clay. There is a pain deep in my back. Deep. I feel it when I flex my fingers, all the way down to my fingers, like the pinpricks when my gas foot comes out of sleep. I hear the whooshing of rounds, like archers' arrows. Zen masters never miss.

We pull into camp for a stand-down. I sit in the hatch with my head and helmet leaning against the lip of the hatch and my arms dangling loose-fingered between my knees, like a spider tangled in a knot of its own silk, swinging round and round and back. My pockets are heavy and full, like a bladder. Full of funny paper money. Paper dimes, paper quarters, and two thousand P, Viet. Poker money. Those dumb town dudes catching on to blackjack. Cross my heart, I will quit forever, but I never miss. Ace-and-a-face-card blackjack till it's coming out my ears; till I am doubling all my bets; till I can't stand it. Blackjack, five and under, and hitting down and dirty on seventeen and making the point the hard way, the filling-an-inside-straight way. Bingo, bingo, bingo, raking in chilly crisp cash and burying busted hands.

I rouse myself and climb down. The sign over the aid-station piss tube says: "Medical Personnel Only." I shuck down my fly and let 'er rip. It's the only bad thing about driving—you've got to wait for the end of the line. But do not worry, my man, it's good training. I stand there spraddle-legged, staring down toward the concertina wire and the grayish, brownish bunkers and the shimmering-hot rubber-tree woodline. I shiver and start to giggle the pissing feels so good.

The Romeo tracks are the only vehicles in the motor pool, but it sounds like a company. The ten Deltas, with Quinn and me among them, stand in a circle out front of the tracks, the warm dust to our ankles. We stand with our hands in half a fist, the calluses pulled tight on the palms. Our eyes red and puffed and stinging with dirt. Our bellies bloated with water from the mechanics' Lister bag and streaked with grit and sweat, stinking of the road and grease and mo-gas. We keep shoulder to shoulder, as though for warmth, passing a couple smokes and a bottle of ready-mix martini donated by the new El-tee. Lieutenant Brian. Graduated Tulane and Bravo Company. A real partygoer. Stepik said he found a bulldog hash pipe in his ditty bag, "big enough to give the Statue a Liberty a buzz." One of the first things he did was promote me to Specialist Fourth Class.

Everyone works his legs, trying to get up the circulation, and rolls his shoulders for the kinks and brushes his hair with fingernails for the dust, while puffing and passing the smokes and taking quick sucking swigs of ready-mix, not bothering to wipe the lip of the bottle. And the conversation goes like:

"Man! Did you see tha' pussy down by Charlie Papa Echo? Lot a meat on tha' one."

"Yeah, an' how 'bout them bunkers in the hedgerow on the lef' jus' outside the ville near the bullpen," says another. "An' which one a you motherfuckers got the goddamn grease gun? I gotta pump up the tread tension on my side. Come on, which one a you liberated that cocksucker."

"An' how 'bout them fucken chuckholes at the lumberyard. Oowee, shit, boy, they is motherfuckers!"

"Say, listen up, Seven-two Delta, don't get yer fucken balls inna uproar. Tha's ma fucken grease gun you so pissed about. An' yeah, which one a you short-timers got tha' son of a bitch, eh?"

"Aw, fuck a grease gun. How 'bout keepin' that bottle motivated; there's some a us come at the tag end a this fucken gang. An' get yer head out yer ass, Seven-seven Delta, we had them bunkers torched the las' time we was at Judith. Roger?"

"Shit. Who's idee was it ta drink this garbage?"

On and on, droning like traffic. I am getting so I cannot listen anymore. If you drive—that's special—because it's the Deltas who do all the work. If you drive point— that's very special—you don't drive in anybody's dust. First out. First in. First to hit an ambush. First to shoot back. Bad, very bad. And driving point drives me crazy. Takes cast-iron kidneys. Takes balls and no brains and a suicide's eye for what's happening. And the tracks burn like paper soaked with tar. Ninety gallons of mo-gas burns a lot of armor, and the drivers, the Deltas, almost never make it out. I know. I've seen.

The rest of the platoon, the TCs and gunners, wander up to the mess hall to catch the cold leftovers. The Deltas stay in the motor pool and after the sun goes down it gets mighty chilly some nights. I beat road dust out of the air filter, pump up the slack in the tread tension with the found grease gun and my ten-pound ball peen hammer, check all the oil levels, including the road-wheel hubs, pour water in the radiator, and check all the bolt heads and nuts. There must be thousands. The nuts on the tread block pins, the drive sprocket and road wheel and idler wheel lugs, the brake adjustment bolts, and the damn fifty-caliber mount bolts. These take a thirteen-sixteenths, this bunch an inch, these the three-quarters. Millions of quarter turns with the socket wrench. Bolts down tight till they squeak, then two more turns for luck with a four-foot lead pipe for leverage. I never got the torque right. Didn't care. Everybody else up at the tents getting quietly zipped up. Four blackjack games going at once. Seven-three Delta still in the motor pool working his asshole into a raisin-sized knot, working up his third sweat of the day, getting ready for the next move-out. Everything got to work, hear? Got to have your shit together twenty-four hours a day. Got to have it piled around you so you can find it even in the dark. Especially in the dark. And if you drive point everything is on your head. Fuck up and somebody is likely to catch their lunch, sell the farm and go home. and then they're square on your neck, like a goiter. And some nights I hear them when I try to sleep, calling me every motherfucker that ever lived. Bad, very bad.

There is no drinking water. It went for the radiator. One of the battalion mechanics is fucked up and sleeping it off on the welder's bench. Rayburn? Fucken Rayburn, where are you? Rayburn went home to his wife two months ago. She promised him the Olympic record blow job. Come on home, she said, everybody's lying for me. The Red Cross never knew what hit them. He sent back a honeymoon post-card of Niagara Falls lit up at night with colored floodlights with two of his wife's curly brown cunt hairs Scotch-taped to it. Everybody took a sniff. Fucken Rayburn, the dufus from Davenport, stalking that pussy on his hands and knees, stalking that pussy with a vengeance. The only dude I knew who would eat Viet snatch, Claymore Face's snatch. "It ain't down home," he would say, wiping his face ear to ear with the back of a greasy sleeve, "but it'll do!" Later we would hear he fucked up his wife; catches her messing around with a couple Davenport cops; does her in with a butcher knife. And wasn't it Rayburn who always said, "Don't force it, Deadeye, get a bigger hammer."

Get the BFH. The Bravo Foxtrot Hotel. The Big Fucking Hammer.

I walk stumble-footed to the tents, one step at a time; my forty-five-and-canteen-and-bayonet web belt hanging over one shoulder. Behind me Quinn and Lavery bang away on the seven-seven, helping the work along with bellowing grunts and abundant curses.

I walk those hundred meters the same way I would turn my back on the Cow Catcher many a night—a hundred times I did that, a thousand times it seems like. My eyes and hands and back sore, tingling sluggishly; my scalp itching. Blood blisters on my fingers and palms that burn and ache. Fingers that bleed around the cuticles and under the nails from slipped wrenches; the backs bleed from catching the sharp gouges along the flat armored sides. Cuts that will not heal. Greasy grit that has worked itself under my belt, rubbing my hips raw. Socks and feet mushy and wrinkled with sweat. The dust I could never wash out of my mouth, crunching in my teeth. Incoherent, fumbling, wasted again, but the work at my back done, and done proper: the gas tank and leaking radiator topped off; those several hundreds of thousands of bolts and nuts as snug and tight as I could manage; the tread tension perfect; the machine guns, cleaned and oiled and mounted, covered with stiff, wrinkled ponchos; and the jump cable hooked up between the Cow Catcher and the seven-six, nicknamed the "Texarkana Poontang," for some reason.

I shuffle past a couple dudes leaning against the platoon bunker, throwing C-ration scraps to a pack of camp dogs, and squeeze by the blackjack game humming along at Whiskey j.'s lawn table, the early sleepers, and half-dressed letter writers. I slump on the edge of my cot, feeling those chill, shivering tingles down my back, and stare over the low sandbag wall and the piss tube at the Alpha Company showers across the way. I untie my boots one eyehole at a time, peel off the damp socks, and undress. I stand in the faint light, brushing through my bush hair looking for crabs and lice and jungle rot and such. Three times I found a dose of crabs.

I grab my towel, slip into my shower thongs, and jump the ditch. Alpha Company is in the field, except for the walking wounded and housecats, and I can take a hundred-gallon shower if I want. I stand under a wing-tank spigot on slippery, moldy planks, letting a single stream of ice-cold water pour over me. I soap and rinse and soap again and rinse again, fighting the mosquitoes. Then I snap the towel to shake out the grit, wrap it toga fashion around me, and go back to the tent. I dress in clean fatigues, still warm from the afternoon sun, dust the inside of my boots liberally with talc, and join the blackjack game.

"Is there anything cold?" I say.

"Naw, Deadeye, there ain't never anything cold," Whiskey j. says, and hands me a canteen cup of grape Kool-Aid. I sit on the end of a mud-crusted footlocker, sipping tepid Kool-Aid and waiting for Stepik to deal the next hand.

The next morning Romeo moves out for Fire Base Carolyne, east and north in the rubber. I sit for two days counting my money, and two thousand P buys a lot of short-time, my man. This one broad has nice tits. Reminds me of home. Not hand-me-downs like most dinks, but handfuls, honest-to-God handfuls all day long. We go swimming in a creek. She shucks down and we fuck on the wet muddy bank, slipping and sliding into the water to our knees. We quit, move up to dry ground again, and slide back. What a ride.

We mount up out of Carolyne and take the battery of 105s with us. The Cow Catcher, Seven-three Delta, me; I pull the whole battery out of the mud. Five tubes and deuce-and-a-halfs and jeeps and lunch baskets and everything. Then Romeo drives the road. Morning here. Afternoon there. Night laager by the Suoi Dau cutoff. The next morning and afternoon and that night, same same. I don't touch ground for three days. Quinn and me stay fucked up.

I bust jungle out to Ap Six, another Chieu Hoi ville. When we break through the woodline the ten Deltas bring the tracks on line and we race the last five hundred meters over dry rice paddy. Some dinks take off for the woods to the left. Seven-seven and seven-eight peel off after them, firing over their heads, then lower. They drop four head of cattle and blow two papa-sans ass over teakettle with the fifties. We drive through truck gardens and in under the shade trees, among the cart trails and footpaths between hooches. I stop at the first hooch I come to with Quinn and the seven-four on my right flank. The others move on. There is an old mama-san sitting in the shade around the side, watching the peanut harvest dry. There's raw peanuts spread all over the back yard. I can see them through the doorways. Trobridge, whom Quinn has now nicknamed Dipstick, and the new gunners, Dewey and Walthers, jump down to check everything out. I shove the Cow Catcher into park, leaving it idle, and stand on the driver's seat with my shotgun Jesse James fashion—one foot on the chicken-wire grill, one hand on the trigger, a round in the chamber, the barrel resting over the other forearm—watching the flanks.

Dewey and Walthers came on the same plane from Cu Chi with Quinn. Dewey did not know, couldn't figure, had no idea what the shaving brushes were for. Stepik said that Dewey was what is known in the trade as a mark, but after a while he caught on. Walthers, a fuzzy-haired guy like Steichen, sat in awe of us for the first week, and it was too simple, too easy to kid him, because he believed every lie we could think up.

Dewey grabs the old woman by the back of her blouse. "No VC!" she shouts, and shakes her gray-haired, wrinkled old head. "No VC. VC numba fucken ten. VC numba fucken ten *thou!*"

Trobridge looks down his ugly lumpy nose at her and says, "Shut yer yap, mama-san." Dewey holds her back while Dipstick and Walthers go through the hooch. Dipstick thrashes around, throwing dishes and saucepans and crockery out into the front yard, while Walthers and Dewey stand and watch. Trobridge and Walthers go out back. Dewey tells the woman to squat, which she does, and goes around the side to cover them. I can hear the muffled crunching of peanuts and more crockery, and then: "Aha!" Dipstick comes chugging around the side of the hooch, holding a crossbow-looking contraption over his head. There is a C-ration can nailed to the business end of it and a stiff wire bolt rigged with a trip wire. It's got to be a home-made mousetrap or something like that.

"Booby trap," says Trobridge. "It's a fucken booby trap! You *lie*, mama-san," he says, leaning down into her face. "You boo-coo VC." The woman squats beside him under the upheld mousetrap, trying to think of a way to explain it. Her lips and gums and teeth are stained red with betel nut.

Quinn and Steichen stand head and shoulders above the weeds and brush on the seven-four not twenty meters away. They stand on the deck, laughing and shaking their heads. "Go gettum, Dipstick!" they yell.

"She's gook!" says Trobridge. "She's gook! Dozer, call the El-tee an' tell 'im we got us a gen-you-wine VC gook!" He is so excited that he cannot restrain himself from jumping up and down, pointing at her broadly with the mousetrap.

"Romeo Six," I say into my CVC microphone, "Seven-three Delta here. Eagle-eye Seven-three says he gotta Victor Charlie, cross his heart and hope to die. Whadaya wanna do with 'er?"

"This is Six. Roger, what is your location?"

"Near as I can make it out, we are directly to your rear. Hang a one-eighty and ya can't miss," I say.

"Roger. Be there in zero five. Tell Seven-three to stand fast. Copy?"

"Roger dodger," I say. Then I turn to Trobridge. "El-tee says ta take a break in place," but it is too late. Dipstick has already torched the hooch and is dragging a flaming rag to the haystack. The woman screams and tries to run after him, but Dewey has her by the scruff of her blouse and keeps pulling her down to her heels. Six-niner, the El-tee's track, comes wide around the smoking hooch just as the thatch catches and a couple small-arms rounds cook off with a muffled pop. Everybody, including me, hunches and flinches for that instant, then looks over at Trobridge as much to say, "Well I'll be goddamned."

The El-tee announces over the radio that Seven-three has a VC hooch. Quinn swings the seven-four around to my rear, facing the rice paddies, and shuts down. Then he and Steichen and Whiskey j. and Dewey go around back. Quinn and Whiskey j. quickly frag the well; find a bomb-shelter entrance, frag it a couple times, and pull off a couple rounds into the opening. Then they move off into the bushes out of my line of sight. Trobridge stands at the side of the six-niner, showing the El-tee the mousetrap. The woman squats on her heels in the middle of the yard, watching after Quinn and the rest. "Fucken GI," she says, and slaps the ground disgustedly.

"Hey, mama-san," I shout.

She looks at me from under the brim of her cone hat. Everybody looks at me.

"You think that's fucked up?" With my gun I point to her hooch, smoking thickly and crackling. A pig squeals. A dog barks. Trobridge shouts nonsense at someone. There is a bull buffalo just to my left with his nose-ring thong tied to a palm tree with a simple slipknot. He has been following the Cow Catcher and Trobridge and the old woman out of the corners of his eyes. He looks over at the burning hooch, looks at the Cow Catcher, looks at the old woman and the six-niner behind her, and tugs at the slipknot, stretching his neck and flaring his nostrils.

"Mama-san, you *really* think that's fucked up?" I shout, and point to Dipstick and the hooch and haystack again. "Well, clap your slanted eyes on this." And I switch the shotgun off safe and take aim on the buff's head from the hip. I work the pump and squeeze off the rounds. Blam. Blam. Blam. Blam. Blam. Blam. I lean forward against each recoil, the slide of the shotgun slippery and sweaty and oily in my hand. The recoil nudges softly against my hip. The buff keeps rolling his eyes, stamping his hooves, and stretching and yanking against the nose-ring thong with flared nostrils and dug-in heels. It takes me six rounds of double-aught buckshot to bring him down. The first round catches him between the flat of his curved-back horns. He flinches and shakes his head and pins back his ears, and pulls back on the nose-ring thong. The second round hits the side of his chest. He flinches again, baring his teeth, and paws the ground, snapping up dirt in small hard chips. The third round hits him square in the snout. He staggers on his forelegs, stumbling, and slacks the thong. He shakes his head again, flinging dribbles of blood in an arc on the damp, packed earth. The woman screams and collapses on the ground, whining and thrashing her arms and pounding on the hard ground with the flat of her palms. I catch the buff again as his head is turned—right on the back of the neck. His flanks twitch. His eyes wide, showing the whites. His jaw slacks and he slobbers gobs of red and creamy foam. The next round catches him under the chin. It blows away the nose ring and thong and a hand-sized chunk of slack flesh and blackened teeth. He falls to his knees, bellows, and shakes his head more violently, which scatters more blood and scummy foam from his lips and the hole in his chin. The last round broadsides him across the face, blowing off the corners of his black bristled lips. He falls to his side, bleeding gushes from his neck and head and snout in front of the hooch, which is now flaming and falling into itself with glowing bits of thatch trailing off with the smoke.

There are other shots off in the distance: the short kakak kakak kakakak of an AK; the quick sharp report of a frag; the crisp, methodical three-round bursts of a semi-automatic M-16—Quinn. There are deep-throated baritone shouts and engine noises muffled in the woods and calls on the radio of more gooks. There is more shooting, fifties and pigs, and frags.

I stand in the driver's hatch amid the thickening hooch and hay smoke which fills the yard. The buff lies on his side heaving his chest and working his legs in fits. It snorts blood, flashing its tail wanly, breathing in hoarse, sucking gasps and sharply exhaled sighs. The woman still screams in the steep-slanted rays of smoky sunlight; crying hysterically, keening. Terrified. Frightened to death we will kill her. The gunpowder smoke rises from the muzzle and open chamber in slow steady wisps. The woman lies on her back with her hands over her eyes, weeping and rocking, knees up. Troopers from the six-niner and other tracks take pictures of the hooch and buff and her, and rummage around the hooch going through her stuff to find something to take with them when we go—cheap hand scythes, bowls and cups, and pots and pans. I reload the tube and the chamber with rounds from the sack hanging on the infrared scope inside. Beside me the engine rumbles at idle.

And it all came on a whim. She was gook. The hooch was gook. The buff was a gook buff. But it always came with that hard-faced, uncaring, eye-aching whim; like hands squeezing down on hands, a sort of rock-scissors-paper trick. Slowly, slowly, so slow it is only glimpsed in time-lapse, those two or three scraps of good and real and soft things left of you are sucked down into a small hard pea. And the rest? Everything else brazes over and thickens and blackens—even the nap dreams. I hear them crunch when I punch them, like walking on a scallop-shell path.

I stand in the sunlit smoky shade with bits of straw ash floating down around me, the woman hysterical and whimpering and the buffalo dead still. And I smell the fear, as

clearly as I can make out Quinn's booming, mumbled baritone voice, and it smells the same as rotted burning flesh.

We wind up the afternoon with three live ones, not
counting mama-san. We torch all the hooches and hay
mounds, frag the bomb shelters, kill and run off the live-
stock, capture, kill, fuck up everybody else we can find.
Seven-seven and seven-eight stroll back from the woodline
with two shot-up body count dragging on the ground behind
them, tied at the ankles. We take the prisoners to Fire Base
Georgianne and that night the ARVN MPs come out with
the resupply to get them.

*

The drinking water goes out the hole in the radiator. I
have buzzing sounds in my head. Radio static—white noise,
they call it. Whispers and shouts and gut-mean curses. That
night a bunch of dinks try for the laager with mortars and
small arms, try to snatch a couple claymores. Cut them off
at the waist, says the El-tee. The incoming mortars come
two rounds at a time. Gristle from somebody's head
splashes around the perimeter. I watch two gooks with the
starlight scope, a night-vision device, try to low-crawl their
asses into grenade range of the seven-four. Just like the old
days with the cavalry trotting up just in time, only this time
the cav was waiting on their ass with pigs and fifties and
claymores and Whiskey j.'s short-fuse frags. All the gooks
look bowlegged, with Boy Scout haircuts they can shake,
chasing flies, like horses. Dipstick burns his ankle when a
hot fifty cartridge drops into his untied boot. He hops
around, whooping and bawling as though some gook had
crawled up and bit him in the leg. The next morning Allen,
Seven-five Delta, carefully adds 卌 to the 卌 卌 I with his
half-pint can of white paint and a stripped cigarette
filter.

And that night I see the woman.

I saw her at night, always after dark. Quinn and Stepik and Steichen and Whiskey j. and Dewey and Walthers and I sat along the benches smoking smokes and playing blackjack, listening to the Alpha Company frequency on the radio. Dipstick stood in the hatch nursing the non-Purple Heart second-degree burn on his ankle, watching the woodline with the starlight scope. I happened to put the red-filtered flashlight to one eye, the other eye staring at the yellowish, grayish moonlit pictures of tits and thighs. First come the scarlet circles, then the black, like a bull's-eye. She stands naked in a field of dwarf tundra flowers and red poppies and stiff mustard blossoms. Who are you? I say. I said it every time. She holds tight to her thighs as though squeezing and rubbing a bruise, half from chill and half from the pain of cramps. And the eyes. Black and red they are, with small points of white fire that flash and fade and flash, like the closest stars or two stars together or Mars or Mercury. Her shoulders and chest and breasts are flecked with faded taupe-colored moles. Her skin is scarlet and the dusty black shadows are the shape of taper candles. And the only part of her that shines and glistens is her pubic hair. It is curled and matted and burgundy-colored. And the line of flesh between her torso and hips seems to smile. No, not a smile. A giggle.

But it is only later—after I fall asleep, dreaming of gray fields of snakes and ramshackle treehouses and the smell of wet-burning hay; after Quinn shakes me awake for the last guard—that I see her close. I look out over the curved gun shield and the fifty barrel and the claymore wires spread out like fingers, and there she is. She never speaks, just whispers in rhymes that could be Russian or French or Basque for all I know. She giggles in earnest and makes teasing faces and climbs into the hatch with me under the blanket, and we make it. Our thighs and arms shiver, our shoulders and backs. We make it until we hear the chickens in a far-off hamlet, squawking and cackling and fighting over scraps. And all that day I see her—as I stand in line for morning chow or take my turn in the hatch for day guard or lounge around the artillery's Lister bag, waiting my turn for the canteen cup—in the corners of my eyes. She sits in the woodline shade with her legs crossed, leaning back against a tree, or walks wide circles in the rangy pasture grass with her hands behind her, dragging her toes lazily, or stands stock-still in the afternoon sun, looking at me straight in the eye. Why does she hang around? What do you want? Are you a witch, I say, or a conjurer? Some soft evil? But she just sits or walks or simply stands, blinking her sparking, fawning eyes, looking at me.

That afternoon the regulars sit in the track as always, playing blackjack. Quinn deals the first cards from the frayed-edge deck. I say, "This woman, you know, has strong and beautiful thighs." It just slips out. Quinn doesn't bat an eye, deals the second cards, snapping them face up with his thumb and second finger; deals me the jack of spades. I look at my down card and laugh. I laugh and they laugh. They think I'm crazy.

"I'll go double on the jacks," I say between humming, closed-mouth giggles, and turn over the jack of hearts.

*

*September —
Chicago, Ill.*

Philip,
Your father and I are fine. We hope you are fine.
Father has been working a lot of overtime this week.
By the way, Eddie has joined the Marines. He is in
Da Nang or somewhere. Would you like some more

113

of that canned fruit? It is very expensive to send,
even fourth class, but we are very glad to do it. God
be with you.

Love, Mom & Dad

Fire Base Georgianne

Mom and Dad,
I am doing fine, although it is God-awful hot all the
time. What is Eddie's address? I'd like to write him
—go see him. We get fresh vegetables, by barter, but
if you send canned fruit that would be fine. Also,
if you could manage a bottle of scotch, Eddie and I
could share it when I see him. (Pack it in popped
corn.)

Love, Flip

October —
Chicago, Ill.

Philip,
We are doing fine. Your father and I went to the track
last Tuesday and put $6 across the board on a mudder
long-shot named Early Wynn. He won going away and
we collected $87.20 altogether. I have sent you the
fruit and more Kool-Aid and the popcorn, but not the
liquor. I am sorry the corn is not popped, but your
father and I are sure you will find a way. You were
always such a clever boy.

Love, Mom and Dad

Dau Tieng

Mom and Dad,
Where is Eddie's address?? Please!? I want to go
upcountry and see him. ONLY ONE OF US HAS TO
BE HERE. Thanks for the fruit and popcorn. I think

*you can slack off on the Kool-Aid for a while, I've
plenty. Why didn't you send the scotch? It's no harm.*

*It's getting too late to write. I'll write more in the
morning.*

Love, Philip

*October —
Chicago, Illinois*

*Flip,
Ma got a telegram yesterday, and some Navy lifer in
his Class-As at the door this morning. Eddie's been
wounded. The clown says he's on the USS Reluctant.
He told us Eddie's deaf and blind, Phil.*

Dan

*P.S. I'll see if I can sneak you some mash. Keep an
eye out. And stay down.*

*

I could see it plain.

There is a flash of light and something cracking him
across the side of his head—a lead pipe and a roundhouse
swing—and then he's bleeding from his ears and the
corners of his eyes. But the pain comes slowly as though
boiled in a cauldron and he gets that dazed, glassy stare
that wounded sometimes get. He struggles to get up. His
lips hang away from his teeth and he can feel them moisten.
He moans because of the blood pounding in his head. He
thinks of his metallic-green '50 Chevy coupe. He suddenly
recalls the way he and I would get up on winter mornings
and dress, standing on the beds because the floor was always so cold, and then head straight for the kitchen where it
was warm. He remembers the rabbit hutch we found abandoned one fall; how we stashed the babies in a cardboard
box behind the furnace; how we fed them warm milk with

an eye dropper; and how their fur came away in our sweaty hands. Where am I? What is this place? What is all this blood for? I'm on the ground looking for water, for worms, but why am I bleeding? A corpsman runs up to him and looks into his face by the light of the fuel-dump fire. The cuts swell and become black gashes that bleed more and more, so fast it won't stop. Eddie mumbles something in that funny way that wounded have and takes hold of the corpsman's leg and the corpsman wants so bad to give him morphine, but he doesn't dare because it's a head wound— a bad wound. And besides, it's my youngest brother, Eddie, and he's wounded, upcountry in the Marines someplace.

I go see the El-tee. "Sir, I'm putting in for a leave," I tell him.

"You wanna leave, Deadeye?" he says. "*Everybody* wants a leave. Get outa my hair." I drop the letter in his lap. He reads it and sends me to the Sergeant Major. I tell him the same thing and show him the letter.

"Well, Specialist, the Red Cross is going to have to confirm this," he says, leaning against the doorjamb of his office.

The Red Cross man has a hooch to himself near the PX. He has a desk and chairs and file cabinet in the front room, a real bed and refrigerator and footlocker and an air conditioner in the back window. He parks his jeep in the shade of the tiled awning.

"You say your brother's on the *Reluctant*, eh?" he says, flopping his hand on the desk, like a fish.

"Yes, sir," I say.

"This fact will have to be verified by the Navy and your hometown Red Cross," he says.

"Yes, sir," I say again crisply. I give him every piece of information I can think of: name, rank, service number, and date of birth. Our home address. Eddie's full name and date of birth. "He's a little on the small side. Light hair. Hazel eyes." He writes it all down to please me.

"Yes, thank you, Specialist. We'll be in touch," he says, and dismisses me.

Well, just snap it up.

So, every morning first thing, and every evening after the mail and dispatches came, I put on a clean shirt, buff my boots, and walk to battalion headquarters to ask if word has come. Romeo goes back to the field, but the El-tee tells me I can stay behind.

"Thank you, El-tee," I say. I wasn't going to the field anyway, not until I had seen my brother. Fuck the field.

I stayed in the tent out of the First Sergeant's way and lounged around the mess hall with Haskins, helped Gonzales with the provision truck of a morning, and spent my afternoons in the EM Club with Staley, drinking beers fresh off the back of Gonzales' truck. Staley was a Charlie Company walking wounded transferred to battalion headquarters, where he clerked and typed in the Awards and Citations office. He got his Purple Heart at Suoi Tre and had done sixty days at LBJ, Long Binh Jail, for mouthing off to the Charlie Company First Sergeant. "He was screaming at the top of his fucken Spanish accent," Staley had said, " 'cause I wasn't limpin' fast enough to suit his ass, I guess. So I wheeled around in the mess-hall doorway and said, 'Listen, you slickass wetback, I'm hobblin' as fast as any housecat I know,' and that cocksucker wrote me up." We'd sit on the stools and Staley would talk about his leg, how it itched and ached nights, and I would listen, but always glancing over my shoulder, past the low sandbag wall and mosquito netting and rolled tent flaps, to the battalion headquarters building. I would tell him how Eddie had been fool enough to join the Marines, but that it didn't mean anything now that he was shot up—blind and deaf,

Danny said. And meanwhile the Red Cross man took his sweet fucking time.

After three weeks of pestering the Sergeant Major twice a day; of late, cold breakfasts; of sweating, drunken afternoons sitting in the EM Club and listening to Staley whine about his leg; of going to the Red Cross man every couple days with my hat in my hand and that fat-fingered housecat giving me that same old speech: "You are *not* the only man the Red Cross is concerned with," when all it would have taken was one fucking phone call to Da Nang, and he knew it.

Three solid weeks of lying up every night, thinking back on all those pillow fights and snowball fights and rotten-apple fights. All those autumn afternoons lying out on the orchard weeds with our coats thrown open for sun warmth, thistles and burrs clinging to the linings. The nights we whispered back and forth in bed and giggled and laughed and argued baseball. What is it going to be like whispering to him if he's deaf? What will it be like to lie up at night with a blind man? Three weeks of mulling all that over and over, and always in the memory, late of a bad evening with the tents and shower to myself, was the floor-to-ceiling picture window between our beds and the hallway stairs we could glimpse through the door. And how many times was it, when we were younger and still believed in snipe hunts and Santa Claus and such, how many times did we swear to each other that we had seen a ghost creep and creep, sliding along the stairway wall?

After three solid weeks the word finally came down from the Red Cross, and the Sergeant Major wrote me up for a seven-day emergency leave, but a lot of good the "emergency" part did me.

I spent two and a half days at Tan Son Nhut Air Base, explaining about my brother and the emergency leave to a running variety of housecats behind the ticket counter, and waited for a standby seat. I drank black-market C-ration instant coffee and Thirty-three beer and ate dark, chewy pastries wrapped in rice paper, and slept on a waiting-room bench. The morning of the third day I finally scrounged my own flight, a plane going upcountry to Phu Cat Air Base near the coast just north of Qui Nhon. We got to Phu Cat after dark. Cargo planes and F-4 Phantoms and Piper Cub spotter planes lined the runways and taxiways. Pickup trucks and step-in vans, hauling trailers of floodlights and generators and racks of bombloads and 20-mm canisters, parked in clusters around this plane and that. The airport terminal was a small building with a counter and desk and chair and file cabinets, several couches and easy chairs around the wall, and overhead fluorescent lights that hummed constantly. I walked in the open screen door and the night-duty man was stretched out on one of the couches, waving a flyswatter at the mosquitoes that came within his arm's reach. I asked him about the Da Nang flight and he sat up on his elbows long enough to tell me it left at 5 A.M. I laid myself out on another couch and slept in my clothes, just like always, with my arm hooked over my eyes because of the lights and mosquitoes. I could only nap on and off, because I was anxious and nervous, and anyway the guy roused me in the middle of the night and told me the Da Nang flight was canceled because the dinks hit the runway, that there would be no flights till the next day. I sat up for a while, staring at the runway through the doorway, hating gooks and working up a hate for that Red Cross man. But as pissed as I was at the dinks and the Red Cross, I just turned on my side and went back to sleep.

I spent the morning wandering around the air-conditioned PX and the streets around the main part of the base, until I found the NCO Club. I rolled my sleeves one more roll past my rank, if I'd had rank patches, and went in. It was a posh-looking place with a real bar and real stools, linoleum on the floor, slot machines and a Wurlitzer juke-box, real glasses and machine-made ice. I sat the afternoon and most of the evening in my scuffed-up boots, faded fa-tigues, and bayonet on my trouser belt, munching Beer Nuts and Fritos and Slim Jims and drinking PX Schlitz and Old Style. The off-duty Air Force NCOs would ask me, "You Army, hunh?" and I'd say yeah, and they'd ask me how come I was carrying a bayonet, and I'd say to open letters with, and they'd buy me beers and ask how the war was going in my neck of the woods, seeing as they never got outside the wire, and I told them it was still there when I left the field, or something like that. Then seeing that I didn't want to sit at their bar and regale them with war stories, they left me alone. I sat till late, eating their bar junk and drinking their watered PX beer, thinking about Eddie and how he would look when I saw him the next day; how he would be laid back on a real bed and clean linen in USN pajamas with his eyes and ears wrapped in cotton bandages with knots of hair sticking up; how I would walk through the doorway and say something like "Which one of you is Dosier from Chicago?" and watch for the dude that pricks his ears and jerks his head; how he and I would sit on his bed and touch and talk—but that can't happen. How, then, I would unbutton my shirt and produce the scotch and we'd trade swigs and wipe our mouths, and offer swigs to the others from the bottle Mother had not sent.

I got the plane in the morning, but I don't remember much about the ride because I was so fretful and excited. The plane pulled up to a warehouse-looking building called Marine Air Freight. The place crawled with Marines. They crowded on the benches and lounged against their seabags, waiting for outbound planes going upcountry and to Okinawa and so on. I asked at the counter where I could find the hospital ship USS *Reluctant*. The Marine sergeant, with crisply folded sleeves and Formica nameplate, looked me up and down and gave me short shrift, saying, rather smartly, that I should hitch a ride to the shore hospital and ask the Red Cross man there.

The hospital was a sprawling group of buildings and quonset hooches connected by enclosed hallways and open-air wooden walks covered with tin awnings. A scattering of foot traffic hobbled and wheelchaired around—dudes dressed in USN pajamas and robes and throwaway slippers. To one side was the dust-off pad covered with a large red and white cross just outside the triage, where they lined up the litters for the operating rooms or grave registration. I went in the front way and walked up to the first dude I came to, a sleepy-looking, pasty-faced Marine in pajamas that bulged with bandages just under the arms. He sat in a lawn chair in the hallway, holding a walking cane across his lap. When I asked him he told me that the Red Cross man had an office between three and four ward, to the left.

I knocked on the office door. No answer. I knocked again. I tried the knob, but it was locked. A corpsman pushing a four-wheel cart of bed linen along the hall said the Red Cross man was in Vung Tau for some kind of conference.

"Okay," I said, "maybe you can help me. I'm trying to get aboard the USS *Reluctant*. It's my brother. Do you know how I can get aboard?"

He stopped. "Look, hey, I'm awful sorry, but the *Reluctant* sailed for Hue and Dong Ha six days ago. Won't be back for a good while is my guess. Sorry." I sat the rest of the afternoon in a chair across the hall from the Red Cross office just on the chance that he might be back, but also I didn't exactly know where else to go.

I hitched a ride back to the Marine transient barracks near the Marine Air Freight warehouse and spent the night on a cot with a long rip in it. The next morning I went back to the hospital and sat in my chair as quiet as ever I sat an ambush, my ankles crossed and my hands in my lap. I made spider-on-a-mirror with splayed fingers, drank ice-cold water from the cooler, and stared at the Red Cross office door, thinking over and over: time will take me . . . time will take me . . . time will take me by the shadow of his hand. But the Red Cross man never came. And the more I sat, the more he did not come. The more he did not come, the more I set my jaw tight and breathed close-mouthed, rasping sighs and snapped my thumbnails and rubbed my teeth with the flat of my tongue.

The next morning I asked the dudes in the transient barracks orderly room if I could use their phone and tried to call the Sergeant Major to get an extension on my leave, but the lines were screwed up. I asked about a flight to Hue at Marine Air Freight. There were none. I went back to the hospital and hunted up the Marine Corps Chaplain. He sat behind his desk, his chaplain's insignia on one collar and his captain's bars on the other, nodding and "humm-humming," while I talked to him. He offered me coffee and a chair and listened, and told me that he was sorry about my brother, but he could not help with an extension and would not help me go AWOL.

Now, there has always been a ritual between enlisted men and officers—the saluting and sirring, groveling and grinning, the bowing and scraping—that is part ossified and ancient custom, part reinforcement that the enlisted men are at the officers' every beck and call. And there are those occasions when razor-sharp trouser creases and lustrously shined boot toes, robustly squared shoulders and puffed chest, blank forward stare, crisp salute, and a loud and snappy, deep and resonant "Sir!" will purchase a weekend pass just as surely as cash. But there is also a way of bracing to salute—leaning forward at the hips and back at the shoulders, touching the chin nearly to the chest, swinging the elbow exaggeratedly to the front and putting a curl to the wrist and hand, then flicking the fingertips away from the brow, like a clay pigeon at the skeet shoot—which parodies, cartoon fashion, that long tradition of respect, making it plain in the mind of a perceptive superior something to the effect that he may take his order or suggestion or vigorous counsel and fuck himself with it. In the Navy, in the old days, it was called mute insubordination. A bread-and-water, whips-and-chains offense, I am told.

I set the chaplain's coffee cup down, gathered in my fatigue cap, said, "Thank you, Captain. Yes, sir, thank you very much," then whipped one of those Fort Knox Armored Cav salutes on his ass, the way we used to do them for the Colonel from across the motor pool, turned on my heel, and left.

That night I straggled to the Army side of the airfield and caught the night flight back to Saigon, a C-130. I climbed aboard angry and hungry and tired. I had to sit on the floor with a bunch of housecatting ARVNs, traveling on standby, who quacked and cackled and yammered and wouldn't shut up the whole trip. The plane landed eighty or a thousand times, I forget which, but no one ever got on or off. We got to Tan Son Nhut late in the morning just ahead of the nonstop Da Nang–Saigon flight. I missed the A.M. Cu Chi–Dau Tieng–Tay Ninh plane, so I was stuck there till the evening. I spent the afternoon in the dink café, drinking Thirty-three beer and thumbing through tit magazines at the concession stand. When I got back to Battalion that night and signed into the company I was one day AWOL, but no one said boo. There was mail waiting for me. Danny wrote

123 |

to say that Eddie was back at Great Lakes; that his hair, which was growing back, would likely hide the scars; that his sight could come back anytime, the doctor said, but that he was stone deaf and would get a pension, disability the VA called it.

And after the first of the year, in January or February or early March, a mortar round or 122-mm rocket hit the Red Cross hooch, hit that Red Cross housecat—in the head, some said—so the inside of his hooch was nothing but *meat*. I was not sorry and did not cry.

*

I got back to the field the next afternoon. Romeo was laagered at Suoi Dau, guarding five 105 howitzers and two eight-inch cannon. I waved at the El-tee as I walked to the Cow Catcher, which faced the garbage dump and the village just like always. No one sat in the TC hatch for day guard. Dewey and Quinn lounged in the back, stretched out on the metal benches, waiting for chow call. After a moment of glad-handing and stowing my AWOL bag and settling in, Stepik arrived. Quinn asked about my brother and I had to tell them he had left Da Nang before I left Dau Tieng.

"Yeah. Well, Flip, it's good to hear he ain't dead at least," said Stepik, slapping me lightly on the knee. "Around here things got shitty right after we left camp. The seven-four got totaled at Carolyne. Steichen and Whiskey j. got dusted off. Trobridge and your new man Walthers and two other new guys are KIA." Quinn and Dewey had been sitting guard on the Cow Catcher by themselves ever since.

That night the four of us sat on the front along the chicken-wire grillwork by the fifty barrel, facing the village. We watched a procession of torches and flashlights zigzag up the side of the Nui Ba Dinh, where the Cao Dai had a temple and the gooks had weapons and ammo caches.

"We was refueling, toppin' off the seven-four," said Quinn, passing me the smoke and reaching in the driver's hatch for the canteen, "before moving outa Carolyne. There was a cargo net fulla fifty-five-gallon drums and Rayburn's electric pump, ya know? And who knows? Maybe it was a spark or some asshole with a cigarette or some shit." He took a long swig on the water. "Anyway, just as I was climbin' outa the hatch the drums blew. I jumped clear and low-crawled my ass outa there, but Whiskey j. and Steichen got splashed. Then the seven-four blew—went up like the head of a fucken kitchen match. Ba-room. Whiskey j., that poor fucker, kept rolling and rolling into mo-gas puddles. When we picked him up to lay him on a litter his skin was coming off in our hands, and Steichen was blinded."

We smoked and drank what there was of the water, talking about the times when Whiskey j. would play football with the platoon athletes, running those weird-ass loop-the-loop pass patterns; the time he stiff-armed Lieutenant Greer and the El-tee got pissed and started calling everybody Pfc and Specialist and everybody called him First Lieutenant Roger Boudene Greer right back; how Whiskey j. could spit out of the sides of his mouth between the spaces in his teeth and how he had thrown frag fuses at that stupid French broad that day in the rubber just to see her hop while she took her pictures, and nearly started a firefight with Bravo Company. Whiskey j. with his straight black hair and Steichen with short fuzzy hair were always together; how Steichen had a way of brushing his bristling hair that scattered dust and dandruff, like scraping the nap of an old sofa. The night that Atevo was killed he was the one who collected flak jackets to cover him and the rest of the night kept whispering in the pouring rain to me, "Hey, Dosier? Hey. Hey, Dosier? You out there? You roger?" His small, close-set darkish eyes and short, thick fingers

looked so funny against Whiskey j.'s thin, long-armed tall-
ness. Steichen, a diehard payday player, never exactly
trusting Stepik's deal, always asked him to leave the deck
on the flat of the blanket. And how he kept his money in
stacks: twenties, tens, and fives and ones.

Dewey, who sat on the end by the muffler, looked bad,
felt bad about Walthers. We could hear it in his voice. He
had tried to talk Walthers out of going, but since we had not
done ambushes for a good long while, Walthers had never
been outside the wire on foot and was curious. Dewey told
about hearing the explosion, and knowing right away what
it was and that Walthers was dead, and Trobridge was the
cause. Walthers was a well-built, good-looking eighteen-
year-old, drafted because he wasn't in college, willing to be
in the infantry because he was young and strong and didn't
really believe his uncle's man-to-man talk. I didn't know
much about him because I didn't pay much attention to
him, but he would always offer to help with the work, and
had good eyes, but not the sense to tell Dipstick to get himself another boy. And Trobridge killed him.

And Trobridge? Or Mr. Mousetrap, as he came to be
called. The man Dewey and I found standing in the hatch
stark-ass naked one morning in the pouring fucking rain,
because he didn't want to get any more uniforms wet, he
had said. The clown who loved the Army and loved the
food, but could hardly sign his full name to pay vouchers;
who hung his flak jacket with chains of pin rings from
smoke grenades to look bad-ass, but smoke grenades are
nothing but colored air, so saving the pins is about the same
as saving Oreo cookie rinds. He had saved that goddamned
mousetrap, too—to take home and mount over the mantel.
Trobridge—who never got any of Cross's insults; who
didn't have a good tooth in his head, and wanted to stay in
the Army forever—got his wish. Sergeant Anson Trobridge,

the platoon dipstick, also called Four-Eyes and High-pockets, even by Surtees when he was in one of his buddy-buddy moods. Good old Trobridge, the platoon stumble artist, dragged Walthers and two other rookies off to a day-light dismounted patrol, "jus' ta show 'em the ropes," and fell over a booby-trapped footlocker full of TNT with enough bang in it to flip an M-48 tank.

"He was supposed to walk them 'round the perimeter and show 'em how to hump," said Quinn. "But he got some wild hair up his ass and took them across the creek and through the brickyard and up the road toward French Fort and Fire Base Grant—the deep rubber."

"An' we heard the fucken explosion," said Stepik, flipping the butt end of the smoke up into the air. "It took seven-seven and seven-five and seven-two 'bout a fucken minute to crank up and get out there, but all we found was the fucken hole and scraps of cloth and gobs of slimy red shit."

We sat the night, exasperated and pissed off and shaking our heads, trading the starlight scope back and forth. We watched the cows raising their tails, dropping streams of shit; a woman pulling a rope bucket from the well hand over hand and then shucking down naked to wash—her skinny drooping breasts and withered arms dripping water; two old men dressed in black pajama-looking pants, trading swigs from beer quarts and puffing a hash pipe; a younger woman walking away from the ice woman's hooch, squatting down near a bamboo hedge, rolling up her pants leg to the thigh and pissing into a garbage dump.

The next day the El-tee called me over to the six-niner and told me that Quinn was moving over to the Cow Catcher as a driver—permanent; that I was in charge over there; that he was putting me in for my third stripe. I sat on the metal bench beneath the radio tuned to Battalion, looking at the El-tee's clean hands and pared nails and Stepik's knees and aid bag.

"Say, El-tee?" I said in a husky, mellow voice. "How much does that work out to in MPC?"

*

Romeo stayed at Suoi Dau for two weeks. We finally gave up playing blackjack because we couldn't stand to look at the three empty places around the blanket. Then one afternoon the whole perimeter was roused from naps and letter writing and day guard by three Bravo Company tracks and three squads of men, cranking down the road from Fire Base Grant and French Fort. A sweep team—two dudes humping metal detectors and earphones and two dudes with bayonets for digging—walked ahead, clearing the road. They came to the bridge next to the brickyard, checked it for mines and charges, and the three tracks laagered around it. The three squads spread out by four- and five-man fire teams among the crumbling brickyard kilns and along the creek banks. Bravo Company had been stung too many times to leave *anything* to chance, even though they were a stone's throw of five 105 howitzers and two eight-inch guns. When the rest of the column, Bravo and Charlie companies, crossed the creek, the three squads remounted the tracks and followed, everybody crowding together on the decks and facing toward the rear. The two companies laagered on the other side of town and we knew the next morning we would be going back to camp for a stand-down. The line companies had no other reason to come out of the woods.

That night after dark the dinks hit their laager with mortars and small arms and RPGs, armor-piercing rocket grenades. As soon as I heard the first crisp chung chung chung of the incoming mortars, I climbed into the TC hatch behind the fifty and slipped on my flak jacket. I cocked the fifty with that quick, hard snick sa-nack snick, and brought up more ammo and grenades and the starlight scope. I scanned the closest hooches and hedgerows and berms and the garbage dump for movement. Papa-sans and mama-sans and kids slipped into bomb shelters among the bamboo, and the skittish oxen and buffaloes and cows nervously flicked their tails and pawed the ground. I quit using the Sierra Sierra when the 105s started lobbing illumination rounds and high explosives over our heads and the hooch roofs, and the range couldn't have been a thousand meters, because the reports came right back. Quinn and Dewey and I stayed behind our guns, watching the reddish GI tracers and the greenish AK tracers ricochet into the air, and the glow of mo-gas fires from RPG hits against the low overcast. We could hear the chung chung chung of the incoming mortars and the quick kakakakak of the AKs on auto and the deeper, badder pom-pom-pom-pom of the fifties, the longer quicker bursts of the light, snappy pigs, and the lighter, snappier sixteens, and once I thought I heard mumbled shouting and engine noises. We kept listening for the first word from the El-tee to mount up and move, but that word never came, just calls back and forth in excited voices: "Anybody got movement?"

"Negative" was always the reply.

That was the first time I climbed into the TC hatch and settled in behind the fifty-caliber machine gun, with a hundred five rounds hanging from the feed tray, the two slippery wooden handles, and the oily butterfly trigger. I had piled the fifty ammo cans into a high pyramid so I could stand as high as possible. The upturned hatch cover behind me, the two armor shields to the sides, and the curved gun shield on the fifty formed a tub around me. From the TC hatch I could look down on the tops of heads, down the fronts of blouses; I kept a gas-mask bag of frags hung on one side and my shotgun—later a captured AK—on the other.

When we drove the road Quinn would drive standing up with his thirty-dollar aviators and black T-shirt and no CVC, using the horn much more than I ever did, but he would giggle and say it gave him a real kick to come pounding down on some poor dink walking his oxcart and honk that stupid fucking horn right in his ear. "Nine times outa ten," he would say, "you spook the oxen and blow them into the ditch." When we went back to pulling convoys, we would barrel down the road, throwing rocks and fifty cartridges at the hamlet hooches and road traffic, and it would not take us a week to get a bad reputation, but then again, who cared? Quinn and Dewey and I traded drags on one smoke after another and tweep-tweeped and bad-assed our way from Dau Tieng to Tay Ninh and back for many a day. One mama-san in a hamlet near the Monza S curve at Charlie Papa Charlie finally got pissed and disgusted at the noise and dust. She came out one afternoon and ran alongside for a way, giving us what-for and shaking her fist. The next morning Quinn slowed down in front of her hooch and whipped a CS grenade—tear gas, riot gas, you know?, the last CS grenade in Southeast Asia—spitball fashion, beanball fashion through the doorway. A perfect throw. Calls started coming over the radio, asking who had torched the hooch, and I said *I* didn't know and the El-tee behind us said *he* didn't know, and *nobody* knew. On the return trip we saw that the hooch had burned to the ground and mama-san had taken off, and that burned-out hooch was good for a grin every time we saw it. Quinn couldn't keep from laughing.

The morning after the firefight Romeo and the artillery packed up and moved out to Tay Ninh. We passed the ice woman's hooch and the Nui Ba Dinh turnoff and the village granary and the rest, but the village was quiet and sobered, eerie. No one stood along the ditches or leaned in doorways. None of those pesky gangs of kids hustled us for C-rations and handouts. There were no oxcarts or three-wheeled Vespas or any foot traffic. Quinn took the hint and started cranking, while Dewey and I kept an eye on every doorway and bamboo hedge and berm.

We gathered speed past the clearing where the two line companies had laagered the night before. The village papa-sans and mama-sans gingerly picked their way among the shallow, water-filled craters and tread furrows, the muck clods and pushed-over berms and swarms of flies, and two burned-out tracks. They scrounged through the firefight junk—helmets and shirts and C-ration garbage, M-16 magazines and cartridge brass and ammo boxes, and dud frags and splayed ends of claymore wires and such—looking for clothing to wear and metal to sell for scrap. Mo-gas fires had bent back the armor plate of the tracks as easily as someone could heat and bend scraps of black plastic, and melted armor lay in dull silver puddles, smudged blackish in the watery muck. The swarms of flies rose and hummed and settled back, as though the clearing was a living, breathing thing, and an acrid smell of cordite and burnt metal and mo-gas filled the air—that stink a fresh night rain never quite washed away. The dinks stopped and straightened up, watching us, almost touching their hats as we passed, but none of us waved or nodded back, as we sometimes did. Charlie Company had lost four KIA: the two Deltas and two grunts.

*

We hauled ass into Tay Ninh Base Camp, as usual, hung a hard right at the airfield, and made for the PX. The

El-tee told us to make our U turn there, and we pulled up along the ditch in front of some abandoned hooches, where we would be staying ten days or so. And that evening, after cold dinners and sun-warmed showers, the mail came. Battalion had been saving it for us—sacks of letters and junk mail and packages.

Letter reading was always sweet and bitter, filled with lonesomeness and a twitching groin and dreamy head shaking when you finished it for the second or third or fourth time. You had to take a hard look around you; the dust-crusted floorboards, the dozen or more canvas cots that smelled of mildew and sweat, the greasy tent-covered hooch, the mud-splattered tracks parked front to rear along the ditch, the smell of gun oil, and the rattle of bootlaces and belt buckles and gruff, mumbling voices.

A red dusk settled on the corrugated roof of the PX across the road. The letter readers lounged on their cots, sitting apart from each other and intent; first reading the script, ciphering the hand, then staring at words and phrases, thinking back, remembering faces and gestures and special-occasion dresses, the tones of voices on the page, and wondering why the letters were always so short. Drawn down into themselves; sighing and smiling, sniffing the lined loose-leaf or onionskin bond or five-by-seven Hallmark, printed with fancy flowers and such across the letter-head and drenched with perfume.

Quinn would get more mail then anybody—letters from Ma and chicks and the wrestling coach and drinking buddies and motorcycle buddies and work buddies. His packages would be filled with large cans of fruit and hard sausage and one-shot bottles of airline booze packed in popcorn. And he had a subscription to the Terre Haute weekly newspaper, which came to be known in the platoon as the *Terre Haute Weekly Township Clarion Gazette Dispatch*

Journal Tribune News and Territory Report. He would sit
in his black T-shirt, with those aviators pushed up on top of
his head, open the letters with his bowie hunting knife, line
up the letters and newspapers according to date, and read
them one at a time, sharing around thick slices of blackish
spicy sausage or ham, spoonfuls of halved pears, sips of
whiskey and tepid water, and handfuls of stale popcorn. He
would sit on the end of his cot and read and laugh and chew
on sausage rind and cough from the booze, reading parts
out loud.

His mother wrote about changed jobs, somebody's new
car, or that his uncle in Flint had had an attack of hives
again. Churchy, family stuff. So-and-so had a baby boy
(she would say). Andrew Prescot Lorenz. The church is
finally going to make some money this year on the bake
sale. (Dandy, that's just fucken dandy, he would say
aside.) Jason is working up near Veedersburg. The job
should be good for eleven weeks' work.

Hey, Buzzsaw! (another would say). Friday some ya-
hoo wrapped up his Harley on 41, right near the courthouse. He racked up his leg and is doing all right, but his
bike is fucken totaled.

I could go to sleep to your picture every night of the
week, Chas. (the chicks would say). Come home, Sweet-
stick, and bring the jewels, I could dig some good down-
home screwing.

Went to Reilly's in West Terre Haute (a motorcycle
buddy would say). Draper, from Cory, you know, that tall
black-haired dude with all the dental work? He got sick
three times. He finally left and Martha didn't find him till
later, that is the next morning, flopped over some machinery in the quonset. Couldn't remember a thing. You
know Doris, the chick who's been sleeping with that bald-
headed motherfucker at the plant? Well, she's knocked up

and went to live with her sister in Fort Collins, Colo. Mia Harper, that married broad over at Clinton with the big knockers. Had a party over at her place last weekend. She got fucked up on Chivas Regal and gang-banged the dudes who didn't bring dates, which was very polite of her. She even did the deed for Haney's kid brother, who ain't never had any. We was standing on the porch listening to them huffing and puffing through the open window. He comes out of the house after, and we asked him, "Well, Haney, how ya like it?" And him pushing the screen door wide open, coming out to the porch, says, "Prime, cuz, downright prime," and smiles this big shit-eating grin. I tell ya, Buzz-saw, I never laughed so hard. Jerry, who's working at the Standard station now, he fell down and cracked his head on the porch swing, he laughed so hard. Anyway, when Harper's old man came back from Memphis, some nosy fucken neighbor *had* to tell him and he beat the shit out of her. They're moving to Cincinnati around Christmas.

Quinn would read a letter like that and say "Aw," or something like, and make a face, but grinning the whole time.

I sit on the edge of my cot with an o.d. towel around my waist. My back beaded with water and sweat; my mail in my lap—letters from Jenny, a girl I met a year ago that spring who goes to school near Fort Knox; Derek, a buddy back at the company at Knox; and Ma.

Jenny's classes were humming right along, but "God, I miss you," she said. Derek had been out a few times. The last time she saw him he was drunk. Sister Francetta let him sleep it off in the visitors' lounge; he kept mumbling about something bad had happened. He hadn't been back since. There was going to be a film festival—all foreign.

Ma was still crying about Eddie. She cried about him until I got home. The nights were getting downright cold.

Two of my cousins were getting married. Somebody, I couldn't make the handwriting out, had had a hysterectomy. Father was thinking about buying a new car. She hoped he would pick another color besides fire-engine red. And why hadn't I been writing? Why hadn't they heard from me?

Derek said that plenty of dudes had been shipping out of the company. Some wound up at jungle school in Panama. One dude volunteered for Ranger training. The rest, two and three at a time, were coming straight over after a month's leave.

Oh, and yeah. You remember Willie O'Neal? Willie wound up in the Ninth Division. Willie wound up dead. Got one of my letters back marked "Confirmed Deceased" across his address. Don't know what happened.

You've got to sit still a minute, so still and quiet it is almost a tingling numbness in the legs, to let it all in. Willie, this small dude, jockey small, but well built. Willie and I had gone through Basic Training together. He could do the monkey bars out front of the mess hall in nothing flat; could knock out eight-count push-ups until a person got tired of counting for him, but had trouble with his full field pack on our first forced march. After Basic he went to Fort Sill. I went to Fort Knox, but we wound up together again at the 32nd Armor there. We stood next to each other in formation. I saved him a gig for a shirttail hanging out on an IG inspection. He had coarse, curly hair, never had to shave, wanted to work in the post office like his old man, and so hadn't minded being in the Army, because the Civil Service gave points for that on the exam. He and I shot some good pool, shared women and rooms at the Brown Hotel in downtown Louisville—his women loving him.

"He's got the cutest little pecker, ain't he?" they'd say, and squeeze him with a hug. I used to borrow his '55 Plymouth for a Saturday night and Sunday and drive to Springfield, where Jenny was going to school. It had four-on-the-floor and a V-8 with a four-barrel carb, and could tear through the Kentucky countryside like a stripped-assed ape. Jenny and I would drive out into the country and park and neck and dry fuck through our clothes and fuck for real, listening to the one Louisville FM station. Willie had taken a weekend guard mount for me just after the first of the year. I tried to pay him, but I couldn't get him to take it. We signed out of the company the same day, leaving for our last leave, me still owing him for two tankfuls of gas and that goddamn guard mount.

Quinn sits across from me on the aisle, his trouser cuffs loose around the heels of his boots, his face shining in the dull light-bulb light, his hair still dripping wet, dripping water on his black T-shirt. He has been reading the letters, dropping them one at a time into his AWOL bag. Every now and again I hear him saying "shit shit shit," under his breath, whispered and close-mouthed. Now he is down to the newspaper. "Shit," he says one more time, and folds it down small enough to fit into his thigh pocket.

"Say, Flip," he says, looking up, "you don't look too cool." I look him square in the eye, then past him at the dust-clogged, falling-down screen, down at the dry-rotted floorboards, his scuffed and brittle boots; out the back doorway to the washstand, splashed with shaving water, where some dude stands naked, drying his legs and thighs. I want to say something about Willie; that he could low-crawl, alligator style, faster than anybody; that he had this fast little car; that I still owed him money and when I tried to pay him he wouldn't take it.

"There's this dude," I say, and maybe Quinn sees the rest in my eyes, and nods.

He folds the newspaper one more time, stuffs it in his thigh pocket, and says, "Let's hat up, hey. Let's get the fuck outa here. I gotta taste for something cold. Come on." I dress and gather up my forty-five web belt and Gabby Hayes bush hat. Quinn waits for me near the door with his forty-five and stainless-steel bowie knife web belt slung over one shoulder, and his black beret crushed in his hand. On our way out we stop at Dewey's cot and ask if he wants to come along. He lies on his back with his arm over his eyes. "No, thanks," he says, not moving another muscle. He still feels bad about Walthers, and talks about him now and again, looking down at his boots and shaking his head when he does.

We walk past the falling-down bunkers and non-letter readers to the Cow Catcher. Quinn picks up his stash of smoke, which he keeps in a Prince Albert tobacco can, a pack of Kools, and a couple packs of White Owl Ranger cigars. He bought an entire case that afternoon—the biggest, ugliest cigars he could find.

Quinn leads me north along the road that parallels the airstrip, past the PX and base camp headquarters. We keep to the high crown of the road out of the dust. The last of the afternoon Huey resupply helicopters come in, skimming along the runway and loping toward the helipad behind us. Several miles to the north and east, beyond the end of the runway, is the Nui Ba Dinh, the Black Virgin Mountain. Even on the clearest, cloudless days a cloud layer wreathes the south slope. In the moonlight the Black Virgin is a cone-shaped, almost breast-shaped, blackened silhouette. The GI rock crusher at the foot of the west slope thumps and crunches away, making gravel, and some mess hall behind us clanks and clatters and hums.

Past the end of the runway we come to a cluster of hooches and trucks. Inside the back of a truck, with a radar dish on top, two housecats sit in front of a reddish, glowing console. One has a headset on and drums his fingers on his thigh. The other leans back in his chair with his feet on the console and his nose in one of those titsy, he-man pulp magazines. Quinn and I go single file along a hard mud path among low dug-in bunkers and housecat hooches— wood-framed, screen-covered, tin-roofed affairs, with ponchos and blankets nailed up for the dust. From the end of the path comes the unmistakable hum and buzz of bar noise—mumbling voices and clanking cans. A yellowish hooch light, shining on the ground and tufts of grass, sil- houettes heads and shoulders and beer cans along the sill. Over the front door a sign reads:

ANDY CAPP'S RETREAT
COUNTER MORTAR RADAR PLT.
TAY NINH

Quinn yanks the door open with his fingertips and we step in. A dozen or more dudes sit in cheap dink chairs and aluminum lawn chairs around mess-hall tables. All of them with clean housecat haircuts, bushy and scrawny and gran- diose mustaches, and bad-ass-looking red and black R & R tattoos. Just for that instant everything stills—the cribbage pegboards and waiting card tricks, even the fingers poised above a white rook. Three yellow light bulbs hang from the rafters. A red plastic room fan blows air through the back doorway. Chill, slippery cans of Old Style, Zippos and packs of cigarettes, line the tables and sills. The screen bulges where dudes have sat and leaned back. I push my hat back on my head, and Quinn and I glance from face to face, skimming them, as much to say, "What the fuck? This private or some shit?" and every eye blinks and glances down and looks away. I catch sight of a hand and arm waving in the darkened background and I nudge Quinn. We move through the chairs and forward-leaning heads to the bar—made from the wood of 105 ammo boxes, sanded and well fitted. Careful carpenter's work, and blackened with a blow torch to look like stain. We each throw a leg over a stool and toss our hats down. The bartender, a wide-eared, dufus-looking guy, wearing shower thongs and pegged civvies and a black and lavender Hawaiian shirt, juts his chin and bugs his eyes and flicks his brow, the way bartenders do, as much to say, "What'll ya have, bub?"

I half stand with one leg on the stool, one foot on the floor, looking something like I did when I drove—elbows tucked, hands to the front, shoulders and back hunched, one foot dead on the gas. Quinn sits low on the stool with his heels hooked on the rungs.

"What's cold?" I say. The dude pulls four cans out of the cooler, sets them on the bar, and slides the opener down. I flash the first two open and give one to Quinn. I take a healthy swig and it feels so goddamn good I take another. Quinn never looks up and never stops drinking. He ticks the can with his thumbnail, as though he's flicking a fly, and drinks it down in long, steady sips. We drink the first two or three rounds the same way anybody does when it's hot and muggy and their throats are dry—quick as hell, sucking on those beers, our eyes watering from the foam in our noses, and throats numbing from the chill—and toss the empties past the bartender's head into the garbage.

We sit and drink our beers and smoke Quinn's cigars, wetting them down from end to end and lighting them in a puffy cloud of smoke, the Zippos flaring with each puff. Quinn slouches and puffs and sips, mumbling. I chew on the mouthpiece until it is soggy and ragged, then spit the tatters on the floor. I fiddle with the brim of my bush hat and stare at the nail holes and printing still visible through the blackened wood, trying to think what the words "Confirmed Deceased" looked like across Derek's neat script.

"Where you guys from?" comes a voice.

"Hunh?" I say, and look up. It's the bartender, coming down looking to be friendly.

"I ain't seen you around here before."

"Say? Oh. Third a the Thirty-third. Triple Tre recon," I say loud enough for everybody to hear. "Dau Tieng. We're laagered up the road by the PX. What're you?"

"You are looking at Counter Mortar Radar," he says, and comes closer. Right away I feel fucked up for asking. He points to a plaque above the bar junk and stacks of cardboard coasters that reads:

Incoming is our business
We catch it on the fly.

When the gooks thump
We hump.

Next to it is another cardboard sign. It reads:

Give blood
Play rugby

"Rounds come in," and he swoops his hand and arm down over his head. "We get 'em on the radar and call in counter mortars. It sucks, just like everything else around here. Still and all, it beats poundin' ground. I used ta be a FO, a forward observer, ya know?" Do tell, I'm thinking to myself. "Worked with the Fourth of the Ninth. That really sucks," he says, and squints his eyes.

"Yeah," I say. "No shit."

"I got fifty-four days to do."

"Yeah? No shit?"

"I tend bar," he says with a sweep of his arm. "Stay stoned. Who cares?"

He gabs on and on about humping. I keep raising my eyebrows, saying, "Yeah. No shit," two or three dozen different ways. I keep looking away and gulping beer and fooling with my forty-five holster and the brim of my bush hat, until he finally gets the message and moves away. And Quinn, slumping over his beers and tossing them carom fashion off the back screen into the garbage, has his Prince Albert tobacco can and pack of Kools on the bar, and has been making smokes between sips and beers.

The bartender circles back on those flapping wingtip ears of his and says, "Hey, buddy, what are you doing?"

"Wazzit look like?" says Quinn, not looking up. He licks the one he's working on and crimps the end.

"Yeah, but what are you doing? Not here, man," says the dufus, leaning secretively against the bar. "What do you think you're doing?"

Quinn starts rolling tobacco from another Kool into a black Cinzano ashtray, raises his eyes, and says, "I'm makin' ice. Tha's wha' I'm doin'. I'm a ice maker. I go here an' there an' stop places an' have cold beers, an' sit low inna stool an' make ice. Why? Makin' ice makes you jumpy?"

"It's not that," the guy says, "but there's officers around here that don't dig it, that's all. Gimme a break."

"Yeah? No shit," says Quinn right back. "Well, I make ice. Stay stoned. Who cares? Johnny fucken Appleseed had his hoe an' hand rake an' tha' fucken seed sack an' his stupid fucken hat. You got your counter mortar radar yellow bug lights an' gen-you-wine beer-mug coasters an' tha' fairy-lookin' goddamn shirt anna fucken room fan, an' Seven-three Delta"—and Quinn nods his head low and pumps his thumb at his nose—"who holds the fucken world's record for bad-assin' yer goddamn convoys, gots his ice. An' sweet 'n' tasty it is, too. Ya kin bet an' take odds,

m' man. Ya don' like m' fucken work, then don' watch."
And he looks at the dude from under his brows, stares him
down. The dude draws his hands off the bar and moves
off.

Quinn scoops up the smokes on the bar and drops
them in his black T-shirt breast pocket under his fatigue
shirt. The two of us sit quiet again, sleeves almost touching,
and continue to drink. I stare at the printing on the burnt
wood under my elbows and the water stains. The same
message repeats over and over: 105 High Explosive 105
High Explosive 105 High Explosive.

"Hey, Flip," says Quinn, almost whispering, "you
wanna see somethin' fucked up?" And he whips out the
folded newspaper and tosses it on the bar. "Third page," he
says. I open it and lay it out to smooth down the wrinkles.
There is a short PTA article, some off-the-wall man-on-the-
street question and answer, and an ad for men's work shirts
and bicycles. Near the bottom of the page is a black-and-
white photograph of five men dressed in khakis and billed
garrison hats, standing in a tight semicircle with hands on
hips or thumbs hooked on belts or arms draped over shoulders. The underexposed reprint gray-tone colors are vague,
clouded shadows. Still, there are highlights. Open collars
and white undershirts. The crescent reflection on the bills of
the hats. The dull contrast of a light-colored two-story barracks behind them. The tingling sparkle of roof shingles
and moist-lipped smiles. The whites of the eyes shaded
under the stiff black brims. The caption underneath says
that so-and-so and so-and-so "of Terre Haute have com-
pleted Basic Individual Training at Fort Leonard Wood,
Mo." Below the caption is a short three-sentence paragraph.
Two of the names are repeated. "Kenneth Corbin, son of
Mr. and Mrs. Robert Corbin, has been killed in action, October 28. Joseph Haney, son of Mrs. Alice Haney, has been

killed in action, October 29. A combined service, Mr. Haney's coffin will not be open, will be held at 3:00 P.M. Monday, Spencer Street church."

"See that dude?" says Quinn, sitting up, leaning over and pointing to the face and hat in the middle with his little finger. "That's me. Kenny an' me was on the wrestlin' team together. He wrassled ten pounds lighter than me. Haney, he graduated a year behind us. He an' I worked in a welder's shop together." Then he sits way up and pulls out his wallet, slips it out of the Baggie, and takes out the same photograph, only in color, being careful to handle it at the border. The cream color of the barracks is just as I remember. The white undershirts and infantry collar brass and belt buckles glow. Every face has different-color eyes and one of them wears a gold wedding band. "That there's Corbin," he says, pointing again, "an' Dick Teleck. Me. Haney. An' Lou Lorenz, who lived a couple doors down from me. He got his shit blown away las' July. He was married. Now Haney an' Corbin's dead, an' that dufus Teleck ain't all that fucken bright." He slumps down again, taking out another cigar. "Ain't that fucked up?" he says, pointing to the color photo with his eyes. "How many letters I get tonight? Eight? An' ever' one a them's gotta tell me 'bout Haney and Corbin and re-min' me a Lou. Ever' one got to blab on an' on how Corbin's mouth looked so funny an' Haney's coffin was screwed down tight, with a bunch a flowers o'er the top. How some fucken lifer an' his goddamn color guard stood at parade rest with Class-As an' rifles an' white gloves an' red eyes, 'cause they was a little high, some said, while Pastor Weber read out the eulogy, and Miz Haney bawled into her handkerchief and dress sleeve the whole fucken time. Jesus H. fucken Christ, Phil, it's like they got their shit blown away nine times, if ya coun' the paper. They got killed an' shipped home an' buried nine

143

times. Ain' tha' fucked up? But ya wanna know somethin' else? It's more fucked up than tha', 'cause it was my fucken camera. We was a little smoked, an' I lined ever'body up, an' we had our platoon sergeant—guy name a Todris— take our fucken picture. An' three a them is dead, an' it was my fucken camera."

And the bartender stands still and the card games hush. Quinn has his hands flat on the bar sucking breath through his teeth, disgusted. I stare at the photo, wondering how roof shingles could sparkle so.

"Tell ya wha'," I say, looking at his flat-palmed hands, thinking back about Willie and his shirttail and as short as he was his khaki trousers didn't come down to the tops of his shoes, the rubbers and road maps I kept in his glove compartment, and that fucken cash—two tens and a five—he kept pushing back at me. "Tell ya wha'," I say again. "Lezz hat up an' go down ta the Charlie Charlie an' smoke up some smoke, eh? Say!" I call out loud, "Say, bartender, wha' ya got 'sides Ol' Style?"

"Well," he says, coming down the way again. "Got some San Miguel, but it's still warm."

Warm. Cold. What's the fucken difference? Cold is nice going down, but I've swilled enough warm, now, so that it don't mean much. A buzz is a buzz. I wave him on for a whole case, heft it under one arm, don my bush hat, and the two of us leave. We stare intently at the dirt path, giving our fuzzy eyes time to adjust to the dark. We stumble over the footbridge and stop on the road, almost leaning on each other, to light our first smokes. We stagger along the right-side wheel rut, Quinn singing to himself in a slow garbled monotone, not minding the tune:

> *So long, it's been good to know ya.*
> *So long, it's been good ta know ya.*
> *So long, it's been good ta know ya,*

Tha' dus'y ol' dus' is jus' nuthin' but jive,
An' I hope ya don' fuck like ya drive.
Tha' dus'y ol' dus' is jus' breakin' m' heart,
An' I hope ya don' fuck like ya park.

"Say, Flip?" he says, stopping dead in his tracks. "You hungry any?"

"Inna sorta gen'ral way, yeah. You mean C's?"

"Negative, m' man, fuck a bunch of C-rats. I mean meat. I mean somethin' like two pounds apiece. I mean steaks," he says, and points to the right. Through some housecat hooches I see the smoke and embers and flare of a charcoal fire—the unmistakable crackle of dripping grease, the sizzling of steaks. Quinn motions for me to stand fast, draws his bowie hunting knife, wipes his eyes with his sleeve, and moves off. I stand with the case of beer between my legs and watch his silhouette move slowly among the bushes and hooches, and then he disappears around the side of a building. A long moment later he comes back, walking toe-heel-toe, with two rib eyes drooping over the flat of the blade. I pick up the beer and we walk. "They a little rare," he says, "but ya can' have ever'thing." We stagger past the camp headquarters, Quinn walking on tiptoes, concentrating on the steaks. We come to another, smaller building. Quinn hangs a left, motioning to me with his head. "Let's go in 'ere an' get some light on the subject." We cross a footbridge over a ditch and walk up a cement path to the base camp chapel, an open-air affair with a low roof and wide eaves, pews for a hundred men, and two yellow bug lights hanging from real electrical fixtures. Behind the communion rail and altar table and crucifix, hanging from the ceiling, I see the silhouettes of the runway and perimeter wire and the Nui Ba Dinh.

"No," I say, stopping just under the eave. "I don' wanna be here. Not tonight."

"I'm gonna have me a wake," he says, and slides into a pew on the left, setting the steaks next to him. What the hell, I say to myself, and slide into a pew across the aisle. I yank open the case of San Miguel and open the first two beers I get my fingers around, tapping the tops of the cans to settle the foam. Quinn begins cutting the steaks into strips.

We pass tepid foamy cans and slices of greasy steak and quiet glances back and forth for half an hour, an hour, maybe more. We sit with our asses all the way back in the seats, the aisle between us, leaning our arms forward over the pews in front, the cans dangling from greasy fingers. We eat the reddish, brownish strips of steak, holding them high over our heads and biting off mouthfuls, fighting the gristle. The steaks snap white flecks of grease into the air when a piece is bitten off. We talk as little as two people can at an arm's length apart.

"Pass a beer," he would say.

"Steak?" I would ask.

We finish the steaks and wash them down with beers, wiping our mouths on our sleeves, and start on the smokes again. I can see the two of us somewhere else, anywhere. His kitchen or mine, sitting backward in the chairs, facing the table crowded with beer-can pyramids, cigarettes, and the salt cellar and pepper mill. Dog-eared stacks of the *Terre Haute Weekly Township Clarion Gazette Dispatch Journal Tribune News and Territory Report* piled on the knee-high radiator. Tin and glazed clay, machine-blown glass and driftwood knickknacks line the bay-window sill; blue floral dinner dishes and steak bones, a clock radio and carving knife on the counter; cricket and cicada noise coming through the screen door, underneath the sound of trucks, gearing down and coasting through town on U.S. 41.

We drink our beers and smoke our smokes one after another and I get drowsy and heavy-headed in a stupid, pleasant sort of way; then it doesn't matter that we are in a chapel, sitting on plain pine pews with stiff uncomfortable backs. Quinn lounges back with his legs over the pew in front of him and we flip crumpled empties and smoking butts out into the dim moonlit dark. I lean way forward with my forearms on the pew back, staring down at the yellowish crescent of light around the lip of the can that dangles from my fingers, and I think back on how Stepik (who would stay on and on in the platoon, and extend for six months and even turn down his month's leave) had reached his head and arm in the back of the seven-three and put his hand over Atevo's blackened eyes, closing them, then slipped me a couple more Darvons and another smoke, after I had had that little talk with the El-tee.

How Willie could low-crawl those four twenty-five-meter laps on that laid-out canvas, back in Basic when we had to low-crawl for time. Willie skittered like a goddamned cockroach, everybody said. How he kept shaking his head, saying, "Naw, naw," sitting in his car with his hands dangling over the steering wheel; me leaning head and ears through the passenger window the day we both started our last leaves. I tried to get him to take the twenty-five for the gas and that guard mount, and got pissed when he kept shoving my hand back.

How Eddie laughed and slid in behind the wheel of his hand-me-down '50 Chevy the day I gave it to him; me with my head in the passenger window, passing him the keys on a bit of kitchen twine. And how he jangled the keys, smiling down at the dashboard. It had eighty-five thousand miles on it, but had a good engine and a handmade, homemade re-built transmission. He cranked it up and slipped it in reverse, hooking an arm over the back of the seat, and backed out of the driveway. And when he drove off I ran to the curb and shouted, "Take good care!" but he was out of earshot around the corner.

And I look over at Quinn, sawing notches along the edge of the pew. He's picking his teeth with his tongue, blinking and squinting his eyes. I ask for another smoke and light it quickly and sprawl back in the pew, sucking those first three or four hits so hard the paper collapses on the leaf.

And I think back on how Jenny pouted and made a face, pulling me by the arm to make me go through the receiving line at the autumn dance a year ago. This bald-headed, wrinkle-necked, full bird colonel from the Officer's Candidate School stood at the tag end, shooting his cuffs between handshakes, decked out in his formal dress blues—fancy piping on the trousers, fringed epaulets, and a gold Armored Cavalry braid looped under one armpit. I tousled my hair and rumpled my three-piece, trying to look as unsoldierlike as possible. But when I slid in front of him and he offered his white-gloved hand, he took one look at my haircut, and sniffed me and stiffened, and told me loud and clear to straighten up and salute him. What kind of a soldier did I think I was and what was my unit? And I had to stand there, in front of God and everybody, and grit my teeth and do it. When I moved away, Jenny said she had never seen me snap my heels so and stand so stiff and look so stern. Maybe that was the night she began to get the message about what it was I did on the weekdays. We left about ten, expressing our regrets to Sister Francetta, the Dean of Women. She asked me why I was so uneasy, and I was a stone's throw from telling her that I didn't have to put up with some chicken fucken colonel's "Salute my ass, Private" crap, on my own time, but I just shrugged my shoulders and excused myself.

I think back on how Trobridge, that puffy-faced dip-stick, had to lean his head way back to look at you, because his glasses were always sliding to the end of his nose. How he never got the hang of booby-trapping claymores, so no one would sit anywhere near him when he tried. How he had a way of slopping gun oil on his shaving brush and slopping the brush all over the fifty, and always had that dusty, greasy, dufus smile on his face, even when he'd fucked up and was in trouble.

How Atevo held his shotgun across his lap and brushed the oil thickly with long, elegant strokes. How he always said, "Thank you," with that boyish grin when Haskins served the dollops of mushy scrambled eggs with one hand and buttered bread slices with the other. How Atevo wouldn't carry claymores on ambush, because they made too much noise, he said, and would tape his trousers at the thighs when he walked point, cat quiet and tiger smooth. And how puckered and swollen and black his face was around the bullet hole—his mouth winced and his tongue tip between his teeth—and how the back of his head was nothing but whitish bone chips and grayish, watery mush. How fuzzy-haired Steichen (who wrote from Japan, saying he was taking blind-man lessons and Whiskey j. was getting some kind of chemical baths and skin grafts) stepped on the little man's arms, breaking them at the shoulders, like somebody snapping damp twigs. And how Whiskey j. slipped the guy sideways into that narrow, shallow grave, and shoveled gobs of muck over him with his boot. How Whiskey j. and I traded long sucking drags on Cross's smoke, leaning against the seven-three—Whiskey j. blow-ing smoke rings with a flick of his jaw into the rain-smell-ing, dead-smelling air. And how Trobridge stood in his TC hatch, leaning over the armor tub with his chin in his hand and looking down at us with those drooping eyes and that idiot grin, as though he'd never seen us, or a dead body, before. And as we made it back to the fire base, my hand still twitched—filthy and water-wrinkled—when I slipped it through the hand strap. And how I couldn't look anywhere but up because of the tears welling in my eyes. I mean, I had seen Atevo's boots plenty anyway, so I didn't have to look at them again.

I reach into the aisle for another beer; the yellow-tinted air warm and thick and stilled around me. I blink my eyes a long achy blink, and turn to Quinn across the way. He sits slouched like me, holding that four-color photograph at an arm's length and sneaking glances at it, squirming and mumbling to himself.

And I've got to think back on Willie's giving me one last ride out to the highway so I could hitch a ride south to Springfield, where Jenny was. I leaned in the passenger window and we shook hands firmly, almost squeezing; me saying, "Take care," and "Be cool," and trying to shove that twenty-five dollars at him; and him saying, "Naw, naw, Flip, I was glad to do it, take care yourself." He revved the engine a couple times and fiddled with the gear shift, so finally I stood back, saying, "Goodbye," and he drove off. He honked and waved, but I watched his eyes in the rearview, looking back at me, and the silhouette of his head in the rear window. He reached down and double-clutched into second, rapping the pipes, and then he was gone. I stood on the shoulder of Thirty-one Whiskey—Dixie Highway—with my duffel bag crammed full, and those two tens and that five folded double in hand. Money I owed him for two tankfuls of gas and a Saturday-night midwinter guard mount. Money I could never spend. Money I would never be able to give away. Money that will follow me around like a bad smell. I might as well have bent down in the gravel roadside, right then and there, and burned it.

I take the last long swig of bad-tasting San Miguel and crush the can and toss it sidearm out into the darkness, and wonder to myself: what in the world has possessed us to come in here? My shirt clings to my back. A numbed pain hums and itches in my throat and the back of my neck and I feel dizzy, but that's okay, because I'm good and drunk. I turn to Quinn. He's looking at me from under those brows, mumbling his mouth as though he's going to say something. His bowie sticks deep in the seat next to him in the smear of steak grease. He motions for another beer and I hand him one, careful not to shake it.

I turn to the front of the chapel, staring into the darkness at the runway and the wire and the Nui Ba Dinh wreathed in silver smoke, and I think to myself that it's a goddamned fucking shame the world is not flat. Then I could sit up or stand up, shade my eyes from the yellowed tinted light, Indian fashion, and see home. I could gaze out under the eaves, and there it would be, morning. Smoky and greenish in the light of a long-shadowed, wet, and chilly sunrise.

"Ain't tha' some shit," Quinn says suddenly. "M' man, somebody 'round here's been fucken up."

"Hunh?" I say, looking around.

He raises his arm straight above his head, pistol-range fashion, and brings it down level with his drooping reddened eyes, pointing at the altar. "Look-it all that sloppy fucken work," he says. He points with his trigger finger to the plain pine crucifix, hanging from a rafter by eye hooks and clothesline rope tied with noose knots. The front edges beveled and nicked. Spike-sized nail holes at each end of the crosspiece and a wedge-shaped pedestal for the feet. A gnarled circle, like a ring of white fire or bleached fishing worms, around the head.

"All that wood's been shellacked, but not sanded. See

them fucken brush marks? An' there's a footprint on the mop board near the corner, left side. Whoever did the crucifix laid it to one side to dry and the shellac dripped off at about a thirty-degree angle. Deadeye, you *gotta* know that there's some asshole 'round here thinks he can work wood, but's lying to himself." He slides out of the pew, taking his beer with him, and walks to the front. He sets his beer on the rail and leans against it with his knuckles, stiff-armed.

"Ya know? I use' ta be a reg'lar churchgoin' fool. I use' ta go on them fucken retreats an' *all* that shit. But that's before I met chaplains an' now I know I've been kidded by experts. 'Do yer duty,' they tell ya," and he drops his voice and puffs his chest. " 'An' yer fucken duty is ta do what yer fucken *told* ta do. . . . Drop 'n' gimme ten eight-count push-ups, trooper, 'fore I gib ya one upside the fucken head. . . . When Ah tells ya ta shit, Ah wants ya ta drop yer fucken trousers an' ask me wha' color does Ah wants. . . . Ah wants ya ta park yer fucken bike an' take this 'ere gun an' go out there an' get me some fucken squint-eyed gooks. Ah'll stay put an' hold the door for ya. . . . Now go! Double time! Hump, goddamn it, hump, hump!' " And he rolls his head back on his shoulders.

"You know what pisses me more than anything, Flip? That aggravates the fucken sweat right out a me? The thing that rankles and itches and just stays sore until I want to chew down hard on something? That gets me so pissed it blurs my fucken vision when I sit quiet and think about it? It was *my* fucken camera," he says, dreamy-slow. "The five of us was *so* fucken tickled about gettin' out of Basic, goin' home on the same bus, and *all* that shit. Teleck and Haney and Corbin and Louie couldn't fucken wait to stand there, all close and chummy, and grin and love it one more time for that fucken lifer. Onnne. Morrre. Timmme. I ran and

scrounged my Kodak out of my duffel and ran back, taking
the five stoop stairs in one jump. We was a little smoked
and grab-assed and poked around and fucked around. . . .
I tell you, my man, I do not know what it was that I was
thinking about. It is the wrongest, dumbest fucken thing I
have ever done." He takes his unfinished beer and tosses it
out the side.

Slow dull footfalls crunch along the ditch, then step up
to the cement walk.

"Well, lookie lookie," comes a voice. It is Surtees,
standing spraddle-legged under the edge of the eave and the
first bug light. *"Here's* you two chicken shits. You birds are
in boo-coo trouble. There's been a move-out and you clowns
has missed it. Seven-three, you are in hot water up to here,"
and he puts his hand up to his eyebrows.

Nighttime call-outs were always bad news. The runner
from battalion operations would come screaming at the top
of his lungs, "Call-out! Recon get down to the motor pool
and move out. Alpha Company (or Bravo or Charlie Company) ambush's hit. Got KIA. Wounded." He'd come stumbling up to the doorway and we'd be awake already and
he'd lick his lips and say it again in hoarse, breathless whispers: "Move out. Call-out. Bad trouble. KIA. Wounded,"
but by that time we were up and pushing past him, shagging
our asses down to the tracks—boots untied, rifles and flak
jackets carried loose, helmets bouncing on our heads, still a
little smoked sometimes and everybody yelling, "Move out,
move out!"

The Deltas would crank up, rapping the pipes drag-
strip fashion—sparks flying from the straight-pipe mufflers like spray—everybody mounted and excited. The El-
tee would come out of the operations bunker at a trot with
a map under one arm and mount up, and we'd move out, flat
out, driving lights out, driving wide-eyed in the moonlight

and starlight or pouring rain. We'd load the guns and bring up ammo and sacks of grenades on the fly, bad-assing up to the gate and blowing through town quick as horses, ready to pound down and open fire on the first funny little thing we saw. And if there was a dink ambush waiting, we would drive straight through it, squeezing off recon-by-fire in ten- and twenty-round bursts, and letting short-fuse frags fly, long-bomb-football fashion. And driving up to the ambush site was always messy—wounded lying in the ditches and defilades, bleeding all over themselves; the survivors standing around dazed and looking at us fuck-you fashion or what-took-so-long? fashion or got-a-medic-or-a-canteen? fashion.

But Surtees' move-out drills always started with some dingleberry housecat from the Orderly Room, standing in the tent doorway and blowing his brains out on a silver MP whistle. The first time he tried it a dozen dudes were up and dressed and had him by the throat before he could suck in another breath. "What the fucken goddamn hell you blowing a fucken whistle for?" we screamed. "Tweety-pie, you blow one more fucken breath into that whistle an' it's gonna be yer las'. You roger that?" "Yes, Sergeant." Surtees stood in the company street, clocking us with his watch, and we piled out of the tents and crowded around his ass and told him to shove his fucking drill, it's one o'clock in the fucking morning. And that black motherfucker made a stink about it to the Major, the one that baby-sat the Colonel, and the Major stood us in formation and read us the riot act till breakfast.

So Quinn leans against the altar rail on his side of the aisle and I'm on my side of the aisle, sitting up at the mention of "call-out," with a funny fuzzy feeling in my head and an itch and trill in my stomach at the thought of having possibly missed the real thing. But that passes quickly when I realize that Surtees wouldn't be standing there, trying to look bad-ass, if it had been. I mean, I'm not so stoned I wouldn't hear them crank. Seven-five is missing on two cylinders and the El-tee has this big booming voice, and we would have heard.

"Go away, Surtees," I say with a croaking voice and an urge to cough. "I ain't in the mood. Fuck your puppy-shit drill."

"Roger that, Deadeye," says Quinn, not looking around.

"Well, now," says Surtees, leaning a hand over his shoulder-holster forty-five, as though he's leaning against a fireplace. "You two chicken shit are in boo-coo trouble. Drinking an unauthorized beverage in unauthorized quarters. Smoking that marijuana. Insubordination. Refusal to obey a direct and lawful order. Yeah, you two chicken shit are gonna do about a thousand years in LBJ." He works his jaw, trying to get up something to spit, and rolls that cheap cigar of his in his fingers.

"Surtees, what do you see around you?" Quinn says.

"I see two of the champion chicken shit in this man's Army desecrating a house of God. An' you two slackers are in plenty, plenty trouble."

"Know what I see?" says Quinn, standing up and turning around. He hooks his thumb in his web-belt forty-five that hangs across his chest Pancho Villa style. "I see Deadeye fucken Dosier and my humble self and a coal-black nigger, and a clear field of fire for a hundred meters around.

"Surtees, you ever hear the one about the kid and the wolf? There was this village, and the dudes there raised sheep. They're so lazy they hired some kid, for some shit wage and room and board, to sit and watch their sheep. The kid watched those sheep every damn night, pulling his pud and whatnot, going a little more squirrelly each night. Well, one night he gets an idea. He starts on a laughing jag, he thinks it's so funny. So he ups and walks to the ridgeline by this big-ass tree, plants his feet and rares back and lets 'er rip. 'Wolf! I say wolf! Eeyooo down there! Help, goddamn it!' And that quick every swinging dick in the village comes lickity-split with their guns and pitchforks and scythes and such, coming flat out up that hill. They run by the kid as if he isn't even there and galumph down toward the flock, looking to lay that wolf out, only there *ain't* no wolf, see? They stand around, scratching their heads the way dirt farmers do and cussing each other because the son of a bitch got away. When they turn to go there's the kid, leaning against a stout low-hanging tree branch, doubled over and having himself a good old-fashioned hawhawhaw. It *is* pretty fucken funny and a couple dudes—churchgoing dirt farmers and coach-house bartenders that got to touch their caps for everybody—why, they just laugh, and laugh it off. But one hefty, football-player-looking dude walks up to the kid and says, 'Wud ya do it fer?' 'Jus' ta see it happen,' the kid says. 'Well, fun's fun, but don' pull that agin, dig?' Dufus says. Everybody mumbles in agreement and goes home. And the sheep stand around in the sharp moonlight, look at each other in that punchy, saggy-eyed, cud-chewy way that sheep have, as much to say, 'What's this guy's problem? Who invited this asshole?' And none of them know, not even the ones that stood in front.

"The kid wanders around, fetching firewood, kicking rocks, and pulling bandit rye to munch on. He sits cross-legged by his fire and after a while he gets to squirming and fidgeting around, and starts feeling cute again. He ambles over to the tree, bringing his rifle this time. He squeezes off a round—KA-BLAMO—and cups his hand 'round his mouth. 'You son-ov-a-bitch! Sayeee down there! He's got me by the leg! Leggo, wolf! HELP!' And those dudes jump outa bed and yank their trousers on, both legs at once. They scramble past the kid, scattering those sheep, and range around and beat the bushes, *looking* for that wolf. And that kid stands by that tree with his rifle over one arm, cow-hunting style, and he's *crying* he's laughing so hard. The villagers gather around him in a gang with big dude in front. The kid straightens up and says, 'Heh-heh-heh. 'Twas a joke. Ya did it faster by a fucken mile this time.' And the big guy steps eye to eye with the kid and says, 'That's twice. Ya fuck wid me one more time an' Ah'm gonna take that rifle and shove it clean up your ass, all the way to the butt plate. Ah'm gonna straighten you out, bub.' Then the villagers straggle down the hill and go home, and everything gets quiet. Even the breeze gets calm.

"Well, you know, there are individuals on this earth who cannot leave a thing set. They've got to tease and tickle and grab-ass with a thing, until it's the other folks that are out of breath.

"The kid waits a good solid hour, sitting by his fire and eating his wine and bread-crust dinner, talking himself up for it, doing all the voices himself. He finishes dinner and brushes himself off. 'Well,' he says, 'it is a *mean* trick, but I don't mean no harm.' He takes one good breath and walks stiff-legged to that tree one more time. He chambers a round—KA-BLAMO. Chambers another. KA-BLAMO. 'Hey, you fucken wolf, get yer sorry ass 'way from those sheep,' he yells. 'Eeeyooo, the village! It's the fucken wolf.' The football player sticks his head out a window. 'Kiss my ass, kid!' 'No, sir, please! He's dragging off the lambs! Hurry! Cross my heart and hope to die! HELP!' So bim bam boom, here they come, wheezing and grunting up that hill one more time, and swoop down into the sheep pasture. They stalk that fucken wolf in twos and threes, guns at the ready, pitchforks down front. They're going to take him out behind the woodshed and beat on his body until it's nothing but a furry sack of pulp and bone chips. Finally they stand among the drowsing sheep, looking straight at that kid. And he's leaning on the muzzle of his rifle, at ease, parade-ground fashion, snickering. The big dude walks up to him and says, 'Wud ah tell ya kid?' and grabs him by the scruff of the shirt, while another dude throws a clothesline-looking rope into the tree. It circles a high branch and the noosed end jiggles near the ground down the slope. They waltz the kid down to the rope and heft him onto the stoutest low branch. The big dude loops the noose over the kid's head and pulls the slack out of the knot. And the kid is talking his fool head off, his voice getting thinner and thinner, saying it in one breath, 'Say now 'twas a joke I need some entertainment just like ever'body ya know? joke's a joke whatdaya guys doin' eh? I only meant ta have some fun come on.' And the big guy says, 'Tough shit, kid.' The other guy pulls the slack out of the rope, and ties it to the tree trunk. Then the big guy kicks the kid in the shin and he takes off. The kid lets out a gagging scream once and for all, flailing his arms. There is a horrible crunching, crinkling sound, like spikes yanked from old timbers with a crowbar.

"Sker-reek. Sker-rauk. The noose rope rubs against the branch bark. The slow tish-tish of the kid's sheepskin boots, bobbing up and down and brushing in the grass. His little-bitty dick sticks out the slit in his trousers, stiff and pale as a one-inch pine dowel. His neck stretched out good and long. His tongue hangs out of his mouth, pinkish and purple like a broken arm, and coated with wine and goppy crumbs of bread crust. The arms thrust out to the sides. The hands look like they're holding grapefruit, and jiggling. The biceps quiver. Sweat pours down his face in streaks, around that bug-eyed stare. His last shuddering breath comes out like a fart, mumbling his cheeks.

"The big guy wipes his hands on his shirt front and walks away, picking up the kid's rifle as he goes, saying, 'That settles his fucken hash.' And the others follow, slow and stumbling."

The chapel bug lights hum. The yellow-tinted air hot and thick around us, flicking with bugs. Quinn stands on tiptoe in front of the communion rail—arms out like a tent, hands and fingers dangling loose.

"You ever hear that one, Surtees?" Quinn says, and turns around, looking at the doorway. I turn around, too, but Surtees is gone. Quinn slumps down on the altar step-up, hot-faced and breathless—the sweat shining like an oil slick, the veins in his neck red and swollen. He fumbles for a smoke, lights it, and takes hit after hit after hit. "If I do so much as one afternoon of bad time because of that spook," he says, "I'm gonna jump dead in his shit with my bare fucking hands. I'm gonna lay him out between stakes and skin that thick-lipped, flat-nosed motherfucker so's he looks like a proper white man, then toss him out a fucken plane or some shit over Harlem an' let the niggers in coon heaven stomp him for an ass-kissing whitey." He says it slow and means it.

All the time he was telling, through all the skippity-skip antics and bear-hug gestures and changed voices and that sker-reek sker-rauk, hanged-man, red-faced, bug-eyed stare, I had watched him. He ran in place and stomped around and stood stock-still—a farmer one minute, a sheep the next, a tree after that, making the ka-blamo gun sounds like a kid playing cowboys and Indians, along with the asides and toothy grins. Through all that I kept saying to myself: where does this dude get the energy, when all the energy I could muster went into the laughing because

Quinn, in his twinkle-eyed, smart-ass, down-home country-boy way of pulling somebody's leg, was laying it out for Surtees that there was going to be a lynching.

Here is a dude who's got this four-color photograph and eight letters and that newspaper and has just about convinced himself that there's a higher and wiser power, some horny-headed motherfucker who has whispered down into his ear, "Die, die, die. I'm gonna pound you down to pulp and bad dreams, pound you down to whimpers." It was the same horny-headed housecat who tied off the chapel cross with noose knots, clomped around the altar lumber in the building of it, using blunt-tipped ammo-box nails and a ten-pound ball peen that left deep circled gouges around the nail heads.

And I've been listening to those horny-headed whispers going on nine months. Die, Atevo. Die, Chingachgook. Well, let Granger live—chopped to shreads. Eddie Dosier, too, but blinded and deafened so all he hears is the blood rushing through his ears. Burn, Steichen and Whiskey j., burn the eyes out of your head. Die, Dipstick, you fool, and the fucken new guys, die and vaporize. Closer, closer, like a spinning spiral bull's-eye, it comes closer, like a kid race down seven or eight flights of spiral staircase—the cheaters and the hotshots using the banister—giggling and screaming their joy and anger. I stand in some mansion foyer amidst the thirty-two polished points of the compass rose parquet, head craned at the oval spirals of mahogany railing rungs, and stomping little feet and corduroy trouser legs thrown over the banisters. Round and round I turn, following the race, round and round. Die, die, the little brats chant, la-la, la-la, upsy-daisy, and then they begin tumbling the bodies out and over. The legs and arms flail, the green jungle shirts with slanted breast pockets, billowing and flapping. The high-pitched, death-rattle, wide-eyed screams echo down the floors. A busful of housecats sit in the hallway entrance with their tails around their feet, meowing and licking their paws and wiping their whiskers, waiting for it to cease so they can go back to their cat-got-your-tongue puppy-shit card games. And the back-in-the-world housecats lounge around the TV in the parlor—haven't got anything better to do than change channels, whisper "Tsk-tsk" and "Can't *someone* get those children to be still?" back and forth. And the generals and chicken fucken colonels and rah-rah senators lean over the upper-most railing, grinning and smiling perfect ear-to-ear smiles, and pound each other on the back jolly-good-show fashion and pass around glad-hand handshakes. They call over their shoulders for more martinis and rotgut bar scotch and another platterful of those tasty liver pâté and beef tartare hors d'oeuvres. And General Westhisface keeps saying over and over, "They're damn fine killers, eh? *Damn* fine," between chomps and swallows and licking dribbled pâté from among the laugh wrinkles, and his eyes squint he's grinning so hard. But the whole time the bodies pile higher and thicker and higher still until I cannot see the door for all the corpses. The compass rose, stone-parquet mandala-looking thing is covered with chips of knees and knuckles and whitish compound fractures and the bubbling, hissing gush of sucking chest wounds and sticky black pools of blood, which seem to be seeping through the stone chinks, like the place was an island sinking back into the sea. Higher and thicker the dead pile until I begin to climb up and out among the corpses, using the leg bones and arm bones, gaping mouths and mushy bellies, and heads of straight black hair for handholds and footholds, like a person would climb the inside of a pile of neatly stacked tires. And by the time I hit the high altitudes, the crisp and thinning air, it's a moonless dark night, but I put my hand over my eyes, scout fashion, and see home——shining and hazy, purple-colored and smoky, back there, round behind me somewhere, gleaming in the midmorning sunshine. All of a sudden I want to wave a broad-armed wave, and shout and hail for help, and maybe I brace myself and try it, one-handed, once or twice. But the air still rains legs and chunks of legs, sawbucks and fivers and black plastic bodybags that float like leaves, the froth of pink and airy bubbles, and reddish streams of junk-gook-booze-and-stale-popcorn barf.

I reach over and snatch up the picture Quinn left in the smear of grease and I stare at it and stare at it. I can almost hear the laughing and red-eyed kidding back and forth; but Lorenz, who was married, is dead, and Corbin and Haney are dead, and I've been in the bushes long enough to know that Teleck, just by the look of him, ain't long for this world. And Quinn, who stands among them, grinning close-mouthed with his shirt tight around his belly and his eyes shining, thinks, only thinks mind you, has this glimmer of an inkling that he's dead as he sits here. I feel pissed and disgusted, because he's sitting not ten feet away. I mean, just because they're dead, and Willie, this short little jockey-looking dude, is dead. Just because I owe that proud little fucker two tens and that five and it was your fucken camera and Eddie is stone deaf and blind and Atevo just happened to sit down in the wrong fucking place and Trobridge, *that* dipstick, didn't have the brains to come in out of the rain. I mean I want to tell him, yell at him, don't die, don't die, goddamn it. Goddamn it, don't die. Just because we're standing in a red-and-black bull's-eye and the shit is falling and bouncing and piling close around us faster than we can catch it or shovel it aside, don't you go off somewhere and die on me, too.

I mean, I've seen too many dudes laid out on litters, waiting for the dust-offs that never come quick enough, screaming and crying the screams. "Shoot me screw me fuck me up God kill me I'm dead." They squirm and itch and bleed gushes from claymore hits or RPG hits or trauma amputations or whatever, and can't get comfortable no matter what, but they keep making fists and squinting their closed eyes closed tighter so they are not tempted to look down at their own mushy bloody entrails, hanging down curled in a red-and-brown field bandage—like a mangled and purplish arm in a bloody muslin sling.

I mean, I am there on my hands and knees in the muck next to him, trying to get him to lie quiet, because every time he moans and hunches his hips a little more entrail squeezes out through the flapping slice across his belly— blackish and slimy and puke-smelling. I mean, he's turning himself inside out each time he winces to ease the pain. He breathes in hoarse sucking gasps, like he's had the wind knocked out of him, and I'm whispering louder and louder into his bloody, muddy face, "Don't die, hey, don't die, don't die, goddamn it," and squeezing his hand. But I feel his hand and arm and face go chill as I touch him. His reddened, shrunken eyes roll back into his head and his lips hang slack, showing tartar-blackened gums. His hand goes limp in my hand though the calluses are still hard and scratchy, like paper on paper. And I shake him by the shoulders and begin pounding fisted, beating, rhythmic blows on his chest at the heart, screaming, "Live, goddamn it, live, goddamn you." And somehow I think it's possible to get down into the prone, to snuggle down into the mud and oil-slick slime with him, and take on some of that sharp, heart-aching pain, some of his dying. Come on, I say to myself as I lie chest-flat, cut me and I'll help you bleed, grab me here at the shoulder and let it come into me, as though pain might be electricity. But all I say is, live, live, in tight-lipped stage whispers, louder and louder and more angry. I pound both fists at once, again and again and again, until I hear the unmistakable crunch of ribs, and that quick the blows go soft and softer and softer still, becoming at last open-handed, flat-palmed caresses across his chest and muddy face, smoothing back matted bloody hair, rubbing the muck from his temples and the ragged gristle of his ears with yellow callused thumbs. I gather the head and shoulders and draw the body to me, chest to chest, feeling a slight warmth there. I cross my arms behind him, my hands clenched into crushing fists again. The shrapnel nicks on his face and neck and chest still bleed some, oozing. I squeeze the corpse tight against me, rubbing my sweaty cheeks through his filthy hair. The blood smears my arms and chest and belly and the tops of my trousers. Then quickly out of nowhere, a typhoon rain begins. First comes a stiff breeze and those great, loud pip-pip-pips on the canvas, then a hard, beating downpour comes at us across the paddy in sheer, roaring sheets. In no time I am soaked and shivering and my hair hangs in my eyes, and I am whispering and whimpering in the ear of a dead man, "Don't die, don't die, don't."

I look up from the dusty concrete floor and that picture of five shining crescent hats, the crumpled beer cans and scuffed jungle boots, and the soft ash of marijuana, and I want so bad to tell Quinn that it's only a fucking photograph, that it doesn't mean a goddamned thing, only he's sitting against the railing in the yellowish air with his knees well up and one arm hooked around his eyes, and he's weeping, I can tell, weeping softly, nodding his head in slow nods and mumbling something I cannot make out. He squeezes his hand into fierce, whitish fists, mumbling and weeping, and rubbing his face raw in his wet sleeve.

*

And afterward, after he cried himself out and the two of us looked hard at each other, each touching the other across rows of pews with glances and smooth flicking gestures—Quinn with his arms hanging over his raised knees; me trying to find something to do with my hands so I wouldn't clasp them and look as though I were praying. After sipping gingerly from one more tapped and opened can apiece, the warm beer tasting like damp, raw grit. After Quinn retrieved his bowie and wiped it on his shirttail, and slipped it noiselessly into its sheath. After a long moment of him walking around the edge of the building under the open-air eaves, like a caged cat, his thick wrestler's hands thrust deep in his back pockets and his reddened, puffy eyes following the edge of the concrete where the smudge of ocher dust was the thickest. He swung around the corner posts time after time with a hooked arm, then stood for a long moment, grasping the crossbeam above his head, apelike. He stretched out, leaning breathless and motionless, gazing north and east from our circle of yellow air at the fuzzy, silvery silhouette of the Black Virgin Mountain—trying to see home, just like me.

After the two of us leaned against the pews in back, pissing the beer in heated, almost painful rushes of urine and listening to it splash and foam in the dirt, we made it back to the tents with the rest of the San Miguel, going slowly and staggering mostly, but making it well enough—our bodies rank and slippery with sweat like heat-exhaustion victims.

It was after we arrived and made it through all the mumbling and grousing and pissing and moaning about Surtees' move-out drill and the fact that we had really done it this time and where had we been and weren't we too fucked up, and our rejoinders that Surtees could kiss our ass and Surtees could suck our dick and that shit-colored lifer could go piss up a rope for all we cared. I mean, after the tent settled down again I rustled around and settled in under my poncho liner.

I crossed my hands over my stomach, closed my eyes,

and right away the whole world started twirling in slow lazy circles that came faster and faster around me. So fast I thought I could feel it pulling on my boots, and it was all I could do to open my eyes and sit up on my elbows, pissed, because I knew I was not going to get any sleep.

Quinn squirmed and pawed and rolled around on his cot, until he let out a long sigh, shoved his poncho liner off, and sat up.

"It's too fucken hot in here," he said. "I'm gonna sleep outside." He got up and took down the cot. He went outside, the cot sort of folded under one arm, the poncho liner over one shoulder, his web-belt forty-five and knife over the other, and his bootlaces trailing loose behind him. He threw the cot down and tried to unfold it and set it up, huffing and puffing. I could hear him softly cursing, sighing, "You goddamn . . . fuck a goddamn . . . come 'ere you pissant mothafucka . . . fuck a gaaa . . . fuck . . . ho ho ho, when I get ma han's on you, you. . . ." Then he started to kick at it and bang it around, but tripped over a tent rope. The whole tent shook. "Gee-zuz H. fuck-king Christ! My knee . . . shit! Ooh, you goddamn . . . get o'er here, you cocksuck . . ." he growled. Everyone in the tent listened, and drunks are funny sometimes and a couple dudes laughed to themselves under their blankets. Quinn stumbled to his feet. The slats of the cot clacked together again. Then he tripped over another tent rope and fell flat with the cot under him, "Sheeit! Gawd damn!" He growled again and spit and then got quiet, and I lay back, thinking that he had passed out or knocked himself out, or just gave up and was falling asleep. I settled back and got comfortable.

Then we heard Quinn's shuffling gait, and he stepped onto the doorway stoop. One. Two. He stood a long moment, his silhouette humped against the moonlight, his bowie in one hand, breathing long croaking sighs. Then he said, "Who's gonna fuck with me?" and threw his bowie roundhouse fashion at the floor in front of him, bending at the waist. Thack. He waited for someone to say something and bent down and yanked it loose. "I say, who's gonna *fuck* with me?" he said, the croak gone from his voice. Thack. "Come on," he said a little louder, staggering more as he pulled the knife up. "Some cocksucker just *try* to fuck with me one time," he said, and made for the middle of the tent. He stood near the end of my cot, holding his arms wrestler fashion. "If there's a gook in this fucken tent and he wants ta *fuck* with me," and he took a deep breath and bellowed, *"Come on!"* Thack.

I felt everybody in the tent rustle and take a breath, the same as happens in a firefight, and I knew that me or Stepik (or Whiskey j. or Steichen if they'd been there) would get up and ease him back to bed, but before I could throw back my poncho liner, Lavery, the platoon tunnel rat—who missed the move-out the same as us, who was a wrestler, like Quinn, and so would stand with him in that circle of Deltas in the motor pool, feigning holds and dodging heads, and who had an ashy tint to his deep black skin because of the sun—Lavery jumped up and shouted in a high-pitched, squeaking voice, "I'll fuck wid ya, an' Ah'm gonna fuck ya up," and just that quick snatched up his sixteen. I heard the sling rattle. We all heard it. He chambered a round—snick, snack—and Quinn stopped short, reached down for the bowie, and held it out front, rolling it in his hand with an easy up-and-down motion. Then he started for Lavery, taking wide, long strides. Lavery shook the rifle again, rattling the sling. "Come on, white-ass," he whispered. "Come an' git it." Quinn crouched and hunched his shoulders, hissing his breath, close-mouthed, with his off hand and arm spread wide, clawed. He let out a low growl and lunged forward,

slashing twice. Sssoo. Sssoo. And everybody jumped. Somebody grabbed Lavery by the hair. Somebody grabbed the
rifle, holding it up. I grabbed Quinn's knife hand from behind, and the rest pushed between the two, and everybody
had a piece of somebody's shirt, jostling and crowding
close to the back doorway and shouting for Quinn to put the
bowie down, put it away.

Stepik had Lavery jammed against the doorway wood,
his arm across Lavery's throat, but Lavery still managed to
scream, "Ah'm gonna kill ya. Ah'm gonna kill him, goddamn. Lemme go!" squirming and pulling on Stepik's shirt
sleeve. Somebody held Lavery's rifle, but did not unload it.
Undeniable proof was needed. I stood facing Quinn, holding his arm that held the bowie, with the flat of the blade
firmly against his chest. Quinn looked past me, stared at
Lavery, and laughed through his nose. "Shee-it!" he said.

Dudes from the other tents started crowding to the
back of the tent, around Lavery and Quinn and the rest of
us in the moonlight.

"All right," shouted Surtees, pushing through the by-
standers. "All right, what're you chicken shit up to now?"

Stepik, now holding Lavery's rifle, said, "Lavery here
got some wild hair up his ass and pulled this sixteen on
Quinn here." Surtees flashed a look at Quinn. "You agin!"
Quinn stood with his bowie in the sheath. Then Surtees
looked at Stepik, still holding Lavery's shirt tight in his
hand.

"No! No," said Lavery, struggling against Stepik's
grasp. "Quinn pulled his fucken knife and came at *me*."

"Bullshit," said Quinn. "I pulled it to defend myself." And everybody from the tent, all white dudes,
nodded heads, and me among them.

"Here's his fucken rifle," Stepik said. "The round's
still in the chamber." And he tossed it at Surtees, who had
to catch it or let it drop.

Surtees took Lavery by the arm. "Lavery, you go down to my tent, eh? Go on!" And Temple and Meeks, two black dudes from the seven-six, and a couple other black dudes from the other tents gathered around Lavery and left. Then Surtees turned to Quinn, trying to grab him by the sleeve, but Quinn flicked his hand away.

"Young specialist," said Surtees, "you are in bad trouble. All of you are in bad trouble, but Specialist Fourth-Class Quinn, your young ass is gonna do some bad time for this. I will see to it personally. Now all of you go back to bed." But we stood looking back at him, looking him right in his gleaming eyes. Stepik, who stood next to him, whispered, "Listen, you shine, we 'bout carved up one jungle bunny t'night. One more would make an even number. *You* roger?" After a moment of staring back and forth, Surtees hefted the loaded rifle, jangling the sling, and walked away, backing away. Everybody drifted back into the tents until only Quinn and I were left. Quinn wandered toward the tracks in a slow sobered arc, and I followed. We climbed into the Cow Catcher—him sitting on the tits-and-thighs side, me sitting on the other.

"Ya know, *nex'* time he tries that I'm gonna *kill* him," Quinn said.

"Probably will," I said, watching him to see if he was going to get up and try something else crazy. I pulled out the blackjack board, laid it on some ammo cans, and fired up the squat stove. We drank San Miguel and smoked White Owl Rangers and what was left in Quinn's Prince Albert tobacco can. I played slow games of solitaire by the light of the squat stove and watched him, ready to talk if talking was what he wanted to do, but he just slouched lower and lower on the bench with his feet up on the water cans and his arms hooked around his knees. He stared out over the falling-down tents and the silent airfield and the quiet wire to the Black Virgin Mountain, the only thing out in that direction worth staring at, but every now and again he glanced down at the games and twice or three times during the night he said, "Red nine on the black ten," or something like.

We polished off the beer and threw the empties out into the ditch and sat the last hour or so in easy, dreamy quiet, trading a canteen cup of water back and forth. When the platoon came out to the tracks for the day's move-out, the El-tee was pissed about the mess, but told us to police it up and nothing more. We moved out with a couple dump trucks and a Payloader to the laterite pits—laterite being a kind of gravel used for roads and sandbags and such. We drove at a walking gait behind the engineer's sweep team, but two clicks from the gate Quinn pulled up and stopped. He stood up and said, "Hey, buddy, that as fast as you can clear this road?"

The guy with the earphones and sergeant stripes pulled one of the earphones away from his head, looked around at Quinn, and said, "Yeah. Damn bet. I don't want to fuck it up."

"Well, shit," said Quinn, settling into the hatch again, "I got myself a heavy fucken date. Move aside," and he waved the sweep team into the ditch, as though he were parting a curtain. Then he slipped the Cow Catcher into neutral, rapped the pipes a couple times, moving it into the high RPMs, then crammed it into low. We jerked forward, the front of the Cow Catcher lifted off its broken shocks, and in no time Quinn slipped through the gears to high. Quinn raced along, leaning forward in the hatch, dressed in his black T-shirt and aviators, teeth clenched and screaming, "Yeah! Yeah! Come on, ya mothafucka! Git some!" Dewey crouched on the back, holding on to his M-60 gun shield for all he was worth. I zipped up my flak jacket and buttoned the flap, climbed out of the hatch and straddled the rim, hunching to one side and averting my face, hoping like hell to avoid as much of the concussion as I could if Quinn hit a mine. He leaned on the horn, though the road was all but deserted, and slipped and slid through curves and around chuckholes all the way to the river. Quinn pulled up with a skid next to the tree that hung out over the water. When he shut down and climbed out of the hatch I said, "What the fuck?"

"Lemme alone, eh?" he said, flicking his hands. "Jus' lemme be. *Skip* it!" he said, and looked me in the eye.

By the time the rest of the platoon showed up with the trucks and the Payloader, he and his girlfriend had their blanket laid out in the bushes. Quinn came out only twice or three times all morning—to urinate in the river and fetch more rubbers from his AWOL bag.

That afternoon the El-tee interviewed each man who witnessed the fight, and everybody lied, and Lavery did one hundred twenty days in LBJ.

THE

PERFECT

ROOM

I want to get drunk, good and drunk. I want to get laid, laid right, laid into a stupor. I want to go somewhere chilly and sunny, even snow-covered some, somewhere cushy and quiet and calm. But not home. I don't know where home is anymore.

*

I put in for an R & R and it came back for the first week in December. I had my pick of Panang or Manila or Tokyo.

Stepik and Quinn and Staley and I sat in the battalion EM Club, away from the harsh, bare light bulbs, the booths and beer coolers, and the housecat barflies huddled three deep around the TV set. We sat in those cheap dink kitchen chairs with the falling-apart backs, the handmade, home-made table crowded with beers and beer-can pyramids, and more cans scattered underfoot. We bought each other rounds by the armful and talked about my R & R, among other things.

Stepik stooped forward, his elbows and cigarettes and banged-up Zippo on the table among the beers and his aid bag slung over the back of the chair. "Well, Panang is out," he said after some thought. "Sounds like a fucken penal colony."

Quinn sat next to him, his chair tilted against the low sandbag wall and his feet on the table. His eyes sparkled with that laid-back, glassy stare, and his face and chest glistened in the light. He took a soggy, ragged White Owl Ranger out of his mouth, spat wet brown tatters at the floor, and said, "Now, I knew a dude in my ol' comp'ny went to Manila. Said the pussy was dirt fucken cheap, but then he was none too quick on the uptake, 'cause he snagged hisself a dose a somethin' er other nobody ever fucken heard of, and wouldn't fix. First off we thought it was crabs, ya know?, those little light-colored motherfuckers with two beady fucken eyes? But the medic had him shuck down an' took one long look, an' said, '*Aw* no, he ain' got crabs. I don't know *what* the fuck it is, but it ain' crabs.' The dude had it all up an' down his dick an' on his belly an' thighs, all scabby-lookin' an' oozin' pus, an' kep' ever'body up nights with his thrashin' aroun'." Then Quinn sat up, shaking his head and laughing. "He finally got his ass dusted off. Ain' that some shit? Dusted off an' gone home witha million dollars wortha gunge on his pecker, all the way ta Michael Reese Hospital, 'cause some fucken lifer wanted ta have a 'look-see.' Who would've ever thought of a angle like that? Shit! It's something one dude pulls once, dig? And it woulda been *that* fucken dipstick. M' man, I ain' *never* gonna be that lucky." Then he shook his head some more and laughed some more, and we all laughed.

Staley sat on the aisle, nearest the door where the house-cats shoved past to go out back to piss, where the reek of grease and sweat and watery beer and watery, ammoniated piss hung the thickest. He sat back with his bad leg up on a chair, leaning his arm on another table, and kept swiping at flies and mosquitoes around his ears and face all night. He said, "Lemme tell ya a secret, Deadeye," and he looked around at all of us. "It don't make a goddamn bit of diff'rence where ya take yer R & R, jus' so ya get yer ass off the fucken mainlan'. All them R & R towns're about the fucken same, annaway." And he nodded his head and everybody nodded their heads. "Say, zit ma turn ta buy?" he asked, and we all nodded yes, so he got up and made for the bar.

There was no reason why I picked Tokyo. It just as easily could have been Cherbourg or Hamburg, Archangel or Savannah, or even Naples. And money was no object. When I boarded the plane at Tan Son Nhut, I had twelve hundred dollars, greenback, in my M-16 bandolier money-belt.

I would float into a hotel lobby. Someone would hand me a tall, chill glass of sipping whiskey. The elevator doors would slide open and I would be wafted to the seventh floor by alpine horns and the singing of madrigals into a large sunny room with a huge, soft double bed. I would shed my clothes with a mimicking shrug. A gesture of the arms and fingers would settle them across the back of a chair. Then I would slither wigglingly between two moist and whispering thighs. . . . Ahhaa.

When we got to Japan and climbed down from the plane everybody was spiffy and scruffy, bug-eyed and tight-lipped, clean-shaved and dust-covered, or just up from a

nap on the plane, bleary-eyed and clumsy. We were the R &
R party—as fair a mix as you are likely to find in any
conscript army. There were the bad-ass Hell's Angels and
Texans and truck drivers, the fuck-up law school dropouts
and Mo-Town and Harlem brothers—walking that walk—
the John Waynes and Boone County Courthouse loafers and
one-eyed Khe Sanh Marines—who had read the JOIN
posters and believed them—the Chicanos and clerks and
dumb-ass lifers, the village idiots and backwoods farmers,
the housecats and walking wounded, and young buck ser-
geants like me. The winners, the losers, the also-rans, and
every notch between. Altogether a hundred fifty dudes.

"The Japanese people frown on dope," the Camp
Zama R & R lecturer told us. That was okay; I was in Tokyo
for a different kind of buzz altogether. "And conduct yourselves so that you will reflect credit on the people of the
United States of America and the uniform which you now
wear." Yes, yes, yes. I had heard *all* the R & R stories. The
fucked-up free-for-all bar fights, the fucked-up fucking, the
R & R falling-down-drunk brag: "Ah kin lick any seven
MPs tha' come through tha' door. 'N' thar ain' a dink
'tween here anna Innernational Date Lion Ah kin't snatch
up by the ears an' toss clean o'er the Annamese Cordillera."

The dude concluded the lecture with a warning to stay
within metropolitan Tokyo, and not, "repeat, *not*," to miss
the plane back. Then a hundred fifty dudes scrambled for
the door with a hundred fifty different ideas of how to go
about getting drunk and getting laid.

I got in line for the Camp Zama R & R Center All
Night PX, the bank exchange, and the tourist office, where
they kept the list of recommended hotels. I shuffled along
in line thinking to myself: What can they do if I miss the
plane? Draft my young ass and slam it into the infantry
and send it to the field—pucker factor, high school di-

ploma, sweat pimples, and all? They've got to wait five days to find me gone, and I can be in Stockholm tomorrow night with better than a thousand dollars, greenback, tied around my belly. Captain, I say! Commodore, I can get down into the front leaning rest and low-crawl my ass into the Tokyo woodwork in an hour and a half. How far do you think I can get on a thousand dollars? Saint Croix? Old Delhi? Trieste? Montreal? Oslo? Columbia, Missouri?

I bought a suitcaseful and some civilian clothes, saying to myself: Edinburgh, Cairo, Perth. I exchanged my greenbacks for yen, mumbling Marrakech, Zurich, Port-au-Prince, Djakarta, Rangoon, and circled into the tourist office, letting the names roll off my tongue, Rio de Janeiro, Marseille, Whitehorse in the Yukon, Cuernavaca, Iron Mountain, Michigan—who would think to look for me there?

At the top of the recommended list was the Fantasy-land Hotel in Yokohama—a favorite with Marines and MPs, no doubt. In downtown Tokyo was the Imperial Hotel, though it was not Frank Lloyd Wright's Imperial. I guessed it was for the officers and civilians, traveling with their dumpy, frumpy fucking wives, so I figured it would cost me three hundred just for the hard-on, and I already had one of those. Then my eye skittered down the other ordinary names and settled, at last, on the Perfect Room Hotel.

My, my, my.

Conjure for yourself the cathouse in soldier heaven. A castle, a palace, a Versailles, just baroque as hell, where every leitmotif and nuance and square inch of pleasure can be explored. Explored, is it? Searched, man, seized. Re-searched. Tasted. Thumped. Squeezed till the pulp runs out between your fingers down to the last particle of sweet and sour ache. A place where the mimosa and acacia trees, the stone-bottomed pasture brooks, and pastel sunlight, flashing off the fountain spray, sings like sexy fucky Gypsy music, the violins shrill and ever rising. Do you want a broad with three tits? They are on the veranda, friend, languishing, pliant, waiting, sucking mint juleps through crystal straws. You like your pussy a little tight? There's a broad there with a snatch no bigger around than the stem end of a tomato. Or perhaps you prefer it a little slack and loose, something to slosh around in like a kid in a thirty-gallon bubble bath. My man, there's a Ceylonese chick there with a twat so cavernous the lips hang down like bomb-bay doors. Or perhaps your forte is fellatio. Why, there's a broad there who'll whip a lip lock on you that'll scorch your shorts and curl the hairs on the back of your neck to look like pig's tails, though in all other particulars she is unremarkable. Then again you would rather perform the sometimes difficult but strangely thrilling feat of cunnilingus. Trooper, there is a chick from the Mississippi River Delta, Rosalee by name, who is *all* cunt—one hundred and ten pounds. No arms, no legs, no asshole. Then again you say that you want nothing more adventurous than straight vanilla, morning reveille, missionary-position screwing. Trooper, there are women for you who are *always* gazing through the skylights (renderings in stained glass of fish and owls and frogs), being as they are nailed to planks of rough-cut Brazilian rosewood.

Perhaps you enter with a flourish and say, "Take me to your apparatus!" Oh, how ingenious of you. There are machines that dangle, machines that swaddle, machines that utter the appropriate hum. There are passive, absorbing and complicated, but rewarding hedgerow mazes. A veritable three-ring circus that would make P. T. Barnum himself twirl in his grave with envy, giggling and cackling and writhing all the while, muttering to himself, "Now, why didn't *I* ever think of that?" Women naked as the day they

177 |

were born with muscular thighs and small callused feet, hanging and hung and waiting their turn at the high wires. All manner of circus freaks dressed in waistcoats, like senators, with fleshy flapping feet, bonking each other with rubber-tree-limb caveman clubs. A reenactment of the Rape of the Sabine Women—the women wearing papier-mâché tits and cunts—the men wearing dildoes the size of small reddish cars, and varnished so to shine. A throng of huge fat ladies with long glistening black hair, each riding bareback on plump, roan-colored, Shire-breed geldings with dappled flanks and braided manes—the women lathered up and sweating like polo ponies. One buxom woman with not a single hair on her entire body, singing a ribald song, loudly, "Roll me over, roll me over, roll me over, lay me down and do it again," aria fashion, longingly, squeezing the middle tent pole between her bovine breasts. Lady elephants in heat, limping and honking and quivering, tails up, round and round the center ring, chased by a rutting rogue bull with a hard-on the size of a church steeple, as purple as a royal robe, the tip dragging in the sawdust chips.

Or perhaps you prefer a home scene. You would like to flood the living room with water, or whatever, and sit on the landing with a pudgy small-town mother/matron/widow, sipping mocha coffee from Haviland china cups, and watch the kiddies play "boat." Then after sending the little brats to bed with crushing hugs and pecking kisses, you drain the water, or whatever, and screw your eyeballs up fucking the very daylights out of her on the strangely waterproof carpet. Well, you'll have to wait for that one, there's a line, you see. But be calm, don't fret. Try the French-trained Arabian twins for a day or so—they'll put a wrinkle or two in your repertoire—then come back. Here's your number.

Whatever your taste, salty or sweet or as bland as cold unbuttered toast, all you have to do is step up to the swinging doors, push through, and enter a veritable playground; mount the pipe-and-plank merry-go-round, straddle the twirling hub, and perform hand-job pirouettes until you do not know whether you are coming or going.

And then you recline upon a rope-and-feather-quilt hammock in the pastel shade of the peach orchard into a warm afternoon nap, when the dreams come slow and calm like driftwood; when the dreams are of sleep. Perhaps you awaken and discover that you are truly satiated, brim full, unable to rise (oh, but this will never happen), and if one more woman offers herself you will take her by the hair and dropkick her out a window. At that moment the women and stained glass and circus freaks vanish, and you are drawn by the soft tinkling of dishes, the mellow, hollow popping of corks, into the banquet hall. Your valet, dressed in silk knickers and a powdered wig, indicates with his eyes and a nod that you are to sit at the head of the table and pulls back your chair. You sit among mumbling playwrights and elegantly dressed turf-race jockeys, opera-freak dirt farmers and brocade-clad women, in a hall lavished with candlelight chandeliers and whale-oil lamps, chamber music and clouds of jasmine incense. The only instruction you receive is to please not tuck your linen under your chin, and then the courses begin. Chilled wines and steaming silver serving bowls of vegetables, platter upon platter of meat and fish and fowl and so forth, delicacies gathered from all points of the compass rose. The courses take you into the small hours, right down to the baked Alaska and Bavarian chocolate cake and plum-duff flambeaux.

Or perhaps, after all, you seek nothing. Not the pleasure of screwing, with all its attendant variations, or sitdown state dinners, the wines served in silver-and-bone

179

flagons, or flashy, dazzling spectator sports. Instead, you wish to sit in easeful comfort, put your feet up, and cipher, reflect, contemplate. Very well. What you require is a small white room, much like the inside of a sugar cube, overlooking the flowers and the flowering trees, the oak and sycamore and lime-tree forests. Done.

The Perfect Room Hotel.

I picked it because of the name, of course—I could not resist—and the fact that it was at the tag end of the R & R bus line that ran twice daily. It was practically on the other side of Tokyo Bay from Camp Zama, something like the distance from Michigan City to the Allerton Hotel, just off Michigan Avenue in Chicago. Most GIs were too horny to get much past La Porte and I wanted to get as far away from other GIs and Army talk and bar fights as the R & R bus could take me.

Sometime after midnight, chilly and raining, the bus pulled up in front of the hotel. There were three of us still left: myself; Hacker, a young clean-cut Marine about Eddie's size; and Christie, a tall extra-Y-chromosome-looking clerk-typist from upcountry somewhere. The bus driver opened the door. I grabbed my suitcase, hit the double glass doors, and stood in front of the sign-in desk in the flick of an eye. I signed for the biggest room they had, told the dude to take my bags there, and asked for the bar. He pointed his arm and hand and black-ink fountain pen toward the back. I walked down the hallway, following the sound of girlish giggling. The women sat along the bar, waiting for us, and since Hacker and Christie were still on their way I had the pick of the litter. As I turned the corner into the bar, a ripple went from dress to dress as they sat up, squaring their shoulders, or lounged further down on their stools, fluttering and fawning—whatever they thought was sexy.

My, my, my.

The one closest to me was thin and flat-chested, which she accented by wearing a long, loose cheerleader sweater, a blasé skirt, and sensible shoes hooked on the rung of the stool. Just Hacker's size. He took her, too. The second was a great fat woman with a flat face, puffy eyes, and hanging jowls. At the other end of the bar was a sallow, horse-faced broad with a high-pitched nasal voice. She had what some folks in this wide world take to be the gift of gab, but that was her whole trouble: she was always jabbering and yammering and clacking her yap. The only moment my ears got a rest was when she yawned, or paused to take a long-winded breath. The second from that end sat looking into her glass, playing hard to get no doubt, after she had looked me up and down. She had thin watery eyes, long store-bought lashes, a salmon-colored wig hung with thousands of tight girlish curls, and long fingernails painted a garish reddish orange. She wore a shiny black hooker's dress, with that slit to the thigh, and shoes with spiked heels. I looked into her face and saw her twenty years from then, liver spots on her sagging breasts, waddling around a hooch chasing after two vomiting brats.

Sitting in the middle was Susie. She had short jet-black hair, a round face, and black almond eyes. She was short with small hands, and well built. A farm girl. She held her glass of Saigon tea with one hand, rubbing the frost with her thumb. She looked at me and looked at me and blinked and looked away.

Just as Hacker and Christie came up the hall I made my move, and by the time they hit the doorway I bellied up to the bar, put a foot on the rail, one hand casually resting across the back of Susie's chair. The two of them hesitated a moment, then Hacker stepped to the end of the bar and Diane, the chick with no body, and Christie circled all the way to the other end, chugging his arms like a Harlem Globe Trotter, and immediately started a conversation with the horse-faced broad I called Peaches. Almost immediately the hooker and the fat lady got up and left. The hooker sashayed out of the bar, flouncing her tits and jiggling her ass, skittering those spiked heels on the two-by-four dance floor as she went.

The bar was just a wide place in the hallway on the way to the dining room. There were the five stools and three velveteen booths, two shelves of bottles, a cracked glass mirror, and sliding glass doors that led to a flower-and-rock-and-carp-pond garden. The bartender—a dude named George, who wore a cutaway Eisenhower jacket with epaulets and fuzzy felt lapels—leaned this way and that taking orders. Later I found out he worked nights to put himself through tailor's school. Hacker ordered bar scotch. Christie ordered a martini.

I looked at the row of bottles. I looked at Susie's face in the mirror. She sat back in the stool, pressing against my thumb. I searched the two rows of bottles up and down until my eye settled on a tall squarish fifth with a black-and-white label. Jack Daniel's "Old Time, Old No. 7 Brand, Quality Tennessee Sour Mash Whiskey, 90 Proof."

My, my, my.

I tapped a finger on the bar and told George I wanted the Jack Daniel's and a tumbler of ice. He filled a tumbler with ice and poured out a long pour with that showy gesture that bartenders have, letting the liquor splash two or three feet into the glass. I had been thinking about a glass of Jack Daniel's and ice for five hours on the plane, and a couple months before that. And when I got tired of dreaming about getting drunk, I dreamt about getting laid. I let the whiskey and ice settle, listening to the warm whiskey crack the ice. I stared at Susie in the cracked glass mirror. Small bubbles of air escaped from the melting ice, Susie's breast was close under the high-necked dress, her thin smile sliced in several places in the mirror.

It was an odd, shy moment. The girl sitting next to me was for hire, make no mistake. I would pay her cash, pay it out every morning, but I didn't want any of that "Say hey, slopehead, fuckie-fuckie? Let's you 'n' me go upstairs, 'cause ol' Deadeye is gonna tear you a new asshole! Guaran-fucken-tee!"

"What's your name?" I asked quietly.

She looked at me in the mirror. "You may call me Susie."

"I'm Phil," I said. She pushed her glass away and ordered a glass with ice and George poured her a shot of Jack Daniel's. When the whiskey melted some of the ice I held the glass to my nose, taking in the bouquet of deep mountain-hickory charcoal, and sour, sour mash. I took a sip, then another and another, and took a breath. The whiskey warmed my stomach. My arm and side tickled in a hundred places by the touch of her short black hair and breast and arm. I held the chilly glass and stared at her in the mirror some more. I could feel that old, old pain down my back, that callused curl in my fingers, that ache in my eyes that made me squint.

"You want to go upstairs?" I asked, quietly again.

"Yes," she said, and straightened up.

"Party," yelled Hacker just then. "Let's have a fucken party. Come on, Dosier. Come on, Christie!" And Hacker and Diane and Christie and Peaches started milling around. Peaches had already hustled Christie for change and shoved it into the jukebox with her thumb. I stood up, pulled out part of my roll and peeled off something like twenty dollars in yen and tossed them out. The bills scattered on the bar. I looked at George and waved my fingers at all the glasses.

"Well, have yourselves a ball," I said. "I'm gonna turn in." Hacker and Christie winked broadly. I took Susie by the arm and we left. We got into the elevator. I leaned back against the wall. Susie leaned against the wall. I looked down at her. She looked up at me.

I had a suite of sorts. There was a kitchenette, a kitchen table and chairs, a couple of easy chairs and reading lamps, and a long, broad double bed we had to climb over to get to the porch. There were draw drapes on the floor-length windows and several darkish paintings and a thatch-weave mat. I went around the room, turning on the lights and lamps, and began to undress. Susie stood next to one of the chairs with a hand on the back, watching me. I looked at her just as I pulled my yellow-gold Camp Zama PX sweater over my head, as much to say, "Come on."

"First money," she said, or something like.

Oh. Yes. I dropped the sweater over the back of the chair and pulled out part of my roll again. "How much?"

She straightened up with her hands folded in front of her, little-girl fashion. "Thirty thousand yen," she said. "Prease." Something under a hundred dollars.

I held the thickly, crisply folded bills in the palm of my hand, the paper beginning to crackle and unfold. Three, maybe four hundred dollars, the rest in my moneybelt tied around my waist. Winnings from payday blackjack games and nickel-and-dime games. That puppy-shit hundred-dollar State of Illinois Bonus I had sent for in July. Money saved from nine vouchers. Money I busted my ass for and sweated for and bent my back plenty for, one breath at a time. Part pay for slipped wrenches and sweat pimples, jammed rounds and blood blisters, hangfires and hot beers and no beers, bad dreams and no dreams, bad sleep and no sleep at all. The toenails lost when Trobridge dropped a can of fifty rounds on my foot. The cuts that never healed, that just stayed sore and oozed pus sometimes. Money I walked all those ambushes for and got dusted off with heat exhaustion for and fought off hordes of mosquitoes and red pissants for. Money owed for helping lay Granger on that litter, and then kneeling there, listening to his whimpering screams. Lump-sum money I had coming the night I heard that round slam into Atevo's face, before I knew *that* was the sound of a face. Cold greenback cash I had gritted my teeth for when I grabbed that little dink, and killed and killed and killed him. All that money, lying thick, folded double across the palm of my hand, crisp enough and new enough to give a person paper cuts.

I counted out the first three ten-thousand-yen bills I came to and held them out between my first and second finger. She reached over, raising her leg for balance—her dress clinging tightly to her thigh—and gathered them in. She folded them once again in her fist and said, "I'rr be back in a minute," turned on her heel and left. I slouched down into the chair and kicked off my low-quarters, still filthy with motor-pool dust.

One-fifty for the room. Something under five hundred for the woman, which amounted to five hundred and some, figuring in dinners and junk trinkets and cab fares, the baths and back rubs every night. I had money left to the tune of five hundred dollars, or something like, to blow away on drinks and parties and whatnot.

Jenny and her fine brown hair; whose skin smelled of Caswell Massey soap and borrowed perfume; who joked, saying it tickled when I touched her, no matter where; whose father appreciated the way I wrote letters (because I never said anything bad, he told me later); who liked farming because it was clean and honest work; who was just the right height in bare feet to dance with, and loved to polka most of all—Jenny, you might as well have been on the other side of the moon. This was between myself and a woman who wanted me to call her Susie, for some damn reason—so I would feel more at home, I guess—when the house and the lilac hedge and passion vines, the crab-apple orchard and wild-grown nursery were the last things on my mind.

The first time Jenny and I made it, the spring I was drafted, she and I stood in the ankle-deep silt in the reservoir on her father's farm on the side of the valley. We held each other around the waist under the water, watching the cows across the road meander back along the mud path to the barns; the slow small cars winding in and out among the rises and farms; the oil smoke rising from the oil breather pipe of the John Deere parked just below us; the quiet restless treeline above; the lowering afternoon sun. The thick green water trailed down her chest among the invisible white hairs; the silt soaking the top of her tank suit, muddy and sexy. Her hair hung, matted and dripping, to the small of her back, and just as we were about to say the words and go behind the orchard shed, peel off our swimsuits, and lay out on the towels, a voice came up from the house. "Jen-ny! Phil-lip! Din-ner!" Mrs. Dahlbeck stood on the back stoop, holding the screen door open with her foot, one hand cupped to her mouth. We drove the John Deere down and ate and went right back up, bringing blankets with us for the chill. It rained at dusk and we huddled under the crumbling eaves of the orchard shed, watching the May rain among the apple trees—the trees crowded thickly with white and pink blossoms. The rain exploded the flowering trees, the air and fields and Mr. Dahlbeck's yard filling with the petals, thick as snow. That mix of smells in the air—the rain and wet dust and flowers, the waterlogged, dry-rotted wood and mildewed spools of baling twine—made us quiet. And while the rain dripped heavily from eaves and splashed in the gravel trough at our feet we screwed under the blanket, quick and fumbling, and felt shy and sweaty and chilly some afterward, but laughed then and messed around some more and screwed again. When we got back to the house, with mosquito welts all over us, I could not mistake the sour-faced, sidelong glances Mrs. Dahlbeck gave me. On my New Year's leave I visited Jenny and we made it in the living room on the couch in front of the TV, listening to the last movie; me dressed in jeans and sweater; Jenny in her print granny gown; her folks long since gone to bed. We screwed on that fuzzy couch, and I brushed her hair, then watched her put it up. Back at Knox, every weekend after that I borrowed Willie's four-speed '55 Plymouth and drove the fifty miles to Springfield, where Jenny went to school. Jenny and I drove into the country toward Harrodsburg or McCreary or Hibernia—out among the legal bourbon stills and dirt-farm-and-grocery-store-and-gas-pump towns—and parked. We screwed in sweaters and coats, steaming all the windows and sweating in the heat and chill in the front seat, because Jenny had this thing about the back seat; me sitting slouched on the passenger's side; she straddling me with her bare feet dangling over the edge of the seat; her sweater bunched to her chin, and her body pressed as close to me as she could manage, for warmth.

After I transferred overseas I didn't get mail for a couple weeks. Then one night Stepik sauntered over to the seven-three, his face shining in the rainy, red dusk, both hands behind his back as though mixing the white and black pawns for chess, and said, "Hey, Deadeye! How many letters you figure you got coming?" "I dunno," I said. "Five. Seven, maybe. One, anyway." And he whipped out a stack that he could hardly hold in one hand. "Deadeye," he said with that down-and-dirty blackjack look in his squinted eyes, "there's seventeen of the little mothers here. This Jenny What's-her-name must think yer pecker's about made a gold. Read 'em an' weep." I zipped them open with my bayonet one at a time and held them down close to the soft, hissing light of the squat stove so as not to miss a word, while the others played blackjack. "Jus' rem'mber, Dead-eye," Cross said over and over in a kidding, smiling way, "Claymore Face don' think yer nothin' but av'rage," shaking his head, but admiring the stack all the while. Atevo rubbed his chill, wrinkled hands on damp knees and kept asking, "What she say, man? What she say?" So I read some out loud and some to myself and some more out loud, and it made me shiver just to see her handwriting.

Susie rapped lightly on the door. I let her in and followed her with my eyes to the middle of the room, where the reading lamp next to the bed silhouetted her body. She turned her back and reached a hand over her shoulder, the way women do, feeling for the zipper. My groin ached already, so I walked up behind her, undid the stay, and pulled the zipper quickly to the small of her back. She kicked her shoes off and flipped them under the bed with her toes, standing there in bare feet with her arms at her sides, her head straight, waiting. I looked down at my hand still holding the zipper. Hard yellow calluses, ragged nails, the smooth curve of her back, the taut strap of the bra, those tensed muscles of the back of her neck, the frayed elastic band of her skimpy shorts, the tip of the cleft of her buttocks. That pleasant smell of clean shining hair. The smell of perfume I found out later was the smell of her sweat, like the stiff aroma of ginger and licorice and cinnamon. I pushed aside the collar of her dress and brushed my fingers on her neck and shoulder, feeling the numb scratchiness of my own hand and her skin lightly dusted with talc. Her throat tensed. Her toes curled. I rubbed the back of her ears with my thumbs. The liquor was quietly murmuring in my head, at the tips of my fingers. She turned her head and kissed the back of my hand, then turned to face me. Her short, clean hair glistened; her eyes sparkled. She began to undress and I began to undress, watching her. She skipped out of her dress, holding it by the collar, and draped it over my yellow-gold Camp Zama sweater. She took off her bra with that shrug-and-catch gesture that women have and peeled down her shorts. We stood naked on either side of the rumpled easy chair piled with sweater, dress, shirt, bra, trousers, red nylon panties, white undershirt, and flap-fly o.d. boxer shorts.

Bare feet; little-girl feet. Red wrinkled shoe marks and round pale toes. Pudgy, dimpled knees and sparse black pubic hair. Wrinkle marks from the elastic around her hips and under her breasts. The sly curve of her stomach and breasts and brown nipples and neck. A small mouth and black almond eyes and short black hair swept downward over her forehead, forward over her ears. She stood there looking at me with her hands and elbows up to raise her breasts while she brushed out her hair with her fingers. Her skin prickled with gooseflesh down her hips and around her nipples.

I walked over to her but she held me at an arm's length. "Make rove, yes, but first we take bath," she said, and grabbed me by the arm and into the bathroom we went.

I want to screw. Hear me? Fuck washing up. I am too fucking horny. I want you and me to get on the bed or the fucking love seat or a kitchen chair or any goddamn place you want, and I'm gonna blow your brains out on the first try. Look, you and me, if we get the torque right, our heads are gonna be buzzing for a month, dig?

But the more I jabbered and pulled back on her arm and shook my head no, the closer we got to the bathtub.

What the hell.

She pulled a three-legged stool from under the washbasin, sat me down, and commenced to give me a bath. She scrubbed with a washcloth and lathery soap, then poured pitcher after pitcher of steaming hot water over my head. And when the tub filled she motioned with a flick of her hand for me to get in.

Now, one does not plunge into a Japanese bathtub. No, you must coax yourself down, foot and leg and R & R hard-on and the rest. Susie followed quickly and squatted next to me chin deep and watched me, giggling cheerily with her hand over her mouth. She laughed *every* time she saw me naked, matter of fact, because I was heavily tanned from the hips up and as pale as a Chicago River whitefish from there down. We squatted in the tub facing each other, the whiskey and ice and hot water buzzing in my head. My skin and scalp tingled and ached, the hot water pressing and squeezing. I rubbed my hand along the inside of her thigh kneading the fleshy muscle. I touched the back of my hand, which dripped water and steamed, to her hair and cheek and down the curve of her breasts. I breathed with flared nostrils and kept wiping the steam and wet out of my eyes, and for a joke took a fingernail and drew it down my arm and showed her the roll of gray-green silt that was oozing out of my body. She screwed up her face, pursing her lips and frowning, as though she had swallowed an entire lemon, and I laughed. She shoved me out of the tub and washed me all over again. She scrubbed and scrubbed, her breasts and arms and thighs and pubic hair hot and steaming and slick where they touched and slid against my back. She tested my arm herself, and scrubbed again and tested again, until my arm and neck and back were streaked with red itchy welts. Then we got back into the tub.

When we finally got bedwards, she scampered gaily across the blankets and turned-down sheets, rolled to her side bulging her breasts, and patted my pillow with her hot little hand, come-hither fashion. She giggled and shook her head, jiggling her breasts, all sexy and fucky. I stared frankly at her, feeling my penis twitch all the while, and stepped forward, ready to climb up, climb on, and show her what fucking was all about. Susie obligingly reached for my crotch. I clenched my teeth, reached to take hold of the headboard, and hit the sheets with my knees, and came before I touched another thing.

I bent my head, exasperatedly, looking down at my penis. "You son of a bitch," I mumbled. "You mother-fucker." I felt stupid—who wouldn't?—kneeling next to her, squirting cum at the loose-weave draw drapes, clean over those fluffy spread-eagled thighs—almost in two/four time. Then I had to laugh. Happens all the time, Deadeye, I chided myself. The fucking draw drapes always get the first dose. Who cares? There's more where that came from. You haven't been in the infantry, in the bushes, for all these months for nothing.

Susie didn't bat an eye. She uncoiled herself and slid off the bed, telling me to wash up again. "Just the privates," she said. Then she swooped into the bathroom, retrieved a damp towel to wipe down the drapes, and changed the bed sheets.

I had fucked Claymore Face, when the ache and boredom got to be too much; it was either Claymore Face or Five-Fingered Mary. Claymore Face and her brother followed us on their Honda—at a considerable distance out of firefight range, but always bringing up the rear. She would do anything for a fiver—fuck regular, ass-fuck, titty-fuck, lick your asshole, suck, fuck with the crook of her elbow if that's what got you off—any-fucking-thing. Once Rayburn told her that Americans didn't call cock a cock, but a one-eyed trouser mouse. So that's what she called it. I finally went to her at Fire Base Georgianne. She waited in the shade of some rubber trees, lounging around her bike and swilling Cokes. I walked down with Cross and Whiskey j.

and a couple others, with my money in my hand. Cross and Whiskey j. insisted that I go first, by way of my being a fucking new guy, I guess. Claymore Face shucked down and laid back on the damp, lumpy ground, pulling me after, and it was like fucking a fat man's fist.

But Susie, she giggled and wiggled and squirmed just fine. I screwed her once quickly, hardly enough to work up a lather. We rested, letting the shyness wear off. Susie boiled water for tea, but before the tea was steeped we were screwing again, and then again slowly, taking time for goosing and grab-assing. We drank tepid tea in bed and smoked, laid back. I stood naked at the window, holding the tea and a real smoke and looking down at the neighborhood streetlights through the loose-weave drapes. The smell of her sweat and my sweat, the smell of the tea and those first clear raspy rushes of strong straight tobacco, made me think of colors—swirling oil-slick colors bubbling up like a spring in calm shallow water. Susie got up to wash herself. A moment later she padded back to the bed, her breasts flouncing, that sweated-up look still in her eye. I sprawled out on the bed next to her, pushing back the covers with my heels.

Susie rubbed my chest with her cheek and kissed the hard muscles and brushed her short black hair along my stomach and thighs, and that first-night all-night, slick cooled hardness was still there. She scrunched down, cupping a breast in her hand, and rubbed the nipple against the purple glistening tip. Then, when I was good and hard again, that itch and ache not meek anymore—like a cobra with its hood spread and stiff doing that slow, twitching dance—she mounted herself and I slipped in quicker than you can pull on an overcoat and flip up the collar. She whimpered and did a little dance with stretched hollowed thighs and arched back and her hands over her head. She gave me closed-mouthed smiles, because it is unbecoming for a Japanese woman to smile and show her teeth, and I arched my back and dug my heels in, pressing against the pillow. She humped and humped, and I came one more time. She finally flopped over on the bed next to me and snuggled in and fell quiet. That's when my dick went soft, and that ache—that slow-grinding rocklike heated pain—left me.

I felt clean—clean and airy and calm right to the back of my head. All that garbage was gone; gone with the damnedest bath I had ever had; gone with the first change of sheets. I hung my head back over the pillow, my chin pointing to the ceiling, arching my back, climbing down. Sweet, sweet climbing down. There was no tension, no tightness, no ache in my eyes. I wiggled my toes and fingers to feel the ripple of the tendons on the sheet. I felt my body ease, felt one small muscle at a time release and drop something, like a newly shattered glass window dropping shards of glass for days and days after—bumped by a moth or fetched by a gush of wind or simply shaken by trucks on the street. I let my jaw slack and felt that tingle, that ease; felt every hair, every pore.

I wanted to get up. I wanted to run to the bathroom, flick on the light, and stare at myself in the mirror. I wanted to see my face change, since I could feel it change, but I didn't have the energy to raise my head. I touched my face with my fingertips and followed the tingling, drawing the skin, listening to it snap back. Susie mumbled and shifted around and got comfortable with her head on my shoulder, her arm across my chest. Her breathing and my breathing finally became the slow deep rhythm of sleep.

*

I awoke in a dull, chill light, coming around slowly. I was startled to see an arm thrown over my stomach. Instead of my bed and Eddie's bed with the window between and

Ma's voice calling, "Fa-ther! Phil-lip! Dan-nee! Ed-die! Break-fast!" Instead of that musty cot with a rumpled and ragged and lumpy sleeping bag and the sweaty, gritty texture of my poncho liner. Instead there was a woman, lying naked, snuggling against me with her fuzzy, chilly arm thrown over me and her quiet breath stirring the hair on my chest. Then came the recollection of steaming-hot baths and sweaty-hot fucks—the way she threw herself back across the bedspread, bouncing—and cold, rasping hits of Jack Daniel's and ice, and a cracked glass mirror.

Outside was the sound of rain or a wet snow on the window, in the porch puddles, the faint ring of water on the iron railing. Someone shouted—I could not make out the words. I stirred on the bed. She awoke and looked up at me and smiled, deepening the sleep wrinkles round her eyes, and twined her legs around my thigh. My cock twitched against her hip. She took it in her hand and stiffened it and rolled languidly onto her back and pulled me by the shoulders after her. We screwed the first screw of my second day on R & R.

My, my, my.

When we finished Susie went for the john, I went for my cigs. I slouched in the chair with my legs straight out in front of me, ankles crossed. She padded back into the room, still naked, and sat down in my lap. We commenced to trade drags on the Camel and fondle and neck, and then we tore off another piece, her sitting on the edge of the chair; me on my knees.

Afterward I called room service to send up a pot of coffee and a steak-and-egg breakfast, and watched Susie dress.

While she was gone I sat in my chair, facing the window, smoking cigarettes and sniffing her scent on my fingers and palm. She came back in a different dress with a coat over one arm, pushing a room-service cart piled with diminutive Japanese hamburgers garnished with sour pickles and bland ketchup, and my medium-rare filet and a double order of sunny-side-up pullet eggs, fried potatoes, toast and jam, and a carafe of weak black coffee.

"What time is it?" I asked.

"After noon."

We sat at the kitchen table and ate. The steak was too small. There were too few eggs and not enough coffee. I asked her if she would like to take a ride. Where to? she asked. Anywhere. Out. Around. Let's see the sights, I told her.

We took a cab to the USO, somewhere in Tokyo above a row of shops near a train station and an expressway. Susie stayed in the cab, double-parked at the curb. Japanese nationals were not allowed upstairs, she told me. I walked up a broad stairway and entered a large room that reminded me of the lobby of some sleazy "men only" transient hotel. Toward the back a portly, motherly-looking woman in a checkered smock sat with her ankles crossed behind a falling-down card table piled with several beat-up paperbacks, a stack of mimeographed handouts, and a shoe box with a slit across the top.

The woman must have heard me coming up the stairs, for she looked up and brightened her face in a grinning, wrinkled smile.

"Soldier! Sold-jer?" she said loudly. The echo—her voice—that word—rattled around the room like a blight of flies banging on a flimsy screen, kamikaze fashion. She waved an arm over her head—the flab swinging to and fro like a crammed-full duffel tied to a short, stout flagpole. I walked to her, my footfalls echoing round the collection of lumpy, ragged couches and dusty reading chairs, the frayed and faded oriental carpets, and dimmed reading lamps;

round a GI leaning over the edge of a dilapidated pool table, an elegantly curved cue stick in one hand and a sliver of blue chalk in the other; round two more GIs, dressed in sweaters and cotton slacks and low-quarters just like me, sitting on swivel stools at a drugstore-fountain-looking thing. They hunched over paper picnic plates, wolfing down cheeseburgers and fries, and cups of Coke, no ice. All the alcove lacked was a cracked marble counter, mahogany and stained-glass display cases, carved-ivory seltzer spigots, hordes of dimple-breasted, pubescent girls hefting armfuls of meaningless books, and the smell of pimple cream and dimestore perfume.

I approached the woman and her card table, wetted a finger, and slid a handout from the stack. The woman, still grinning that apple-cheeked grin, scooched forward on her folding chair, and revved up to tell me about the baked-ham raffle later that evening, the sock hop Friday night (with officers' daughters accompanied by beefy chaperones, and conducted like every other puppy-shit high school gym dance in the world), the round-robin pool tournament on that pitiful table, and the eight-hundred-thousand piping-hot chocolate-chip cookies that would issue from the oven any minute.

She spoke with slow and careful pronunciation in a low, hawking alto voice—the dusty, gravel-like timbre trilling from wear and tear, and half a dozen vodka martinis before dinner for forty years—that called to mind East Coast finishing schools where everybody studies art history (because they've got to study something), and the effortless, leisurely life of telling other people what to do. I asked, as politely as I could manage, what else was doing in town—I had no reason to be uncivil, she was obviously somebody's mother—and scanned the list of plays and puppet shows, movies and restaurants, and so forth. She listened aptly, leaned forward even more and widened her eyes, then dove back into her spiel about sitting down and writing a nice letter home and bellying up to the bar for a nice tall chocolate phosphate, and the rest of that sorry hustle. And I laughed, I tell you, on the inside. I roared with pity and glee. I tried not to smile, bit the inside of my lip, but could not suppress just the slightest smirk, because while the woman blabbed on and on, a hundred-dollar-a-day whore waited for me at the curb, warming her hands and that fluffy raffle ticket of hers in a fur-collared coat; a woman who drank what I drank, ate what I ordered, and fucked, eagerly, any way I wanted to fuck.

I went back downstairs.

"Where to?" Susie asked.

"Downtown. Around," I said.

We drove along boulevards, past narrow footpath streets among the neighborhoods, along the masonry embankments for the trains, glass-and-steel buildings, thousands of people dressed for the cold, walking and standing with their faces turned to shopwindows, or waiting at the corner curbs for the lights to change. Everything unbelievably clean and chill. A lowering sky. The threat of a rain or wet snow. Buses, cabs, drab overcoats and polished oxfords. Lighted signs and neon signs in incomprehensible Japanese characters. Susie and I watched out the side window and necked and copped feels back and forth. She and the driver mumbled between themselves. I read the poop sheet. A Bolshoi troupe did *Swan Lake* the week before. Some symphony would be performing the week after. A Nō performance in Osaka—too far to go. Shadow puppets the next week. So on and so forth. I had picked the deadest week of the year, but who cares? I thought to myself, and Susie nuzzled closer.

That night we went to the Tokyo Enlisted Men's Club

on the top floor of the *Stars & Stripes* building. The head gazook made me rent a tie. There were perhaps thirty tables and a plain wooden dance floor and a bandstand and a dude in the men's room to pass out hand towels. We took a table away from the dance floor among the other R & R GIs and smartly dressed whores. I sat with my back to a concrete pillar so I could look out the large windows and keep an eye on the rest of the room. There was sterling-silver service and white linen serviettes and cut-glass water goblets and crystal-clear ice. When the waiter came around and bowed and stood there, his pencil poised above a note pad, I asked for a large medium-rare porterhouse, an order of those smallish boiled potatoes garnished with parsley and celery salt, artichoke hearts with butter-and-lemon sauce, asparagus with hollandaise sauce, a side order of creamed onions, and rye bread or black bread with whipped butter. Any sort of bread but white bread, dig? Oh and yeah, bring a tumbler of ice and a double shot of Jack Daniel's right away. And a cup of very strong coffee. Susie ordered pretty much the same thing in Japanese, except for smaller portions.

The drinks came and we drank with relish. The meal came and we ate with gusto. Steak, potatoes, artichokes, onions, bread and butter, coffee, sips of whiskey. By God, real food. After eating cleverly disguised paper and flakes of graphite and lumps of puppy shit dusted with orange dirt for nine months—a real sit-down dinner. I called for more strong black coffee, another double shot of whiskey. I ate slivers of steak and hollandaised asparagus dipped in hot butter and lemon. Onions one at a time and an artichoke heart and another sliver of steak, and called for more bread, more coffee, bring me *more!* I ate a potato and an onion, then an artichoke heart and another sliver of steak. I bent my head over my plate and kept busy for the better part of an hour, calling for more whipped butter, more whiskey, more water, bring another cup of your excellent coffee, Charles—no living person enjoyed a meal any more than I. Susie had long finished and sat in a low-cut, fluffy burgundy dress, watching me eat. I ate and ate and ate and when I sat back, finally—wiping my mouth and both hands and folding the linen more or less the way I found it, then reaching for the last of the coffee and whiskey and a cigar —I could not help saying to myself that there sits this Susie, here is a cleaned plate, and at an arm's reach are one or two sips of whiskey. This was what it's all about.

We ate there almost every night. There was creamed herring and double orders of shrimp cocktail appetizers. There was pressed duck and chicken Kiev and an entire Chateaubriand (with grilled Bermuda onions), late-night four-egg Texas omelets (with chilled applesauce). There was sweet corn and creamed corn, baked potatoes with sour cream and chives, zucchini and acorn squash and creamed spinach and succotash and white turnips and wild rice and brussels sprouts and baby peas and waxed beans and boiled cabbage, red and white. There were chef salads and tossed salads and quartered heads of lettuce with Russian or garlic, olive oil and wine-vinegar dressing, or Roquefort cheese dusted with paprika. There was rye bread and wheat bread and raisin bread and black bread, Italian bread we had to break by hand, and Parker House rolls. And for dessert there was cherry cobbler and chocolate mousse, devil's food and angel food cake, lemon meringue and mince and peach and Dutch apple pies. And when I pushed myself away from the table, and took the last sips of whiskey and ice and strong black coffee, we got up and joined the wild, milling crowd on the dance floor—Susie in her low-cut, busty dress; me in my cotton slacks and yellow-gold Camp Zama PX sweater and rented tie. We danced every dance after that and the windows steamed over, and we always left when she got tired and made it back to the bar at the Perfect Room Hotel. We drank a few drinks—schnapps and beers or Irish coffee, or brandies sometimes—talking with George while he polished glasses and closed up. Then Susie and I went upstairs (me copping feels inside her dress, or the two of us dry-fucking until the elevator doors slid open), with a bottle of sake for a hot bath and a bare-ass back rub, and those hot fucks on the cold sheets or the couch or one of the plushy, itchy reading chairs.

We necked and finger-fucked and dog-fucked and tit-fucked and crawled over each other on the bed, copping feels, and played silly games of tag (to see who was going to do what to whom), and drank warm sake and laughed and lay on the shag rug in front of the couch, nuzzling and tickling, drinking and fucking. Sometimes we just plain wrestled, but play got a little rough once when Susie grabbed me around the neck from behind, a breast against the side of my face, and I wheeled around suddenly and keeled her over with a punch square in the middle of her chest. Then we screwed to show there were no hard feelings; Susie on top dancing that little dance with her hands and breasts; her hips and thighs and breasts covered with goose pimples, but her skin warm, me with my unfailing R & R hard-on and dug-in heels, rattling the mattress for all we were worth. When I got sleepy we curled up against each other. And it got so I could nod right out; could sleep through to the afternoon without being startled awake by the maids banging on the door or the hallway traffic or the traffic on the street below us. I would wake easily, slowly, that warmth—someone lying naked—which pleased me, always there.

One evening we went to see *King Lear*, in Japanese and traditional dress. There was a bare stage except for a spiral ramp that rose fifteen or twenty feet above the stage, and everything was ramps and levels. A bunch of soldiers, dressed in shakos and leather jerkins, handling pikes, came tramping down one of the ramps and stood around and the jabber commenced. Then somebody galumphed in from another direction and threw up his hands, and the only thing I could think of was that sorry old joke about "Hark! Is that a cannon I hear?" and then they all came alive as though somebody had mentioned money, and tramped off, all in step, of course. The stage was deserted for the count of three or six or ten; then a couple of women, wearing clown white and shiny black wigs and bathrobes with sack bustles tied just above their butts, sort of ambled down. They stood and yakked and a moment later some dude, carrying a samurai sword, sneaked his head around the proscenium and giggled and laughed, talking to himself and rolling his eyes the while, then left. Then Lear—I guessed it was Lear, because he outdressed the rest—came out and screamed and yawned and jumped around, ran up the ramp, stood on the pinnacle; then somebody turned on a wind machine that twirled his long stringy gray beard. He screamed and spit, threw down his hat and danced on it, and did every kind of desperate choking and gaggling. I thought to myself: Lear doesn't die, does he? He did everything but throw himself off the damn thing. Susie and I sat arm in arm in the very last row on the ground floor, and I kept chuckling all the time, because I was a fool to try to understand what was being said. When it was over and the corpses had been carried off and the houselights came up, an older couple who sat in front of us looked sad, and nearly everybody looked sad. Susie looked sad and puzzled. My ass was sore from all that sitting and so we walked for several blocks just so I could get the circulation back into my legs. Susie asked all kinds of questions about the play, but I couldn't answer any of them.

"Then, Phirip, why do you raugh? It was very sad

story. A father such as Rear does not cry and curse his ordness for nothing? Was not Rear a great king of Engrand? To raugh at such a thing is a disgrace." I could not answer and I felt stupid. We were riding in a cab in the dark. A wet snow covered the windows. The traffic was very heavy. That night when we screwed she was put-offish. There was an archness, a sadness.

The next night we went to see an American movie, *The Dirty Dozen*, in English with Japanese subtitles along the right-hand margin. It had everything. A group of condemned convicts were recruited, with promises of clemency, for a pre-dawn Normandy Invasion Day suicide mission. There was the crazy major who in another life will blow us all away, and the beady-eyed shell-game carnie who had a look on his face as though he were constantly toting and retoting the odds. There was the village idiot who didn't know his own strength and couldn't count, and the moron with sloping brow and slobbering lips. Then came the bald-headed psychopath who swore up and down that God talked to him all the time, and the token black dude who talked like a football player and ran faster than a grenade could fly. And lastly there was the blue-eyed, cute-faced, blond-haired MP who never loaded his grease gun and never raised his voice. The highlight of the entire movie came about halfway through the evening. The moron, impersonating a general traveling incognito, was asked to inspect an honor platoon, forty of the straightest-looking Airborne dudes you are ever likely to see. He put his hands behind his back and walked up and down the ranks, looking at boots and zippers and belt buckles and buttons and open-breech rifles. About halfway through the last rank he suddenly stopped in front of one guy, rocked back on his heels and asked, "Whar ya from, son?" the way they do. The guy with his M-1 at inspection arms smiled weakly—a nice touch there—and said, "Po-Po-Pokorneyville, California, s-s-sir," or some such place. The moron giggled and smirked and shook his head at the ground, the jeering laughter welling up in his chest, and said, "Ne-ver heard of it." And then all of a sudden the subtitles were going a mile a minute, a gobbledygook of dashes and squiggles and things that looked like cartoon trees. The whole theater sat quiet, expectant, waiting for the next comprehensible thing to happen, and I sat on the aisle, belly-laughing at every inspection I had ever been put through. I mean, I *guffawed*. I *shrieked*. Tears came to my eyes. I held my sides and damn near slid out into the aisle, I laughed so hard. Susie had me by the arm; shook me and dug her nails in trying in vain to get me quiet. The whole theater looked at me, thinking what they have always thought of Americans—GI boo-coo dinky dau, savvy? And that night we went straight back to the hotel, bought a bottle of Jack Daniel's, and went straight to the room. We called down for dinner and a bucket of ice. We ate dinner at the table, in our robes. After I finished and poured myself a drink, I walked over the bed in two quick strides, opened the draw drapes, and stood looking down at the dark faint city. I could hear Susie fooling with the dishes, stacking them, gathering the silverware, sliding the cart out into the hallway.

"Susie!" I said. "Susie. Do you know who I am?" I turned my back to the steamy window, a glass of ice and whiskey in one hand, a Camel in the other. She stood by the big deep chair with her robe wrapped tightly, all the curves shrouded, but plain. She heard the serious stupidity in my voice. It was one of those questions that demand, first, simple answers. She looked down embarrassed, pulling the robe tighter. I could not help but respond with a twitching groin.

"You are Phirip," she said, holding the robe closed at

her throat. "You are Vet-nam GI. You stink just rike the others the first time. You have rough hands, strange brue eyes. You tark kind to me. You are quiet, not rike so many others. You make rove nice, too."

Don't we all.

"You are funny man. You raugh at odd things. . . . That pray was not funny. . . . The movie was not so funny. . . . You are too quiet. You tark in your sleep. You wake me sometimes. Donard, who I was with rast week, he dreamed arr bad dreams."

"Do you know what I do? Do you know where your money comes from?" I said.

"You fight VC. You kirr some, too. I know. I hear. You fight sometimes in your sreep, just rike Donard, but not so much rast night or maybe tonight. You touch me nice, though, not as some others." She rubbed her hands up and down her arms. "You go back tomorrow. Yes? You write me?"

"Yes, I'd like that," I said, and lied. She came over to the bed, climbed on, and stood on her knees near the head. I put the drink on the night table and reached over and pulled the slipknot loose on her robe and pushed the lapel and shoulder and sleeves off. She did the same for me. We lay on the bed screwing and drinking until I fell asleep.

The next afternoon we went to an art gallery on a broad boulevard near the old Imperial Palace. I took Susie's arm and we ascended a wide curving staircase, entering the mezzanine gallery—paintings in one room hung along the walls, mounted on plain wooden easels, and wobbly cork-covered screens; the other room crammed with pedestals and sculptures cordoned off with limp velvet ropes; and a heavy glass partition between. Susie left me with the paintings—to find the most comfortable chair, I supposed.

In one corner hung several canvases by the same man. A short biography said he lived in Paris; knew Monet and Gauguin and Van Gogh and those guys—and could probably swill absinthe with the best of them.

All of his paintings were seascapes.

Water falling on water thick with swells and grayish foam and whitecaps. Cracked longboat oars and shredded knots of manila rope and chunks of caulked and painted wood flotsam, glowing in a strong clean light.

A sea shining like frosted, rippled glass. Pile upon pile of thunderclouds as far as the eye can see, brilliantly white and black around the folds and creases, facing a lowering sun; the thinnest light along the horizon ten miles distant. Livid, smoky shafts of yellowish light shallowly slanted for miles and miles, scattering dappled specks over the water, and mutely reflected along the charcoal gray and russet undersides of the low cloud cover. A light I've only seen on the prairie in an autumn dusk.

Here and there and yonder random lumps of craggy rocks and smoothed boulders, rising clear of foamed shoal water in harsh moonlight. The foremost crags ragged with mossy grass, furling and unfurling among calm high-tide swells. And on the left, more clouds—softly, quickly done —the ridges and fissures and billows looking for all the world like a rearing horse's head; the heavy brows and hollow highlights of cheeks; the curl of thin, bristling lips; the flared curve of the nostrils; a mean pinch to the chin. That wiry shock of windblown hair hanging into dark sunken eyes—one eye squinted wildly.

I stood with my arms folded over my chest, hip cocked, then sat on the edge of a concrete bench, fascinated by the sharpness—that backbreaking, painstaking thoroughness—the meanest oaken slivers on the oars; the lines of shadow between chipping deck paint and bare wood; the slyest bluish glint of madness in the corner of the horse's eye.

I suddenly shivered with chill. My ears rang. I rose and shoved my hands into my pockets, and walked into the other room, looking for Susie. The room was ringed around with a bizarre variety of sculpture—pink porcelain and taper-wound copper wire, elegantly polished car parts, clay parings and chips of ebony flint sprinkled with cinder crumbs, and varnished panels of Japanese newsprint papier-mâché—displayed on tall black lacquered pedestals, broad rectangles of swirled marble, and ordinary fruit crates.

Dribbled, blackened gobs of welder's brazing rod, titled "Dwarf, with Flowers."

Skinny chunks of close-grained, sinuous driftwood with a handful of tenpenny common nails pounded round about, and painted with kindergarten tempera and a two-inch scrub brush, titled "Benjamin Eating."

A thin sheet of riveted roofing tin creased sharply, origami fashion, to look like a gull with fiercely downswept wings, titled "Emperor's Waltz."

I stood just inside the doorway with my shoulders hunched and my fists lumped deep in my pockets, skimming them quickly.

My man, I thought to myself, are you ever in the wrong racket. I should have brought some of Granger's letters he kept in a pouch under his seat, with the return address: Sandra Davis Granger, Denver, Colorado. Some of the letters heavily blood-spattered and filthy; some only flecked; some, strangely, perfectly clean; some tattered as though a cat had chewed them; some with dog-eared corners as though he had marked the place; some with orange dirt ground into the creases or finger-smudged around the edges (even though Granger always washed his hands before);

but each opened across the top with a quick snip of his bayonet, and oil-splotched and ragged, like paper folded once and torn by hand. Letters Whiskey j. and I decided to throw away when we gathered Granger's personal gear to send home.

I could have mounted the letters and envelopes on a slab of cheap whitewashed plywood, collage fashion, and scribbled "Dear John" in high school drafting-class block print with a borrowed 2H pencil. I could have sold it on the spot for cash, commissioned a bogus passport, and retired to the sunflower and wine-grape fields of southern France, amid the gush and clack of every junk-art junkie on Honshu Island.

In the middle of the room, and facing away from the door, a large stone nude of a woman (pockmarked to resemble lava rock) reclined on a marble block the size of a ten-place banquet table. The woman was flat on her back with her knees well up and feet together, thighs spread-eagled, and hands clasped behind her raised head, gazing out between her knees. The exaggerated, bulbous features smooth like some of Picasso's women—a thick stiffened neck, broad shoulders and arms, fat unbending fingers, and large flattened breasts. Susie stood to one side, looking up at the back of the head, thoroughly engrossed. I settled myself on a concrete bench and watched her watching it. She sidestepped around it, reaching up gingerly on tiptoes to touch the bundle of hair or the tendons and hollows back of the knees, and slid the flat of her hand across the stomach. She swept her fingertips along the edge of the marble, making a pouting face with her lips and nose; then she saw me, peeked under the small of the woman's back and winked, like she did in the bathtub every night. Finally she came to me, smiling, and sat close, putting her hands on my thigh. She beamed, her eyes sparkling. Then she squeezed my leg and jogged her head toward the statue, excitedly searching for the words, but she said it as much with a vigorous back-and-forth gesture of a hand as in her broken English, "Her, me, same same."

That night I had to sign back in at Camp Zama by midnight, so Susie and I had dinner at the hotel and went back up to the room. We quaffed San Miguel and peppermint-schnapps toasts, screwing on the bed with the sheet wrapped tightly around us, and standing against the kitchen sink, and back to belly on the thatch mat. Then after one more piping-hot bath and a back rub, I dressed in my beat-up low-quarters and cotton slacks and yellow-gold PX sweater, packed my suitcase, kissed Susie—or whoever she was—and left.

Christie and Hacker and I rode the bus in silence. At Zama we changed back into our khakis, exchanged our yen for greenbacks, and the R & R party boarded buses for the airport. I bought two bottles of schnapps at the duty-free all-night liquor store. The flight was one long buzz of jet engines, sad and dreamy. Most everybody nodded out, I could not sleep. Halfway there Hacker slipped a pint of scotch out of his shirt, and we traded swigs back and forth, talking in low whispers.

We arrived at Tan Son Nhut just before dawn. When the stewardess opened the door that flat and tasteless, basement-smelling air in the cabin became sticky and sickly and humid. There was no mistaking that smell—a raunchy, shit-foul, tenant-dirt-farm stink. The smell of junk left where it fell; of grease-trap garbage and cow shit, spilled mo-gas and urine ammonia, rice-paddy muck and sun-scorched iron.

B Y

T H E

R U L E

Christmas Day was a truce day. That's the only reason I remember it.

On the twenty-fourth Romeo pulled out of Dau Tieng with a battery of 105s and laagered at some no-name fire base in a stand of old, wild-grown rubber trees. At four o'clock the next morning Quinn roused me for guard. I slipped on my field jacket for the chill. I wrapped my blanket around my shoulders and sat behind my fifty with my knees drawn up, but a breeze came between my legs from inside, and I couldn't help shivering. The ground looked moist and even wet in spots, on the verge of frost. I pulled the blanket up over my head, blew on my fingers, and still I shivered. Christmas Day.

It was not very dark, not as dark as three or three-thirty, say. A cast of gray-green half light filled the sky, thin black shadows that faded into dull hues of mere darkness. At three it had been pitch dark. At four a fluorescent pale lightness shown, like a low-watt lamp through opaque glass. Not shadows but not really day. If such a light falls across a just-born, he is marked. He will be a strange and moody child; a withdrawn and silent man. He will always be at the edge just on the brink of everything, looking up at love and work and people. He will push a broom. He will slide the slop bucket along with his foot, slapping the mop from wall to wall in quick and easy figure-eights, and on the day he dies there will be no sign, no revelation, no mourners. He will die on one of those days when fog hangs low over cities and airports are closed.

Christmas Day. There would be no tree hung with silver icicles and jumbo candy canes and homemade, handmade cookies; no uncles snoring in the front-room chairs; no living room scattered with paper and ribbons and boxes; no big sit-down dinner. Just the stink of bodies and fire-base rubble, and a rubber-tree woodline, always some fucking woodline. But then Quinn did have his Prince Albert tobacco can and I had that brandy fruitcake Jenny had sent me.

When the sky got light enough I boiled a canteen cup of instant coffee and sat the rest of my guard, warming my hands on the cup and letting the steam rise into my face, sipping now and again.

In the middle of the morning the resupply chopper came, dropping off mail and packages from the Red Cross. Each man got a couple books, a Red Cross pen and letterhead paper, toothpaste, cigarettes, a cigar, and a bar of Hershey's Tropical Chocolate. Whoopie. I kept the cigar and traded Dewey one of the books and threw the rest away.

After lunch Quinn and I spread out in the back, smoking our smokes and munching fruitcake and washing it down with beers scrounged from the artillery. Dewey and a fucking new guy, Teddy, napped under the track in the shade.

I was breaking Dewey in as a driver, since Quinn decided that driving was out. "I'll set beside that left-side pig. I'll fucken hump ambushes, if we ever do any again. But I'm getting too old to drive. Dewey'll drive," Quinn had said. "I already asked him." Dewey read the manual, stuffed more sandbags under the driver's seat, scrounged a brand-new grease gun from somewhere, and sent home for a pair of aviators, like Quinn's.

Teddy had arrived in the platoon when I was in Tokyo. He came from upstate New York and had short fuzzy hair, like Steichen. He'd just graduated from the Tiger Brigade Infantry School, at Fort Polk, Louisiana, and kept saying, "Shit, man, this ain't nothing like they said in Tiger School," every time he turned around.

Later that afternoon one of the crewmen from the 105 howitzer parked behind us came over and slid onto the bench. He was built like Quinn—all arms and shoulders, but then all those artillery dudes were built like that, because all I ever saw them do was hump rounds and fill sandbags. After a couple pulls on a smoke he said, "Say, listen, there's gonna be a gun duel in a minute. Cap'um wants ta find out who's the best gun. What the fuck? Might be good for a grin. Prize is four cases of beer. Come on."

The CO and the First Sergeant and a couple clerks, carrying the beer, walked up behind the gun. The Captain picked the target—a tall barkless tree, easily the tallest tree around, to the south about three hundred meters. "And the first gun crew to blow off the left fork wins," he said as he explained the rules to the crews.

Our crew went first. Everybody sat back of the gun, on stacks of wooden ammo boxes or sandbags or the sandbag bunker by their mess tent. The gunner, a sharp-eyed Greek with black curly hair, stood behind the gunsight with his eye squinted in the eyepiece, hands on his knees. The Captain stood right behind him at parade rest. The Greek worked with elevation a couple cranks, the windage a crank or two, then stood up, and grabbed hold of the lanyard. He looked at the Captain, who doffed his PX baseball fatigue cap and nodded his head. So the gunner yanked the lanyard with a snap of the wrist and the round was off. I blinked at the concussion, as though someone were flicking wet fingertips in my face. The round sailed in a slow arc through the fork of the tree, like a pebble from a slingshot, and blew a couple hundred meters down range. And just that quick the loader slapped open the breach, slipped the smoking cartridge out, and tossed it underhand behind him. Then he stood there with the second round cradled in his arms until the Greek nodded his head. The loader eased it snug into the chamber, and closed it slowly.

"It's a little high and about two feet right," I said, pointing.

The Greek nodded, but didn't seem to pay attention.

"Say, m' man," Quinn said to one of the clerks. "Might as well put that beer somewhere outa the sun, hunh?"

The Greek put his eye to the gunsight again, touched one of the cranks with his fingertips, nudged the gun with his boot, and smiled. Then he stepped to the side, and eased the slack out of the lanyard, and squeezed off the second round. Whacko! The tree limb took off, like somebody pushed off a building, and chunks of twigs and shrapnel showered the ground. The Captain shook hands around, had the beer moved to their bunker, and walked away.

The next day we loaded up and moved off to rejoin
Alpha and Charlie companies laagered in a field near the
road. The dinks had blown one of the bridges, so we would
have to build a temporary. We loaded the timber on the
first three Romeo tracks.

The stream was right on the edge of the jungle. Dewey,
standing up as far out of the hatch as he could manage
(with Quinn sitting right behind him), pulled the Cow
Catcher to the edge of the bank. Alpha and Charlie companies pulled up behind. On the other side was a small
flood plain of rice paddies and a hamlet. The bridge, a
French-made concrete through type, was split across the
middle and sitting in the water. The engineers' sweep team
cleared the sight and moved across. In half an hour we had
the wooden bridge thrown together. The sweep team was
two hundred meters down the road, one of the sweepers
passing the detector back over a spot, holding the earphone
tight to his ear. Another guy came up behind him and
squatted over it, carefully pushing his bayonet into the dirt.
I signaled Dewey with a wave of my hand to bring the Cow
Catcher across. I heard an explosion. I dropped to the
ground, rolled over the side of the embankment, and down
into the ditch. I searched the woodline. I heard no firing
and saw no movement, so I crawled up the embankment.
Dudes were running down the road to the engineers and
then me with them. Men were lying on the road, but began
to stir. The engineers' Lieutenant counted his men. Everybody was all right, but not really.

The guy who had been stooping over the mine was not
there. We checked the ditches and looked up and down the
road. I found his ID card, a little bent but all right, and
handed it to the Lieutenant. Down the embankment some-

one found a scrap of boot and part of a trouser leg. We searched the paddies again. The engineers' Lieutenant stood over the hole holding the card, the piece of boot, and the trouser scrap. Someone found the ends of commo wire used to detonate the mine.

If it had been a contact mine and the guy touched it, then it would have been his own stupid luck. But this was command-detonated. Nothing in the world you can do about those. In a couple days his family will be gathered around a hunk of a boot, a piece of trouser, and his ID card. His headstone will say Such-and-so is buried here, but it isn't so. They don't see the body, the Army won't open the coffin.

I didn't even look to read the card. Why did I want to know the guy's name? There's nothing in knowing who he was. I walked back to the bridge. Some gook sat in that woodline and picked the guy he was going to kill—he *picked* him. No, not him, he's too skinny. Not him, not enough rank. *Him*. That's the guy. *One. Two. Three. Whomp.* Guts and teeth and chunks of bone let fly. Something inside me bore down, I tell you; some clamp slammed home, I say. If that motherfucker wanted a fight, he just bought it. Fuck with me. Come on, just *fuck* with me. I'll kill you with my bare hands, just like the other one.

I walked to the edge of the bridge and gave Dewey the come-on signal with a snappy jerk of my arm. When I saw him making it without my help, I turned and walked away, watching the engineers still standing around the hole.

There was another explosion, right behind me. I dove for the embankment and rolled down again, holding tightly to my steel pot. I looked up and saw a cloud of water and timbers big as a man's thigh. Then came the hollow ringing sounds of chunks of wood bouncing on the road, and the funny familiar feel of mist across my face. The bridge.

They blew the bridge. I jumped up, the air still raining garbage, and scrambled for the track.

"Shit *gawd*-damn. Gawd-*damn* shit," I said in whispers, then shouts.

The front of the track had settled into the water.

"Dewey! Dewey?" I screamed, coming to the stream bank. All I could see of him was the top of his CVC in the hatch.

"Jesus H. fucken Christ!" he said from inside.

"Is anybody hit?"

"Did anybody see what happened? Man, all I saw was the fucken river go up right in front of my face," he said, and sat up, his face dripping wet and black with silt and sand. I jumped onto the deck and leaped to the back. Quinn crouched behind his gun, looking out over the gun shield at the nearest hamlet hooches, his hand on the pistol grip, his finger on the trigger. Teddy stood inside in knee-deep water, looking down at the water already leaking in.

"Get the guns and shit and move out," I said. We dismounted the pigs and sloshed around for some ammo and moved over to the El-tee's track, just behind us. The Colonel and the El-tee and the Alpha Company CO stood behind it, looking at the hamlet on the left. The Colonel sent an Alpha Company squad into the jungle on the right and told the El-tee to form a skirmish line with the tracks behind the ditch berm, facing the village. Quinn with his pig ambush style, Dewey, soaked to the skin and dripping water, with his sixteen and thigh pockets full of magazines, and me with my shotgun and gas-mask bag of shells got in the prone between the El-tee's track and the seven-one. The Colonel brought up the ARVN interpreter. He yelled something at the hamlet. The hamlet was quiet. He spoke again, cupping his hands. Still no answer.

"Open fire on that first hooch," the Colonel said, loud

enough for everyone to hear. Everybody on line started putting out rounds, then a fifty tracer set the thatch roof afire. When the fire caught well enough he ordered a squad to check it out. Quinn and Dewey and I jumped up and moved forward. We spread out on line—me and my shotgun, Dewey with his sixteen on automatic, Quinn with that shoulder strap over one shoulder and a fifty-round belt hanging off the feed tray and draped over his shoulder— with another fire team from Alpha Company, moving at a slow walk. By the time we came around the front of the hooch it was smoking thickly.

"Lah-dee, lah-dee," I yelled, going into a crouch.

"Chieu Hoi, dink," shouted Quinn, leveling the muzzle to the ground in front of the doorway and taking a broad stance for the recoil.

We heard nothing, so Quinn took a grenade from his flak jacket and rolled it underhand into the mouth of the shelter. When it blew we walked back to the road, passing twenty meters in front of the woodline, while Alpha Company went on ahead into the hamlet. Then a sniper round zinged past our heads and just that quick Quinn turned on his heel and fired a ten-round burst into the woodline with his pig, leaning forward. I dropped to the prone and turned. Quinn sloughed the ammo belt from his shoulder, went down on one knee, and put out a long, long burst, holding the muzzle with a stiff arm, and walked the rounds in and out, in and out of the woods in front of us. He caught sight of the target the same time I did, a gun slit in a low bunker. I blew off round after round and he opened fire once more with another long burst, using the rest of the belt. Dewey fired then, two quick magazines. We heard a muffled, hustling noise and then two dinks climbed out, eyes wide.

We *had* them, a kid and an old man. Dewey and I rushed up and grabbed them. I was red-faced with rage.

| 216

Quinn stood on the path, reloading. The kid had a hole in his shoulder, was bleeding but not bad, but the old man had a gash across the side of his forehead that went to the bone. I took the kid by his wounded arm, squeezing and jerking him as we walked along. The old man went into shock and fainted, so Dewey simply picked him up in his arms and carried him. When we crossed the ditch berm I pushed the kid down on his heels. Stepik had pulled out a litter and motioned for Dewey to lay the old man out, and went to work on him.

"Fuck the kid," he said, looking at me. "Let'm wait. El-tee, better get a dust-off for this one. He's in shock bad."

An Alpha Company medic came down and wrapped the kid's arm.

The kid squatted in the sun. His wounded arm hung painfully to the ground, his other hand holding the bandage tight, almost squeezing it. I put the muzzle of the twelve-gauge right in his face. He stared into the blackest hole he was ever likely to see, front-sight blade and all. He took long sweated breaths. His face became flat and pale. I judged him thirteen or fourteen, and watched the wrinkles come at him sudden, out of the corners of his eyes and mouth, while he watched the gun and me and Stepik working on the old man. He sat motionless in the ditch dust, aging. I stood there, hip cocked, aging too, in my own way. You fucking little squint-eye. Move, kid. Just move. Go ahead and take off on a run. It would be so easy to kill him and say he made a grab for the gun. Kid, I'm going to blow your fucking head off, at the eyes. I wanted to reach down and crush his fucking face, disembowel his little asshole. He sat on his heels, looking at the old man. He sat in that fucking woodline, peering out through the brush. He saw that engineer bending over the mine—a dud bomb by the look of the crater—and as easy as he would thread a needle he touched that wire to that battery and click!—all he needed was the slightest spark. No kid could watch a man die. You goddamn skinny gook punk. I should just go ahead and blow your fucking brains out. By the rule he was a man, and the rule says to the hilt with your fucking anger, to the fucking hilt.

My jaws would ache later, that thought would grind so hard. I bit the fleshy inside of my cheek and did not feel it then, but later that night my mouth would burn as I ate greasy cold chunks of salted meat.

I flicked the safety on and off and that was the sound and motion, quick as horses, the two of us listened to and watched. I stood there watching his black blinking eyes, moving my finger from trigger guard to trigger and back; not knowing that days later I would see enough bodies and black blood to cauterize and seal smooth the cure.

I snapped the shotgun sharply to port arms, and turned my back on those reddened eyes and that shock of dusty black hair and wounded arm, and Alpha Company torching hooches. I walked away and gave the gun to Quinn, saying to the El-tee and Stepik and the rest, "I can't fucken watch him anymore. Somebody else do it. I'm gonna do something fucked up if I gotta stand there one more minute." So Quinn took the gun and walked up to the kid and leaned down, with a hand on one knee, resting the muzzle on the kid's shoulder and saying, "Die, gook," slow and loud so the kid wouldn't need the interpreter. The kid's eyes started to tear, as much from the dust in the air as from hearing one or two final facts shouted down at him from the barrel of a twelve-gauge.

I walked away from the El-tee and the others, expecting to hear the crashing report of the shotgun, hoping that Quinn would do it, expecting that he would, because he was the only man for five hundred meters around who *could* do it—and get away with it, like he got away with so much else. I wanted that smooth, smug, slant-eyed fucking face ground into meat, transformed into spray. I walked to the edge of the stream where the water swirled round the concrete bridge. The Cow Catcher had settled to the bottom and filled with water. Someone's waterproof floated in the crew hatch. I hung my thumbs on the armholes of my flak jacket and stared and stared at my TC hatch, wondering where I'd be if I'd been standing there, and looked back at the kid, squatting on his haunches, and hated him more. My breath hissed in my nose; that creamy yellow bile bubbled in my throat. I walked in slow wide circles in the roadway, like a horse will pace the perimeter of its paddock until it wears a path. My body tensed and went slack, then tensed quickly again, just the same as the mounts I used to walk between polo chukkers at Onwensia Stables—walking hots we called it—the lathered, snorting horses skittish and shyful after someone had run their asses off for fifteen minutes or so. We walked them four at a time and if one went crazy, they all went crazy.

When I calmed down some and wiped the sweat off my forehead with the back of my sleeve, I went to Quinn and took back my gun. He shrugged his shoulders and sat down again with his sixty.

And I waited my chance. The kid knew what I wanted to do. He saw it coming like flatland farmers can see company coming three days off. He looked at me with those wrinkled eyes and shoveled his wounded arm around in the dust and then looked down at my boots. I kept glancing over my shoulders, picking a time when no one was looking, and when that moment came, when even Quinn was fooling with his M-60, I clicked off the safety, looked again, and blew the top of his head off. The fucking round hit him right in the forehead and he flew back over the berm ass over teakettle as though somebody had dropkicked him under the chin. I hated him when he was alive and I hated his corpse.

Then everybody crowded around me, jostling and yapping, and some dude from Alpha Company snatched the shotgun out of my hands; me all the while telling them he made a grab for the gun, goddamn it, he made a grab for the gun and pulled the muzzle. Then Quinn elbowed his way through the crowd and stood next to the Colonel, who screamed in my face, but I wasn't listening. I watched through the crowd for glimpses of those black dusty feet and splayed arms and that mushy no-expression face on the corpse I had made. And Quinn said, yeah, the gook panicked and grabbed the gun. Then Stepik and the El-tee listened and repeated it—the El-tee looking at me the whole time, blandly blinking his eyes. They said they happened to turn around, catching sight of the detainee making a snatch for the muzzle. Too bad about the gun being off safety, but an accident's an accident, and the Colonel seemed to be satisfied. He even handed me back the shotgun, taking a long stern look at me when he did. I could have cared less what he thought, the dink was dead.

Vengeance is that quick vicious turn of anger that swings and hacks until you cannot lift your arm; until you cannot step but on the corpses. The day after Christmas I stood over a weak wounded kid and saw his grave and my grave, and the grave of those around me—a deep smooth-sided shaft and you will never fill it.

*

Brigade sent out an eighty-eight-ton VTR, a retriever for tanks the size of a small house, to pull the Cow Catcher out of the creek and tow us into camp—the first time the

Cow Catcher had to be towed anywhere. The four of us were covered, crusted, filthy-scabby with the VTR's dust by the time we rolled into camp, around dusk. The dude dropped us off near the mechanics' shack, where the mechanics had the lights to work by. The battalion stayed behind—stayed the night, sent for more lumber, built another bridge, and crossed the next morning.

Four dipstick-looking mechanics with their canvas tool bags gathered around the Cow Catcher's upraised hood, committee-meeting style—scratching their heads and scratching their asses and putting their heads together like a gaggle of hens. Rayburn, fucking Rayburn, where were you when we needed you? Rayburn was breaking rocks some-fucking-place, doing twenty years to life, he wrote and told us, for doing the big deed on his wife. The mechanics craned their necks and stuck their heads inside and flashed a flashlight here and there. The engine wasn't beat up, just waterlogged—everything was waterlogged—but they pulled spark-plug wires and ran their fingers over the dripping four-barrel carburetor and tapped the water-filled air-filter housing, the way mechanics do, and put their heads together again, mumbling, "Hrum, hrum," among themselves. They thumped the slimy valve covers and gawked at the firewall asbestos and twiddled with the distributor cap and the crankcase-oil filler cap and squeezed the radiator hoses, the one with that mysterious leak, between their fingers, and scratched their greasy heads some more. They took turns sticking a finger into the sludge and oily silt at the bottom of the engine compartment—jungle compost and spilt oil and piss and the carcasses of rats; gunk and garbage and God knows what a couple inches thick that had been accumulating going on two years and stank to high heaven.

They put their heads together one more time, hrum-

hrumming and mmm-mmming; then the first mechanic, a short guy with a paunch and the only set of Allen wrenches in the battalion, took a step back and put his hand to his chin and made a long face, like he was contemplating a fucking painting or some shit.

Quinn and I stood on the chicken-wire grill, gazing down between our feet at the flitting flashlight and shifting our weight back and forth. Dewey stood knee deep in the driver's hatch, hands on hips and chewing the ass end of a White Owl Ranger like a pro. Teddy, the fuzzy-haired new guy, stood behind him on the deck, waiting to find out if he should dismount the guns and clean them or go to the tents or what. The four of us stood above the four of them, chewing our cud, brushing the dust off our flak jackets, and shaking the dust out of our hair.

"Well," he said finally, "I judge it needs a new engine," or something like, and waved a finger in the air.

Quinn pursed his lips, blew a raspberry, and mumbled, "Oh, my achin' fucken back," and said out loud, "No shit, Sherlock."

We unloaded all the ammo cans and most of the gear so the mechanics could take out the rear firewall panel. While they began turning bolts the four of us made for the mess hall to see if we could scare up something to eat, brushing more dust from our hair and spitting dust out of our mouths and carrying our guns and such Pancho Villa style. We pushed through the screen door. Haskins stood behind the griddle with a putty knife and GI kitchen cleanser and a pot of steaming water, scraping it down for the morning. I stood in front of the serving line with one arm slipped through my forty-five web belt, like it was a sling, and said, "Say, m' man, anything round here to eat?"

"Wall wall wall. Whar did *yo* come from?"

"Haskins? Anything to eat?"

"You betcha! How 'bout san'wiches?"

Anything. Just to sit inside the wire and rest my eyes was enough.

"Yeah. Is there coffee?" I stood there staring at the gray floor behind him and the two black ovens against the wall. Always coffee. Even here. Especially here. He pointed to a small vat. We ladled coffee for each other and sat down at one of the NCO tables. The mess hall was dimly lit. The chairs stood neatly at the tables. The cooks lounged in the kitchen, drinking beer out of the meat locker and laughing. I put my arms on the table and put my head down, hoping to fall asleep. After a moment Haskins brought the sandwiches and a plate of stale lettuce. "Sorry, Deadeye. That's all they is," he said. Thick slices of white bread and chunky slabs of meat. The meat was cold and slick with grease and heavily salted. I ate slowly, chewing the meat, leaving the bread. My mouth burned. It was no use trying to enjoy the food, there was too much road crud in my mouth. Jaws so tired from anger that chewing was painful. Just eat it and leave. Quinn folded a piece of lettuce small enough to fit in his mouth, then came the slow sound of his devouring it whole.

Haskins came back to the table with beer, pulled up another chair, and sat, leaning over the back of it.

"Where's the res'?" he said.

"The rest of what?" I said.

"The platoon. Ever'body else. Ya know, Rom-e-o."

"In the field. Cow Catcher is down. We got towed in."

"Yeah. I heard 'bout the engineer an' the firefight. Say, how'd ya like ta smoke a smoke?"

"Yeah." So Haskins pulled out a pack of smokes and offered them around.

"Say, Haskins," said Dewey. "Ain't you a little 'fraid the number one over there will turn you in?" and Haskins and Quinn and I looked over at him.

"Who? Him?" said Haskins. "Ain't none a those lifers got time on my ass. 'Sides, he's from Alpha Company, an' thinks his shit don' stink. What's he gonna do? Sen' me ta the field? Say, Ah wuz readin' in the *Stars & Stripes* 'bout this doctor, what wuz his name?" Haskins pulled out a week-old *Stars & Stripes* from his thigh pocket. "Here 'tis, 'Doctor Arthur T. Dreese.' Now ain't that some honey of a name? Annaway, he wrote this thing 'bout co-lester-oil. Whatever the fuck that is. Lemme read this to ya. 'Ah propose that eggs,' *eggs* that is, 'eggs contain dang'rous a-mounts of co-lester-oil, an' kin be the cause a heart trouble, if con-sumed as habit'al fare at the breakfas' table.' Unquote. Wall, Dosier, Ah tell ya, Ah may be jus' a dumb Michigan nigga, but Ah been in this man's Army fer goin' on three years. 'N' Ah been *here*, cookin' eggs fer all comers since before yo wuz borned. Ah may not know a *hell* of a lot, but Ah know a *egg* when Ah see one. Why, Ah kin spot a egg inna room fulla golf balls. Ah kin cook a egg on its side. Goddamn, Ah kin jus' 'bout talk chicken talk. Ah looks three hunnurd eggs straight inna eye ever' damn mornin' 'fore any a these other housecats is up, so Ah figure Ah knows m' eggs. So, who is *this* housecat? Where the hell he get his info? Ah tell ya, Ah kin walk outa that do' anytime a the day 'r night, rain 'r shine—an' Ah ain' *bull*shittin'—an' eggs is 'bout the mos' harmless thing Ah kin lay m' eye on. If God come to me 'n' He said, '*Haskins, it is yo misfortune to die of a dose of co-lester-oil pois'nin*,' then Ah'd know tha' Ah wuz gonna live fo' about a thousan' year. But if what this bub says is true, why Ah tell ya what. You 'n' me'll load up the mess-hall jeep, 'n' we'll go out of a mornin' an' throw eggs at the sons a bitches. Better yit,

we'll hand 'em out, like the Army did way back, givin'
Indians the blankets offa smallpox deathbeds. 'Here,
Chingachgook, have a egg. How 'bout a smoke fer later?
Thar ya go!' Give the village headmen panatelas, kids
under ten years Camels. Makes 'bout as much fucken sense
as anythin' else Ah seen this fucken battalion do, annaway."

"Haskins, you're goddamn fucken crazy!" I said.

"Hey-heh-heh, *ain'* it the truth. Deadeye, *ever'*body
knows Ah'm nuthin' but a *cray-zee* nigga," he said, bugging
his eyes and grinning for all he was worth and pointing to
himself with all his fingers. "But shee-it! One a us brothas
gotta be the Crazy Nigga roun' here since Snowflake Surtees
—that chicken-shit fucken shine—took off. Say, m' man,
eat up, hunh? Ah don' make it ta keep m'sef ennertained.
Ah mean, ah'm sorry tha's all they is, but shee-it, Deadeye, ya'll 'uz late fer suppa. Eat up now, ya git sick otha-
wise. Come own. Ah gotta finish up, hey. Ya dudes take yer
time, hunh, an' take it light."

Switching engines—which would have taken Rayburn
till midnight—took those rookie mechanics till dawn, and
later that morning we mounted up and rejoined the battalion on the Tay Ninh road near Check Point Charlie. The
battalion turned north and rolled along at a walking pace
around the Nui Ba Dinh and laagered that night at Prek
Klok. The next morning we moved out early. The road
narrowed and the jungle seemed as close as a crowd. In the
afternoon we pulled into Katum, the last of the backwater
base camps, where we broke for lunch. All the hooches and
mess halls and so forth were well dug in and sandbagged,
and more than a couple were chewed up with mortar hits.
We headed east then south toward Suoi Cut, an abandoned
village. The sun went lower. Jungle dusk was closing in.
The whole column—three line companies, Romeo, Bat-

talion, and a battery of 155-mm self-propelled howitzers—perked up, shivered and awoke, alerted to every funny noise. We had to be getting close. We had to. We had never driven at night, not even the Tay Ninh road, our own turf —except for call-outs.

I called the El-tee. Were we getting close? Within two hundred meters. Then I saw troopers along the ditch, and there were straight-leg grunts lying prone in the ditch all the way to Suoi Cut. (We said the name of the place like we were calling hogs, "Soo-wee! Soo-wee!") On the Rand McNally map it is not the width of a finger away from the Cambodian border. A cart trail split the clearing in half, but there was not one hooch mound, not one stick of cut wood, not the least sign that anyone had ever lived there. Slowly and calmly with each season of rain the jungle gathered it in, like an old spider teasing a dying fly.

Suoi Cut was nothing but a circle on the map, a ragged circle.

Alpha and Bravo companies took up positions on the west side of the laager. Charlie Company and that battalion of straight-leg grunt infantry, the Fourth of the Ninth we heard, moved in on the east side. Romeo pulled into a laager around the battalion headquarters, between the 155s and two airlifted batteries of 105s. By the time we pulled in and shut down, it was dark.

By New Year's Day, Suoi Cut looked completely different. Truck trails and sandbag bunkers, stacks of artillery rounds, deuce-and-a-halfs parked here and there, and bare-chested men walked around with rifles and dusty flak jackets, and the ground was pulverized to dust. The line-company ambushes came in. Relief for the LPs went out. The five Romeo tracks that had been filling in among the Bravo Company tracks dropped off the line. The line companies' dismounted day-sweep patrols left. Chinook resupply choppers came in with C's for the grunts, makings for the artillery mess tents, and ammo all around, escorted by gunships packing fifties and multi-barreled mini-guns, belt-fed grenade launchers and rocket pods. While the Chinook unloaded, the gunships circled low over the woodline.

Davey Cooper, Whiskey j.'s replacement on the six-niner, came around with a note pad where we were leaning on our shovels, filling sandbags for a bunker we would never use, and asked if we needed any supplies. We looked around at each other and looked at him sitting at the edge of the ramp like a person would sit on the edge of a desk. I said, "Shotgun ammo, double-aught buck if I got a choice," took a pause and said, "Cloth sandbags, these plastic motherfuckers ain't for shit," took another pause and said, "And flyswatters. Do ya think we could get some o.d. fly-swatters—the flies is awful thick nights." Cooper let out a laugh and wrote it down.

New Year's Day was another truce day, from six to six. That night the first half of the platoon took its turn on the line. The seven-four pulled in among the Alpha Company first platoon tracks in the ditch by the road. Akins, the TC, was a guy I knew from Basic. There were only two other dudes on the track: Moody, a good driver and a decent mechanic; and Wrye, a tall skinny kid with big brown eyes and bad nerves. The Cow Catcher was assigned to Alpha Company's second platoon, and the seven-two and seven-one pulled on line to the left with the third platoon down the way.

We loaned some claymores to the bunkers on either side of us. The night before, the four of us had celebrated the New Year at ease, with a little smoke and a couple hours of ghost stories, and since January first was New Year's Eve back-in-the-world we hauled out the smoke and the rest of that dried-out fruitcake and celebrated all over again. So while Teddy lounged in the hatch above us, Quinn and Dewey and I lounged on the benches, sitting knee to knee, talking in low voices. Well after dark, we could barely see each other's faces in the starlight. Dewey was telling us about the last New Year's Eve party he'd been to.

"I got so fucken ripped. Wound up passed out under the buffet. Next morning I woke up on the porch mat without a stitch on, and this fat pig of a broad was lying on the floor next to me. *I* don't know what happened, but *she* had a big shit-eating grin and kept hugging me."

"Don't ya know if ya got laid?" asked Quinn.

"Fucken-A, Quinn. I don't even remember taking my clothes off."

"M' man, ya better get yer shit to-gether." And just then a claymore blew. Quinn and I shot our heads up through the crew hatch. To the left a grayish cloud of smoke rose straight into the air, and two troopers lay belly down behind their bunker, looking around themselves. The Alpha Company second platoon leader came over the air.

"What was that? What's going on?"

"Two-six, this is Two-eight," came another, younger voice. "Disregard. Just some short-timer getting one off for the back-in-the-world New Year."

"Send that man to my location," said Two-six, sounding peeved. "And everybody turn down the radios. I can hear all of you."

Quinn turned down the volume until it was just audible. And we sat back again, but barely a moment later the second platoon's LP, three dudes sitting shoulder to shoulder in a foxhole twenty meters into the woods, came over the air. The dude spoke in halting and careful whispers, giving each word its own breath. "Lima. Pa-pa. Two. Got. Move. Ment." I looked at Quinn, then Dewey, and began to rise. The tracks on line got very quiet; quiet enough to hear light sneaking footfalls in the perimeter behind us.

"Lima. Pa-pa. Two," the dude softly whispered again. I knew that he sat scrunched down over his lap, put the mouthpiece ever so close to his lips, and covered his secret message with his hand. "Count six—eight bodies—coming your location."

"Roger," said Alpha Two-six. "Eh, Romeo seven-three? Gimme some recon-by-fire."

I gave him a roger and climbed into the hatch, pushing Teddy up and out. I put on the CVC, cocked the fifty, and swung it around square to the front. Beginning ten meters in front of the woodline, I squeezed off a long burst, walking the rounds up to chest high. I moved the gun to the left and fired, then the right. I swept and fired. A long burst. A short burst. Another long burst. The hundred rounds were gone, scattering hot fifty brass and links around the gun mount and inside around my feet. I reloaded quickly and listened. The LP came back over the air again, whispering quickly, this time giving it in one breath.

"More - bodies - twenty - thirty - boo - coo - can - we - pull *back?*"

"This is Two-six. Negative," the dude said flatly. In other words, goodbye. And all that night I listened for the LP's dying words, a booming shout through the jungle as the gooks stood over them, zipping them up with bursts of AK. "Hey, Alpha Two-six! Fu-uck you! See you in god-damn fucking hell, Two-six!" (But the next morning the three of them, all black dudes, would stumble out of the woods without waiting for relief, dragging the radio and their rifles and such, soaked to the skin and ass-whipped. Their eyes *that* big around as though they'd seen something that would last them to the grave. The dudes would walk past the Cow Catcher, shaking their heads at one another and mumbling, "Nev-ver fucken a-gin, man. Nev-ver fucken a-gin, you hear me?")

Quinn and Teddy moved in behind their guns, bringing boxes of frags and ammo with them and standing on the benches. Dewey took my shotgun and stood in the crew hatch just behind my armor shield, not sure what to do. Teddy, with those lean arms of his, watched Quinn in his black T-shirt and flak jacket all night long, doing what he did.

Then it began—fifties and sixties and frags and AKs and RPGs—down toward the road where the seven-four had parked—frags and claymores and sixteens on auto and more AKs, lots of AKs—on the south side of the laager by Bravo Company and to the east by the grunts. And a moment later Quinn and Teddy and Dewey and I started in, because there they came. First the muzzles and sight blades, then the khaki trousers and handmade, homemade rubber sandals, the black-cloth web gear and straight black hair. A squad of dinks, maybe more. And we all began at once— machine guns and AKs and grenades and RPG rounds coming in hitting somewhere, spraying ice-blue and red and whitish shrapnel. I picked a silhouette or shadow or shirt and pulled off rounds with both thumbs on the butterfly trigger. Long bursts and short bursts. And Quinn and Teddy took turns lobbing grenades, pulling the pins with their thumbs, tossing the pin rings back over their shoulders, counting one thousand one, one thousand two, then heaving the grenades up and over the canopy. Sometimes they got an air burst. A burst of automatic AK fire would tangtangtangtang against the fifty gun shield where I stood, crouching behind the gun. All that noise like cackling and throaty rattling, a junk box poured out on the ground, all clatter and jangle and screaming. The three batteries opened up, firing at will, sailing HE rounds into the jungle, and the shrapnel came back into the laager, whizzing hotly, and sometimes banging against the gun shields with a clang. Then word came down that air strikes were coming in, watch your head, so we slacked off a minute and waited. The Phantoms came in low over the treetops, one after another, dropping canisters of napalm with each pass. Then somebody said that they were calling in the eight-inch and 175 guns from Katum and Suoi Dau. Someone else said there was a break in the line over by the grunts and they were doing it hand-to-fucking-hand, Romeo get ready to pull off the line and move over. And I said, yeah, I could dig it, and Quinn slapped the sixty gun shield with the heel of his hand as much to say, yeah, come on, let's go. But we never did. The Phantoms kept coming, shrieking and screaming low over the clearing, setting napalm fires with each pass. The fifties and pigs and gunships and mini-guns and small arms kept putting out rounds. The dinks kept coming up to the woodline, out into the clearing. We could hear the booming volley after volley of eight-inch and 175s whistling in, getting air bursts, because they could set the fuses for time and had the time down right. The 155s and 105s behind us squeezed off canister rounds point-blank above the screaming and yelling, and Quinn and Teddy lobbed grenades and worked the pigs and I banged out ten- and twenty-round bursts, walking the rounds in and out, in and out of the woodline just as Quinn had done a couple days before. I could hear the Alpha Company CO screaming bloody fucking murder over the radio, screaming so loud we heard him well enough without. And I never moved so fast in my life, tearing open ammo boxes, cocking and firing and cursing, sweated up and squinting with the rest. Alpha Company fire teams moved back and forth behind us trying to find clear fields of fire. There were more incoming mortars and rockets and Chicom grenades, and somebody said a 105 crew got blown away, tube and all, and then gunships came around again with mini-guns and fifties and belt-fed grenades. God, my God, I could hear the wounded screaming, behind us and in the woods and down front. The medics came up to the track on our right and dragged off two dudes, one dude screaming nonsense at the top of his lungs, fuck you fuck you fuck you. There was a rattle of straight-pipe mufflers backing off from high RPMs, and everybody was trying to talk on the radio at once. We kept putting out rounds and more Phantoms came around again, more and more yet—every Phantom in War Zone C, every Phantom in Cochin China—and there was a constant clatter of the mini-guns, spraying red-orange tracers like a cow pissing on a flat rock. The green tracers of the AKs arcing upward, and heavy incoming hit the LZ and battalion oper- ations. And, Jesus, somebody said over the air, Jesus shit, they said, there they are, get'm, get'm, kill'm. Get down and get some.

And the rattle started all over again. A call came for medics and litters and extra hands to report to the LZ on the cart trail, but we just put out rounds and watched the silver and black light from the 105 illumination rounds swinging the shadows back and forth. Another bunch of dinks broke through the woodline off to the right, the dude in front with a pistol and the guy behind with an RPG launcher, locked and loaded. Then blap-slap-slide, there was a whomp! and a blast of gray curling smoke, and when the smoke cleared they were gone and the woodline right behind was in shreds. That's when I remembered our claymores—we still had a dozen claymores out. The gunships—with blinking running lights and landing lights—circled, one behind the other, firing long bursts, brrrrrrap, and the eight-inch and 175s and 155s and 105s came in volleys, ka-rack, and thack- thackthack as the shrapnel caromed through the woods. The medics came back for three dudes in the bunker on our far left and the air strikes settled in on the Bravo Company side of the perimeter. I saw three mo-gas fires and another blew while I looked straight at it—black and gray and scarlet, a brilliant black and fiery orange mushroom, one guy flying off the back in flames. The El-tee came over the air ("Seven-three? Seven-two? Seven-four? Seven-one?" You could hear the worry in his voice as though he was lost himself and hadn't talked to another human for days. Hello? Anybody?), and asked if we were all right. I piped up on the CVC, "Fucken-A bet yer sweet tooties, El-tee." Seven-one and Seven-two answered right after that, but we couldn't raise Seven-four and Dewey wanted to go down and see, but I reached around and grabbed him by the shirt and screamed at him to stay put.

I went through box after box of hundred-round belts, grabbing the fifty with both hands, shoulders hunched and tense, and rolled out twenty-round bursts with both thumbs on the butterfly trigger. The rounds chopped up the corpses that lay in front of us and chewed up the woodline to chest high. The sound, the feel, the thick smell of gunpowder and gritty sweat and smoking thirty-weight oil mixed with a sniff of fear—that sweet sticky ooze—and the sheer physical joy at the noise the fifty made as it tore into the bodies and the woods. The recoil worked its way up my arms until it blurred my vision; until it was an aggravating overpowering ache in the small of my back that dragged me closer—nose to nose—to the sputtering gun flashes and a senseless, rhymeless, fluid madness. But it was not panic. No, it was never panic. Panic does not explain that crackle in the air. It almost amounted to a spark arcing between the thumbs. My body was all used up; all screams and gasps and migraine ache. The barrel smoked and stank white hot, so I poured some thirty-weight on the barrel and feed tray, and it steamed and smoked and smelled of grease. The firefight slacked and thickened, slacked and thickened all night long.

We ran out of grenades and claymores and one of the pigs hanged fire, so Quinn wound up with the shotgun and I used my forty-five, squeezing off well-aimed shots, just like the range.

*

Suddenly the sun rose over the trees. I stood behind the fifty, leaning back against the damp armor shield; my mouth so dry and thick I couldn't work up anything to spit. The air strikes were gone. The Huey and Cobra gunships were gone. The artillery had ceased fire. I stared at shot-up trees and beaten-down woodline grass, blinking my aching eyes, and only when I saw a movement of an arm and flak jacket—some dude stepping gingerly among the corpses to the right—did I understand that the firefight was over. Then I saw the bodies, dozens it seemed like, and a litter of ammo boxes and packing cardboard and the cartridge brass, the dud Chicom grenades and frayed ends of claymore wires—firefight junk—jungle junk.

Quinn still stood in the crew hatch, the shotgun over his forearm, his chin on the stock, his hand and fingers at the trigger.

"You okay?" he asked slowly.

"Yeah," I replied. "You?"

He stirred, laid the shotgun on its side, and rubbed his eyes with the grimy heels of his hands and wiped his mouth on the short sleeve of his black T-shirt. He nodded his head a couple times and muttered, "Mmmm." Then he stepped back a step and slumped down inside next to Dewey, who sipped water from a canteen, spitting each mouthful out the doorway. I bent over to climb down and pain shot up my back. I thought I might be wounded and did not know it. I stood straight, arching my back, and reached under my flak jacket, touching the small of my back with the back of my hand. No, it was nothing, just that old pain. I climbed down then, ignoring the pain, and slouched down next to Teddy, who sat against the battery box, asleep, leaning his head against the empty Igloo cooler. The three of us traded swigs from the canteen to get that flat taste of cordite, gunpowder, out of our mouths, but it wasn't much good. After a while I motioned for Dewey to get into the hatch. Quinn reached into his AWOL bag, got two cigars and gave me one. He wetted his from end to end, lit both of them, puffed a couple puffs, turning the cigar in his mouth as he did. Then after a long moment he said, "They're fucken maniacs, ya know. Crazy fucken goddamn maniacs. They gonna kill us all."

He poured some water on his hand and rubbed it on his face. I climbed out the rear door and turned east, walking down the line of Alpha Company tracks toward the seven-four. I limped on both legs. A warm itching pain tickled my thighs. My knees cracked from the stiffness. My feet prickled and felt swollen. There was a sore cramp in my thumbs and palms and wrists, and the calluses were red. My body was hot and my flak jacket slid back and forth across my shoulders on the sweat and grit. I walked behind the Alpha Company tracks in a fog of cordite and morning mist. The men sat behind the tracks, facing away from the woodline, not twenty meters distant, sitting on their steel pots with their rifles in their laps; on somebody's waterproof which ballooned like a bean-bag chair, eating C rations with plastic spoons; laid out on the ground with a poncho liner drawn over their eyes, asleep; cross-legged and bare-chested, cleaning rifles; or busy setting out live claymores. All of them bare-headed and sweaty filthy, trading swigs around, talking among themselves; not noticing me much. Pale, greasy faces, weary wary tones in the voices, a slump to the shoulders, those morning-after darkened, sunken bleary eyes—squinting, the faces almost grimacing in the sharp sunlight. Brownish teeth and that hangdog know-nothing expression; that slow, death-march measured movement, like I remember from so many ambush mornings. They oiled guns and ate breakfast and washed up and changed clothes—standing naked for that moment—almost anything to keep from looking over their shoulders at all those corpses.

In the trampled grass between the tracks and the woodline lay the groups and gangs, ragged lines and files and clusters of the dead; six or eight or ten here, three or four behind a fallen barkless tree limb, ten or so over there, and blood trails leading back into the jungle. One corpse leaned against a tree, one hand on his stomach, the other on his chest, sitting in a pool of sticky black muck. A young NCO, a dusty-tinted black guy with dark freckles and orangish hair, and more energy than most, said he had watched the guy crawl there. The dink died sometime around dawn, he said, but he wasn't sure; didn't really know; could care less.

The seven-four straddled the near ditch, the fifty barrel pointing to the sky. There didn't seem to be anything wrong, except no one was in the hatch, watching forward. On the ground around it were M-16 magazines and cartridges, a couple dozen empty ammo boxes and packing cardboard, helmets and the plastic wrappings of field bandages and so forth, scattered like someone had cleared a workbench of junk with a sweep of an arm. I stuck my head in the rear door, expecting to see Moody and Akins and Wrye sitting in back, eating breakfast or wiping down guns, or taking a break. There was no one, just more empty ammo boxes, brass cartridges and links and more empty magazines, rifles and loose sixteen ammo, bloody shirts and ragged blood-soaked flak jackets and bloody handprints on the floor, and two RPG holes—one on the right side next to the TC hatch and one square to the front of the driver's seat, in front of Moody's face, if he'd been sitting there—and a thick scatter of shrapnel nicks. Opened and unused cans of fifty and sixty ammo lined the bench. The machine guns were still loaded, just abandoned. Grenades hung from a couple hand straps, like strings of onions; beat-up shot-up waterproofs packed in along the sides; and somebody's leg—boot and bloused trouser and all—just back of the driver's seat. Moody's, by the look of smeared grease-gun grease just above the knee. I jerked bolt upright, sucking a long breath, and turned quickly on my heels and moved to the side and leaned against the chill, damp armor, looking toward the woodline not twenty meters away and the high crown of the road and the shallow, grassy ditches. The night before, all the yelling and the slamming of bolts, all the bloody screaming for medics had come from here. In front of the seven-four, along both ditches and the edge of the woodline and among the low wet bushes in the open, were the bodies. Thirty, fifty, maybe more. Their issue khakis nicked with shrapnel and bullet holes, stiff with blackish blood and streaked with grass stains, and web gear soaked through with the morning wet. The bodies laid among AKs and thirty-round magazines and Chicom grenades and dud U.S. grenades, the frayed ends of blown claymores and dud claymores, chunks of trees and jungle junk blown out of the canopy, and a soft film of grayish dust. The gray dead faces shone with a sweaty grease. The dew droplets in their hair sparkled, like cobwebs sparkle in a cool and damp sunrise. They sprawled in grotesque clown postures with the shrieks frozen to their eyes and lips, and the curled fingers and filthy nails clinging with chalky dust and damp bits of grass. Some had been dead all night, some had lain there and struggled and died, crying and calling for water in dry-throated whispers under the pounding of the guns. Some had managed to crawl off to lay out and die among the trees, and some had shinnied, low-crawl fashion, close enough to the seven-four to reach up and touch it. And among the corpses moved the body-count detail, stepping over and around the bodies like they were holes in the earth, looking very much like the bodies on the ground, smeared with greasy dust and morning wet, and dressed in flak jackets or o.d. T-shirts or bare-chested because they couldn't find shirts. "Forty-seven, forty-eight, forty-nine, fifty," that young NCO counted, pointing with two fingers here and there and yonder. The others counted, too, agreeing with nods and yeahs. The only guy wearing a steel pot held a sheet of 25th Division blue-lined letterhead writing paper in his hand and scratched dit dit dit dit slash, crinkling the paper with his bit of pencil as he wrote. The other men coming along behind stripped the bodies for the clothes—the bright tin web-gear buckles with the embossed star and the rubber sandals, the wallets and the cash—stepping where the detail stepped and whipping out their Minoltas and Nikons and Kodak Instamatics, snapping shots and staring down at the bloody faces and bloody ashen hands and saying among themselves, "Yeah, *this* here's the dink," and *"I* shot this one here, I *'member* this cocksucker. Watch out for that dud there, Franny," and *"Shit*, boy, will ya look at this one," his buttocks all but torn off, ragged lumps of spine exposed, and black with flies already. That's when I noticed that hum; that itch in the air; that dimmed quality to the sunlight. Swarms of flies. The bodies lay in odd groups, some on top of the one before, and stared back at the onlookers, but never twitched the slightest twitch. The detail walked slowly into the woods, going carefully for fear of the bodies being booby-trapped, which had happened to Bravo Company more than once.

Quinn walked down the line with my shotgun over one shoulder, carrying a canteen cup of steaming C-ration instant coffee and looking at the corpses I was looking at.

"Here," he said, turning to look at me. He handed me the shotgun and the canteen cup. "It's fucken garbage, I know, but it'll help ya get that fucken taste a gunpowder and shit outa yer mouth. An' the El-tee called an' wants ta see ya. He's over that way some-fucken-place," and he pumped his thumb south. "That's fucked up, ain't it?" he said pointing to the corpses with his eyes. "Moody? Akins? Wrye? Where you at?" he shouted.

"Gone," I said. "I'll ask the El-tee." I turned and walked off toward the center of the laager, sipping from the canteen cup. The coffee was scalding hot and bitter and gritty with dust. I spit it out and threw the rest in an arc on the ground. I limped on sore feet and aching knees and cramped thighs, leaving Quinn peeking in the back of the seven-four. I walked through the artillery batteries, where the artillerymen were busy clearing away, filling more sandbags, unpacking more rounds, and burning the unused bags of cordite. The wooden ammo box fires crackled, then sparkled and flashed as the dudes tossed bagfuls of charges into the flames, and that thick gunpowder tang hung in the air for days and became a parched and bitter, nauseating dryness in our throats.

I found the six-niner and the seven-zero parked back to back on the other side of the battalion operations command tracks. Sergeant Corso—Surtees' replacement as Platoon Sergeant—squatted on his steel pot, among a group of walking wounded, watching a No. 10 can of water on a fire of C-4 chunks. The fire hissed and crackled and burned white hot.

Corso was in his middle thirties, early forties; had

touches of gray hair. When he grew his handlebar mustache it was sprinkled with gray, too. He had been one of the NCOs at the tank range at Fort Hood—a number-fucking-one housecat job if there ever was one—but mouthed off to some chicken colonel, he said, and was on the next plane. He was a decent scrounger; had hustled Haskins for eggs and bacon and No. 10 cans of fruit, and real ground coffee.

That's what he was doing when I walked up, making campfire coffee.

"Mornin', Deadeye," he said, looking around, as though I'd pulled up to a crowd of hardware-store porch loafers, leaning against the plate glass. Then everybody there, the track crews and walking wounded—still waiting for dust-offs—howdied and mumbled, "Glad ta see ya" and "Wasn't that a pisser?" and I rogered back, nodding. Everybody had a bit of story to tell; how they came to be wounded, how they came not to be wounded—what had happened. We sat around that C-4 fire on uncomfortable water cans and empty 105 fuse boxes, flimsy wood-and-wire cases of machine-gun ammo cans, and along the edge of a bunker. Some tried to laugh and make light cracks, but the wounded sat stoically, trying not to jostle, and waited for the coffee to boil and steep. Stepik was trying to sleep on the top of the bunker with his arm over his eyes—his aid bag lumped on his bare stomach—so while the conversation jumped around I hunted up a poncho liner and covered him. "Thank ya, Flip," he said. When the subject came around to the seven-four Cooper said that Akins and Moody were not KIA, just dusted off. The crew of the seven-five, two dudes from the seven-eight, and all four dudes from the seven-six, the Texarkana Poontang, got dusted off, too.

All I could think was: the poor seven-six gets it in the neck again.

"And what about Wrye?"

"He's inside," Corso said, "but he ain't a hunnurd percent. He's just waiting for the next load of walking wounded to be called for. Altogether there's twelve, maybe thirteen dudes hit. Dano, from the seven-six, nobody knows for real. Bravo Company thinks they dusted him off, but they ain't sure. This morning Bravo Company ain't too sure 'bout anything, 'cause they got troubles a their own. Three a their tracks burned and they got boo-coo wounded and boo-coo KIA. They 'bout hangin' in there by the slack in the skin on their balls. Charlie Company got boo-coo dusted off, same's that battalion a grunts. But, Deadeye, dig this: Brigade figures it was a fucken *regiment* that hit us; some off-the-fucken-wall major was already here this mornin' and I heard him tell somebody at Operations there could be five, six hundred bodies, 'cause there's fucken body count all *over* the fucken place," and he pointed with his chin in an arc and a wave of his hand at the perimeter.

"Yeah. No shit. Say, m' man, the El-tee said he wants ta see me," I said.

"Yeah," said Corso, pouring out cups of coffee at last, "but it can wait for the coffee. He's in the back there with Wrye, sacked out."

I sat down on somebody's duffel bag, my hands warming around the canteen cup, then I pressed them, palm and fingers, firmly against my eyes. Behind me, among the Colonel's collapsible map table and aluminum-and-plastic lawn chairs, two housecat captains buzzed back and forth with that morning-after command-bunker bullshit conversation, saying, "Whooie! Plenty dinks bought the fucken farm *last* night. Major says I'm in for a Silver Star," and so forth.

The El-tee was asleep on the gas-tank side bench with one hand thrust between his thighs, the other thrown over some ammo cans under the TC hatch. Wrye sat on the other bench, his elbows on his knees, his hands around half a canteen cup of coffee that someone had just given him. A filthy tan bandage was tied round his chest, tied tight with two thick knots. His shirt, stiff with blood under his left arm, was simply draped over his shoulders. A wounded tag, a shipping-tag-looking thing, with a morphine syrette pinned to it, was wired to one of the buttonholes.

Wounded change. He had blackish leathery wrinkles around his reddened eyes, that stare that wounded sometimes get. Granger had it. Wrye's skin was pale, almost grayish, even though he'd been in the field four or five months. He stared down at the cup in his hands, or maybe his stockinged feet, or maybe the dusty mud-crusted floor, or maybe nothing. Maybe he contemplated the holes in his side—which ached every time he inhaled, he said, like he'd had the wind knocked out of him—the scratchy feel of a blood-stiffened shirt, the warmth of the coffee in his filthy, callus-stiffened hands. Maybe he was thinking back. Moody blown off the side by the concussion, leaving his leg, which gushed blood for a couple more beats; Akins standing in the TC hatch, pounding out rounds at the top of his lungs, but sinking lower because his legs were going numb and he couldn't hold himself up anymore, and so ended up firing those last long bursts into the air.

"Wrye?" I whispered. "Hey, Wrye, you okay?"

"Dosier. . . . I don't . . ." His hands shook the cup and some coffee splashed. "Don't look at me. . . . They just . . . We had . . ." Then he took a breath. "We just kept firing. . . . Akins kept killing them. . . . I *saw* them die. . . . The way the heads exploded sometimes, the bellies, *arms* came off. . . . They just wouldn't stop coming at us, shouting. And the whole time Akins screaming like a crazy man and bleeding from the legs, and Moody . . . Moody's leg sat there the whole time . . . Laces tied and all." He winced and jerked his head to the side, sniffed in a breath and winced again in pain. "God, Dosier, we had to do it. . . . Didn't we? A grenade hit me on the side of the face. . . . It stung, like it was a baseball. . . . You ever get hit with a baseball, Dosier? I'm s'posed to be dead," he said, whispering more than ever and shaking his head slowly from side to side. "I should be dead, shouldn't I?" And then tears welled in his eyes, sparkling them, and rolled down his face one right after another. Then he dropped his chin to his chest and the tears dropped to the floor between his stockinged feet.

Then all of a sudden the El-tee sat up. "Donny," he said. "Listen up, Donny, gimme that coffee, and you lay down. I'll get Stepik to give you some more Darvon. It's okay, Donny. You're not going to have to do it anymore. Akins did not die. Moody is going to be all right, you'll see." He took the cup out of Wrye's hands and pushed him over so that he lay on the bench and slipped a folded poncho liner under his head. "Come on, Dosier, we can talk outside."

The El-tee rubbed his face and found his steel pot and rifle, and poured himself a cup of coffee. "I want the Cow Catcher to take up the seven-six's position. There's more ammo and shit comin' in later this morning, so no sweat about that. They're bringing in fresh troops, too, as soon as they can get the choppers.

"Now go on, Coop will show ya where to set up. Wrye's goin' home. Alpha Company put him and Akins and Moody in for Silver Stars; says the seven-four counts for thirty-some bodies."

"Yes, sir, I know. I had a look," I said.

To the south on the Bravo Company side of the laager, the woodline was thirty meters down range. Just back of the perimeter three burnt-out tracks wallowed in puddles of shining aluminum-alloy armor plate. Whole pieces were scattered between, rounded and warped by the heat, and soft-looking. The gun mounts and decks, all the sides—everything but the steel plates in the floors—had been incinerated. The rubber pads on the tread cleats and solid-rubber tires on the road wheels were burned away, and the treads lay slack, like huge rubber bands. Ashes of rags and scraps of unopened metal ammo boxes—that had been cooking off all night—and a greasy, shiny soot covered everything. And the stink of rubber and gunpowder and scorched iron was thick and heady.

Line-company tracks carried lots of gear and a little ammo. The Romeo tracks carried lots of ammo and a little gear: six or eight thousand rounds of fifty and sixty ammo, boxes of frags and a couple dozen claymores, and C-4 and blasting caps and detonation cord. So the seven-six, the one in the middle, had all the cooked-off ammo boxes. Shivers had third-degree burns and lost an arm. Temple and Meyer, the gunners, had been blown off the back, burned some and cut up some.

Dewey brought the Cow Catcher around and pulled on line. The four of us gathered around the seven-six, looking down at it—the bottom of the driver's-seat post still bolted to the floor, the oily ammo boxes, twisted and exploded a hundred times by the cooking ammo. Heat rose in waves and there was the whiff of rubber. And then I saw. The ridge of the temple, an eyehole, the bones of fingers at an arm's length, the tips and ridges and hollows of a pelvis among the ashes and engine parts too hard to distort by fire. A body covered with that rubber and cloth smudge, like a carcass picked clean, then brought in with an oil-slick tide, half in, half out of the sand.

It could be a trick. I was so tired. My eyes and fists and thighs ached. I stared down at it. The eyehole, the hip, the small bones of the thumb.

"Dewey," I said. "Go get the El-tee. That's Dano. Go get the El-tee and Stepik and a poncho."

He looked down. His mouth opened and he took a long breath. Then he looked over at me.

"Get a fucken poncho or a bodybag and the El-tee and a fucken medic." But he did not move. "Do like you're told. Git!"

A moment later the El-tee and Stepik came, stumbling over clods of dirt and sandbags and junk, coming fast.

"Where is he? Where is he?" they said as they came. I pointed to the body, the ashes, the sooty chunks of junk. Dewey came back with a long-handled spade and his brand-new poncho.

"Go ahead, Dosier," said the El-tee. "Get it. Get it quick. Do it. You there, lay out that poncho, and you, Dosier, you dig."

I stepped closer and put a foot up. The wreckage was still hot; it would have smoked if it could. I grasped the shovel tightly until my knuckles turned white, and with the blade end pushed and scraped aside the boxes. The flesh was burned away; the carcass—almost unrecognizable as a human corpse—charred black. The skull was torn and snagged with pieces of shrapnel and cooked-off fifty-caliber slugs, and the greasy ashes of waterproofs and duffels full of clothes smothered the bones, like sludge. I worked the shovel under the pelvis, pushing and pulling until I could pick it up. As I lifted him out and set him on the poncho, feathery flakes of ash fell off in the breeze. There was flesh still clinging around his pelvis and the short length of backbone that came with it. I put him down quickly and turned to look for more. I shoveled out a belt buckle and shards of bone and snips of shrapnel and fingers and boxes. Then I threw down the shovel. Stepik made to bend down and pull the corners of the poncho together, but I pushed him away.

"I'll do it all," I said, and drew the corners together.

Stepik pulled a roll of wounded tags from his thigh pocket. We filled in the information the best we could and then Stepik twisted the wire around the gathered corners.

The three of us went back to the six-niner. The poncho banged against my leg as I walked, and everyone we passed turned and looked at the poncho and knew there was a body in it, a body light enough for one man to tote. The greasy bones and blackened flesh and shrapnel pieces and poncho rubber made soft crunching noises each time it hit my leg, and I walked fast, trying to hold the sack away from me. The wounded tag flapped against my wrist and the wire cut into my hand. I set the poncho in the shade of the El-tee's track, and turned away, rubbing the wire cut on my palm, spitting on it and working the spit into the cut with my thumb. The three of us stood looking down at the body until Cooper went into his waterproof and came back with a bottle of back-in-the-world gin his father had sent him too late for Christmas. He broke the seal and took a long pull, then passed it to me. I raised it to my lips and closed my eyes. I don't like the taste of gin, but took three quick sucking swigs. My eyes teared and I choked before I could take the bottle away from my lips. My throat and mouth and stomach and head burned. We passed the bottle back and forth until it was empty, and then I walked back to the Cow Catcher.

Dano was one of the new guys. He wore a gun glove and we used to laugh at him because he didn't want to get calluses on his gun hand. Once we were called out in the middle of the night, and I watched him running down to the motor pool with his flak jacket and grenades, pulling that glove tight on his hand, trying to keep his running balance with his shoulders. But none of that meant anything anymore, because the poncho didn't weigh twenty pounds.

Dewey and Quinn sat in back, rolling smokes from his Prince Albert tobacco can, and Teddy stood in the hatch.

We sat and smoked and tried to eat and cleaned guns one at a time. When the Chinook resupply choppers came they parceled out the ammo, the fifty and M-60 ammo and frags and double-aught buckshot. Out front a bulldozer scraped up a ditch and the Bravo Company detail began burying the bodies, dragging them out of the woodline, stripping the gear, and rolling them in. They put out a call for more men to work.

Quinn? Dewey? Fuck off, they said.

Later that morning a Chinook came in with a load of newsmen, looking so bad-ass spiffy in their Saigon-cowboy suits—starched tiger fatigues, spit-shined boots, and silly fucking bush hats.

Yessiree! The Great Truce Day Body Count! All you got to do to get on the dinnertime news is blow away more people than live in Hadleyburg; sit up all night nipping gooks, and then lounge around the grave site cleaning your nails and picking your teeth, waiting your turn to be interviewed by some housecat with a dick job and a shorthand notebook—but don't forget to sweep up a little so the folks think you're neat, and comb your hair a little like the old days so Ma knows it's you. There was a free-lance camera clown, Korean or Japanese, and a network newsman with slicked-back gray hair, slinging a tape recorder over his shoulder with the mike to his mouth, looking for all the world like a playground director. He and the dude with the 16 mm walked fast, making it around the seven-six just in back of us, not even taking the time to look down and figure out what it used to be, like it was garbage in the gutter, and went straight for the grave.

The dude with the 16 mm waltzed up and asked if he could stand on the deck so he could get a better shot.

"Shore," I said, getting up from the bench. "Why, just *any*-fucken-thing for the workin' press!"

"But first ya got to take ma fucken picture," said

Quinn, flicking his ash and pointing to himself with his smoke. "Take *all* our pictures. An' I'll take *yer* fucken picture. Jus' let us get our guns an' shit, an' take our picture an' you kin stan' any-fucken-place you wan'. Stan' on yer fucken head, f'rall I fucken care." So the guy stood there with that camera resting on his shoulder, while we dragged out clean shirts and our bush hats and some ammo belts and bandoliers and pineapple frags, machine guns and rifles and forty-fives, worn low on the hips, and my shotgun. We stood in a loose semicircle and John Wayned it for the guy, standing there spraddled-legged and reared back, grinning real bad-like and laughing, having ourselves a good old-fashioned hawhawhaw. He panned back and forth a couple times and then said that was it, so I helped him up to the deck with an oopsie-whoopsie-daisy and he stood behind Teddy's sixty and took his movies. By then the reporter had the Bravo Company CO by the shirt and the two of them stood in front of the grave while Bravo Company helped the bodies into the ditch with a flip of a boot—the dude with the 16 mm clicking and grinding away to a fare-thee-well.

"And Bravo Comp-nay did this an' we did that, ya see. Now, the straight-leg grunts o'er there was dukin' it with the gooks hand ta hand, but that ain't nuthin', 'cause Bra-vo Comp-nay, why, we is jus' 'bout the most evil bunch a motherfuckers in this whole val-ley. Yessireebob, if it hadn't been for Bra-vo Comp-nay—the name is Rock, Captain Richard Rock, Are-oh-cee-kay, sir—if it hadn't been for the Bra-vo Comp-nay these gooks'd be coming ashore at San Dee-ay-go. No shit!"

I leaned against the armor smoking my smoke, watching Mr. Network slick back his hair, taking down every lie with a straight face. I wanted to shout: Hey, dipstick! Come on over here! See this garbage here? A gun-glove freak burned right down to his socks at this very place. All this silver junk and that black junk used to be just like the Cow Catcher here. See that there, that's fingers and that's most of an arm, and under that box is an ankle and foot. I'm sorry about the rest, but if ya want ta catch it, go on down to the six-niner and the El-tee will be tickled pink to show you the sack, or maybe you can catch it before they throw it aboard the KIA dust-off. But he just kept standing there, jacking his jaw while Bravo Six, that skinny fucking lifer, rapped him a crock of bullshit.

Then some dude with a red Santa Claus beard and a 35-mm camera slid up to us as we sat around the back, smoking.

"My name is Fuziozoopopolis," he said, or something fucked up and dufus-sounding like that. "I'm from UPI," or was it the AP?

"Yeah?" I said, looking up. "No shit."

"Yes," he said, putting a leg up on the ramp, chummy fashion. "Say, what do you men think about all this?"

I glanced over at Quinn. "Say? Think?" I said, "Am I s'posed ta think something?"

"My name is Quinn," said Quinn. "Cue-you-eye-en-en."

"You were here last night, right? I mean, what's on your mind right now?" the guy said, bending forward, note pad poised.

"His name is Dosier, Dee-oh-es-eye-ee-are," said Quinn.

"See that garbage back there? Found a dude in that this morning. See them dinks in the ditch? Fuck 'em. But say, m' man, lemme ask you a question. Why the fuck you come out here?"

"Don't you know? I'm a journalist. You're news this morning."

"Yeah? No shit. You wanna real story?" I said.

"This is Dewey, Dee-ee-double-you-ee-why," said Quinn.

"Yeah, that's what I'm here for."

"Up 'ere is Teddy, Tee-ee-dee-dee-why," said Quinn, looking straight up through the crew hatch. "Take a fucken bow, Ted."

"I'll fix it with the Colonel so you can ride with us, and get the real lowdown. Coming out here after it's all over is candy-ass—*his* speed, dig. But a young buck like you? Why, a couple of one-man ambushes, couple of weeks on the line, couple of no-shit firefights like this one, and a little luck, why, you'll probably run out of paper. How about it? It'll be worth millions. They'll probably whip the Pew-litz-er fucken Prize on your ass."

But he said no. His mama didn't raise no fool.

"And tell the folks back home that we're all gonna re-up an' stay on till the last fucken dog is dead," Quinn said, nodding his head.

Back home they'll broadcast the two minutes of film showing the detail collecting the weapons in one pile and the khaki scraps in another, but not the footage of Bravo Company stumbling around in a gunpowder fog with all the sweat run out of their bodies, trying to catch their breath long enough to choke down C's to keep their water up, nor the puddles around the seven-six. You'll see the Chinooks bringing in fresh meat with full packs and ammo and the touching scenes of the rows and rows of bodybags, but not the lumpy ponchos. And while the dude with the 16 mm watched the three dudes from the Bravo Company LP sitting exhausted on a bunker and passing a warm can of Ballantine—the last beer in the company—he missed the eight litters coming up the road covered with blankets and shirts and flak jackets, the arms and feet dangling over the side and bouncing up and down as the litter bearers humped along, not looking too well themselves. The Bravo Company ambush had eight KIAs a half hour before Bravo Company ever fired a shot.

Even though the detail had been working the better part of the morning there were still bodies all over—mutilated by 105 canister rounds and claymores and point-blank fifty rounds and grenades and a crack across the face with a two-by-four; wrapped around trees or hunkered together like books or sprinkled along the ditches. An entire platoon got caught on the road fifty meters down and laid out to a man by Phantoms and gunships. Bodies lay in groups and gangs among the AKs and Chicom grenades and blood in the deep grass, and the detail could hardly make a dent in getting rid of them. In the mass grave each tier of bodies was covered over with shovelfuls of dirt and bags of quicklime. Then the detail would go back for more. One trooper on each arm, if there were enough arms, and shuck it down—field gear in one pile, rifles in another, personal shit in the third. Then they'd heave-ho. Sometimes the heads would meet, hard enough to raise a lump and a migraine, and loud enough to hear.

And Bravo Company just digging the hell out of it—though some of the fucking new guys started to wear o.d. handkerchiefs over their mouths—going through the gear, snatching up the silver belt buckles with the embossed star and the little pouches of smoke and the cash, the Ho Chi Minh tire-track sandals and letters from home scribbled on Victory Newsletter tissue paper, signed Ma or Sis or You-Know-Who. I sauntered up to one gook, face down in the burned-out grass with the back of his shirt full of holes and stiff with blood, like a piece of cardboard, and twitching with flies. I yanked his AK out from under him, scrounged a sandbagful of thirty-round magazines, and let it go at that.

The collage of death poses, the pale gray skin, the curled fingers scraping the grass ash and filmy dirt. Some sticking their tongues out of bloody black mouths, one dink with his head sheared off at the jaw with his black tongue laid out on his lowers, looking for all the world like somebody took his head off with a swipe of a hand. One dude with eyes tight, lips open, the wrinkled laugh lines and frown lines, and black blood down to here from the mass of dried shredded junk hanging from the chest—the dink caught a claymore fair and square. And the dudes behind him hanging on to one another. The dead leading the dead, all in line, and all laid out. Another dude fell on a trip flare and it burned and burned, so he got buried with the ass end of it sticking out of his ribs. Thousands and thousands, the parade of dead men keeps coming. You get so tired of watching, like at a boring ball game. The pitcher leans over chewing his cud, looking for the sign, then he skylarks around kneading the rosin bag, hanging on it like a tit, while twenty thousand housecats hope he throws it for the mouth. More and more bodies came out of the woodline. A couple lay in the ditch in front of us with their knees up and their heads back, flies in their eyes and ringed round the bullet holes, like horses round a windmill well. All afternoon everybody on the perimeter got to take snapshots of them. And we kept finding bodies in the jungle for a month, leaning against trees with their pith helmets and rusted AKs in their laps. The skin drawn tight and humming with jungle bugs.

Cooper came around with a sandbag full of forty-five magazines and the flyswatters and told us that Westhisface was coming out to see for his own lonesome self, but later that afternoon we had some incoming rounds, so I guess he called it off. The El-tee told us to clean up a little anyway, but we kept smoking our Cambodie smokes and took turns trying to nap and swatted flies.

There was more incoming down along the LZ where the mo-gas and ammo and C's were stacked, and just that quick the whole laager opened fire. The LPs didn't even ask what was happening, they just squeezed down into their foxholes and froze. All the gunners, and me among them, kept it up until the guns smelled of thirty-weight oil and burnt frying pans. The dinks were back—they were there by the thousands. It was almost like an echo; you could hear the loud sloppy smacking of lips as everybody bent over to kiss their assholes goodbye, then did John Waynes, all hunkered down and cannibal, waiting for the dink hordes. Quinn and Dewey and Teddy and I looked the hardest, because they burned the seven-six to the ground the night before and I was too young to die. But it never happened.

We had air strikes for three days solid, and constant H & I from Suoi Dau and Katum. That night the ground shook with a B-52 strike, and later in the morning when it was still dark we had two more and nobody got any sleep, and it was that way for something like a week. The ground buzzed hotly with flies, always murmuring, and began to stink that jungle stink, saturated with a death stench like the thick smell of sleep around an unmade bed. It soaked into our clothes and eyes and settled in our food and clung to our skin like the dust.

A couple days after the big firefight Romeo and the other line companies left the laager, pulling sweeps during the day and sitting on tight laagers at night, and we had incoming every night but one. And everywhere we went was a free-fire zone. One afternoon we drove up to a cart and buffalo, standing out in the middle of nowhere, chewing his cud. I blew him away with a quick sweeping burst of fifty. That night we sent the cart in with the resupply and Headquarters Company set it up in front of the Orderly Room with a sign: "Captured by Romeo Seven-three." The next day we rolled along a trail, looking for rice caches and finding them, and surprised three dinks leaning against an anthill, taking a break. We blew them away as they ran for the woods. We piled the rice, something like a couple tons, I guess, nice and high and poured mo-gas on it and burned it right then and there. It burned slow and popped and the embers glowed all night, silhouetting everything. Another afternoon we fought our way into a battalion-sized base camp and found two bunkers stacked with o.d. Ho Chi Minh bicycles, so we took the rest of the afternoon off and got a little higher, and dicked around with the bicycles until dark. Quinn came across a GI waterproof with a pair of dink shorts and a couple shirts, a greasy plastic baggie of NVA dope—some real garbage—a comic book crammed from cover to cover with bad drawings of Yankee gangsters, evil-eyed henchmen, and the lackeys of the imperialist conspiracy biting the dust left and right, and cross my heart and hope to die, two powder-blue medium-sized sweat shirts with the manufacturer's stamp that read: "Made in Hanoi" —in English, I kid you not.

Another afternoon Bravo Company called us out to scrape up one of their platoons that got ambushed. We busted jungle for the better part of a morning, and when we pulled up the four dudes left huddled back to back in the tightest perimeter I have ever seen, with the wounded in the middle and the KIA outside. We loaded everybody up and backed off because the El-tee called in an air strike, and I came over the air and asked if he could get them to burn that whole fucking woods.

We kept moving around. Up near the border. Back this way. We moved and sat the night, and moved again the next morning. I made a deal with Stepik for some Darvons. I'd sit the last guard, pop a couple Darvons with my morning coffee, do a smoke, then we'd mount up and break camp. We busted jungle and deep rubber with happy-go-

lucky Deadeye ("a dozen smiles to the mile") Dosier leaning gunslinger fashion against the armor tub—my shotgun
and gas-mask bag of shells on one side and my AK and
sandbag full of thirty-round magazines on the other—humming some catchy little tune and regaling Dewey on the
crew phone with incredible stories of incredible R & R
fucks. Right around that time word came down for us to be
very careful in the rubber trees, because the U.S. Government had to pay the Michelin Rubber Plantation fifteen
hundred dollars, or something like, for each tree we demol-
ished. So after that we never missed a chance to take a poke
at one, even if we only nicked it.

And then it was the middle of February all of a great
sudden and the whole can of worms picked up and went
back to camp. The seven-seven towed the seven-four. It
would be stripped and turned in for scrap. The bulldozer
dug a hole for the seven-six and buried it. We cranked south
along a cart trail, then took the road past Suoi Tre and Fire
Base Grant and French Fort and Suoi Dau, then hit the convoy road in the middle of the afternoon. The Cow Catcher
finally gave out, so the six-niner towed us the rest of the
way, and being towed is like sitting in a piping-hot steam
bath while some clown pours bushel basket after bushel
basket of vacuum-cleaner dirt over your head. Our part of
the convoy finally rumbled through the gate around nine or
so. The next day Quinn and Dewey would discover slivers
of RPG shrapnel in the gas line.

That night the line companies and Romeo parked
among the perimeter bunkers because of some rumor of an
attack on the camp, but the Cow Catcher crew fired up the
squat stove and laid back, smoking our smokes.

The next morning the gas-line shrapnel settled in a
corner long enough for the Cow Catcher to limp into the
motor pool on its own. We drove at a walking pace along

the perimeter road, past the rear of the Romeo tents where a bunch of fucking new guys stood leaning out the doorways and over the low sandbag walls, watching us pass. Somebody dismounted from each track at the motor-pool entrance and walked ahead. One at a time we pulled up, backed into place, and shut down. The seven-seven dropped the seven-four near the mechanics' shack, then pulled up and shut down too. And for that moment the twenty-some of us stood and sat and slumped motionless, letting the grinding, rattling echoes die away.

One by one we roused from our stupor and slowly climbed down. We stood in that ankle-deep silt, wearily glancing up and down the line of tracks, looking blankly into one another's eyes. Then we straggled off to the mess hall in a gang, hangdog fashion—one foot in front of the other. Nobody bothered to unload the fifties or sixties or take off their flak jackets or wash up or change into clean fatigues—nobody had clean, anyway—and we lined up last of all at the screen doors, feeling raunchy and scroungy and pissed off. That stink of garbage and jungle junk and such followed us, and even the dink KPs held their noses when we crowded in. Akins sat there with a GI cane hung on the back of his chair and his legs still bandaged, but he hadn't seen Moody or the others in a month.

I want an egg and some bacon. Fuck the bread. Fuck the apples. Fuck the Kool-Aid. There was tepid powdered milk and the ass end of scrambled eggs, and Haskins, who looked like he'd lost some weight, even Haskins, whose head did not fuck easily, mumbled something goofy while he doled out hefty scoops of mushy eggs. I told him about the seven-four and the seven-six and the bicycles and the sweat shirts, but he did not laugh or even crack a smile. "Glad ya made it, m' man," was all he said. The five Romeo TCs left sat at one table on the NCO side, filling it with guns and elbows and mess-kit tablespoons and tin mess-hall trays, still dripping wet with soap. It soaked into the eggs and they tasted bitter and slippery. And the housecats, the young looies and senior NCOs that had more brains than to go to the field, asked us to eat outside; we were smelling up their mess hall.

Well listen, buddy, I wanted to say, if you don't like the way I eat, blow it out yer ass. I just got back from thirty-some days on the border, counting fucking dinks, and if you can't dig it—if you can't fucking dig us coming into your mess hall, write your fucking Congress. I'm taking a break. Go shuffle yer papers.

We stayed and stayed until Haskins finally came around and bought us off with a couple smokes.

*

The next morning Dewey flew to Bien Hoa with a couple other dudes to pick up replacement tracks—he was going to be the new TC on the seven-six. I took him aside the night before; took him by the shirt, telling him that the seven-six was jinxed, nothing but bad luck, but he wanted badly to be a TC and didn't listen. They came back that night and he showed me a gunmetal-black ankh cross made of coat-hanger wire, and about the size of my palm, hanging around his neck on a leather thong.

"This take care of it?" he said, dangling it under his chin.

"No," I said, but that was all I said.

The day after that Romeo went back to work, pulling convoys. Out in the morning. Back in the early evening. Parties every night. I slept in the track. I just could not sleep in the tent. The lumps in the sleeping bag wouldn't settle. The canvas felt odd. The blanket scratched my arms. The rats under the floorboards would not get quiet. At night the armor was still warm and I could light the squat stove and read Jenny's letters and my brother Danny's letters in peace. I could smoke my smokes and stay as high as I pleased and sit on the bench with my AK in my lap, just looking at it and wiping it down with gun oil. I could swing, cross-legged, in my hammock and put that red-filter flashlight to one eye and see that woman, and nod off when I got good and ready. Some dudes in the platoon said I was crazy for staying on the Cow Catcher, but I didn't care, I told them. The platoon would come down to the motor pool in the morning for the move-out, wake me, and I'd eat a C-ration breakfast on the fly. I was down close to going home, within weeks of getting on that plane.

I started slacking off. Quinn moved back into the driver's hatch. "What the fuck," he had said. "Who cares? You care? I don't care." So he and I would get smoked up on the morning outbound run, and get laid noontimes, while the platoon laagered in a rubber-tree grove just outside the Tay Ninh gate—waiting there for the return convoy because the MPs wouldn't let us in the gate anymore. Claymore Face and her brother followed us on their Honda, and we took turns going first on her.

"Serg'n' Deadeye," she called me, her very own One-Eyed Trouser Mouse.

"Serg'n' Deadeye," she'd say, "you nee' a haircut, but oooh," she'd squeal, "you look boo-coo han'sum with a mustache." She and I would neck and cop feels in the back of the Cow Catcher, while the other whores and honchos and brats strolled among the other tracks, hustling Coke in cans and Thirty-three in quarts and illustrated Japanese fuck books. Then I started hustling Claymore Face, freak-sideshow fashion, to the fucken new guys, standing on the back of the Cow Catcher and bragging in grand style that "Claymore Face is the damnest piece of ass this side of the Saigon River—flash some tit for the gentlemen, sweetheart —and I certify that her snatch possesses ancient and mystical powers. To short-time Claymore Face—never mind how

God-awful ugly she is, boys, just slip a sandbag over her head—is to guarantee a sovereign cure for everything from sweat pimples to tumorous blood clots. Step r-r-right up!" And every now and again a couple would line up, taking the dare and laughing, with their money in their hands. But every once in a while some wise-ass would finish up, getting the blouse in his trousers just so, and comment, "She's pitiful, Dosier. Just pathetic. The world's worst." And I'd lean way over from above him, my hands on my hips, and say, "M' man, she's as good as it gets 'round here."

Quinn and I set her up in back of the Cow Catcher with ammo cans and the blackjack board and blankets and she'd short-time the dudes there. Quinn and Dewey and a bunch of old-timers would climb on the back and watch through the crew hatch. It got so a regular crowd formed.

One time Quinn and Dewey and Teddy and Stepik and Cary, a transfer from Bravo Company, and I were sitting around the crew hatch with our legs dangling in— smoked on Cambodie smoke, as was usual—watching Claymore Face fuck some new guy from the new seven-four crew. He had thick black hair on his asshole and halfway to his shoulder blades, and was pounding on her for all he was worth. We looked down, bug-eyed, clapping and shouting encouragement. He got flustered and pissed and picky about having an audience, so he turned his head and said, "Hey, now, how come you guys got to watch, eh?"

"We got to make sure ya gets yer money's worth, m' man. Ta make sure ya do it right," said Quinn, " 'cause if ya fuck funny, yer ass goes to the line, dig? So hump, m' man. Pound, I say! Bounce, goddamn it!"

And Claymore Face did so well we dug into our pockets for some MPC, crumpling the quarters and dollars and tossing them down. We asked the dude to move his head so we could throw the money at her face, and she blinked and squinted when they hit the mark, as though she was looking up at a monsoon rain. When the dude popped his nut and climbed off, the six of us gave him a hearty round of applause. Claymore Face jumped up and scrambled around, snatching up the money, bare-ass—her jugs just jiggling, like somebody was slapping them with open-handed slaps, her meaty, sweaty thighs smeared with cum. The fucken new guy sat back on the bench, hitching up his baggy trousers, watching her climbing around and grunting. He watched us laughing and pointing to her upturned ass cheeks, and shouting, "Cool. Warm. Real warm. Oh, yer *hot*, sweetheart. *Real* hot," and then she'd see it and grab. When she had all the crumpled bills she could hold, she stood up in the crew hatch among that circle of legs and crotches, smiling that God-awful-ugly no-tooth smile of hers, hugging the money to her chest.

"Hey, sweetheart. That money ain't for free," I said, bugging my eyes and shaking my head slowly. "No, no, negative, no. You all got to suck me off. Matter a strict fact, you got to suck everybody." I unbuttoned my fly and eased out ol' Deadeye and pointed at him with my eyes and a sawing motion of my hand. She made a face and giggled, lowered her head and shook her shoulders, acting real dumb and dufus, as though she thought I was kidding. But when I made a show of reaching down and unsnapping the flap of my forty-five holster she jerked her head up and stiffened, like somebody had kicked her dead in the ass when she was asleep and told her to move on. She dropped her money on her clothes and stepped between my legs and put her lips down over the tip, free-handed. She sucked in her cheeks and slobbered and licked some and glanced up at me, as much to say, "Okay. All right. I'm going. I'm *going*." It wasn't number one or anything, but it was all right. At least I didn't have to worry about teeth. When I came she popped me out of her mouth and looked around, and there were six more dangling out over the crew hatch.

She went from cock to cock, among the giggling and jostling and dudes poking her in the back, and by the time she came around to Deadeye again her lips and chin and neck were smeared with spit and cum. I was hard again and everybody was hard again, so I told her to go around one more time.

We just sat in that circle while Claymore Face went the rounds again, her eyes darting from gun to gun. And that fucking new guy sat inside all the while. "You guys are fucked up," he kept saying. "You dudes are crazy, you're nuts!" He went to Sergeant Corso and the El-tee and some other dudes in the platoon, but nobody paid any attention to him until Stepik finally told him not to be such a fucking Boy Scout.

After that Claymore Face didn't come around much, and nobody much cared.

*

The dinks started playing silly convoy games, pulling logs across the road, digging shallow trenches, making dirt castles. The first couple of times, I'd dismount with my AK and check them on foot, but that got old awful quick. After that I just had Quinn hang back some and pulled off a burst of fifty and if there was a mine it would blow. A couple times they did. Every day it was some hassle, some real hard-core puppy shit—an ace of spades, goofy-looking religious symbols, dead goats, junk like that. Lots of puppy shit.

"I wish'd they'd cut the games and just do it," Quinn said one afternoon. And then they did. Just the other side of Charlie Papa Golf where the jungle came to the road— RPGs, automatic weapons, the whole nine yards. We rumbled into the ditch on the ambush side and opened fire. Thirty machine guns all going at once, not waiting for the gun flashes or the heads or the sounds. We pulled out of the ditch, rolling at an idle right up to them and firing down on their heads. Then the El-tee called an air strike, so we had to back off to the other side of the road, with the fifties reaching over the high crown, watching for dinks that might turn and run. The Phantoms came in low and slow along the ditch with napalm. Tumble, tumble, crash, splash. One Phantom did the napalm, the other would strafe, starting from a couple thousand feet and diving straight down with 20 mm, moving the rounds into the bull's-eye, one gook at a time. They buzzed the ambush for the better part of half an hour, with flat-out bomb runs and screaming, strafing dives. We just leaned back, watching from the other side of the road. A sack of RPG rounds cooked off. The Phantoms left and we moved up.

We found fourteen corpses, dragged them to the road and laid them out, like fourteen baked potatoes. We stripped the bodies for the clothes and hung around looking at them. Quinn stood in the wheel rut with an AK easy in his grip, looking down at one of the blackish, reddish corpses. He heaved his chest and laughed a little to himself, then he puffed his chest and clenched his jaw.

"You goddamn . . ." he said, and swung the AK around like an ax, clubbing the body across the face with the metal butt-plate end. He started screaming slowly, "You fucken gook! You fucken gook!" pounding on the corpse with each word, putting his back into each swing, as though it were a work chant. The first couple blows all but glanced off, then something cracked and the head quickly became blackened, reddish-grayish junk. Charred bits of skin and chunks of flesh and splashes of blood flew like wood chips—like spray—the body hunching, as if Quinn were beating a rug. Cary stood on the driver's seat of the seven-zero, looking back at Quinn and yelling with his hands cupped around his mouth, "*Fuck* that cocksucker *up!*

That's the gook took a shot at me with his RPG. Fuck 'im *all* up!" Everybody else, thirty-some dudes, jerked their heads round and stood stock-still and stared, listening to the crunch crunch crack—Quinn chanting and pounding, roundhouse hard. The El-tee turned on his heel and walked to the front of the tracks so he could say, in truth, that he had seen nothing, in case he was ever asked. Finally he shouted, "Mount up and move," from around the front of his track, and people started to walk and mount up, but Quinn kept right on grunting and swinging and hacking at the head and chest and hips, thrashing the corpse into hideous, mushy lumps. Then the El-tee shouted louder and Quinn stopped, breathing deep breaths. He walked away, dragging the AK behind him, but quickly turned back, shouted "Gaaaa!" and clubbed the body one more time. Then he dropped the rifle where it hit, walked to the Cow Catcher, and climbed up. We left the bodies on the road and drove back to camp at a jogging pace, dazed and tired and sobered some, and did not look back. The cook who served that night had heard about the count—*everybody* had heard about the fourteen count. He wanted to talk about it as we sidestepped through the serving line, but we shuffled quietly along the way we did everything now. Only Quinn looked the dude dead in the eye as he ladled out the corned beef and steaming, tasteless cabbage.

"Yeah, a fourteen count. Big fucken deal. Who cares?"

The next morning when we strolled by with the sweep team the bodies were gone.

*

The day of the first big monsoon rain, we came in from convoy soaked to the skin, laughing and giggly, and there stood my replacement in the doorway of the tent.

He had three stripes and looked old enough to be my father. He was large and cushy, but after a tour he would leave lean and know that he had been someplace. He had pudgy, clumsy hands, bulbous features, and a thin mustache, and his eyes, dark and dull-shining things, seemed more bewildered than most I've seen.

"Howdy. I reckon you're Recon, ain'tcha?"

We looked him up one side and down the other.

"I guess we are. What're you?" Quinn said.

"Well, howdy. Name's Fitzwater," and he shook everybody's hand as they crowded past him. "I'm s'posed ta go ta the 34th Armor, but I'm here jus' on a kinda temporary basis, ya know?"

"I don't doubt," I said.

"Say, did you guys get inta trouble ta-day?"

"I don't care," I said, lying back on my old cot.

He sat on the cot next to mine. "Ah'm from Ama-rilla. Neat little town, Ama-rilla. J'ever been there?" Next to him was his duffel bag and two Samsonite suitcases. He reached into his duffel and pulled out a quart mason jar of peppers.

"Ma wife an' Ah went to Nogales jus' afore Ah come over, an' bought these peppers off a Mex," he said, unscrewing the top. "Have a pepper!"

He dug one out of the jar with his fingers and gave it to me. I put it in my mouth—what the hell—then turned my head and spit it out over the low sandbag wall in the direction of the piss tube.

"*Say* now, this here fella down at the training station at Cu Chi says that somma these gook women put razors in they pussy. J'ever hear a that?"

I looked over at Quinn and he looked at me and winked.

"Shore did, Fitz," I said. "There was a dude, name a Gumpp. *You* remember, Quinn."

"That's for true," said Quinn, leaning forward across the aisle. "Had three fingers and a glass eye. His ol' dick got *plum* sliced up. Bled like a stuck fucken pig. And the language! *Shit*. I ain't heard such language since I worked in a packin' house back home. I wish'd we had a record of it. It was Claymore Face that done it, she spread out for him just as nice and easy as you please, so Gumpp stepped up, dropped his trousers, just like always, and slid in just ordinary like. Then that smile of his kind of dripped off his face. Now, he was holding himself up at an arm's length, and ducked his head in the general direction of the pain, and dropped his jaw real slow and let out *the* loudest, *most* evil-sounding word ever to fall past the lips of man. Kinda like a rebel yell or the sound of a thousand Indians running out of the woods, coming down to lay out a wagon train, gonna kill everything and pillage and rape everything with a hole in it. Lord, *Lord*, I wished we coulda got a record of it. So Gumpp grabs Claymore Face by the throat and chokes her to a fare-thee-well. Kills her. But he had trouble getting up, 'cause she was kinda tight in the first place, don't ya see, and him all slicked up and lost his hard-on and all. Well, he finally worked himself loose and stood there with his trousers down around his ankles, bleeding gushes down his legs and all over himself. Now Doc, the medic, came running up, but he took one look and burst out laughing. He fell down he laughed so hard, pointing and squirming around and holding his stomach like he had appendicitis or some shit. Well, Gumpp got pure desperate, took his rifle, and shot Doc in the leg. Doc jerked his head around, but he started laughing all over again, so Gumpp took better aim and shot him in the head three times."

"You mean he killed the *medic*, too?" said Fitz.

Quinn looked him square in the eye. "*Shore* he did. Wouldn't you? I mean, what fucken business is it of his where you hurt? Shit, I would have purely stomped his ass for carrying on like that. It was good we got rid of him anyway. He wasn't a very good medic to begin with. Couldn't tie a fucken granny knot if you bet him a month's pay."

"And what happened to Gumpp?"

"Aw, he bled to death. Ya see, he was shooting at everybody 'cause we was all laughing. We stood behind trees and shit, watching old Gumpp stumble around, still bleeding gushes, till he turned ash pale and fell over, stone dead."

"Gee" was all Fitz could say.

Finally we got up and went to chow. Fitz tagged along behind, bringing that mason jar of peppers and a bottle of black greasy sauce. There was lamb and potatoes and carrots and mint jelly. Quinn and I sat facing Fitz. He plunked down his tray and poured the black sauce on the meat and potatoes, smearing it around and working it in with his fork, then he sprinkled the peppers around and cut across the tray with his knife and fork, mixing the potatoes and carrots and lamb and jelly and peppers all together. Then he commenced to eat, shoveling the food into his mouth, using the knife to gather it on his fork and smooth it. He held the fork close over the plate and bobbed his head down and made a grab for the food. Lamb and peppers and potatoes and carrots and mint jelly, thick slices of bread and gulps of water. He worked his jaw like a cow chewing a wad of cud, his cheeks flashing and his mustache going like a pump handle. I looked over at Quinn and he looked at me with that look that says, Jesus, is this guy fucked up. Has *this* dude ever got shit for brains. We shrugged our shoulders, dropped our forks, and got up and left.

The El-tee put Fitz on the Cow Catcher. I had to break him in and then stand down, stand back, and wait for my orders. But Fitz couldn't get the hang of using the radio or getting the convoy check points straight or something simple-ass, like how to hang grenades on a flak jacket.

Fitz came up to me one night and said, "Now, Dozer, Ah knows that you an' Quinn and Ted and a couple others are smoking that dope on convoy and nights, but Ah ain't gonna say nothin'."

"That's real white of ya, Fitz," was all I said.

The next afternoon I went up to the El-tee in the motor pool and told him, "This dude is a cartoon. Nobody can be *that* dumb. However, do not ask me to come back to the field."

The El-tee and the Colonel finally discovered just how dumb-ass and dufus Fitz was when he fell out of the TC hatch and broke his arm, so they palmed him off on the 10th Armored Cavalry, and Teddy—who had been gunning all this time—moved into the hatch. Quinn quit driving, too. He could not, would not, be roused mornings for the move-outs, so the Cow Catcher got a new driver—a guy named Janecek—and two gunners I never did meet.

I took to sleeping late, taking my shower early. Mornings I would do some smokes with Gonzales and Haskins, and I sat out my afternoons in the EM Club with Staley and Quinn.

Then every night the platoon came back with wounded and towed tracks. The convoy hit something every trip—mines or RPGs or sniper fire or firefights. One day the Cow Catcher hit a mine that blew off all the driver's-side road wheels. The concussion catapulted Teddy out of the hatch. Janecek died on the dust-off, we heard later. The new dudes on back broke legs, got torn up.

The battalion wrecker brought the Cow Catcher in at the tail end of the convoy. Quinn and I took one of the medic jeeps and drove to the evac hospital to pick Teddy up. His head wrapped thickly, he looked woozy with that dazed and glassy stare that wounded get. We drove him back to the platoon. He slid out of his seat, went inside his tent, and lay down. He stayed in his cot that night and the next day, and the next night.

Quinn and I hustled a case of beer out the back door of the EM Club and went down to the motor pool—down to the Cow Catcher. We threw the beer inside and walked around it. The smooth filthy sides, those old claymore gouges, the cracked road-wheel hubs dripping oil, the words "Cow Catcher" hand-painted with a cigarette filter because I couldn't find a brush, the faded numbers, the streaked mud-colored stain of mo-gas down the side, the drive sprocket I could turn with a finger, the greasy canvas tool bag, the upraised fifty. I touched it all with the flat of my palm, the back of my hand. I used to live here.

We had been drinking steadily all day, smoking Cambodie smokes since noon, and popping Darvons since we got up. Quinn sat with his back to those tits and thighs; me with my back to the Igloo cooler—just like we had always sat. The Cow Catcher was totaled—fire panels ripped away as easily as tinfoil; engine parts scattered on the floor; radio smashed; my hammock gone; my camera some-fucking-place—I never did find it; my waterproof punched with holes; blood all over the driver's hatch and dashboard and infrared scope. The next morning that bunch of dipstick fucking hack mechanics would strip it for parts and turn in the rest for scrap.

We sat with the beers between us, drinking quickly, furiously, knocking them back—boom boom boom—and flinging the empties out the door, up through the crew hatch.

Coming all this way, riding the Cow Catcher all this way. Why the hell was I sitting in camp while Janecek drove around looking for a mine? Sure, he was a fucking new guy, but he was doing all right. Give the dude a break. All this fucking way. All this way down to this. Goddamn.

And I slapped the underside of the armor deck so hard my hand stung and started to itch. I threw an empty out and opened another can. Atevo and Steichen and Whiskey j. and Granger and Trobridge and Walthers and Willie and the engineer and Eddie, and on down to Dano and Janecek and the Cow Catcher, and so on and so on until I couldn't remember anymore and gave up trying. The dinks were getting close, circling in on the bull's-eye—walking the rounds in, and picking and choosing along the way—but getting the range; getting in closer just the same. And the longer I stayed, the more chances I gave them.

"Who do we think we are?" I said.

"I am one bad motherfucker. Mean bad," said Quinn, thumping his thumb against his chest.

"Yeah hey, but where were we today?"

"What the fuck ya talkin' about?"

"Shit, m' man, all's I know is, if we'd been there it woulda gone different. Tha's all. I'm tellin' ya it woulda been different."

"Aw, fuck off, *Dead*eye."

"Well, take a fucken look at it. If you 'n' me'd been where we 'uz s'posed ta be, Teddy 'n' Janecek woulda been on the back 'n' the fucken new guys woulda been someplace else. I'm sayin' you 'n' me fucked up."

"*Oh* no, m' man. I don' need ta hear it, dig? Not from you er Corso er the El-tee er anybody. People been pounding that buddy-buddy shit up my ass half a my life, an' I'm goddamn sick an' fucken tired a listenin' ta how fucked up I am." Eleven months and some in the bushes and it all came down to a fucked-up box of junk and two stoned and mumbling, bitter drunks. "Look. Flip," he said, and leaned forward, nose to nose. I could feel his breath puffing as he spoke, as close as we would ever be. "You an' me is tight. You an' me been through our shit. You be gettin' yer orders any day, be going home boo-coo soon. Fuck this war. Fuck these dinks. Fuck Janecek. Dig? An' me? I give a fat fucken squat. I could care less." And he slumped back hard against the pictures of tits and thighs, mumbling, "I care . . . I fucken care . . ." and rolling his head from side to side, his eyes squinted shut, pinching his face together.

The Cow Catcher right there all the time. My ride home. I knew it like I knew I couldn't feel anything in my fingers anymore; like I knew I couldn't taste food anymore; like I knew that Quinn and I would not see much of each other anymore—probably never after I went home. A person does not like to look into another man's face and see all those bad days and bad feelings reflected back, as though the other face was a fisheye lens. The seven-three was a piece of my arm, and a piece of your arm doesn't fall off without your bleeding and screaming the pain. Fucking war, fucking dinks, fucking Janecek. Quinn and I sat knee to knee, drinking the warm beers and smoking the last of his Prince Albert tobacco-can stash. We fell asleep, sitting bolt upright, hot and filthy, cramped and crowded by the wreckage.

C O M I N G

H O M E

H I G H

I gave everything away. My orders came, so I dumped everything I owned on my cot—shirts and trousers, socks and towels, R & R civvies and such—and stood looking at it. Give it all away, my man. What can you do with a footlockerful of junk? I pulled my AK down from the nail and sat on the pile of clothes, holding the gun across my lap and working the safety back and forth. I have to give it away, too. It is the first thing I will give away. The day I took it most dudes stood around, taking pictures and gawking and laughing at all those funny gray faces, snatching wallets and dope and gear, but I put a palm on an AK and let it go at that. I didn't keep his wallet, so why should I keep his AK? Besides, what do I need an Automat Kalashnikov 47 for back-in-the-world?

So I gave everything away, and what I couldn't give away I threw away.

I wasn't getting much rest since I moved back into the tent. The platoon would straggle in from convoy and jack around and party and laugh it up, and I just couldn't get any sleep. So I would go down to Staley's hooch and hang around there until late, when I guessed everyone would be in bed. Sometimes I would catch Akins sitting up by himself in the dark, scratching the itch in his stitches. So he and I would share one more smoke before turning in. In the morning I would waken with the rest of the platoon about an hour before dawn. Everybody would stumble out back to piss in the ditch and then troop off to the mess hall. They would leave for the motor pool and their convoy, and I would go back to the tent and sleep until nine or ten. I started hanging around the laundry tent just back of the Orderly Room. Some mama-san and her son and daughter ran the place. The daughter was real nice—she asked me if I spoke French. We could talk better in French, she said, because GI English sounded so fucked up. She was from Vung Tau, a town on the coast, the in-country R & R center. She called me "Serg'n" all the time and smiled every day when I dropped in. I kept asking her if she'd like to make a quick five hundred P. We could go over to the tent, I said. It would be number one, I told her. She kept saying no. She was a convent girl, saving her pennies to go to France and be a model. Well, Chingachgook! I says, here's the easiest five hundred you'll make today. She kept saying no, but I kept going back. Then the day before I shipped home I went over late in the afternoon to pick up my khakis. She asked if I was going on R & R. "No," I said, "tomorrow I'm going home." "You go 'merica?" she asked. "Yeah, you know, home." "Serg'n, tomorrow you come early, I present you, you present me." She said it sweetly and smiled. I didn't think she was going to let me into her shorts, but was really going to give me something. That had happened to Staley. His girlfriend was the Colonel's housegirl. At Christmas the Colonel had given her a twenty-four-carat gold Buddha on a gold chain, and she turned around and gave it to Staley. He wore it, too. That night I went to the PX and bought two bagfuls of bath towels, soap, a good fountain pen, stuff like that.

Evenings, Quinn and Staley and a bunch of us would sit by Staley's beat-up bunker, smoking and listening for the incoming mortars. It became something of a game to sit and listen for the thump, then the soft plushy whoosh of the rounds as they sailed overhead. We never worried about getting hit, because the gunners always made for the airfield or brigade headquarters or the PX. Let the housecats crawl for a change. When we heard one we would jump down from the bunker and bet where it was going to hit. If it was close, a short round, we could hear it coming down whistling like a woodsman and see the quick flash of fire and hear the snappy crack. Sometimes we could even see the sparks from the tube shower upward into the rubber trees.

The night before I left Staley threw a party. We moved the cots against the wall, and everyone danced and drank quarts. Quinn and Staley stood in the middle of the floor passing a pipe of Cambodie smoke back and forth; Quinn had a foot up on Staley's cot and Staley leaned back against his table, watching Quinn puff long sucking puffs and blow Cambodie smoke rings. Quinn wore a bright yellow baseball cap with the word "CAT" across the front that someone had sent him, three or four days of scroungy beard, and my AK hanging from his shoulder. He leaned his arm over the wooden pistol grip the way Surtees used to lean on his shoulder-holster forty-five. "Say, m' man? Hear ya goin' home inna mornin'," was all he said, slow and drawled. Staley had a four-hour tape—the Rolling Stones and Lou Rawls—laying smoke across the floor and every stash in the platoon was on the table. Then Staley and Quinn got the idea of going over to the mess hall and cooking up something warm. Gonzales, the little dude who drove the provision truck and had arms like *that*, sashayed up to Staley and announced that he knew where he could steal some frozen pizzas and rib-eye steaks, so the party moved over to the mess hall. I stayed behind because I didn't care about pizza and steak, and besides, Lou was just getting wound up. They came back sooner than I expected. Staley was pissed off at somebody for not letting them use the oven, but everybody else was laughing and poking each other. We opened another round of quarts and started the tape over and started dancing again. Some dudes hooked arms and danced couples, but most jigged around, singing along and stomping on the floor. Every now and again someone let out a whoop and threw an empty into the company street.

Akins hobbled down with the mail. I got two letters from Jenny and the two fuck books, the ones with yellow covers, I had sent for back in December. I put the letters away and opened the package. I dropped the wrapping ceremoniously on the floor and began to read one of the books. The dudes dancing near stopped and listened. Pretty soon they crowded closer, trying to read over my shoulder.

". . . then the straps of her gown and the dress now hung by her breasts. Her eyes half closed, she was aware only of the warmth of his fingers on her thighs. She reached up and pulled the dress away from her breasts and the gown gathered in folds around her waist, hesitated, then floated to the floor and gathered in a pool of black silk. . . ."

One of the dudes behind me let out a whoop and hopped around, yelling, "Yahoo! Get'm, tiger! Yahoo!"

". . . lifted her and placed her spread-eagle across the head of the bed, then undressed as quickly as he could."

"Sounds like my brother," someone yelled. "When he gets worked up, he looks like one of them two-dollar cucumbers." Whoever said it walked away, but turned and came right back. By this time I was drawing a crowd and continued reading, only louder so everyone could hear.

". . . he kneeled on the floor and put his face in front of her muff, his neck outstretched, and breathed deeply like a cook will do sometimes when he takes just a taste of a fussed-over sauce. Then he worked his nose past the bristled brown hair, nestled it in her crack and wiggled it like a fat old rabbit. . . ."

Lou was saying something nasty cool, and a couple dudes hooked arms and began dancing in circles, chanting: "muffdiver—muffdiver—muffdiver," and stamping their feet in time with the music, while I kept reading.

". . . Irma let out a squeal as though somebody had tickled her once and for all, clamped her legs tightly around Roger's head and locked her ankles, stretching her toes. As Roger worked his tongue into her puss she squirmed and wriggled her hips so all that Roger could hear was her hip joints scratching together. Her fingers were spread on her stomach and as she whimpered and moaned, her hands moved to her breasts and she began massaging her swollen nipples lightly with the palms, pressing down harder and rotating so that the fingers interlocked and touched the other breast. . . ."

"Yippie," someone yelled, and jumped into the air, coming down heels first and landing with a loud crack on the floor.

". . . Roger began humping the side of the mattress and reached up to grasp Irma by the arms for leverage. Soon Irma caught the rhythm and the bed began to buck and bang against the wall. Irma started to cry in earnest and call Roger's name.

" 'Roger, Roger. Oh, Roger. Uh, oh. Oh, Roger. Roger.' "

And everyone in the tent took up Irma's cry. "Roger. Roger. Roger. Ra-jer. Ra-jer."

They clapped their hands and stomped around.

RA-JER. RA-JER. RA-JER.

*

Back at the tent everyone was asleep. Akins snored softly, scratching his nails on the canvas. I had not slept well for weeks. It was too close to my time. I had no need for sleep. I had been stoned and drunk every night for a long time, and anyway I was going home in the morning. Staley and I had smoked a bunch of smoke on many a night, driving the perimeter road so stoned that we kept driving well after dark, and had to break into the mess hall to get something to eat. When I was tired or drunk enough to nod out, I slept in starts and fits, dreaming of flat-out chases with fast black rabbits, my hands and feet jerking, pacing the quick obliques and sharp flanking moves. But I was always quick to awaken. The slightest noise, even the subtlest shadows on shadows of the first man to sit up and yawn, was enough to make me open my eyes. But on the last night sleep was not possible, not even the sleep so familiar to guards when the body stiffens and nods, but the mind still churns along, listening, sniffing, seeing past the heavy, heavy eyelids. I will sit by the table and watch the wire and listen for the soft plushy sound of the incoming, and when they come I will hear them, screaming like the dead scream, and count them on my fingers. I will sit through everything—the mortars, the rockets, the skinny fucking sappers hugging their packs while they crawl along the ditch out back—and I will be silent, because I am going home in the morning.

I know they cannot kill me.

Everyone talks about what they are going to do when they get home. Home. The magic word spoken with no small reverence—everybody-goes-home, I'm-going-home, back-in-the-world, the land of the big PX and the twenty-four-hour generator. A mountain held to the ground by trees, green like the color green that dripped from the hand of God. The green of all green. That's where I'm going in the morning. God or the devil could walk into the tent and call me, saying, "Come with me, I will take you to my house and give you soft fine clothes—your fondest, most cherished wish—simple rest. Come." But I would not go with him, because first of all, first before anything, I must go home. I have come too far, done too much, seen too many things to deny myself the ritual of stepping back from all this. You hear stories about dudes going home and getting themselves killed in car accidents and such, and everybody feels so bad, but it doesn't mean anything. I mean, he's seen home, and whatever it means to him, he's seen the thing he sat up nights scratching his head about, and bragged about and dreamed about.

And now it's my turn. It's owed. But I have to go home the way I came. That's why I have given everything away. The dream is dead. Only the ritual remains. The dream lies draped among the scrub bushes near where Atevo died, the neatest small puncture in his face. He was only the first. There were others. Always more. The dream died quickly, but I hung on to it for a long time, until I didn't know whether the stink of it was the dream or my flak jacket or just somebody's dirty asshole. It had me around the neck and hung down my back and whispered to me in my sleep that this was not the place, farther on, always farther on, and soon I was walking on my knees. Then one morning close to Christmas, as I sat guard wrapped in a blanket, it slipped off my shoulders. It cried and fell away and screamed goodbye. Suddenly there was no caring, except for the things I could reach out and grasp with a hand. There is too much sleep and good feeling lost, and it has been too long since I have seen someone smile, and I have had my R & R already and a grunt only gets one, and I don't care. I don't care for anything except the dudes I can touch and talk to today, and going home is simple-ass wishful thinking. Nobody goes home from here. But if any of those dinks give me any shit I'll grease their ass and chalk it up as body count, but there's too many dead now for me to go back and do over, and I just don't care anymore. Come on, fuck with me. I killed one dude with my bare hands. I broke a couple bones in his throat and squeezed until his eyes bugged out and pounded him into the mud until I could hardly lift his head and the son of a bitch clucked and jiggled his arms, and died. I don't care—one more, ten more, a thousand more, it doesn't mean anything. I'll fill your sandbags or burn your shit or wander around in the bushes because I simply do not care about anything but a drink and some smoke and laying my head down every once in a while to rest my eyes. I'll piss where the urge takes hold, short-time any broad with two legs, blow snot holding a finger to the other nostril. The war works on you until you become part of it, and then you start working on it instead of it working on you, and you get deep-down mean. Not just kidding mean; not movie-style John Wayne mean, you get mean for real. You start volunteering for the weird missions, all the goofy ambushes, loaded to the teeth with grenades and knives and your cool-ass AK, and run the road throwing out rounds just to hear the fifty buzz in your ear, and race through hamlets on the road missing the dinks by *that* much, and you laugh and throw empty cartridges at the kids who stand there begging C rations. I dug free-fire zones because we could kill anything that moved, and all I wanted to do was kill and kill and burn and rape and pillage until there was nothing left. Then I'd volunteer to get a shovel and turn every square inch I could get to, but even then I would get down on my hands and knees, looking for earthworms and grubs to squash with my palm heel.

You go crazy and see dudes crack up all around you and dinks keep coming at you and you grease one, then the next, and still they come out of the woodline and your hands get sore from holding the handle on the fifty and your thumbs get cramps all the way to the elbows from pressing on the butterfly trigger, and your driver goes crazy helping you reload and the dinks keep rushing out of the woodline and you keep greasing this one and that and lob grenades, and the bodies pile up and still they keep trotting out of the woods and you grease them by the squad and they pile higher until you reach up with your arms, as though you're looking for a hand up and *scream* your lungs flat. The war has swallowed me, it has clamped off all the veins, and I'm high on dope and Darvon and mo-gas and sick and tired of the fucking footrace, so I jump down in front of the track, with the bowie knife between my teeth, and snarl.

How did I come to love it so? What evil taller than myself did I grapple and wrestle and throw to the ground? Subdued. Did it come with a night moon, or is it something inside, this pain in my chest? Did it enter quickly, leaving this crablike scar on my eye, or does it hover here like a poltergeist, whispering?

I can never go home. I just want to see it. I won't say a thing, cross my heart. I just want to see it one more time. I want to smell it, touch it ever so lightly, put my ear to it and hear it tap, tap, tap.

So, now only the ritual remains. I have not been getting closer, only farther away. Faces are incomplete, tinted scarlet and edged black like fine thin lace. All the familiar things, the kitchen smells, the single words of old friends, are beyond the grasp of my arm. Only Jenny is there. Jenny of small thick letters about working summers and the thousand dumb, funny things that mean nothing, but fill up letters. Mail from home, hand-stamped and written in script. Somebody knows I am not dead. I want to look at you, Jenny, hear you breathe, be with you. Say a word, any word. I want to hear the sound, the timbre, of your voice. I want to put my hand to your neck and feel it vibrate when you speak, as though I were a deaf-mute just learning.

I have lost a good deal. My hands are stiff and cold, they ache with the changing of the season. The backs are wrinkled and spliced with small scaly cuts, and the fingers shiver when I hold them out. The nails are long and hard, discolored and chipped. The palms are drawn and chapped, and calluses have grown on the insides of the knuckles and joints. There is not the slightest inkling of texture or coolness or warmth, and everything I do now has a slack baggy feel to it. All touch is the same: the small shards of wool at the edge of a blanket; the wood of my shotgun stock; the oily wooden handle of the ball peen hammer; a clean shave; the inside of a thigh. I can no longer maintain smooth effortless motion, even when I am stoned. When I first came into the platoon, that was what struck me about the tracks. They were huge and lumbering, stunted animations of some slow and wild thing. Noisy and fat, grunting cartoons, smelling of thirty-weight oil and gunpowder and beer piss, with a meanness designed in as surely as the bore and stroke.

And I am filthy all the time. I feel that grit, that crawl of the skin, something itching all the time, and greasy. But not because I worked in grease. It is something inside, some white silky liquid, gathering itself around blackened marrow, like ambergris. It is more than stink, something more than stench. It is beyond the sweat and salt stains, distilled into something more rank, more uremic, some powdered poison. It has been sucked and sweated out, and baked and faded and fire-assayed until it falls off in flakes. A thing I did not understand, or even see, until I went on R & R and saw it shine like an oil slick in my bath. That's why my first flak jacket smelled like something had died in it; indeed, someone had. The taste in my mouth has gone fallow. It has faded back and back, like someone running downhill full tilt, shouting over his shoulder with the wind at his back, in his face. You cup your hand around your ear, but all you make out are swallowed snatches, and the sharp rush of grass and dust. Everything tastes like chalk on my tongue; the gums so soft they bleed when I eat C-ration crackers. I started out smoking Camels, then cigars, then bigger cigars, then dope, lots of dope—just to feel it hit my lungs, to feel anything hit my lungs. I have lost the simple rhythm of breathing. It must be due to the humidity. I seem always to be breathing as fast as I can, as though to catch up, like a cross-country runner who stops to lean against a tree; hysterical for breath to the point of vomiting. Also, it is plain that I have lost the ability to sleep. One night I tried to do it right, stayed sober, did all those nighttime things. I lay on my sleeping-bag cot, motionless and wide awake for several hours, until I finally gave up and strolled down to Staley's, and stayed the night.

So here I am, clumsy and slow and very tired, going home in the morning. That is why I am leaving all my things behind. Whatever real value fatigues are—warm, fast-drying, mosquito-proof—they will drag me down and hold me back. They will always stink that stink. That special itch will always be there in the sleeves. I have to leave everything. I don't dare take any of it. It took me less than a year to get used to not wearing underwear and sleeping well enough in a hammock, and it will take me less than a year to get back to real clothes and driving in traffic and homemade soup.

*

It rained early in the morning. Simple rain. There was no breeze, no heavy smell of wet air, no thick spray of mist. It splashed onto the tent, like thimbles dropped on taut linen. It dripped from the tent ropes and splashed lightly in the doorway light. I sat by the table with my feet outstretched, smoking my smokes and sipping from a C-ration can of fruit cocktail. I ate it without a spoon, tipping it to my mouth and sucking at the fruit. I flipped the butt of the doped Kool out the doorway. It stuck, smoking and hissing. I can go one of two ways. I can go home and be crazy in peace, or I can stay here, be crazy, and get killed. If I stay they will kill me. If I go home people will cast down their eyes and offer condolences when I walk the ward of an afternoon. They will visit me, bringing meaningless little gifts, and sit for the obligatory ten minutes, talking to me in simple sentences. Politicians will pump my arm for the camera, all the while asking me what my name was. Total strangers will walk to the outside of the sidewalk. I will spend my waking hours in the corners of large cathedrals, lighting candles in my own behalf. I will sell shoelaces at elevated stations; be a postman; till the soil; sleepwalk. I will be crazy in peace.

The air was quiet except for the sound of the rain, and Akins breathing heavily through his nostrils. Even the 105 battery down the way was between fire missions. There would be no surprises tonight. I felt a great rustling urge. I am going home. Death himself could walk into the tent, shrouded in his yellow slicker, mumble his little speech and raise his arm, but I will not move. He will step forward, startled by flat refusal, and raise his voice so that several men stir in their sleep, and call my name again. I will look at him and laugh through my teeth. His image will smoke with rage, then pass through the mosquito netting. Only the soft stench of salt ash will linger. Akins will think I have pissed on the floor.

Everyone woke as usual. We went out back to piss and left for the mess hall. I sat with the TCs and Haskins and Stepik and a couple others, drinking coffee and swapping addresses and such. I told them to look me up if they were ever in Chicago, and they all said they would. I traded Dewey the shotgun and gas-mask bag full of rounds for his M-16, and gave my forty-five web belt to his Delta, another fucking new guy—a strapping, chunky-looking kid named Guttierrez. When they got up we shook hands around, saying, "Take good care," and such things, and then they left for the road sweep before the convoy. I watched from the back of the tent one more time as the tracks headed down the perimeter road, raising a billowing dust. They cranked through the gate and hung a right into Dau Tieng. The dust hung and settled slow, like a yellowish rolling fog, and then that faint grinding and squeaking, crunching rattle settled, too, on my heart it seemed, and they were gone.

I shaved and trimmed my mustache, packed my suitcase, and changed into my khakis. I took the two bagfuls of Ivory soap and bath towels and junk trinkets to the mama-san at the laundry, telling her to thank her daughter for me. Then I turned in Dewey's M-16 and a couple magazines, signed out of the company, and hitched a ride to the airfield.

A small crowd of GIs lounged around some packing

crates, waiting for the planes. Some going home, some going on R & R, and some Viet workers, sitting on their heels hogging the shade. I had my stripes and division patch sewn on, but none of the ribbons. It didn't mean anything, the no ribbons, the sloppy salute flashed quick and wide, front-line style, the less than soldierly spit shine, the starch wrinkles all over my shirt. I was going home. Who cared?

Our plane came in low and fat, with no armament. It was painted brown and o.d. and gray, and rolled to a stop. The NCO called the roster. Is he really going to call my name? It was like anything else, maybe it would happen, maybe not. If it wasn't this plane, there would be another. They have to send you home sometime, your tour is finished sometime.

"... Brown, Caniel, Carlson, Dosier—"

That's the one. I grabbed my suitcase and climbed on board. Men already sat on the floor, ARVNs and GIs from Tay Ninh. We piled our baggage into a cargo net hanging near the ramp and sat on the floor, too. The benches along the bulkhead were for officers and senior NCOs; the EM and young NCOs sat on the floor in rows with a cargo strap across their laps. I sat down with my legs crossed, and held on to the strap with both hands. There was something missing. No one had a weapon. The crewman had a thirty-eight, but what if we were shot at, shot down, what's a goddamn thirty-eight? Why did I turn in my bayonet?

The engines revved, then we were rolling. I held the strap with my forearms against my chest. The plane rose sharply and turned south. I could see nothing out the windows but sky. I wanted to go to the window and take a good look at the base camp. No, it was better this way. Don't look back, don't ever look back, because you might turn around and go back. The crewman lit a cigarette. There were two dudes in front of me from Bravo Company. One of them pulled out a smoke.

"You Bravo Company?"

"Yeah. Who are you?"

"Recon. Romeo Seven-three. Say, you know Clay? Eland Clay."

"That crazy bastard? He's the dude with the sandbag full of gold teeth and ears. He goes home next week. They put his ass in for a Bronze Star. Ain't that some shit? Seven-three, hunh? Cow Catcher? Have a drag." We smoked and talked. Everybody on the plane caught a whiff. Some took the hint. One of the lifers looked like he was going to start taking names. When we got to Tan Son Nhut a truck was there to meet us. There were seven dudes going to the 90th Replacement Detachment. The roads were just like back-in-the-world, asphalt and broken white lines. Along the way were small compounds of barbed wire. A gas dump, a lumber dump, the wood stacked high, whole sections of prefab roof rafters, dudes walking around without weapons, some in jeeps wearing civilian clothes.

Where have I been? All these dudes getting hostile fire pay. Fifty-five a month for doing this. I just know these housecats think they got it bad. "Man, I am bored to tears. Positively tears. Stone bored." "You going to the movie tonight? Some dude says there's some tit in this one." "No, I think I'll stroll on down to the day room and hustle some snooker." Can't you just hear it? Hot and cold running water, real toilets, everybody has a jeep, eight kinds of eggs for breakfast, and round-eyed pussy walking the streets just like back in Des Moines. Red Cross Donut Dollies that put out for everybody. We get the ugly ones with a limp; these dudes get the fish right off the boat, come to smooth out the wrinkles in a hardship tour.

Housecats!

"Hey, Bravo Company, I'll put all the cash in my pocket on it, that all these dudes for ten miles around never sleep alone." Not one night. Beer so cold you've gotta wear a glove. Smoke so mellow somebody gets blown away every time it rains hard. Dudes making a killing on the black market with refrigerators and greenbacks and fans and stereos and cameras. Jesus fucking Christ, combat pay. We've been had. This is a champeen ream job. What would anybody *do* with all this shit? Real beds. Sheets once a week. Three hots a day. Round-eyed pussy, reasonable. The dudes standing around during duty hours with their thumbs up their asses and fingers in their mouths, bored to death. It's a laugh. Just don't sit anywhere near me, pissing and moaning about being bored, don't even whisper. When I come through just drop the subject. In my whole life I never heard of anybody, not one dude, that dropped dead of boredom. Can't you just see it? A bunch of housecats strolling down the avenue to the USO. One of them suddenly clutches his throat and stumbles to the ground in gagging convulsions. "It's boredom! He's got boredom. My God, get a medic. Get a blanket, get a chaplain, get a dust-off! This man has boredom. Stand back, it's boredom, all right." The plague spreads. Long lines of litters crowd the dispensaries. Nothing cures it, not Olympic swimming pools, not all the Red Cross pussy in Southeast Asia, not even soaking their balls in Epsom salts. Like some disgusting consumptive gunge, some lingering and lethal, virulent plague, a combination of amoebic dysentery, the clap, and teething pain, it sweeps back and forth across the rear echelon. Thousands succumb.

Watching these dudes piss away a hardship tour in a combat zone is enough to make a person go somewhere and laugh until blood squirts out his ears. A nonstop three-day laugh, clutching his stomach with both arms, turning red, then black and blue, laughing at those dudes sitting there playing circle jerk; laughing so hard his skin breaks into open sores and he blows out his eardrums with the screeching. Tears come. His feet swell and burst his boots. He rolls around, and every time he looks back at the housecats the laughing starts all over again. He laughs so hard it blows a hole in his kidneys.

Back at Dau Tieng we had Red Cross. They stalked around the evac hospital and ran the puppy-shit paperback library. They even came to the field once, packing home versions of daytime-TV game shows—"Password" and "Concentration"—under their arms, to entertain the artillery. We had come in from ambush, up past our ears with being awake, but the El-tee said we had to go over and help out—to make it look good; to let the Red Cross know they were appreciated. I just wanted to take a piss and take a nap. Then they were all over the tracks, bullshitting us while we sat around stripped to the waist, trying to eat what was left of breakfast. Two of them stood on the ramp of the seven-three, playing with Trobridge's field glasses, watching an air strike off in the direction we had come in from. They gaggled about how the dude in the Phantom coming straight down for the strafe must be a bachelor, because no married man would do anything *that* crazy, but ain't that the cutest thing you ever saw. And meanwhile the 20 mm is tearing some poor dink a new asshole. Lady, I got to take a piss. Why don't you go down to the seven-four and harass them for a while? I walked around to the front of the track and leaned back against the armor, and undid my fly and whizzed the all-time-feel-good whiz, arching the piss high so maybe they would see it in the glasses. They'd go in that night and write all their undergraduate friends about what a bunch of evil uncouth motherfuckers those dudes in Romeo were.

The Red Cross, what a bunch of walking wounded.

When we arrived at the 90th Replacement Detachment a placard arched across the roadway, proclaiming to the fucking new guys going the other way:

WELCOME

The Rules

1. *Speak nice to the dinks.*
2. *Don't piss just anywere.*
3. *Shave once a day for the sake of public relations.*
4. *Recreational pharmacology is frowned upon.*
5. *Do not get the gunge. When the Army wants you to have it, it will be issued to you.*

> *Signed,*
> *General Westhisface*
> *Commanding.*

It had all changed around. The whole compound was surrounded by incredible piles of concertina wire with bunkers and guard towers every thirty meters or so, looking out over clusters of hooch slums. All those pale faces standing around with uniforms still cracking with sizing. The truck pulled up in front of one of the first buildings. The driver told us to report to the window around back, a hole cut in the wall and a counter with a pfc. sitting there, fanning himself with the *Stars & Stripes*.

"You guys a little late, ain'tcha?"

Just remember, no hassle, speak quietly, be polite, and they won't fuck up your orders. "Excuse me?"

"I said, how come you guys are getting here so late?"

"Talk to the driver about it. We're reporting for transportation to CONUS."

"Lemme see your orders. Here's some blankets. Be in the area for your name to be called and the shakedown. And don't get caught with any dope around here. Got it?"

We walked down the line of hooches and took the last one in the row, nearest the latrine. That night the two Bravo Company dudes and I sat on the roof, smoking our smokes and watching the lights of the city. One of these nights this city is going to catch it square in the teeth—then watch these housecats do a low crawl.

The next morning some young looey stood in the doorway and called everybody's name. We went to the briefing room and exchanged our MPC for greenbacks, and unpacked for a shakedown. One hundred-and-some dudes stood behind their gear with Class-A stashes of Cambodie smoke taped to their calves or stuffed into M-16 bandolier moneybelts. We laughed and grab-assed and smiled that smile, because weren't we just getting away with the crime of the century. But the shakedown NCOs looked for live ammo and grenades and such that crazy housecats wanted to sneak home and show around, along with scraps of Chicom mortar shrapnel and knife-fight scars. They loaded us on buses with heavy screens on the windows, and drove us to Bien Hoa Air Base, but none of us knew we had arrived until the buses stopped and opened the doors in front of a shed-looking building with a flat fiberglass roof and rows of benches, facing the airfield. In one corner at the back a couple dinks ran a PX snack bar, and there were no bunkers, and no one I saw had a weapon.

Some officers arrived later in staff cars and congregated along the front row of benches, marked "Officers Only."

I paced the edge of the concrete, keeping to the shade, looking out over the runways and along the flight line. Behind us were rows of two-story barracks and buildings, trucks parked along the curbs, and air conditioners in almost every window. I sat with the two dudes from Bravo Company.

"You know what? There ain't no bunkers here."

They glanced around, then back at me.

We were not home yet. This was still the Zone. We were so close to going home. The waiting was a nervous, fidgety challenge. We kept moving around, sitting here to watch the airfield, moving to the snack bar for a Coke, or standing in small groups that moved back and forth across the back of the building. Some dudes stretched out on the benches and slept. The CIBs, the grunts with the Combat Infantryman's Badge, fidgeted and paced, staring at the runway more than the rest. The Phantom air strikes went out by twos and came back, refueled and reloaded and went back. Somebody was not having a good day.

Then there it was, coming in a steep dive for the end of the runway. Everybody stood, the CIBs in front. There was a thrill of breath. A chill came across the airfield. A few dudes cheered. This, too, was part of the ritual, these last few minutes. Our 707 hit the end of the runway with a splash of tire rubber, coasted to the end, and taxied along the flightline at a good clip, with a face in every window. It pulled up in front of us and the ground crew rushed out with the stairway.

Closer, my man, ain't we getting closer every time you turn around.

They began to file off the plane, officers and senior NCOs from the front, and enlisted men from the back. Bright-eyed, bushy-tailed, some wearing dress greens, some wearing mustaches already; all of them squinting in the sun. The officers walking that walk.

Then it started: the catcalls, the fingers, the lewd and snide remarks.

"You'll be sa-ree! Goddamn fuck-king sa-reee!"

"Wha's yer fucken sister's phone number? Address? I'll drop by an' tell 'er I saw yer ass, an' it was still in one piece."

"Keep an eye peeled, dufus, there's nuthin' but gooks for a couple hundred clicks aroun'!"

The CIBs stood on the benches and sat on the backs, shouting and gesturing the loudest, and knew that twenty-some dudes walking down from the back of the plane would go home strapped to a litter or trundled in a bodybag.

We lined up according to the numbers on our tickets, taking our sweet time, playing the number game. "Where's number one-one-five?" "Who's got number four?" "We're waiting on your ass, number four." "I think they should do this according to height." "I'm sixty-nine. I'm sixty-nine. I'm sixty-nine." We climbed aboard and I took the first window seat. There was no mistake about this plane going back to Travis, but I wanted to witness for myself half the world go thataway, as though it might not happen if I didn't see it. Like the man who insists upon witnessing vital emergency repairs, to make sure all the parts are replaced, that just the right torque is put to the bolts. The engines wound up and we rolled off to the end of the runway. How were we going to do this? Take a running start and squeal the tires on the turn, or stop dead to work up the rpm's with all the brakes on? I decided that there would be a quick turn onto the runway, then the pilot would punch it and off we'd go. Very cool. He wasn't getting combat pay. Why should he stop and work up the rpm's? But the plane swung around to the end of the runway and stopped. Keep going, my man! Lay some rubber, get me off the ground. The engines revved, all brakes on. The plane vibrated slightly. The wingtips flapped and still they fed more torque. The engines whined even louder, and then all of a sudden my arms lifted from the armrests and I was pushed back into the seat. I looked quickly out the window at the wheels and the blur of rubber patches on the cement. Then that was it. The wheels pulled away from their shadows and we were in the air ten feet, twenty feet, more. The plane went into a steep climb, the horizon nearly vertical in the window. There it was one more time. Pale orange dirt roads, shallow-pitched thatch roofs, buffalo sunning themselves in puddles that flashed brilliantly white for an instant, reflecting the sun, the bouncy-soft canopy of the jungle green and gold and green. I felt a quickening of blood in my neck, a muted gushing in my ears. Several of the dudes let out a cry, but there wasn't much joy in it, not the incredible shriek one would expect. This was part of the ritual also—the sighing and banging of fists on the armrests, the cheers and hat throwing and streamers pulling tight between the troopship's sundeck and the open-air warehouse crowded with girlfriends, the mooses and shacks, watching their meal tickets sail for home and a discharge. And then the final gesture, a mouthful of phlegm gathered and flung into the harbor with the tongue. But there is no ship, no crowds, no streamers. It is no occasion for cheering or special gladness or sweet-sad crying, just a moment of strange triumph, held tight at the edges because we are only one planeful, and bottomed out shallow, because the plane that is taking us home brought other men.

The plane followed the river for a time, then turned due east. We passed over jungle stranded among rice fields, small hamlets and sandbagged fire bases, making for altitude all the while. And then there it was, sand dunes and short tough grass and the South China Sea. The surf must roll to the beach like that from every ocean on the globe, the soft laying of the thinnest foam on waterlogged sand. To have been stationed somewhere near the coast—to have to walk near it every morning on the way to chow; to stroll down of an evening and watch it roll up to my feet; to listen to that roll and splash at night as I swung in my hammock, the murmur of it, the touch of it—would have pushed me into insanity. I know that one night I would have tried to swim it. No matter how far home is, at sea distance becomes a state of mind.

I watched the ocean until we came into Guam. I hadn't unbuckled my belt from the takeoff. We came into the airfield, lined with B-52s painted in dark camouflage colors or plain flat black. We had to get off the plane for the refueling. I was getting to feel more cool all the time, because about the only thing I remembered about San Francisco was that it was cold in March. Not freezing cold, just wet, shivery cold, the sort of cold that makes you hold a coffee cup with both hands. So the only piece of issue gear I had with me was my field jacket, smelling of sweat and mud and wood fires. We straggled off the plane and burst into the terminal. In the cafeteria three broads walked in wearing hats that looked like fezzes, and sat at the counter and quietly ordered coffee. Their legs were crossed, their skirts high on their thighs. I had never seen skirts so short. You're back-in-the-world, my man. You've got to expect that things have moved around a little since you left. Three of the tallest broads I had ever seen. Long legs that wrap around your head and turn you deaf. They looked prime and round-eyed for sure. Not a dude in the place was thinking about anything but walking up to those broads and saying, "Baby, I dig your body, how'd you like to go some-where and get laid; we'll all chip in." But nobody said boo to them. Those broads looked like they could chew off your leg and spit out the bones. We just sat there watching every-thing those amazons did, and said to ourselves, "Look at that round-eyed pussy, wouldja."

Back on the plane the stewardesses showed a couple movies and served a meal. I kept ringing for more coffee until the girl would walk by every now and again with the pot. It was dark, but I kept watching out the window. Twice I saw the lights of ships, small pinpoint dots, like the glow of a cigarette at two hundred meters, only cold and white. First light came easy and quiet, like it never did on the ground—a clean, straight shot of warm sun. There was none of that gray-green funny business. It came like a good cook will slice homemade bread, quick and sharp, letting the slices fall away better than could be arranged by hand. First gray, then white, then golden on the front edges of the wings and engine cowling and all across the horizon.

I kept drinking coffee and tried to remember all the things I was going to do when I got home. I couldn't decide much beyond buying a good pair of dark glasses and taking a bath. I hadn't had a bath, a good bath, since R & R. And the glasses, I wanted dark glasses to cover my eyes. In January, when we started getting replacements, their eyes seemed funny, their faces pale. Even the black dudes had that paleness before they grew a crust. And when they did, their faces squinted, their hands became accustomed to holding a weapon, and their shoulders slumped the same as ours. But at first the dark around the eyes, the saggy wrinkles, and the way we had held our hands in half a fist, that must have surprised them, and frightened them, too. It is the look of the eyes, for a long time called the thousand-meter stare, that blatant sparkle of light which does not shine. The glassy milky eyes not of the trenches, but of the ambush. It is the thousand-meter stare cranked down to fifty, to five. It is seemingly perfect concentration; blind rage; simple pleading; incomprehension. A surrender to cool perfect murder that defies sleep and warm soapy water. It is a reach to see everything at once; the limit of wakefulness; an urge to live; to stay awake. Because to let the eye wander, to drop that gaze, to fall asleep and slip into dreams, is to die.

I would buy a pair of dark glasses, the darkest lenses I could find, and save myself the trouble of people leaning close to me, whispering, "Dosier. You know, you've got the oddest, strangest look in your eyes. Why is that, hey? What have you seen?"

Later that morning we pulled into Hawaii. I made for the gift shop, where they sold dashboard hula-hula dolls and dufus kid-toy coconut handbags and genuine lava-chunk paperweights. I bought the first pair of glasses that fit my head and didn't look too goofy. Some dudes crowded into the bar to swill down as much booze as they could without getting sick. Some dudes strolled into the snack bar for a hamburger and shake. I slouched on one of the benches with my arms stretched out on the back and my legs out and ankles crossed, stoned on airline coffee and Darvon and a smoke, watching the pussy that wandered around. There were blond-haired ladies, waltzing around with those mama-san outfits that started at the chin and went two feet past the floor, decorated with hordes of flowers and brown bamboo. There were short flat ones with huge cheeks, old mama-sans built like footballs with faces hidden under necklaces of flowers, young sweet-tasting virgins, fourteen or so, hanging on to Daddy's trousers for all their worth and flashing their faces to the floor whenever one of us looked them in the eye, and the ones you know put out for somebody because they're carrying some short round of a kid on one arm.

The call for our flight came. By the time we got down to the gate a mob of officer types and dependents traveling standby were crowded thick as hair around the guy behind the counter, waving their tickets in his face.

"Stand aside there! Make way." We pushed through the crowd flashing our tickets in the guy's face, leaving those farmers flagging their standby tickets in the breeze.

We took off again around noon or so. We passed over two ships going toward Hawaii. I put my eye close to the glass and looked as far ahead as I could. There it was, a thin black line, a rock wall, the coast of California. I sipped coffee and watched the water. The sea had never looked so strange and cold. The coast kept coming closer, rising black and gray out of the water beyond the reach of the surf that splashed high and swirled back into the undertow. The sea did not roll slowly up the sand, chasing sand crabs and driftwood, but struck the rocks that rose straight out of the sea. The rocks struck level ground and the stiff pale grass that stretched from there to the shores of the Carolinas and Virginia. There were small spindly trees hung with withered fruit and houses clustered three and four together and small smooth-rolling cars on the blacktopped roads. Then the plane glided over it. The place where people have dragged themselves for a hundred years to stand at the edge of the rocks and curse the ocean because this was where the land finally fell back into the sea. There was nothing to think about or dream of or pound my fist for, not anymore. Over there growing things were lush and thick and the deepest green. Weeds and rice and jungle grew and pushed at footpaths and roads and hamlets. Everywhere something was spreading wide, getting tall, grabbing for the sunlight. But here the growing things seemed to have run out of energy, stunted short like all growing things are in the sea air. The green of things was pallid, more anemic than anything else, as though the green of the earth had been sucked up, cut and baled, then stored thick somewhere and left. It looked as though it needed a good spread of manure and a season in clover, then turned under and planted right.

We circled Travis Air Force Base once with our gear down and touched ever so softly. I began to shiver. We rolled the length of the runway and taxied toward the terminal. A throng of people, dressed in heavy coats and scarves and gloves, crowded close to the railing on the roof, waving their arms like crazy and yelling at the plane. Trust the Army to leave nothing out. We would probably get off the plane, be issued fatigues and packs and rifles, and marched to Oakland Army Terminal. I think it would have been more fitting if we came back the way we went, packed to the doors in the middle of the night on the other side of the field. That's the way they ship home the wounded, loaded in C-133s and unloaded into the backs of ambulances. The plane came to a smooth-rolling halt. Right on the mark. They turned off the engines and two guys with the ground crew rolled up the stairway and ran up to help with the door. It is hardly possible to sit here and recollect the feelings as the engines wound down, or the shudder that went through the plane when they slammed the stairway against the side, or the sight of a thousand strange huddled spectators screaming "Yoo-hoo" at the top of their lungs, waving handkerchiefs and mittens and fat babies. It was a powerful, glad feeling—a chill shivery breathing; the short snappy twitching of sore fingers; the itch and tickle of gooseflesh up and down my sides. A sweet and bitter moment. I think I will never again be rushed with such an incredible physical joy as I was just then. I had actually lived. There were no folded sleeves or litter of cartridge boxes, no guns, no sandbags. I would never again be yanked out of the first sound sleep in months by freight-train eight-inch howitzers, or hold a rifle and know "you bet your sweet ass it's loaded," or have to police up a battle-field—weapons in one pile, whole bodies in one pile, stray arms and legs in another, spread over with quicklime, but the lime never quick enough.

There would be no more midnight alerts, the platoon taking to the road in the middle of the night to clean up a fucked-up ambush. There isn't going to be any more of that smelling like some fetid and dying thing, because of no water to wash in, and my flak jacket stinking acrid and dead like a crapper buzzing with horseflies and maggots. There isn't going to be any more dust and shit between my teeth and in my lungs from driving the road, of which there isn't a one-mile stretch anywhere that's straight and level and well tended. There will be no more drinking brackish flat water, no more flies up my ass when I take a squat, and for a long time now there would be real food and nobody, or at least very few people, standing along the road trying to hustle me for C rations and Camels and Hershey's Tropical Chocolate.

But most of all it will be quiet. One morning I will be reaching sleepily for the burner to make the coffee or slipping a fresh blade into my razor or bending over to pick up a snippet of thread on the floor, and that buzzing in my head will cease—simply pass away. There will be honest, hearty laughing and the joy of communal drinking, celebrating being in one piece and breathing air that does not stick in the throat or reek of gunpowder and rice-paddy muck. No longer will there be that gamey crawl to the skin I got so tired of scratching. No more drinking all but the last half inch in my canteen cup because of the grit and rice chaff and bugs. There will be comfortable sleep, the deepest, most restful kind, unaided by a case of PX beer and three or four smokes. Sleep honestly come by. There will be sheets and blankets—maybe two—and streetlights and the sounds of taxis.

I was not the first off the plane. I had heard an ugly story. It seems this dude was killed and his old lady came down to meet the next plane. When they started climbing down, the woman walked up to the first dude and said, "If my son can't come home, neither can you," and shot him four times before the MPs could grab her. No, sir, being first just doesn't count anymore. I had the rest of my life to climb down that stairway. I pulled on the field jacket and walked down zipping it up, watching the eager beavers going down on their hands and knees to touch the ground. A regular finale. Be cool, Dosier, get through customs, get your separation, and dee dee mau—take off.

The luggage came in and I lined up to go through customs with the two dudes from Bravo Company. This fat dude with his customs get-up came down the line. The three of us stood there behind the long silver table with our bags, our CIBs shining blue and silver, and the customs dude went through the first Bravo Company dude's stuff, pulling out the pockets of trousers and shirts, unraveling socks, even going through his ditty bag and looking in the envelopes of opened and saved letters. He pulled the once-over heavy and hard, looking for anything. Then he stepped over to me.

"You got anything to declare?"

I had one pair of back-in-the-world underwear, some letters tied in a bundle, one of Quinn's "Made in Hanoi" sweat shirts, that gold-yellow Camp Zama PX sweater, and, of course, my one and only, never fail, bulletproof Gabby Hayes bush hat.

"No, sir." He looked at my spread-eagled suitcase in a glance and moved on to the next Bravo Company dude and started on him. These two dudes had CIBs, the Purple Hearts, the Bronze Stars, and all that. They were also black. Tall and thin with long pale-brown fingers and dark glasses and dope taped to their legs just like everybody else. Two days before, they had been on the line, humping fifty-pound packs, necks draped with green towels, sporting bandoliers of M-60 ammo and faded camouflage covers, and sweating out going home as only the grunt infantry can sweat. The three of us stood together facing the fat man who shook everybody down as they came through, looking for live ammo and puppy-shit pornography and flammables and so on. But he couldn't have called the Bravo Company dudes "nigger" any plainer than if it were the only word he knew. "Boy, Ah knows you tryin' ta sneak some damn shit inta this country, something evil an' nasty an' gook-like, an' Ah's gonna find it, whate'er it is. So stan' back, 'fore Ah give ya one upside the head. You home now, boy, an' Ah don' care what ya got hangin' on your sleeve, jes' stan' back." I looked at the first Bravo Company dude, who had a livid whitish mark on the back of his hand, like a burn scar. Then I looked over at the other Bravo Company dude, who had an AWOL bag crammed with cameras and lens cases and packets of film. And a look of the eyes made the sign. I've seen it, done it so many times. Follow me, fire and move, fire and move. I want body count, body count. Get down in the front leaning rest and crank out some goddamned body count, young sergeant.

We rolled through hamlets two or three times, and every trip we got a couple sniper rounds, and each time we'd call and tell the El-tee. Maybe it takes him a couple more trips to get the handle on things, or somebody gets hit; then he orders everybody to hang a hard right, pull off the road on the ambush side, and open fire at nothing in particular, just kill everything that breathes. And we do it, cranking forward all the time, over hooches and buffs, until everything is run off or dead.

The two Bravo Company dudes and I stared at the customs man the same way Lavery had stared, had hated us with his eyes—Quinn and Stepik and Dewey and me—when the MPs cuffed him and slid him into their jeep. He had stiffened his back and turned his head to us, blinking his eyes to keep from glaring. And Quinn looked right back at him, leaning forward a little. Then the MPs drove away with a crunch of tires, but Lavery turned and stared at us through the dust. Stepik and Dewey and I turned away, but Quinn stood at the high crown of the road, staring back at Lavery until all we could see of the jeep was the dust, billowing out. My God, how he hated us. How he must hate us still.

The three of us hated that customs man the same way. If that room had been empty of witnesses, I say, if it had been just the three of us and the fat man, I tell you, we would have taken him into a corner away from the glass partition where the spectators stood, and cut him. I sit here and remember that silver customs badge and that gesture of his, the flipping of the last pair of socks off his fingertips, and that "Hey, nigger" look in his eye, and I say in the simplest words I know we would have killed him with the same spirit we killed dinks and gooks and slant-eyes, and all the rest. It is the coldest murder.

Our group made it through with nothing confiscated, nothing palmed; no one held back. We loaded into buses that would take us to Oakland. It was well past dark. We were taken to a converted warehouse at the Oakland Army Terminal, just off the entrance to the Bay Bridge. The dudes being reassigned went to one building; those of us getting out altogether went into another. In one large room were bleachers in front of a broad floor, marked something like a basketball court. All around the bleachers were various counters and rows of desks and a large black fan set on a platform on one of the columns. A bunch of clerks, wearing dress greens with stiff poplin shirts, sat at desks or walked around with coffee cups, trying to stay awake. Next to one of the large sliding doors hung a large four-color poster of some dude in battle dress—pack and patches, bloused boots and bayoneted rifle, shit-eating grin and all. The caption said, "He works for ZERO defects, so should you." And I thought if the dude knew what the poster said he would jump down and blow away every poplin shirt in the place, screaming, "ZERO fucken defects up your ass!"

I was the first to arrive.

"Where are you going?" one of the clerks asked.

"Home."

"Are you separating?"

"I guess that's what you call it. This the place?"

"Have a seat."

I put my suitcase on the floor and stretched out and fell asleep. I was awakened by one of the Bravo Company dudes just in time for this young looey to hand out forms and say his little say. We handed these in and were given more. By this time it was very late. We were taken to our complimentary steak-and-eggs breakfast about midnight or so. The young lieutenant said that we would not be separated until the morning, when we would take our physicals and draw our pay. The barracks at Oakland were the new type, four stories with eight squad bays and tile floors. Replacements going the other way were billeted there until their planes came. The mess hall had tin trays and real tables and stout chairs. The steaks were not bad, but it didn't mean anything anyway. On the way back to the bleachers some of the dudes stopped at the ground floor Orderly Room to see if they could find someplace to lie down. A young slick-sleeve private stood behind the counter next to a pile of unfolded blankets.

". . . I'm sorry, but my orders don't say anything about putting you guys up . . ." He waved a plywood slab in someone's face. It was his general orders, stapled and covered with acetate and green tape.

"Fuck yer orders, kid! All I'm talking about is a place to lay my body out for a couple hours. How fucken difficult is that?"

One of the dudes standing in the back saw the stripes on my sleeve and turned to me. "Man, ain't this some shit? They got all kinds of racks upstairs and this kid is worried about orders. Why don't you try?" I walked to the counter with as stern a look as I could manage. The kid looked right out of training, no division patches, brand-new boots, and his belt buckle still had shellac on it, scratches and all.

"Private, what's this about no bunks?"

"Uh, Sergeant, the CQ didn't leave me any orders about these guys. I don't want to get into trouble. They are not authorized blankets or anything."

"Who said anything about blankets?" I turned to the Bravo Company dude with the cameras. "Is there a squad bay?"

"Yeah, third floor left. Nobody in it."

"Well, Private, just let these dudes sleep up there till morning. If anybody gives you a hassle, just send them to me. I'll be over at the bleachers."

"Yes, Sergeant," he replied crisply.

As if he would know where the bleachers were. He nodded when I said it, but he was thinking to himself: well, goddamn, here's something else nobody told me about.

All the dudes who wanted to sleep for a while went upstairs, which was everybody but the second Bravo Company dude and myself. I went to the bleachers to get a towel, then went back to the barracks to take a shower and, for the first time since R & R, put on underwear. Back at the bleachers he and I drank coffee and more coffee and popped the last of my Darvons. His name was Jonah Washington, lived in Sacramento, would be home by the middle of the afternoon. He was supposed to be on that Bravo

Company Truce Day ambush, but was bumped by some poor dude who had to do it for punishment. We lounged on the polished wood benches and talked school and women and getting work, to keep each other awake. We sat side by side with our feet up on the benches below us, like we were at a basketball game. We talked in near whispers with easy, weary voices. He gestured with those large elegant brown hands of his and long and bony wrinkled fingers. He had watery black eyes and a lumpy razor rash, and said he thought he was through being a nigger when we started talking about that customs dude. We talked about cars and dudes we had both known and the Black Panthers and R & R and more school. We talked and paced up and back to keep from dozing, and yawned and stretched and took turns buying bad machine coffee until we both ran out of change; until it was morning and the others began straggling in. We were taken down to the medical section and given our physicals—blood, short arm, psychological, the whole she-bang. The guy in psychological asked me if I was having any problems. I told him I was having terrible nightmares and bad headaches. I found out I had high blood pressure. Only two dudes were held over for observation. The rest of us were trotted down to finance to draw our pay. Then we had to sit through a character lecture by a chaplain about cleaning up our language, and then an old man in a wheel-chair talked about the GI Bill and made a pitch for the VFW. We were issued new uniforms. I would wear mine home and throw it away. My outfit was baggy and smelled of talc and mothballs, but it didn't mean anything because I would be home by midnight. By the time we changed into our Class-As, our DD-214s—our discharges—and other papers were ready.

"Is everything there?" the clerk asked, sliding mine across the counter.

CIB, ribbons, rank, yeah, that's close. I signed my last voucher, picked up my suitcase on the fly, and split for the cab line. Bye.

I wanted so badly to stop in the doorway. I had an overwhelming and undeniable urge to turn around and shout some snarling invective—at once obscenely sibilant and plosive. But I caught myself in midstride and shook it off. It will keep, Dosier. Let it soak some. It will save.

I walked up to the first cabbie I saw. "You know how to find San Francisco Airport?"

"Sure, trooper." The cabby sat up, smiling that smile that says tips, tips, tips. I watched the traffic, but quit after a while because of the way the guy was driving. I finally closed my eyes and hummed to drown out the click of the meter. When we got to the airport I whipped out my elephant-hide wallet and leafed through the greenbacks, five hundred dollars' worth. Money left from my last two vouchers, accrued leave, and the last of my blackjack winnings. I flipped through the bills quickly, crumpled a ten to make sure it wasn't stuck to anything, paid the dude, and he touched his cap to me. Then I went into the terminal, walked up to the first counter, and slid my suitcase onto the weighing machine.

"When you going to Chicago again?" I said, pushing my dark glasses up.

"Sir?" said the woman behind the counter.

"I say, when are you going to Chicago again today?"

"Oh. Ah, six-thirty, flight 106."

"What's the cheapest seat?"

She fooled around with the ticket while I pulled the greenbacks out of my elephant-hide wallet again, counted out the fare, and slid it across the counter. When she handed me the ticket she said, "Sir, the bar is down that way, first right. The USO is upstairs." She smiled, looking at my sunglasses. I smiled back and said, "Thank you," very slowly.

I went to the bar and slid into a booth. The waitress came over, dressed in one of those getups that make a person look all tit. She handed me a menu.

"I'll have a double Jack Daniel's, a New York cut, hash browns, a sliced tomato, and brussels sprouts. You got brussels sprouts? I guess that's all." She brought the drink and left for the kitchen.

I reached for the glass and clicked it with my fingernail, making it ring. "Well, Dosier?" I said to myself. "Here's to Deadeye and the Cow Catcher and all that. Peace to the ashes." And I drank, feeling like some bad-ass white hunter just arrived in Mombasa or Nairobi or some such place, sneaking through another carload of poached ivory and bleeding from a handful of hemorrhoids. I finished the whiskey and ordered another. The girl came with the steak. I ate slowly, chewing each mouthful, and ordered another drink. I finished that and ordered still another. I had to call my folks and tell them I was home, tell them when to pick me up at O'Hare Airport. I went out to a row of pay phones on the concourse, sliding into the first one I came to. I picked up the receiver, but then I had to laugh because I couldn't remember the number. I sat there with the dial tone buzzing in my ear, looking down at my shoes, trying to recall the number we'd had for as long as I could remember. I remembered that short bit of bedroom hallway, like an alcove almost. I remembered the brought-from-the-old-country wall clock—the tock-tock-tock rhythm in the house, a rhythm in my life. The clock hung opposite a rosewood-veneer nightstand, where the phone had always been set on a pile of dog-eared phone books. Then the number came to me and I dialed. I suddenly felt very queer. I was back in San Francisco, calling home as though no time had passed.

My folks, my brothers, Eddie and Danny—sure I would be glad to see them. I would be more than glad to see them, but I would always be a boy in that house.

I have traveled to a place where the dead lie above the ground in rows and bunches. Time has gone somewhere without me. This is not my country, not my time. My skin is drawn tight around my eyes. My clothes smell of blood. I bleed inside. I am water. I am stone. I am swift-running water, made from snow. I am stone, chipped from giant granite boulders, small shards, jagged and sharp-edged, sliding down the rockface past the timberline. Chips and flakes break away from me, and sparks sometimes. I have not come home, Ma. I have gone ahead, gone back. There is glass between us, we cannot speak. I hear voices, I have seen a wraith, Ma. He wore black boots and britches and strange livery. He talked to me, he whispered, he laughed. He touched my stomach with the back of his hand, like people will put an arm on your shoulder when they speak, and it burns.

"Hello," someone said. The voice quaked, shivered, sounded unwell. Was *that* the sound of Ma's voice?

"Hello, Ma?" I blurted. There was a long pause. "It's me, Phil. San Francisco. I'm home, Ma. I'm all right. I'll be flying in tonight, flight 106." There was another pause. "Ma?"

"Yes, Philip, I'm here," was all she said.

"It's me. I'm home. San Francisco."

We talked some, but then she had to go, she said. Pop told me later that she didn't eat dinner and stayed in their bedroom, crying.

I went back to the bar. You've got to beat your brains out, trying to make it home, but when you bump up against it, it doesn't sound like you know it should. There is not that resonance, that solid ring. You drink double whiskeys, ice

and all, and every time the woman bends down to pick up
the glass you look down the front of her getup, as though
she had anything different. She looks at you funny, not
because you're looking at her, but she has never seen anybody drink quite so fast, ice and all, or put their feet up on
the leather, or mumble quite so loud, talking about ivory
and headaches and a man called Atevo.

And being drunk never felt so sweet. Everything
slowed down to a nice hazy crawl. Mellow, like sun-warmed
bath water.

The flight was called. I sat in an aisle seat and drank
coffee and stayed strapped in. Then we were flying low over
lighted streets and theater marquees and neon signs hung
high over bars and tall gaudy airport hotels. We hit the end
of the runway and dashed quickly to the terminal. Planes
were everywhere. The only things that made it real were the
dress greens and the ribbons and the sweet smell of perfume the stewardesses laid so thin when they walked by. I
was the only one on the plane who knew what they smelled
like. Like the mist that sprays when you pierce a lemon
with your nail or the back of clean hands. I walked out, my
blouse unbuttoned, tie pulled loose, collar wide, that orange
motor-pool dust still on my shoes. The first one I saw was
Eddie in his Marine uniform, wearing a pair of wrap-
around dark glasses and leaning on one of those thin white
canes. He looked taller and heftier. He took blindman lessons at Great Lakes Naval Hospital during the day and
lived at home. All the rest of that week I watched him
struggle with his food at dinner, sit on the edge of his bed at
night, trying to read braille, and refuse everybody's help,
until I just couldn't stand to watch. Danny stood next to him
with his hands on Ma's shoulder. Ma told me later that he
cried into the phone when she called him at work to say I
was home. Ma had gray hair, curled short, just like I

remembered. She wore her beige coat, which she held tightly with both hands, the way women do. Danny had written and told me she had been sick with one thing and another since Eddie had been wounded. Pop stood next to her, dressed in his one suit and his old overcoat, his hands deep in the pockets, and a shaving cut on his chin. He looked as haggard and harassed and tired as Ma, and had lost some more hair. I stopped just in front of them, looking at each one, as though they were stiff and propped there. I walked up to Eddie and shook his hand. We are both home, Eddie. While we stood there holding each other by the hand I reached up and put my other arm around him and gave him a great hug. I held him and he put his arm around me. I could feel the excitement he felt. I had never felt a heart thrill so. After a moment I turned and did the same to Danny and Pop, then turned to Ma. She and I hugged, then the five of us left.

The outside was very cold. Pop wanted to buy me a drink, so we didn't get home until after one in the morning. Everybody went to bed. I drew some water for a bath. The bedroom upstairs was cold, just like always. The bathroom was steamed and hot. I scrubbed myself pink, drained the water and drew fresh, a little hotter, and scrubbed again. The third time I drew water I sat back and soaked, turning the water on to keep the steam in the room, until Pop came in around four to get ready for work. We had breakfast together. He fried the eggs and made the bacon and toast and coffee, and the two of us sat in the dining room at the places we always sat—him with his back to the windows, me with my back to the old buffet, still and always piled with mail and catalogues and the sterling-silver case and a mantel clock. Pop asked me if I was going to look for work.

"I expect," I said. "I want to go to Springfield and be

with Jenny. I sent her some money. I already have an apartment."

"You and Jenny going to get married? Gee, she sounds like a nice girl."

"I don't know, Pop," I said. "I guess."

"You going to stay in Springfield or go off to Pennsylvania or come back to Chicago?"

"We'll see, Pop," I said. "Probably stay in Springfield for a while. I got to see what it's like."

"What kind of work you going to look for? Factory work? You don't want to work in a factory, do you?" he said. He looked down at his plate, thinking about his own day-foreman job at a metalworking place. "You could get a restaurant job, like you had before."

"I don't know, Pop," I said with a wave of my hand. "I got to take a look around. Worse come to worst I can always get a job at a stables, following horses around with a coal shovel, like I did at Onwensia."

All that day I sat in the living room, reading some and napping some and watching out the window. Late in the afternoon I called Jenny. I sat on the cold cement basement steps and we talked on and on about this and that, and every once in a while she'd say, "Excuse me, Flip," and stop somebody walking past the dorm phone there, saying that I was home; that she was talking to me in Chicago. Her voice was muffled and rang on the phone, but she sounded warm and happy. She worried about the apartment she'd rented for me because she'd had to sign a six-month lease. I told her that it was okay; that it didn't mean anything; that no one had ever been shot for skipping out on a lease. We talked for a good hour, then she had to go to dinner.

Early that evening I borrowed Danny's car and drove to a cut-rate liquor store, picked a bottle of Jack Daniel's, and took it to the counter.

The clerk, a tall, young dude with a Skil saw pencil pocket, looked at me.

"You got an I.D.?"

I pulled out my driver's license.

"You got a draft card? Did you know this license is expired?"

"Well, hey, I just got out of the Army yesterday. I was overseas when the license expired. When I went into the Army they took away my draft card and gave me an I.D. I haven't had time to reapply. Don't you believe I'm Philip Dosier?" I pulled out my 214. "How's that?"

"So?"

"Look, here's my citation for the Combat Infantryman's Badge. Here's the orders for my sergeant's promotion. Is that good enough?"

"No." He stood there shaking his head. "And I cannot sell you any liquor. That's the rule, kid."

Kid? Rule?

I stepped back from the counter to put the papers back into my billfold and let another civilian buy a case of beer. The dude looked at me fold the papers while he waited for his change. Just remember, no hassle, no trouble, keep it quiet even though your heart is pounding like a madman at steel doors. The civilian with the beer started for the exit. I looked at the kid behind the counter and grabbed for the whiskey and threw it over my wrist. It hit a bottle of Gallo and bounced to the floor and smashed. I walked for the door.

"Hey, you . . ."

Fuck off. Fuck with me, m' man, and I'll wrap your ass around the neck of that bottle and stuff it down the goddamned plumbing. There was no use telling that guy what I was thinking, that two days before I would have cut him in half, wrecked the store—bottles, picture windows, and all. I sat in the car shaking. That swift rush of anger; that jumping up at the first word given—halting on the road to do an ambush from the tops of the tracks—the swarthiness, the swagger, the brag. It had to stop. It's all over, it's two days ago. It's history. It's dreams.

I left slowly, driving on the right, suddenly unaccustomed to the night lights and the cars and the cold. All the fucking around and sleeping stoned and drunk, shaving in cold water and the slack sound the fifty makes when you cock it. It is over. I was going to step back from all these people and get some peace and quiet. I had to get away from Chicago and fucked-up civilians and raw March weather. I wanted to get to Kentucky and Jenny as quick as I could.

That night I had clean sheets and real blankets, and my old beat-up pillow. I found Eddie sitting on his bed, going over his braille. When I touched his knee to let him know I was there he said, "You don't have to do that, Flip. I can tell by your footsteps."

And without thinking I said, "I just wanted to touch you, hey."

As I undressed he finally talked about getting wounded and being laid up for so long and the dumb-ass braille lessons and about all the things he had time to think about. "Zillions of things," he said. "But it could have been worse, Flip. There was dudes in that bunker that got killed. So it could have been worse." Then I hugged him again, not knowing any other way to respond, and felt his eyes water when he hugged me back, wanting so bad to hear my voice, but then he pushed me away and slipped his dark glasses back on, and went back to his braille, skimming his fingertips across a stack of flash cards that he held in his lap, whispering the words to himself, and sometimes spelling out each letter to make sure.

When I pulled back the covers and climbed into bed, I thought to myself, this was it, the way I had dreamt of sleeping for God knows how long. Arms spread under the pillow, elbows and legs stretched out, nothing but room compared to that hammock, and warm and dry besides. But it didn't feel right. There was a tightness in my shoulders, an odd texture to the linen, a strange convulsion in my stomach. I got up after a while and took a couple aspirin. I lay on my back, one hand on my stomach. There it was, that tightness, that itch, that slow-motion growl. Then voices, mumbled, swallowed in the rain. The sounds of a night fire, the long green and orange streaks of tracers ricocheting off the ground into the air, the orange and blue and white flashes of RPGs and the stubby scarlet and black incoming. The bad nights had begun. I got out of bed and stripped it. I laid one blanket on the floor, pulled the other on top, and slept on my back with an arm under my head, my legs cramped and tight.

I wanted to get south where Jenny was, where the weather was milder, just as soon as I could get a bus or a plane. Pop asked me why I should go to the expense. "Besides," he said, "I want to meet this girl. You wait for Saturday, then I'll drive you down. You can wait—can't you?" And I thought to myself that I had waited this long, a couple more days didn't mean anything. Not anymore. So Wednesday I called Jenny and told her that Pop was driving me down Saturday afternoon; that he wanted her to meet us in the lobby of the Brown Hotel in Louisville between three and four.

CLIMBING

DOWN

We made an early start that Saturday, and all the way
down Pop kept up his unending questions about work—and
I'd answer, "Yeah"—and getting married, again—and I'd
answer, "Yes, Father"—until he came to his last question,
again, "I guess it was pretty rough over there, eh, son?"
And I'd fidget a minute, pushing my dark glasses up on my
nose whether they needed it or not, and look out over the
dusty dashboard and down the road, and say, "Yes."

   I sat cramped on the passenger side and smoked and
watched out the window, glancing at the blur of working
farms and ramshackle farms, the bungalows and ranch-
style homes and the jacked-up house trailers, the dogwood
groves along the creek banks and the poplar sapling wind-
breaks, turned earth and fallow earth and reddish, rusted
barbed-wire fences. It floated by and I took it all in, following it with quick glances—the open stretches of rows of
corn stumps and the litter of harvest junk, the kid toys on
the gravel driveways, the old cars and old tractors and such
behind falling-down barns, and dotted here and there the
farmyard, barnyard elms crowded around wood-frame
houses.

I had three hundred dollars in my wallet—cashed-in Savings Bonds the Army made me buy—and two thousand more in the mail from my Armed Forces saving account. I will blow where the wind blows me, go where the wind takes me. What happened after I got to Springfield, after I settled in some, didn't much matter.

We crossed the Ohio River into Louisville around three, found the Brown Hotel, and circled the lobby to see if Jenny was already waiting. The place crawled with GIs on weekend passes from Fort Knox. They were GIs all right, no one could mistake those Saturday inspection skin-head haircuts, the just-so trouser creases, and spit-shined shoes—that clean-shaved, bright-eyed, open-faced sharpness. They milled around the lobby furniture and stood in line for single rooms and hung over the mezzanine rail, gazing down and scratching their heads, "Well-Fred-whadaya-wanna-do-now" fashion.

Pop and I sat on a couch near the main stairway. I watched the broad steps, hollowed and rounded, and the brass handrails and the glow of the street on all that marble; watched the hordes of GIs move around, taking those shining stairs two at a time or standing in small gangs, at-ease fashion. I watched them until I couldn't stand to look at them, so I gazed at the two dusty equestrian portraits hanging over the front desk. One was Aristides, who won the first Kentucky Derby in 1875. He stood in loose dirt to the fettocks in front of a split-rail fence. Sleeked neck and flanks, swollen girth, small wooden face and eyes. The jockey, a skinny-legged, no-face kid, sat stiffly with a large bouquet of roses hooked over one arm.

The other portrait was Man o' War, who never ran in the Derby, standing parade-ground fashion, in the shade of a paddock tree with green rolling meadows and white rail fences behind him—his coat speckled with sun and shadow. Huge. Squat. Supple. Thickset, like a plow horse. Long, curled muscles in his neck and legs. Beads of muscle in his shoulders and flanks. With his head cocked and ears pricked, nostrils flared and yellow teeth grinning, he looked as though he were on the verge of laughter. He peeked out of the corners of his eyes, the keenest sparkle there. Princely. The look of eagles, as horsemen say.

I sat on the edge of that couch for the longest time—smoking and squirming, rubbing my softening, sweaty hands on my knees—then there she was, coming slowly up the stairs, sliding her hand along the brass banister and looking in every face, and every face looking back at her, the way GIs do. She wore a raspberry-colored dress, and her brown hair, which shone auburn in the summer, was longer than I remembered.

She stepped up to the edge of the carpet, sailing her hand off the end of the banister, and stood holding a small red leather purse in front of her. Quickly she tossed her head back to shake out her hair, fluffing it with her hand, and looked among the crowd with slow sidelong arcs of her head, and darting eyes. I sat forward, catching glimpses of her through the crowd, but her face was silhouetted against the sunlight glow of the marble behind her. Then she saw me. Her eyes brightened and she grinned, then nudged her way through the crowd, and stopped—a step or two between us. I stood up. The soft, ringed wrinkles of baby fat on her neck were gone. A keener, fuller light shone in her eyes; she smelled different. I tried to recall the tone of her voice—when she was excited and happy; when she was sleepy; when she was irked; after a couple of drinks. I tried to recall the way she held her cigarettes, the touch of her lips, how she walked barefoot, the feel of her small, round breasts on the backs of my hands. Any of that.

I had traveled halfway around the world to that spot on the carpet, and it all fell away—Quinn and the platoon and whatever was left of the seven-three. I was suddenly tired and felt my shoulders go limp.

I caught myself staring and blinked and took a breath. "Hello, Jenny," I said, almost in a whisper.

"Philip," she said. Had her voice dropped? It sounded smoother somehow. She held out her hand, fingers twitching. "Philip?" I shivered back of the ears, but I reached over and touched her hand, running my palm up her arm and around her neck, and then she put her arms around me and we embraced. She pressed against me, leaning forward on her toes—her warm fingers spread wide on the back of my shirt, and her forehead squeezing into the nape of my neck. My God, how long had it been since anyone touched me like that. I felt her body through the clothes, the warmth and slickness of the nervous sweat, the thick pressure of her breasts, and her lips on the side of my face, brushing against the eyes and chin and lips. I wanted to gather her in; hold her tighter than ever I held anyone; tighter than Eddie when I first saw his puffy face and reddened unblinking eyes. I wanted to draw her into me so she would know the sheer release and relief I felt; so I wouldn't have to explain it—since the saying is always awkward.

I wanted to get rid of my father, somehow, nicely; thanking him for the ride down and the offer of dinner, but pumping his arm and moving him for the car all the while. I wanted to head south to Springfield and the apartment Jenny had rented with money I sent her in February. I wanted to climb out of my clothes and get Jenny out of her clothes, then lay her on her back and love her, again and again and again. I wanted to boil water for coffee and loll on the edge of the bed and watch the sun go down. I wanted to feel Jenny's damp stomach and warm thighs curl against me. I wanted her to hook an arm over my shoulder and look up at me and ask for a sip of coffee. I wanted to lie back and talk in hoarse, throaty whispers and not have to listen to any of that "but-but-but-but" I had listened to all week.

I felt her chest tense and her hands jerk, and then she dropped her arms, but I held her wrist. I felt an itch in my eyes and blinked and felt glad. I introduced my father and he said what about dinner and I was thinking, the hell with dinner, but said, "Where to?" He led us to the big dining room. I sighed and thought: Why not? You've waited this long, one more afternoon doesn't mean anything, remember?

We ate steaks, Jenny and I hardly saying a word back and forth, just trading glances. She and Father did most of the talking; she telling him about school and her folks and the farm; he telling her stories about me. She laughed the loudest and longest when he told that sorry story about my first nickname. "We called him 'Wall Pounding Shorty' because he used to stand in his crib and beat on our bedroom walls with his little fists. Yes, and at the most—well, how to put it?—the most awkward times." I said something like, let's go, I'm god-awful tired from the trip, let's go, but Father said, "Philip, I have been good enough to buy you dinner, the very least you can do is sit still while I get acquainted with my future daughter-in-law." The waiter hovered and hinted and a-hemmed and pawed the rug like a cart pony. And by the time Father finally got the message and we walked out to the car for my suitcase, it was dark. Father gave Jenny a hug and kiss and shook my hand, and left. Jenny and I drove south through Louisville and Fern Creek and out into the country. I straddled the transmission hump with both hands along the back of the seat, fisted, and Jenny drove with both hands tight on the wheel. I watched the glow of the dashboard lights silhouette the profile of her face and the front of her dress. She talked quickly, nervously—blah, blah, blah, school paper, blah, blah, blah, so-and-so did this, blah, blah, blah—and I uh-hummed, answering with yeses and I-don't-knows and I-guesses.

We finally pulled up in front of the apartment. The place smelled of dust and old varnish, cracked and sticky to the touch, but looked clean enough and well kept.

Jenny walked sideways up the stairs ahead of me, still talking. "And I don't know if you'll like it, but this was the best I—that is, we, the girls and I—could find. And Mrs. Kinney—she's the landlady—Mrs. Kinney says it's clean and quiet and you did mention *quiet* in your letters. Mrs. Kinney is this old lady, very nice, who didn't even come up when we came to have a look. She says she can't climb stairs. Now the front door sticks and the toilet is awful noisy and I hope you like it, Phil." Then she stopped at the threshold of the top floor, thrust her arms out, dropping her purse, and said, "God, Phil, I'm glad you're home, I love you so." I put the suitcase on the landing and we leaned against the wall and held each other and kissed for the longest time. Then Jenny picked up her purse and fished around for the key—a thin brass skeleton key—worked it in the lock and tried to get the door open, but it was stuck, so I gave it a whack with my shoulder. She went in and flipped on the light and I came in after with the suitcase and shoved the door shut and I was home.

*

Jenny rushed around the room, touching the several chairs and lamps and so forth, saying, "This is the couch and this is a lamp and this is the rocker," and so on. She opened a dormer window, saying, "The street is right down there, and you can't see it but there's a park across the street, and now for the kitchen." And she grabbed my hand and dragged me toward the back, opening the refrigerator to show me two beat-up ice trays and some frozen meat and the rest. She threw open the cupboards above the sink. "This is all silverware and dishes and cups and things we filched from the cafeteria. Here's the sink—hot water and cold—and here's the gas stove," she said, flipping on a burner that popped and burned blue and white before she turned it off. "And here's your table and kitchen chairs. These curtains—as a matter of fact, all the curtains here"—and she gave a sweep of her arm—"we bought at a farm auction and Sister Francetta made them over. You like them? And back here, Phil," and she zoomed into the next room, leaving me standing in front of the stove. "Phil? Come on! This, uh, is the bedroom," she said, flicking on the light, letting me catch a glimpse, and flicking it off. "The bathroom is just next to the bed. Do you like it?" she said, standing in the kitchen again. "I hope you like it. Honest, we looked all over. Even *farm* places. This is about the best there was. Did I do all right? Phil?" She stood with her hands on the back of a chair. I stood in the bedroom doorway—the darkened room behind me.

"It's fine," I said. "I like it. It's just fine."

"Well, what do you want to do now?" she said, backing into the front room. "We could drive out to Egan's and get some wine. Or beer? Do you still drink beer?"

"Jenny," I said, looking her right in the eye, "let's not go anywhere. Make some coffee or something and let's stay right here."

"Well, I . . ." she said. She closed the window and fixed the latch, looking at me. Then she fiddled with a lampshade, looking at her feet, but abruptly turned, slipped off her shoes, and bounced over and put her arms around me again. We leaned against the kitchen doorjamb, nuzzling, feeling for the warmth and old touches. Then she let go and went to make the coffee.

She clanked around for a minute and said, "There's

no coffee, but how about tea? Do you think you would like tea?"

"Sure. Tea. Fine," I said.

The apartment was painted a dull blue color. The tiles were coming unglued in the bathroom. The linoleum in the kitchen curled in the corners, and the roof leaked just in front of the refrigerator. The rocking chair, which became my favorite place to sit, had broad runners and broad flat armrests. At night I would open all the windows and sit with my feet on the sill and listen to the night sounds—the crickets and frogs; the semis going through the gears making their way through town; the hum of the streetlamps. And every once in a while the soft boom-boom-boom-boom of a night fire at the Fort Knox tank range, like someone softly slapping two pillows together. A sound I never thought I would hear again.

Jenny came out with a cafeteria teapot and two mugs. She sat with her toes curled over the edge of the cushy easy chair, I slouched in the rocker, and we drank steaming mugs of weak pekoe tea laced with brandy from my suitcase. She wanted to know everything—what I saw and what I did and who were some of those guys I wrote her about. I told her about mixing Kool-Aid in the drinking water to smother that heavy chlorine taste; the difference between the chalky tang of warm beer and the light, sharp taste of cold (and she made a face). I told her about giving up underwear because of the heat and ticks and chiggers (and she shivered, spilling tea and brandy on the rug). I told her about getting dusted off with heat exhaustion—gulping down a handful of salt tablets and canteens of tepid water, and the slippery, itchy, greasy feel of my skin (and she grabbed hold of the armrest and looked at me funny).

After we got married I told her all of it—the ambushes and firefights, and getting stoned with Atevo and Cross and Haskins and Rayburn and Quinn (Jenny looking at me, saying, "Dope?"), and going to see Eddie; Clay-more Face and Susie and the stone sculpture; the old woman and that water buffalo and Trobridge's mousetrap. And on those nights we'd make love and make love and *still* I couldn't sleep—even after I started popping Hines V.A. Hospital prescription Librium. We'd sit in the living room on the floor and I'd work my way down to Stepik shooting up that V.C., and the V.C. by the bridge the day after Christmas, the big body count, and Dano and Wrye and Moody, Quinn and Surtees and Lavery, that little Viet in the rain and the powerful madness that settles over a person when he stares at a corpse for hours.

But that first night I talked about the little things—mushy scrambled eggs and shaving brushes, what a pain in the ass the rain was—until I looked up and said, "Why don't you come over here for a minute." And she put her tea and brandy aside and uncurled herself and came over. After a minute of just holding each other, necking and copping feels just like the old days, I wanted to say, "Let's screw," but hung back because I was through pushing at people. But soon enough she was warm and I was warm, so we got up and went back to the bedroom.

We undressed quickly, standing back to back at opposite sides of the darkened room. I heard her rustling around, and she whispered for me not to look yet, and then I heard her feet pat-pat across the floor, and she said I could turn around if I wanted. She stood in the doorway, silhou-etted by the light coming through from the living room, wearing a sheer and lacy lavender nightgown—her shining hair falling just so over her breasts. Every last curve was shrouded but plain, and my groin twitched.

"Am I pretty?" she said, holding a handful of gown in her hand because the hem was too long. "Do you like?"

"Yes," I said. "Very lovely." I went around the bed and walked up to her. I made to take hold of her, but she whispered no, and took hold of the hem and pulled the gown over her head, and again I said she was lovely. She put her hands on my chest and said she liked my muscles; said she didn't remember me being so well built. And I put my hands on her thighs and said that touching her for real was nothing like I remembered. I looked at her and touched her for the longest time, despite that aggravating pain in my groin, but then she got playful and silly, giggling and squirming, so we yanked back the covers and threw aside the pillows, and made it. *That* was the itch I wanted to scratch. And we scratched it until it burned like a mosquito welt, and then we scratched it some more. When I finally rolled onto my back Jenny went into the bathroom and closed the door. I wiped the sweat from my eyes and threw my arms out. I had forgotten what climbing down was— lying back easy, feeling that pleasant ache; feeling all that weight and tightness sink into the mattress. Even that sharp shooting pain in my back—which used to just plain wear me out until I had Quinn beat on it one night with the flat of his fist—even that seemed to blink and go out.

Then the toilet flushed and Jenny padded into the living room, coming right back with a mug of tepid tea and brandy, her feet making quick and slippery thaps on the floor. The bed jostled when she climbed over to me. She sat cross-legged, drawing her fingers up and down my chest and stomach, rubbing my temples and smoothing back my hair.

"That feels nice," I said. "Thank you." And she bent way over and kissed me. She skimmed my face and neck and chest with her hand, and I closed my eyes, listening. The springs creaked—sker-reek, sker-rauk—as she rocked back and forth, and I could not help but wince and jerk my head to the side. A dog scampered along the sidewalk, clicking its nails—snick-snick-snick—stopped, and raced off, and I winced again.

"Phil?"

"Mmmm."

"What is this scar?" and she pressed her finger gingerly to the side of my brow, just above my left eye. I sat up on my elbows, took a swig of her tea, and told her how Trobridge—this guy I knew—was sitting on guard about two or three one morning, and dropped a two-by-four through the hatch, and it hit me; how I couldn't see and thought I was blinded and the medic—a guy named Stepik —came over and laughed a little and sewed it up with a piece of catgut about a foot long, which was why the scar looked like a crab.

"So it wasn't when you were fighting?"

"No. Matter of fact, I was asleep. Say, how'd you like to rub my back?" and I turned over on my stomach. She rubbed me with those warm fingers of hers, and we shared cigarettes, and made love again and again, and then it was nearly midnight and she had to go. So she dressed, kissed and hugged me, and left.

*

I lived in a mansion. It was a mansion on a street of old mansions—fine homes of handmade brick and sparse lawns; cut-stone curbs and brick and black iron fences; the pastel shade of sycamore and pecan and walnut trees; and cobbled driveways laid out herringbone or scallop fashion, the mortar lines mossy and grassy and damp in the morning. Out back the coach house smelled of chaff and cobwebs, bare lath firring and mildewed timbers, and odd pieces of harness leather hanging on nails and slick with white powdery fuzz.

Mrs. Kinney occupied the entire first floor. I saw her every morning when I went out, sitting barefoot in a wicker chair on the porch, among pots of herbs and pelargonium

and her dog—a sand-colored mongrel-looking mutt named
Spice. She always wore a floppy straw hat, long skirts, and
plain blouses. "I never wear shoes, Philip, when the
weather gets warmer," she would say in a thin high voice.
"I am old enough to do what I like. Don't you think?"
"Yes, Miz Kinney," I would always answer. "Yes, ma'am."
She sipped tea from hand-painted bone china cups or
passed a small embroidered handkerchief from hand to
hand, squeezing it, stretching it between arthritic fingers,
fingering the embossed texture of the blue and white and
cream flowers and stems, like a rosary. She had the languid,
crisp aroma of warm and wet Sweeting apples about her. If
I had mail she tied it with a brown ribbon with a card
slipped under the knot that read, "Mr. Dosier. Third floor
east." Sometimes she invited me to sit and poured a cup of
strong black Irish tea.

"Philip," she said the first time I sat with her, "what is
it that you do?"

"Well, Miz Kinney," I said, "I don't do much of
anything. I just got out of the Army."

"Yes," she said, "I know. That girl Jennifer, from the
college, she said that you were in the Army and overseas.
'Fighting,' she told me. This fighting is bad, but I guess you
know that, don't you, Philip?"

"Yes, ma'am."

"So, what is it that you do?" she said again. "I see you
leave in the morning and not again until after dinner."

I walked—around town at first—past the old shoe
store and the five-and-dime and the main-drag restaurant
called the Texas Lunch; over by the L & N siding for the
feed and appliance store and lumberyard; down into the
neighborhoods—old brick houses painted in black trim and
carefully tuck-pointed, with Springfield Township Histori-
cal Society "circa so-and-so" plaques over the doors.

Farther afield was the "colored section"—gray houses and falling-down picket fences and dirt streets and the smell of old wood; beat-up flatbed trucks and pickups parked along the ditches with hand-painted signs on the doors; a thousand barefoot kids gawking at me as I walked through, and the women sitting on porches in kitchen chairs, peeling potatoes or snapping green beans and shooting the breeze.

And when I covered the town pretty well I would walk along the highways and gravel roads and dirt section roads, out among the creeks and woods and so forth, the worked farms and beat-up farms and fallow farms. I filled my eyes with the blooming orchards and damp, turned earth and the "shuff-shuff" of a breeze in an aspen grove—the good and peaceful things in this world. I sat for an entire afternoon watching a stone-bottomed creek pool, thick with leaves, and schools of bullhead and minnow and bass fry skittering in and out in the rippled and dappled shade. I listened to the slow, deep spring thaw trickling down the rockface and into the pool dammed with stones and silt. I watched a hawk circle and circle with its wings outstretched, until it suddenly swept its wings back and swooped down behind a woodline. I walked and watched clouds of dust follow a tractor and harrow, and yearling horses chase each other around a tree while the mares calmly grazed and the foals nuzzled for milk.

And Jenny was always near—nervous from all the waiting and nervous from finally having me around. But the two of us got comfortable, and kind, and more loving as I stayed and stayed. Every once in a while we drove south to visit friends of hers, who worked a dairy farm and lived in an enormous L-shaped stone house surrounded by huge flowering trees that bloomed yellow and white. Here and there around the several acres of yard huge patches of jonquils grew wild, and a lilac windbreak lined the front fence. Around the back the Lewises kept junked tractors and junked cars, rusted plows and manure spreaders, spools of greasy winch cable and nail kegs filled with engine parts, among the puddles of rusty water and reddish tail-light glass and weeds as tall as a man. Time after time the cows would stand and drink and flick their tails, watching me watching them at the gate. My gaze went from the rusted, sagging barbed wire to the pasture path, trampled to a slippery mush by thousands of trips to the barn. The memory of watery muck and bowlegged Viets, and dead fetid things would be strong then—the coming down from all that still lagging back, still aggravating my sleep nights. But then I would jerk my head and blink a good long blink, and smell the bushel baskets of jonquils in the back seat of Jenny's car, and hear the crackle of frying chicken. So I would put an arm over Jenny's shoulder, smelling the aroma of her skin, coming around.

Most afternoons I joined Jenny and her bubbling, squawking girlfriends for dinner. And since someone always had a diet going, I never bought a meal. They loved the way I ate and ate and ate, and made a big fuss over me, making me feel at home, and for a while I was prince of that apple town. I would lean back in my chair and watch out those tall windows with rippled panes of handmade glass. Outside stood a statue of the Virgin or St. Catherine or somebody—one arm raised, thin fingers extended, the other hand hidden in the mystery of her gown. Her toes peeked out from under the hem among the windblown leaves and twigs, and that smooth-faced downward glance with its limpid expression of peace and calm. I watched her, and the pear and apple orchard behind her, almost every evening, slowly, slowly bloom in front of my eyes.

For Easter vacation Jenny and I drove to Pennsylvania to visit her folks. Her mother wore the same cotton dresses and flowered apron, and her father his overalls and flannel shirts. After dinner he told me he was glad about my mild letters and wanted me to tell him all about it, but I shrugged him off and shrugged him off until he finally gave up.

Later that week her mother wanted to know if we were going to get married, looking me square in the eye when she asked, and I looked at her and then Jenny, and said yes we were. Jenny looked at me puzzled, because we hadn't decided anything for sure one way or the other. But then she smiled and her mother jumped up and got all excited and called her husband into the kitchen. Everybody hugged and shook hands, and by the end of the week I was never so glad to get out of a place in my entire life.

On the trip back we messed around in the car and couldn't wait to get back, but when we got to Springfield, just short of the apartment, we ran out of gas. We pushed the car to a gas station and I told the guy, this heavyset, grease-covered kid, to fill it up and go over it in general, then left for Mrs. Kinney's to check the mail. I was expecting a letter from Staley, who shipped home about a week after I did. There was no letter from Staley, but there was one from Dewey. I walked back to the car and slid in on the driver's side. Since I left the platoon he had made a third stripe and Romeo was really hitting the shit. The dinks had the motor pool zeroed in. A 122 rocket hit next to the six-niner. Corso and Lavery, who was back in the platoon, and a couple others got it bad and there were ambushes on the road every couple days, and Romeo could only field six tracks now, and there were boo-coo fucken new guys, and the old-timers and the short-timers just stayed fucked up. Toward the back, down toward his signature, he wrote:

I don't really know how to say this, Flip, except to say Quinn got killed last . . .

I didn't read any further. Quinn was dead.

Everything went flat calm. I could feel a rush of tears, tears I hadn't felt since I was a kid. Then my face burned with tears, just the quietest tears coming faster and faster. Jenny stood next to me in the opened door and put a hand on my shoulder and asked why I was crying all of a sudden and who's Quinn? And then I was ashamed of my crying and turned away from her, sloughing off her hand. So I thought of the pale, rocky coast of California and the smell of mothballs and talc, hot black tea and those bushel baskets of jonquils, and Jenny's warm and gentle hands—and the thousand things I could never tell her. I mean, Quinn was this short, light-haired guy, quick and clever as anything and smart as hell. Asleep and dreaming nightmares he was arm and leg better than any three dudes I ever rode with. Stoned or sober or ass-whipped tired, he knew the tracks and the killing and the staying alive. I mean, he and I stood back to back many a night. So how come? You cover me and I'll cover you and we'll all go home, and I read Dewey's letter again. And I cried like a kid, the tears coming like an old man's birthdays; like old women keening over a coffin—that special feeling for kin laid out among candles. He took frag shrapnel in the back just before we came back from the border, and instead of going for the Purple Heart he made us dig out a couple dozen scab-like slivers of spring steel. That was the way he wanted it. And he wore that shirt until the shrapnel nicks frayed into tears; until it hung down his back in shreds; until the Colonel made him throw it away. I was in a rage. People would die. At that moment I could have destroyed whole cities, whole civilizations, whole fucking races of people. If Quinn can't make it back, none of us can.

*

The first chance we had Jenny and I got married—me because I could not stand sleeping alone anymore; she because she did not know how else to help. I picked her up at the dormitory one morning. We walked over to the chapel, surprised a hundred nuns at morning prayers, and exchanged our vows in whispers. Back at the apartment with a wet spring snow hanging off the gable, Quinn is dead. Reading snatches of the *The Agony and the Ecstasy*, with Herbie Mann blowing smoke across the floor on the FM, Quinn is dead. Michelangelo busting his ass and going blind at the Sistine Chapel, that flute coming nasty and breathy and shrill, Quinn dead in a truck accident—the truck on top of him. The coffin never opened.

I do not know how many days it was that I sat in that flat-runged rocking chair and wept into the crook of my sleeve the same as he had. Jenny nuzzled me and hugged me close, asking who Quinn was, and I began by telling her that Quinn was this dude who liked her just by the sound of her letters.

I wake up one morning—I've go to *do* something—remembering that Quinn lived in Terre Haute. Jenny takes off for school. I take off for Terre Haute with a coat and tie and that stupid line from an old John Garfield movie. I get to Terre Haute in the afternoon and recon the town. Where is the best place to track him down? The newspaper. Everybody in Terre Haute reads the newspaper.

"Say, m' man, you know a dude name of Quinn?"

"Yes, sir. Lives such-and-so."

I go over. Knock. Twice. Nobody home. The next-door lady says Mrs. Quinn teaches school. I leave to get some lunch and feed a headache. An hour later I go back. I walk up to the door and try again. My man, my man, what are you doing here? A woman comes to the door. I see her through the curtains, coming from the kitchen, wiping her hands on her apron. Didn't Quinn mention once that his old lady loved to cook and bake and such? She pulls the door open.

"Yes?" she says.

"Uh, Mrs. Quinn? You, uh, don't know me, but I knew Quinn overseas."

She drops her apron and her face flashes a dull kind of happiness.

"Please come in, won't you," she says.

"Yes, ma'am. Thank you."

"And you are . . .?"

"Uh, Dosier, ma'am. Philip Dosier."

She says oh, and seems to recognize my name. On the bookcase is a photograph of Quinn in his dress greens and that picture from the last day of Basic and an oil painting of the Last Supper on dark velvet. I remember the day we went to the PX to pick it up and the hassle we got into with the medics for borrowing one of their jeeps.

"Philip, would you like to come into the kitchen? I'm just getting dinner. You will stay for dinner?" she says.

"Yes, ma'am, thank you," I say.

"You knew Charles from . . ."

"The Triple Tre—Third Battalion of the Thirty-third," I say, and sit down. "I, uh, drove up from Kentucky to see you, to say I'm sorry. I don't know what else to say." Well, Jesus, what could I tell her? I'm sorry he got his shit blown away in that fucking dumb-ass war? That it's likely he was so stoned he never knew what hit him? That I'm sorry I came home and he didn't? "I'm just really sorry, that's all."

Mr. Quinn comes home. A tall man, outside all his life. Big rough hands and Quinn's giggly grin and blue eyes. He shakes my hand as though I were a son.

"We were hoping someone, a friend, would come," he says. We sit and eat and after dinner Mr. Quinn says, "You know, after Edward was killed some letters and things came in the mail." And he hands me a blue medal case and a stack of letters of condolence—from the El-tee, the Colonel, the brigade commander, the division commander, General Westmoreland, the Department of the Army, the Governor of Indiana, senators, congressmen, and the Commander in Chief. And they all read pretty much the same. "You may feel proud, however, that your son gave his life in the defense of his country and countrymen. He was a credit to the uniform of the United States Army, a sterling example of American manhood and devotion to duty, and it was a high honor, a distinct and rare privilege, to have him serve under me." The El-tee's was the only letter written in script, but it sounded sarcastic coming from him, even though he was trying to sound sincere.

And the Bronze fucking Star. The medal, the ribbon, a lapel pin, and three copies of the written citation. Just the kind of trick those clown-suit lifers would try to shove off on parents, as though a deuce-and-a-half falling on his head was an act of courage.

That evening we sit in the living room and watch *all* the slides that Quinn sent home. There it is again, but all jumbled up and as tall as the wall was high. The border and Stepik and Steichen and Whiskey j. and Quinn's Saigon shack and me on Christmas and the day after and our tent right after he transferred in and body counts—the whole nine yards.

Bzzt.

"This is Suoi Dau," I say. "Just after Quinn transferred in."

Bzzt.

"This is Tay Ninh Base Camp. That's me and Quinn and Stepik, the medic, and the seven-three."

"What's that in the background?" Mr. Quinn asks.

"That's the Nui Ba Dinh. The Black Virgin Mountain."

"We're glad you could come, son."

Bzzt.

". . . This is the Truce Day body count."

"Uh, how many is that?" Mr. Quinn asks.

"They say it was four hundred fifty."

Bzzt.

"Now here are some Viet kids we used to swim with."

Bzzt.

"And this is Quinn's girl from Tay Ninh."

"Edward's girlfriend?" says Mrs. Quinn, leaning forward on the sofa and putting a hand on Mr. Quinn's hand that holds the projector buttons.

"Well, she was part French," I say.

"She has lovely hair," Mrs. Quinn says.

Bzzt.

"This is a body count I do not recognize."

And on and on until late. We go through trays and trays of slides and photographs. When we finish Mrs. Quinn asks me to stay the night—I could sleep in Quinn's old room.

I say no, thank you, no, and make up some lie about having to be back first thing in the morning.

She says, you will come and see us again?

Yes, ma'am, I'd like that. I promise. Thank you. Thank you again for the dinner, it was very good. It was good to meet you, I say.

Mr. Quinn says, come back again, son.

Jenny and I stayed close to the Quinns, Rollie and Jason, by letter mostly. They dropped in on us that summer on their way to Yellowstone. Two Christmases later we called on them on our way to Pennsylvania. We sat in the kitchen, shaking out the cold, when I looked up past Jenny into the pantry, and told Rollie that I wanted to see Quinn's grave. I had been thinking about it since the first time I was there. Jenny and I had never talked about it, but she knew

I was going. Rollie came out of the pantry and looked at Jenny, then me, and nodded her head slowly, smiling, and said fine. I drove out to the cemetery on Route 41, along the Wabash river. In the center stood a small memorial statue. Civil War veterans in front. World War I on one side, World War II on the other. Korea and Vietnam in back. Four pyramided rows of white crosses, names only. I sat in the car with my collar up, looking down at the names—Quinn and Corbin and Haney and Lorenz and Teleck, among them. His grave was in the newer part of the cemetery, and the stone bigger than I expected. Across the top was the word.

Quinn. Thin, tall letters. Rollie's and Jason's names were there, too, but the grass in front was unbroken. Under the name Charles E. was a low mound of dirt sparsely laid over with grass, and a thick paper vase with red and green flowers. I stretched and folded my hands, looking at the stone. There was a lowering sun. It started to get colder. The air was brisk, chill. I opened the door and got out.

I put my hands in my jacket pockets to keep them warm, and there we are, jumping and rushing for that hooch by the stream—Quinn trying to blow away that kid before he is a POW and it is too late, and then lying for me, lying like a rug. And the second or third time we sweep through Ap 6, his flak jacket hanging from his shoulders, looking pissed, staring down the El-tee. The El-tee saying, I thought I tol' ya ta check out that well. And Quinn saying, well now, El-tee, why don't you just go piss up a rope, and hefting his gun. And taking some old woman by the hair and giving her a shake when he finds a Chicom claymore, and those kids giving him room, like they could smell the kill. The night he came close to killing Lavery, Quinn drunk and pissed, throwing his bowie at the floor and shouting, who's gonna *fuck with me?* And me lying for him and

Lavery going to jail. And Quinn saying, ya know, nex' time I'm gonna *kill* that nigger. And later him saying that he admired me because I had somebody like Jenny and would have my shit together when I got home. And me answering back that he had his shit together, too, but him saying, no, I ain't going home, it don't matter what I do, I don't care anymore. He knew it way back then, that he had changed, and laid himself out for it and gathered it in and worked on it with his arms in a hug, hands fisted, grinning that grin of his. Him finally getting everybody to sing the verses and choruses to his El-tee song, while he scat-sang, dancing around in his shower towel and waving his arms as though he were conducting. Quinn getting all decked out the day of the big body count and bad-assing for the guy with the camera—grinning and John Wayneing and clowning and kidding and pulling that guy's leg to a fare-thee-well. And the rest of us stoned to high heaven and hardly keeping from laughing. That Honcho—the kid from town who swept floors and washed glasses in the EM Club—razzing Quinn about something or other, and Quinn taking him out back of the mechanics' shack by the scruff of the shirt and stomping on his head, and Honcho crawling off and never coming back. I walked around and around the grave, my boots crunching on snow-covered, ice-covered grass just up the way from the river. I woke him out of a sound sleep to say so long the morning I left—him all bleary-eyed and pasty-faced, asking me to hold off the wedding until he could make it home; it's one fucken shivaree I do not want to miss, he said. We held each other at the shoulder, wrestler fashion—and him taking my hand and shaking it slow and firm, then grasping it slam against his chest at the heart and telling me to take good care. I circled that grave, trying to think of something to say out loud to myself; resolve that sad and bitter feeling I saw chiseled into the stone. Quinn the laugher. Quinn so mean and evil. Quinn dead a year and a half but the grave looking fresh, as though the dirt was still loose and the flowers were colder than his body. I stopped and drew my hands out into the cold, making fists and letting go. "Goddamn you, Quinn."

APPENDICES

PHONETIC ALPHABET

Alpha	November
Bravo	Oscar
Charlie	Papa
Delta	Quebec
Echo	Romeo
Fox Trot	Sierra
Golf	Tango
Hotel	Uniform
India	Victor
Juliet	Whiskey
Kilo	X-ray
Lima	Yankee
Mike	Zulu

GLOSSARY

AIT—Advanced Individual Training.

AK-47—Automatic Kalashnikov-47, a Soviet-make auto/semi-automatic assault rifle, the weapon of choice of many successful national revolutions; reliable and dependable.

Annamese Cordillera—The Central Highlands.

Aqua Velva—A cheap brand of after shave lotion sometimes used by derelict alcoholics when real liquor cannot be obtained. Dreadful to drink.

Armored Personnel Carrier—An M-113, or APC; also called A-cav or track.

Article 15—Non-judicial, company-level punishment which involved forfeit of pay, confinement to barracks, and extra duty. From Uniform Code of Military Justice.

ARVN—Acronym for Army of the Republic of South Vietnam.

Artillery Base—A temporary base camp where a battery of artillery, typically 105mm howitzers, would set up to support ground troops; also called forward support base or Landing Zone (LZ).

AWOL—Absent Without Leave.

AWOL Bag—A small bag with just enough room for one change of clothes and light enough to carry in one hand.

Azimuth—Compass heading.

B-40—Another name for an armor piercing Rocket Propelled Grenade (RPG).

B-52—The heavy American bomber which carried out the strategic high altitude bombing missions. The Vietnamese called them "Whispering Death."

Back-in-the-World—Slang for the continental United States. The same as the Land of the Big PX and the Land of the 24-Hour Generator.

Berm—A narrow ledge or shelf of dirt; a dike or dam; the built up walkways or paths between rice paddies.

Black Panthers—A militant and influential black power political group of the 1960s.

Body Count—The tally of Viet Cong and North Vietnamese dead; the act of tallying.

Boo-Coo—From the French *beaucoup*, meaning many. GI pronunciation.

Bowie Knife—A hunting/fishing knife with a 15-inch blade; named for Jim Bowie, killed at the Battle of the Alamo.

C-4—A malleable plastic explosive which comes in one pound slabs.

C-Rations—Boxed field rations. Also called Cs or C-Rats.

Capp, Andy—A comic strip character who spends most of his time drinking, watching football, and dodging work.

Chicken Colonel—Slang for the rank of full colonel, the insignia of rank being a spread eagle which is said to resemble a chicken. Always derogatory, i.e., chicken [shit] colonel.

Chicom—Abbreviation for Chinese Communist, as in Chicom Claymores or Chicom frags (hand grenades).

Chieu Hoi—In Vietnamese it means "Open arms"; it was a program whereby enemy soldiers were repatriated to the South Vietnamese government. American troops would shout this to get VC and NVA soldiers to surrender.

Chinook—The CH-47, a cargo helicopter with large triple rotor blades at each end; it could carry a platoon of (40) men and more. It was huge, lumbering, and noisy.

Chingachgook—The Indian character from James Fenimore Cooper's *Last of the Mohicans*. A play on words; a racial slur.

Church Key—Slang for bottle and can opener.

CIB—Combat Infantryman's Badge.

Class-As—The full dress uniform. In Vietnam it consisted of low-quarter oxfords and black socks, khaki trousers and short sleeved khaki shirt, and an overseas soft cap (also called a cunt cap).

Claymore—An antipersonnel mine about the size of a shoe box top, curved slightly outward, filled with C-4 and many hundreds of small steel balls somewhat larger than double-ought buckshot. They were usually set out in front of a night perimeter in gangs of a dozen and more from each Armored Personnel Carrier.

Click—Slang term for kilometer.

CO—Commanding Officer; also Conscientious Objector, a Selective Service (draft) classification.

Cobra—The AG-1H; an assault helicopter fitted out with rocket pods, machine guns, etc.

CONUS—Acronym for Continental United States.

Coon—A racial slur for black American.

Cordite—An explosive.

CVC—Head gear resembling a football helmet worn by track and tank crews, and containing radio earphones and a small microphone.

Darvon—A barbiturate easily obtained by the medics.

Day Sweep—The same as a Search and Destroy mission.

Dee Dee—(Also dee dee mau) From the Vietnamese *didi*,

meaning to run; get the hell out of here; go. GI pronunciation.

Delta, The—Nickname for the driver of an Armored Personnel Carrier. From the phonetic alphabet.

DEROS—Acronym for Date Estimated Return from Overseas; the day when a soldier ended his tour and rotated back to the United States.

Die-wee—Captain; from the Vietnamese *dai wi*. GI Pronunciation.

Dick Job—An easy job or task.

Dink—A racial slur meaning any Vietnamese.

Dinky-dau—From the Vietnamese, meaning crazy. GI pronunciation.

Dipstick—Slang for fool; a man who cannot be reformed or improved, he is a fool for life. Always derogatory. Literally: the gadget used to check the oil level in an engine's crankcase. Figuratively: A dipstick is only good for one thing.

Ditty bag—Small kit in your pack for shaving gear and toilet articles.

DMZ—The De-Militarized Zone at the 17th Parallel between North and South Vietnam agreed upon in the 1954 Geneva Accords.

Deuce-and-a-Half—A large truck that carried two-and-a-half tons in troops and cargo.

Dust-off—Slang for medical evacuation by helicopter (Medivac). The word "Dust-off" was the personal radio call-sign of a Major Kelly, one of the original Medivac pilots of the 57th Medical Detachment at Tan Son Nhut, killed making a Medivac near Tay Ninh in 1965.

El-tee—A nickname meaning lt., the abbreviation for lieutenant.

EM Club—Enlisted Men's Club.

F-4—Phantom jet fighter-bomber. Provided close-in tactical support for ground troop.

FCC—Federal Communications Commission.

FNG—Fucking New Guy.

FO—Forward Observer; traveled with the infantry and spotted rounds for the artillery.

Forty-five—A .45 caliber automatic pistol.

Frag—Slang for fragmentation hand grenade.

Fragging—The assassination of an officer or ranking NCO by member(s) of his own unit. Usually an act of revenge.

Gook—A racial slur for Vietnamese. First used by Americans during the Korean War, it is a Chinese word meaning, literally, country (the land and the people).

Gunge—Slang for a horrible infection.

Harlem Brothers—Black soldiers from Harlem, the black section of New York City.

Ho Chi Minh Sandals—Sandals worn by North Vietnamese troops, made of automobile tire rubber with inner tube straps.

Hooch—A ten- to-twelve-man billet; a wood frame and screen wire hut with a tin roof, but sometimes only a tent or temporary bunker. A hooch was never anything very wonderful; a place to sleep out of the rain.

Housecat—Nickname for a soldier with a permanent base camp job, such as clerk, cook, and the like, who never left the base camp—just as a housecat would never venture out of the house. Always derogatory.

Huey—Nickname given the UH-1 helicopter, the ubiquitous symbol of the Vietnam War; also called a slick. Used to transport troops and for resupply—ass and trash, as the pilots would say.

H & I—Harassment and Interdiction; random night artillery fire at predetermined locations, typically a trail intersection frequented by the VC and NVA.

IG Inspection—An inspection by the Inspector General, the granddaddy of them all. To fail an IG was very serious.

Jungle Rot—Slang for immersion foot; a fungus skin disease. Called trench foot in WWI.

KIA—Killed In Action.

KP—Kitchen Police; to work in the mess hall.

Laager—From the Afrikaans; a defensive perimeter of armored vehicles. It came to mean any temporary perimeter.

La-dee—From the Vietnamese *lai di*, come here. GI pronunciation.

Laterite—A reddish, ore-like soil used to pave roads, make bricks, fill sandbags, etc.

LBJ—Long Binh Jail, the US Army stockade at Long Binh; also the initials of Lyndon Baines Johnson, President of the United States and Commander-in-Chief of all US armed forces, an irony not lost on the troops.

Lifer—Slang for any career military personnel. Always derogatory.

Line Company—Same as infantry rifle company.

Lister Bag—A large canvas bag with several spigots used to store potable water; usually hung from a tree or the like.

LP—Listening Post, usually set up at night some distance to the front of a laager.

Low-quarters—Dress oxford shoes that are part of the Class-A uniform.

M-16—The issue assault rifle of all the American forces in Vietnam; regarded as not as good a weapon as the AK-47.

Mark—A sucker; an easy victim.

Mermite Can—Large insulated food container, about the size of a portable camping cooler, from which cooks served hot food brought to the field.

Mo-gas—Motor gasoline; as opposed to diesel fuel.

Mo-town Brothers—Black troops from motor-town, i.e., Detroit, where most American cars are manufactured.

MP—Military Police.

MPC—Military Payment Certificate; scrip; issued in lieu of genuine money, to keep US currency out of the black market. Totally worthless, but used among GIs and Vietnamese as legal tender.

NCO—Non-Commissioned Officer.

NVA—North Vietnamese Army. Name for North Vietnamese soldier.

Number-one—Slang for the very best; of the best quality and absolutely supreme; nothing finer.

Number Ten—Slang for poor quality; the rock bottom.

Number Ten Thou[sand]—If number ten is absolutely the rock bottom, then number ten thou is the epitome of the irremediable, unsurpassable worst.

OD—The color olive drab.

One-Eyed Trouser Mouse—Slang for penis.

PA & E—Pacific Architects & Engineers.

Pancho Villa-style—Used to describe how the troops wore belts of machine gun ammunition crisscrossed across their chests.

Payloader—A piece of earth moving, road building equipment.

Pedicabs—Rickshaw-like contraptions attached to bicycles, for hire.

PF—South Vietnamese Popular Forces; nicknamed Ruff Puffs.

PFC—The rank of Private First Class.

Piaster—Vietnamese monetary denomination. Commonly called "P."

Pig, The—Slang for M-60 machine gun.

Piss-tube—A sanitation device; a sump, usually a long tube filled with stones and other debris, buried in the ground, to urinate in.

PX—Post Exchange where soldiers could buy food and cigarettes, personal items, clothes, cameras, fans, stereos, and the like at prices heavily subsidized by the government.

PX Aviators—Dark glasses of the style worn by pilots bought at the Post Exchange.

Quaker's Meeting—A Sunday religious service characterized by meditation where no one speaks unless moved by the spirit.

Recoilless Rifle Jeep—A jeep with a 106mm recoilless rifle mounted on the back.

Romeo Apple Pie—Reconnaissance Platoon nightly Ambush Patrol; the radio call sign.

Romeo—Radio call sign and nickname for Reconnaissance Platoon.

RPG—An armor-piercing Rocket Propelled Grenade; also called B-40.

RPM—Revolutions Per Minute.

R & R—Rest and Relaxation. Usually a five-day leave.

RTO—Radio Transmitter Operator; the radio man.

Ruff Puffs—Slang for South Vietnamese Popular Forces. Always derogatory.

S & D—Search and Destroy.

Sebbo-twee—Vietnamese pronunciation of the number seven-three.

Shack—Verb, as in "shacked with" or "shacked up." A couple living together but not married. Also called a shack job.

Shivaree—A noisy, mock serenade; lots of noise—very little music.

Short-time—Very quick sexual intercourse, as with a prostitute.

Shuck down—To undress quickly.

Sierra-Sierra—The starlight scope, a night vision device which uses available light and looks like a telescope. Compared to an infra-red scope which uses its own light source.

Sit Rep—Situation Report; given over the radio.

Slopehead—A racial slur for Vietnamese. Also slowped.

Smoke—Nickname for marijuana; also a smoke grenade used when a helicopter is landing to give position, wind direction, etc.

Stand-down—A rifle company's return to base camp for refitting and rest, usually for several days.

Steel pot—GI helmet.

Sundance—The tongue-in-cheek nickname of a Wild West Outlaw.

Tanker Bar—A long and heavy, stout steel bar used in tank and track maintenance.

Tee-tee—From the Vietnamese *ti ti*, very small or very little. GI pronunciation.

TC—The main hatch on a track where the .50-caliber machine gun is mounted; also track commander.

Thirty-Eight Special—Small .38-caliber revolver; sometimes called a Saturday-Night Special.

Trip-Flare—A ground flare set off by the enemy tripping a wire.

Tube—Slang for artillery piece.

Tunnel Rat—A soldier who crawled into tunnels to search, usually armed with a flashlight and .45 automatic pistol.

USN—United States Navy.

VA—Veterans Administration.

VC—Viet Cong. Spoken phonetically, Victor Charlie.

VFW—Veterans of Foreign Wars. A paternal lobbying association usually regarded for its cheerful and determined pro-war attitude.

VTR—A large tracked vehicle used to tow disabled trucks, tanks and tracks.

Wayne, John—Movie actor; nickname for anyone who acted foolishly macho brave. Always derogatory.

WIA—Wounded in Action.

Yogi Bear Hat—Nickname for campaign hat, characterized by a broad, round, flat brim.

MISCELLANEOUS

105—Field howitzer with a 105mm bore.

155—Field howitzer with 155mm bore.

175—Field howitzer with a 175mm bore.

1049—Request For Transfer form number; to transfer out of a unit.

BAR—Browning Automatic Rifle; an M-1 modified to fire automatic.

C-130—Large cargo plane.

C-133—Large cargo plane.

E-5—Rank of sergeant, a non-commissioned officer.

E-6—Rank of staff sergeant, a non-commissioned officer.

E-Deuce—Nickname for the M-14E-2; an M-14 modified to fire automatic.

C-130—Large cargo plane.

C-133—Large cargo plane.

DD-214—The form number on your final discharge, a very important event and a very important document.

M-1 Carbine—A small rifle.

M-14—The assault rifle that replaced the M-1.

M-60 Machine Gun—A light machine gun.

M-79—Forty mm grenade launcher; also called the blooper or thumper because of the sound.

For a complete list of books available from Penguin in the United States, write to Dept. DG, Penguin Books, 299 Murray Hill Parkway, East Rutherford, New Jersey 07073.

For a complete list of books available from Penguin in Canada, write to Penguin Books Canada Limited, 2801 John Street, Markham, Ontario L3R 1B4.